The Pleasure is All Hers...

WEE BOOK INN

10310 - 82 AVENUE 432-7230
8101 - 118 AVENUE 474-7888
10328 JASPER AVENUE 423-1434
15125 STONY PLAIN RD. 489-0747

"I do not mean to disturb your schedule."

He blinked. "That's, ah . . ."

He seemed to lose his train of thought, possibly because she'd started unbuttoning his waistcoat. She concentrated on the brass buttons and the slitted holes, aware that her breathing had quickened with the temptation of his proximity. An awful thought intruded: How many other women had had the privilege of undressing him?

He cleared his throat. "Uh, kind of you."

"Is it?" Had he been with another woman tonight? He was a man of known appetites.

She had no idea where he went in the evenings. Her fingers fumbled on that last thought, and she finally identified the emotion flooding her brain: jealousy. She was completely unprepared for it. She'd known before they'd married who he was—*what* he was. She believed she would be content with whatever small part of himself he would share with her. The other women, when they came, she would simply ignore.

But now she found she simply couldn't. She wanted him. All of him.

"There's enchantment in Hoyt's stories that makes you believe in the magic of love."

—*Romantic Times BOOKreviews Magazine*

"Elizabeth Hoyt writes with flair, sophistication, and unstoppable passion."

—Julianne MacLean, author of *Portrait of a Lover*

Please turn the page for raves
for Elizabeth Hoyt and her novels.

Praise for Elizabeth Hoyt's Novels
To Taste Temptation

The Serpent Prince

more . . .

The Leopard Prince

more . . .

The Raven Prince

OTHER TITLES BY ELIZABETH HOYT

The Raven Prince

The Leopard Prince

The Serpent Prince

To Taste Temptation

ELIZABETH HOYT

To Seduce A Sinner

FOREVER

NEW YORK   BOSTON

Copyright © 2008 by Nancy M. Finney
Excerpt from *To Beguile A Beast* copyright © 2008 by Nancy M. Finney. All rights reserved. Except as permitted under the U.S. Copyright Act of 1976, no part of this publication may be reproduced, distributed, or transmitted in any form or by any means, or stored in a database or retrieval system, without the prior written permission of the publisher.

Cover illustration by Alan Ayers
Hand lettering by Ron Zinn

Forever
Hachette Book Group USA
237 Park Avenue
New York, NY 10017
Visit our Web site at www.HachetteBookGroupUSA.com

Forever is an imprint of Grand Central Publishing. The Forever name and logo is a trademark of Hachette Book Group USA, Inc.

Printed in the United States of America

First Printing: November 2008

10 9 8

For my father, ROBERT G. McKINNELL, who has always been incredibly supportive of my writing career. (But you still can't read this book, Dad!)

Acknowledgments

Thank you to my wonderful editor, AMY PIERPONT, and to her industrious assistant, KRISTIN SWITZER; to my fantabulous agent, SUSANNAH TAYLOR; to the energetic Grand Central Publishing Publicity team, particularly TANISHA CHRISTIE and MELISSA BULLOCK; to the Grand Central Publishing Art Department, especially DIANE LUGER for another wonderful cover; and to my copy editor, CARRIE ANDREWS, who has once again saved me from public embarrassment.

Thank you all!

To Seduce
A Sinner

Prologue

Once upon a time, in a nameless foreign land, a soldier was marching home from war. The war he'd fought had waged for generations. It had been waged, in fact, for so many years that in time, the people fighting it had completely forgotten the reason that they fought. One day, the soldiers looked at the men they battled and realized they did not know why they wanted to kill them. It took the officers a little longer to come to the same conclusion, but eventually they had been prevailed upon, and all the soldiers on both sides of the war had laid down their arms. Peace had been declared.

So now our soldier marched home on a lonely road. But since the war had gone on for so many years, he no longer had a home to march to, and really he marched to nowhere. Still, he had a pack with some food on his back, the sun shone overhead, and the road he'd chosen was a straight and easy one. He was content with his lot in life.

His name was Laughing Jack. . . .
—from LAUGHING JACK

Chapter One

Jack marched down the road, whistling merrily, for he was a man without a care in the world. . . .
—from LAUGHING JACK

LONDON, ENGLAND
MAY 1765

There are few things more unfortunate in a man's life than being thrown over by one's prospective bride on one's wedding day, Jasper Renshaw, Viscount Vale, reflected. But being thrown over on one's wedding day whilst suffering the lingering aftereffects of a night of heavy drinking . . . well, that had to set some kind of damnable record for bad luck.

"I'm so s-s-s-sorry!" Miss Mary Templeton, the prospective bride in question, wailed at a pitch guaranteed to bring a man's scalp right off his skull. "I never meant to deceive you!"

"Quite," Jasper said. "I expect so."

He had an urge to rest his aching head in his hands, but this was obviously a highly dramatic point in Miss Templeton's life, and he felt it wouldn't show the proper gravity for the moment. At least he was sitting down. There was one straight-backed wooden chair in the church vestry, and he'd commandeered it in a very ungentlemanly manner when first they'd entered.

Not that Miss Templeton seemed to mind.

"Oh, my lord!" she cried, presumably to him, although considering where they were, she might've been calling on a far higher Presence than he. "I could not help myself, truly I couldn't. A frail wreck is woman! Too simple, too warmhearted to withstand the gale of passion!"

Gale of passion? "No doubt," Jasper muttered.

He wished he'd had time for a glass of wine this morning—or two. It might've settled his head a bit and helped him to understand what exactly his fiancée was trying to tell him—beyond the obvious fact that she no longer wished to become the fourth Viscountess Vale. But he, poor dumb ass, had tottered out of bed this morning expecting nothing worse than a tedious wedding followed by a protracted wedding breakfast. Instead, he'd been met at the church doors by Mr. and Mrs. Templeton, the former looking grim, the latter suspiciously nervous. Add to that, his lovely bride with fresh tears on her face, and he'd known, somewhere deep in his dark and heavy soul, that he would not be eating wedding cake today.

He smothered a sigh and eyed his erstwhile bride-to-be. Mary Templeton was quite lovely. Dark shining hair, bright blue eyes, a fresh creamy complexion, and nicely plump titties. He'd been rather looking forward to the plump titties, he thought morosely as she paced in front of him.

"Oh, Julius!" Miss Templeton exclaimed now, throwing out her lovely, round arms. It was really too bad that the vestry was such a little room. Her drama needed a larger venue. "If only I didn't love you so!"

Jasper blinked and leaned forward, conscious that he must've missed something, because he didn't remember this Julius. "Ah, Julius . . . ?"

She turned and widened her robin's-egg-blue eyes. Really, they were rather magnificent. "Julius Fernwood. The curate in the town near Papa's country estate."

He was being thrown over for a curate?

"Oh, if you could see his gentle brown eyes, his butter-yellow hair, and his grave demeanor, I know you would feel as I do."

Jasper arched an eyebrow. That seemed most unlikely.

"I love him, my lord! I love him with all my simple soul."

In an alarming move, she dropped to her knees before him, her pretty, tearstained face upturned, her soft white hands clutched together between her rounded bosom. "Please! Please, I beg of you, release me from these cruel bonds! Give me back my wings so that I may fly to my true love, the love I will cherish in my heart no matter if I am forced to marry you, forced into your arms, forced to endure your animal lusts, *forced* to—"

"Yes, yes," Jasper cut in hastily before she could enlarge on her portrait of him as a slavering beast bent on ravishment. "I can see that I'm no match for butter-colored hair and a curate's living. I retire from the field of matrimony. Please. Go to your true love. Felicitations and all that."

"Oh, thank you, my lord!" She seized his hands and pressed moist kisses on them. "I will be forever grateful, forever in your debt. If ever—"

"Quite. Should I ever need a butter-haired curate or a curate's wife, et cetera, et cetera. I'll keep the thought in mind." With a sudden inspiration, Jasper reached into his pocket and drew out a handful of half crowns. They'd been meant to throw to the rabble outside after the wedding. "Here. For your nuptials. I wish you every happiness with, er, Mr. Fernwood."

He poured the coins into her hands.

"Oh!" Miss Templeton's eyes grew even larger. "Oh, *thank* you!"

With a last moist kiss to his hand, she skipped from the room. Perhaps she realized that the gift of several pounds' worth of coins was an impulse on his part and that if she stayed longer, he might rethink his largess.

Jasper sighed, took out a large linen handkerchief, and wiped his hands. The vestry was a little room, the walls the same ancient gray stone as the church he'd planned to be married in. Dark wood shelves lined one wall, filled with the detritus of the church: old candlesticks, papers, Bibles, and pewter plates. Above, a window with small diamond panes sat high on the wall. He could see the blue sky with a single puffy white cloud floating serenely. A lonely little room to be once more left alone. He replaced the handkerchief in his waistcoat pocket, noticing absently that a button was loose. He'd have to remember to tell Pynch. Jasper leaned his elbow on the table beside his chair and cradled his head, eyes closed.

Pynch, his man, made a wonderful pick-me-up to settle a sore head after a night of overindulgence. Soon he could go home and take the brew, perhaps go back to bed. Goddammit, but his head hurt, and he couldn't leave just yet. Voices rose from outside the vestry, echoing off the vaulted ceiling of the old stone church. From the sound, Miss Templeton was meeting with some paternal resistance to her romantic plan. A corner of Jasper's mouth kicked up. Perhaps her father wasn't as swayed by butter-yellow hair as she. In any case, he'd far rather face charging Frenchies than the family and guests outside.

He sighed and stretched his long legs before him. Thus was six months' hard work undone. Six months was the amount of time he'd taken to court Miss Templeton. A month to find a suitable lass—one from a good family, not too young, not too old, and pretty enough to bed. Three months to carefully court, flirting at balls and salons, taking her for rides in his carriage, buying her sweets and flowers and little fripperies. Then the question put to her, a satisfactory answer, and the chaste kiss on a virginal cheek. After that, the only thing left had been the calling of the banns and various purchases and arrangements made for the upcoming blissful nuptials.

What, then, had gone wrong? She'd seemed perfectly complacent to his plans. Had never once before this morning voiced any doubts. Indeed, when presented with pearl and gold earrings, one might even go so far as to say she'd been ecstatic. Whence, then, this sudden urge to marry a butter-haired curate?

This problem of losing fiancées would never have happened to his elder brother, Richard, had he lived long enough to seek his own viscountess. Perhaps it was him,

Jasper thought morbidly. Something in him that was anathema to the fairer sex—at least when it came to matrimony. One couldn't help but make note of the fact that this was the *second* time in less than a year that he'd been handed his congé. Of course, the first time it'd been Emeline, who—let us be fair, here—was more sister than lover. Nevertheless, a gentleman might very well—

The sound of the vestry door creaking open interrupted Jasper's thoughts. He opened his eyes.

A tall, slim woman hesitated in the doorway. She was a friend of Emeline's—the one whose name Jasper could never remember.

"I'm sorry, did I wake you?" she asked.

"No, merely resting."

She nodded, looked quickly over her shoulder, and shut the door behind her, closeting herself quite improperly with him.

Jasper raised his eyebrows. She'd never struck him as the dramatic sort, but then his perception in this area was obviously faulty.

She stood very straight, her shoulders square, her chin lifted ever so slightly. She was a plain woman, with features that a man would be hard-pressed to remember—probably why he couldn't remember her name now, come to think of it. Her light hair was an indeterminate color between blond and brown, and worn in a knot at the back of her head. Her eyes were a nondescript brown. Her dress was a grayish brown, with an ordinary, square-cut bodice that revealed a meager bosom. The skin there was rather fine, Jasper noted. It was that translucent bluish-white that was often compared to marble. If he peered closer, no doubt he would be able to trace the veins that ran beneath the pale, delicate skin.

Instead, he raised his eyes to her face. She'd stood there, unmoving, as he'd examined her, but a faint flush was now visible high on her cheekbones.

The sight of her discomfiture, however slight, made him feel a cad. His words, in consequence, were rather sharp. "Is there some way in which I can assist you, ma'am?"

She answered with a question of her own. "Is it true that Mary will not marry you?"

He sighed. "It appears that she has set her heart on capturing a curate, and a mere viscount will no longer do."

She didn't smile. "You do not love her."

He spread his hands. "Sadly true, though it marks me as a blackguard to confess it."

"Then I have a proposition for you."

"Oh?"

She clasped her hands in front of her and did the impossible. She straightened farther. "I wonder if you might marry me instead."

MELISANDE FLEMING MADE herself stand still and look Lord Vale in the eye, steadily and without any hint of girlish fluster. She wasn't a girl, after all. She was a woman in her eight and twentieth year, well past the age of orange blossoms and spring weddings. Well past the hope of happiness, in fact. But it seemed that hope was a hardy thing, almost impossible to beat down.

What she had just proposed was ridiculous. Lord Vale was a wealthy man. A titled man. A man in the prime of his life. In short, a man who could have his pick of simpering girls, both younger and more beautiful than she. Even if he *had* just been left at the altar for a penniless curate.

So Melisande braced herself for laughter, scorn, or—worst of all—pity.

Instead, Lord Vale simply looked at her. Perhaps he hadn't heard. His beautiful blue eyes were a trifle bloodshot, and from the way he'd been holding his head when she entered the room, she suspected that he might have overcelebrated his impending nuptials the night before.

He lounged in his chair, his long muscular legs sprawled before him, taking up much more space than he should. He stared at her with those shockingly bright green-blue eyes. They were luminescent—even whilst bloodshot—but they were the only thing about him that could be called lovely. His face was long, creased with deep lines around the eyes and mouth. His nose was long, too, as well as overlarge. His eyelids drooped at the corners as if he were perpetually sleepy. And his hair . . . actually, his hair was rather nice, curly and thick, and a lovely reddish brown color. It would've looked boyish, perhaps even effeminate, on any other man.

She'd nearly not come to his wedding today. Mary was a distant cousin, one she'd spoken to only once or twice in her life. But Gertrude, Melisande's sister-in-law, had felt ill this morning and insisted that Melisande come to represent their branch of the family. So here she was, having just made the most reckless move of her life.

How odd fate was.

Finally, Lord Vale stirred. He rubbed a large bony hand down his face and then looked at her through long, spread fingers. "I'm an idiot—you must forgive me—but for the life of me I can't remember your name."

Naturally. She'd always been the type to hover round the edges of a crowd. Never in the center, never drawing attention to herself.

While he was just the opposite.

She inhaled, tightening her fingers to still their nervous trembling. She would have only this one chance, and she mustn't bungle it.

"I am Melisande Fleming. My father was Ernest Fleming of the Northumberland Flemings." Her family was old and well respected, and she didn't deign to elaborate. If he hadn't heard of them before this, her protestations of respectability would do her no good now. "Father is dead, but I have two brothers, Ernest and Harold. My mother was a Prussian émigré, and she is also dead. You may remember that I am friends with Lady Emeline, who—"

"Yes, yes." He lifted his hand from his face to wave away her credentials. "I know *who* you are, I just didn't know . . ."

"My name."

He inclined his head. "Quite. As I said—an idiot."

She swallowed. "May I have your answer?"

"It's just that"—he shook his head and gestured vaguely with long fingers—"I know I had too much to drink last night and I'm still a little dazed by Miss Templeton's defection, so my mental facilities may not yet be up to par, but I don't see why you'd want to marry me."

"You are a viscount, my lord. False modesty ill becomes you."

His wide mouth curved in a faint smile. "Rather tart-tongued, aren't you, for a lady seeking a gentleman's hand?"

She felt the heat rise in her neck and cheeks and had to fight the urge to simply fling open the door and run.

"Why," he asked softly, "amongst all the other viscounts in the world, why marry me?"

"You are an honorable man. I know this from Emeline." Melisande stepped cautiously, picking and choosing her words with care. "From the brevity of your engagement to Mary, you are anxious to wed, are you not?".

He cocked his head. "It would certainly appear so.".

She nodded. "And I wish to have my own household instead of living on the generosity of my brothers." A partial truth.

"You have no monies of your own?"

"I have an excellent dowry and monies that are mine besides that. But an unmarried lady can hardly live by herself."

"True."

He contemplated her, apparently quite content to have her stand before him like a petitioner before the king. After a bit, he nodded and stood, his height forcing her to look up. She might be a tall woman, but he was a taller man.

"Forgive me, but I must be blunt in order to avert an embarrassing misunderstanding later. I wish a real marriage. A marriage that, with God's grace, will produce children begot in a shared marriage bed." He smiled charmingly, his turquoise eyes glinting just a little. "Is that also what you seek?"

She held his eyes, not daring to hope. "Yes."

He bowed his head. "Then, Miss Fleming, I am honored to accept your offer of marriage."

Her chest felt constricted, and at the same time it was

as if a fluttering wild thing beat against her rib cage, struggling to burst free and go flying about the room in joy.

Melisande held out her hand. "Thank you, my lord."

He smiled quizzically at her proffered hand and then took it. But instead of shaking to seal the bargain, he bent his head over her knuckles, and she felt the soft brush of his warm lips. She repressed a shudder of longing at the simple touch.

He straightened. "I only hope that you will still thank me after our wedding day, Miss Fleming."

She opened her mouth to reply, but he was already turning away. "I'm afraid I have an awful head. I'll call on your brother in three days, shall I? I must play the forsaken lover for at least three days, don't you think? Any shorter a period and it might reflect badly on Miss Templeton."

With an ironic smile, he gently closed the door behind him.

Melisande let her shoulders slump with the release of tension. She stared at the door a moment and then looked around the room. It was ordinary, small and a bit untidy. Not the sort of place one would associate with her world turning upside down. And yet—unless the last quarter hour had been a waking dream—this was the place that had seen her life take a new and completely unexpected diversion.

She examined the back of her hand. There was no mark to show where he had kissed her. She'd known Jasper Renshaw, Lord Vale, for years, but in all that time, he'd never had occasion to touch her. She pressed the back of her hand to her mouth and closed her eyes, imagining what it would be like when he touched his lips to hers. Her body trembled at the thought.

Then she straightened her back again, smoothed her already smooth skirts, and ran her fingertips across her hair to make sure everything was in order. Thus settled, she began to leave the room, but as she moved, her foot struck something. A silver button lay on the flagstones, hidden by her skirts until she'd stepped forward. Melisande picked it up and turned it slowly in her fingers. The letter *V* was embossed in the silver. She stared at it a moment before hiding the button up her sleeve.

Then she walked from the church vestry.

"PYNCH, HAVE YOU ever heard of a man losing a bride and gaining a fiancée on the same day?" Jasper asked idly later that afternoon.

He was lounging in his specially made, very large tin bathtub.

Pynch, his valet, was over in the corner of the room, messing about with the clothes in the dresser. He replied without turning. "No, my lord."

"I think, then, that perhaps I am the first in history to do so. London should put up a statue in my honor. Small children could come and gape whilst their nannies admonish them not to follow in my fickle footsteps."

"Indeed, my lord," Pynch replied in a monotone.

Pynch's voice was the perfect tone for a superior manservant—smooth, evenly deep, and unruffled—which was just as well since the rest of him wasn't much like a superior manservant at all. Pynch was a big man. A very big man. Shoulders like an ox, hands that could easily span a dinner plate, a neck as thick as Jasper's thigh, and a big bald dome of a head. What Pynch looked like was a grenadier, a heavy infantryman used by the army to charge breaches in the enemy line.

As it happened, a grenadier was exactly what Pynch had originally been in His Majesty's army. That was before he'd had a slight difference of opinion with his sergeant, which had resulted in Pynch spending a day in the stocks. Jasper had actually first seen Pynch in the stocks, stoically receiving spoiled vegetables to the face. This sight had so impressed Jasper that immediately upon Pynch's liberation, Jasper had offered him the position of his batman. Pynch had readily accepted the offer. Two years later, when Jasper had sold his commission, he'd also bought out Pynch and Pynch had returned to England with him as his valet. A satisfactory series of events all around, Jasper reflected as he stuck a foot out of his bath and flicked a droplet of water from his big toe.

"Have you sent that letter to Miss Fleming?" He'd dashed off a missive politely stating that he'd call on her brother in three days if she did not signify a change of mind in the meantime.

"Yes, my lord."

"Good. Good. I think this engagement will take. I have a feeling about it."

"A feeling, my lord?"

"Yes," Jasper said. He took up a long-handled brush and ran it across the top of his toe. "Like the one I had a fortnight ago when I wagered half a guinea on that long-necked chestnut."

Pynch cleared his throat. "I believe the chestnut came up lame."

"Did it?" Jasper waved a hand. "No matter. One should never compare ladies to horses, in any event. The point

I'm trying to make is that we are already three hours engaged, and Miss Fleming hasn't yet called it off. You're impressed, I'm sure."

"A positive sign, my lord, but may I point out that Miss Templeton waited until your wedding day to break the engagement."

"Ah, but in this case, it was Miss Fleming herself who brought up the idea of marriage."

"Indeed, my lord?"

Jasper paused in scrubbing his left foot. "Not that I'd want that fact to leave this room."

Pynch stiffened. "No, my lord."

Jasper winced. Damn, he'd insulted Pynch. "No good would come of hurting the lady's feelings, even if she did rather fling herself at my feet."

"*Fling,* my lord?"

"In a manner of speaking." Jasper gestured with the long-handled brush, spraying a nearby chair with water. "She seemed to be under the impression that I was desperate to be married and therefore might take a chance on her."

Pynch arched an eyebrow. "And you didn't correct the lady?"

"Pynch, Pynch, haven't I told you never to contradict a lady? It's ungentlemanly and a waste of time to boot—they'll just go on believing what they want anyway." Jasper scrunched his nose at the bath brush. "Besides, I have to get married sometime. Wed and beget as all my noble forefathers have done. It's no use trying to avoid the chore. A male child or two—preferably with at least half a brain in their head—must be fathered to carry on the ancient and moldy Vale name. This way it saves me months of having to go out and court another chit."

"Ah. Then one lady would do as well as any other in your view, my lord?"

"Yes," Jasper said, then immediately changed his mind. "No. Damn you, Pynch, for your lawyerly logic. Actually, there's something about her. I'm not sure how to describe it. She's not exactly the lady I'd choose, but when she stood there, looking so very brave and at the same time frowning at me as if I'd spat in front of her . . . Well, I was rather charmed, I think. Unless it was the lingering after-effects of the whiskey from last night."

"Naturally, my lord," Pynch murmured.

"*Anyway*. What I was trying to say was that I hope this engagement ends with me safely wed. Otherwise I shall very soon have a reputation as a rotten egg."

"Indeed, my lord."

Jasper frowned at the ceiling. "Pynch, you are not to agree with me when I compare myself to a rotten egg."

"No, my lord."

"Thank you."

"You're welcome, my lord."

"One can only pray that Miss Fleming will not meet any curates in the coming weeks before the wedding. Especially yellow-haired ones."

"Quite, my lord."

"D'you know," Jasper said musingly, "I don't believe I've ever met a curate I liked."

"Indeed, my lord?"

"They always seem to be lacking a chin." Jasper fingered his own rather long chin. "Perhaps it's some type of necessary requirement to enter the English clergy. Do you think that's possible?"

"Possible, yes. Likely, no, my lord."

"Hmm."

On the other side of the room, Pynch transferred a stack of linens to the top shelf of the wardrobe. "Will you be at home today, my lord?"

"Alas, no. I have other business to attend to."

"Would your business involve that man in Newgate Prison?"

Jasper switched his gaze from the ceiling to his valet. Pynch's usually wooden expression had a bit of squint about the eyes, which was Pynch's version of a worried face.

"I'm afraid so. Thornton's to be tried soon, and he's sure to be convicted and hanged. Once he's gone, any information he has dies with him."

Pynch crossed the room with a large bath sheet. "Always assuming he has any information to impart."

Jasper stepped from the tub and took the sheet. "Yes, always assuming that."

Pynch watched him as he dried off, that same squint in his eyes. "Pardon me, my lord, I don't like to speak when it isn't my place—"

"And yet you will anyway," Jasper muttered.

His manservant continued as if he hadn't heard. "But I am worried that you are becoming obsessed with this man. He's a known liar. What makes you think he'll speak the truth now?"

"Nothing." Jasper threw aside the towel and strode to a chair where his clothes lay and began dressing. "He is a liar and a rapist and a murderer and God only knows what else. Only a fool would trust his word. But I cannot let him go to the gallows without at least trying to learn the truth from him."

"I fear that he is merely toying with you for his own amusement."

"You're no doubt correct, Pynch, as you usually are." Jasper didn't look at the valet as he pulled a shirt over his head. He'd met Pynch after the massacre of the 28th Regiment of Foot at Spinner's Falls. Pynch had not fought in the battle. The valet didn't have the same drive to find out who had betrayed the regiment. "But, sadly, reason does not matter. I must go."

Pynch sighed and brought him his shoes. "Very well, my lord."

Jasper sat to draw on his buckle shoes. "Buck up, Pynch. The man'll be dead in another sennight."

"As you say, my lord," Pynch muttered as he picked up the debris of the bath.

Jasper finished dressing in silence and then went to his dresser to comb and club his hair back.

Pynch held out his coat. "I trust you haven't forgotten, my lord, that Mr. Dorning has made another request for your presence on the Vale lands in Oxfordshire."

"Damn." Dorning was his land steward and had written several appeals for his help with a land dispute. He'd already put the poor man off in order to get married and now . . . "Dorning'll just have to wait another few days. I can't leave without talking to Miss Fleming's brother and Miss Fleming herself. Remind me again, please, when I return."

Jasper shrugged on his coat, grabbed his hat, and was out of the room before Pynch could make another protest.

Jasper clattered down the stairs, nodded to his butler, and strode out the door of his London town house. Outside, one of the stable lads was waiting with Belle, his big bay mare. Jasper thanked the boy and mounted the horse, steadying her as she sidled sideways, mouthing her bit. The streets were crowded, necessitating that he keep the mare to a walk. Jasper headed west, toward the dome of St. Paul's, looming above the smaller buildings surrounding it.

The bustle of London was a far cry from the uncivilized woodland where this whole thing had started. He remembered well the tall trees and the falls, the sound of roaring water mixing with the screams of dying men. Nearly seven years before, he'd been a captain in His Majesty's army, fighting the French in the Colonies. The 28th Regiment of Foot had been marching back from the victory at Quebec, the line of soldiers strung out along a narrow path, when they'd been attacked by Indians. They'd never had time to form a defensive position. Nearly the entire regiment had been massacred in less than half an hour and their colonel killed. Jasper and eight other men were captured, marched to a Wyandot Indian camp and . . .

Even now he had trouble thinking about it. Once in a while, shadows of that period appeared at the edge of his thoughts, like a fleeting glimpse of something out of the corner of one's eye. He'd thought the whole thing over, the past dead and buried, if not forgotten. Then six months ago, he'd walked out the French doors of a ballroom and seen Samuel Hartley on the terrace outside.

Hartley had been a corporal in the army. One of the few men to survive the massacre of the 28th. He'd told Jasper that some traitor within the regiment had given their position to the French and their Indian allies. When Jasper had joined Hartley in searching for the traitor, they'd discovered a murderer who'd assumed the identity of one of the Spinner's Falls fallen—Dick Thornton. Thornton—Jasper had trouble calling him anything else, though he knew it wasn't his true name—was now in Newgate, charged with murder. But on the night they'd captured him, Thornton had claimed that he wasn't the traitor.

Jasper nudged Belle's flanks to guide her around a pushcart piled high with ripe fruit.

"Buy a sweet plum, sir?" the pretty dark-eyed girl next to the cart cried to him. She cocked her hip flirtatiously as she held out the fruit.

Jasper grinned appreciatively. "Not as sweet as your apples, I'll wager."

The fruit girl's laughter followed him as he rode through the crowded street. Jasper's thoughts returned to his mission. As Pynch had so rightly pointed out, Thornton was a man who told lies as a matter of habit. Hartley had certainly never voiced any doubt as to Thornton's guilt. Jasper snorted. Then again, Hartley had been busy with a new wife, Lady Emeline Gordon—Jasper's first fiancée.

Jasper looked up and realized that he'd come to Skinner Street, which led directly into Newgate Street. The imposing ornamental gate of the prison arched over the road. The prison had been rebuilt after the Great Fire and was suitably decorated with statues representing such fine sentiments as peace and mercy. But the closer one drew to the prison, the more ominous the stench became. The air seemed heavy, laden with the foul odors of human excrement, disease, rot, and despair.

One leg of the arch terminated in the keeper's lodge. Jasper dismounted in the courtyard outside.

A guard lounging beside the door straightened. "Back are ye, milord?"

"Like a bad penny, McGinnis."

McGinnis was a fellow veteran of His Majesty's army and had lost an eye in some foreign place. A rag was wrapped about his head to hide the hole, but it'd slipped to reveal red scarring.

The man nodded and yelled into the lodge. "Oy, Bill! Lord Vale 'as come again." He turned back to Jasper. "Bill'll be 'ere in two ticks, milord."

Jasper nodded and gave the guard a half crown, insurance that the mare would still be in the yard when he returned. He'd quickly figured out on his first visit to this dismal place that extravagantly bribing the guards made the entire experience much simpler.

Bill, a runty little man with a thick shock of iron-gray hair, soon came out of the lodge. He held the badge of his trade in his right hand: a large iron ring of keys. The little man hunched a shoulder at Jasper and crossed the yard to the prison's main entrance. Here, a huge overhanging doorway was decorated with carved manacles and the biblical quote VENIO SICUT FUR—*I come as a thief.* Bill hunched his shoulder at the guards who stood about by the portal and led the way inside.

The smell was worse here, the air stale and unmoving. Bill trotted ahead of Jasper, through a long corridor and outside again. They crossed a large courtyard with prisoners milling around or huddled in clumps like refuse washed upon a particularly dismal shore. They passed through another, smaller building, and then Bill led the way to the stairs that emptied into the Condemned Hold. It was belowground, as if to give the prisoners a taste of the hell they would soon spend eternity in. The stairs were damp, the stone worn smooth by many despairing feet.

The subterranean corridor was dim—the prisoners paid for their own candles here, and the prices were inflated. A man was singing, a low, sweet dirge that every now and again rose on a high note. Someone coughed and low voices quarreled, but the place was mostly quiet. Bill stopped before a cell that held four occupants. One lay on a pallet in the corner, most likely asleep. Two men played cards by the light of a single flickering candle.

The fourth man leaned against the wall near the bars but straightened when he saw them.

"A lovely afternoon, isn't it, Dick?" Jasper called out as he neared.

Dick Thornton cocked his head. "I wouldn't know, would I?"

Jasper tsked softly. "Sorry, old man. Forgot you can't see the sun much from in here, can you?"

"What do you want?"

Jasper regarded the man behind the bars. Thornton was an ordinary man of middling height with a pleasant, if forgettable, face. The only thing that made him stand out in the least was his flaming red hair. Thornton knew damn well what he wanted—Jasper had asked often enough in the past. "Want? Why, nothing. I'm merely passing the time, seeing the sweet sights of Newgate."

Thornton grinned and winked, the facial expression like a strange tic he couldn't control. "You must think me a fool."

"Not at all." Jasper eyed the man's threadbare clothes. He dipped his hand in his pocket and came up with a half crown. "I think you a rapist, a liar, and a murderer many times over, but a fool? Not at all. You wrong me, Dick."

Thornton licked his lips, watching as Jasper flipped the coin between his fingers. "Then why are you here?"

"Oh." Jasper tilted his head and gazed rather absently at the stained stone ceiling. "I was just remembering when we caught you, Sam Hartley and I, at Princess Wharf. Terribly rainy day. Do you remember?"

"'Course I remember."

"Then you may recollect that you claimed not to be the traitor."

A crafty gleam entered Thornton's eyes. "There's no claim about it. I'm not the traitor."

"Really?" Jasper dropped his gaze from the ceiling to stare Thornton in the eye. "Well, you see that's just it. I think you're lying."

"If I lie, then I'll die for my sins."

"You'll die anyway, and in less than a month. The law says that convicted men must be hanged within two days of their sentencing. They're rather strict about it, I'm afraid, Dick."

"That's if I'm convicted at trial."

"Oh, you will be," Jasper said gently. "Never fear."

Thornton looked sullen. "Then why should I tell you anything?"

Jasper shrugged. "You still have a few weeks left of life. Why not spend it with a full belly and clean clothes?"

"I'll tell you somethin' for a clean coat," one of the men playing cards muttered.

Jasper ignored him. "Well, Dick?"

The red-haired man stared at him, his face blank. He winked and suddenly thrust his face at the bars. "You want to know who betrayed us to the French and their scalping friends? You want to know who painted the earth with blood, there by that damned falls? Look at the men who were captured with you. That's where you'll find the traitor."

Jasper jerked his head back as if a snake had struck. "Nonsense."

Thornton stared a moment more and then began laughing, high, staccato barks.

"Shaddup!" a male voice from another cell yelled.

Thornton continued the odd sound, but the entire time his eyes were wide and fixed maliciously on Jasper's face. Jasper stared stonily back. Lies or insinuated half-truths, he'd not get any more from Dick Thornton. Today or ever. He held Thornton's gaze and deliberately dropped the coin to the floor. It rolled to the center of the passage—well out of reach of the prison cell. Thornton stopped laughing, but Jasper had already turned and was walking out of that hell-damned cellar.

Chapter Two

Presently, Jack came upon an old man, sitting by the side of the road. The old man's clothes were rags, his feet were bare, and he sat as if the whole world rested upon his shoulders.

"Oh, kind sir," the beggar cried. "Have you a crust of bread to spare?"

"I have more than that, Father," Jack replied.

He stopped and opened his pack and drew out half a meat pie, carefully wrapped in a kerchief. This he shared with the old man, and with a tin cup of water from a nearby stream, it made a very fine meal indeed. . . .

—from LAUGHING JACK

That night, Melisande sat at dinner and contemplated a meal of boiled beef, boiled carrots, and boiled peas. It was her brother Harold's favorite meal, in fact. She was on one side of a long, dark wood dining table. At the head of the table was Harold and at the foot was his wife, Gertrude.

The room was dim and shadowy, lit only by a handful of candles. They could well afford beeswax candles, of course, but Gertrude was a frugal housekeeper and did not believe in wasting candle wax—a philosophy that Harold heartily approved of. Actually, Melisande had often thought that Harold and Gertrude were the epitome of the perfectly matched husband and wife: they had the same tastes and views and were both a trifle boring.

She looked down at her grayish portion of boiled beef and considered how she was to tell her brother and his wife of her understanding with Lord Vale. Carefully she cut off a small piece of beef. She picked it up in her fingers and held the bite down by her skirts. Under the table, she felt a cold little nose against her hand, and then the beef was gone.

"I am so sorry to have missed Mary Templeton's wedding," Gertrude commented from the foot of the table. Her smooth, wide brow was marred by a single indent between her eyebrows. "Or rather, her *not* wedding, for I am sure that her mother, Mrs. Templeton, would have appreciated my presence there. I am told by many people, *many* people, that I am a comfort and a relief to those whose fortunes are in decline, and Mrs. Templeton's fortunes are *quite* in decline at the moment, are they not? One might even say Mrs. Templeton's fortunes are abysmal."

She paused to take a tiny bite of boiled carrot and looked to her husband for his concurrence.

Harold shook his head. He had their father's heavy jowls and thinning light brown hair, covered now with a gray wig. "That gel ought to be put on bread and water until she comes to her senses. Throwing over a viscount. Foolish, is what it is. Foolish!"

Gertrude nodded. "I think she must be insane."

Harold perked up at this. He was always morbidly interested in disease. "Does lunacy run in the family?"

Melisande felt a nudge against her leg. She looked down to see a small black nose poking out from beneath the table edge. She cut off another piece of beef and held it under the table. Both nose and beef disappeared.

"I do not know if there is lunacy in that family, but I would not be surprised," Gertrude replied. "No, not surprised at all. Of course, there is no lunacy on *our* side of the family, but the Templetons cannot say the same, I'm afraid."

Melisande used the tines of her fork to scoot the peas to the edge of her plate, feeling rather sorry for Mary. Mary had only followed her heart, after all. She felt a paw against her knee, but this time she ignored it. "I believe that Mary Templeton is in love with the curate."

Gertrude's eyes widened like boiled gooseberries. "I don't think that pertains." She appealed to her husband. "Do you think that pertains, Mr. Fleming?"

"No, it does not pertain at all," Harold replied predictably. "The chit had a satisfactory match, and she threw it away on a curate." He chewed meditatively for a moment. "Vale is well rid of her, in my opinion. Might've brought a bad strain of insanity into his bloodline. Not good. Not good at all. Better for him to find a wife elsewhere."

"As to that . . ." Melisande cleared her throat. She would find no better opening. Best to get it over with. "I have something I've been meaning to tell you both."

"Yes, dear?" Gertrude was sawing at the lump of beef on her plate and didn't look up.

Melisande took a deep breath and stated it bluntly, because really, there didn't seem to be any other way to do it. Her left hand lay in her lap, and she felt the comforting touch of a warm tongue. "Lord Vale and I came to an understanding today. We are going to be married."

Gertrude dropped her knife.

Harold choked on the sip of wine he'd taken.

Melisande winced. "I thought you should know."

"Married?" Gertrude said. "To Lord Vale? Jasper Renshaw, Viscount Vale?" she clarified as if there might be another Lord Vale in England.

"Yes."

"Ah." Harold looked at his wife. Gertrude stared back at him, quite obviously at a loss for words. He turned to Melisande. "Are you quite sure? Might you have mistaken a look or . . ." His sentence trailed away. It was probably quite hard to think of what else might be mistaken for a marriage proposal.

"I am sure," she said quietly but clearly. Her words were steady, though her heart was singing inside. "Lord Vale said he would call upon you in three days to settle the matter."

"I see." Harold stared in consternation at his boiled English beef, as if it had turned to Spanish stewed squid. "Well. Then I offer my congratulations, my dear. I wish you every happiness with Lord Vale." He blinked and looked up at her, his brown eyes uncertain. He'd never really understood her, poor man, but she knew he cared for her. "If you are sure?"

Melisande smiled at him. However little they had in common, Harold was still her brother, and she loved him. "I am."

He nodded, though he still looked worried. "Then I

shall send a missive informing Lord Vale that I will be glad to receive him."

"Thank you, Harold." Melisande aligned her fork and knife precisely on her plate. "Now, if you will excuse me, it's been a long day."

She rose from the table, conscious that the minute she exited the room, Harold and Gertrude would discuss the matter. The skitter of claws against the wood floor trailed her as she entered the dim hallway—Gertrude's economy of candles prevailed here as well.

Their amazement was only to be expected, really. Melisande had shown no interest in matrimony for many years, not since her disastrous engagement to Timothy so long ago. Strange, to think now how devastated she'd been when Timothy had left her. All that she'd lost had been unbearable. Her emotions had been sharp and burning then, so awful that she'd thought she might die from his rejection. The pain had been physical, a deep cutting thing that had made her chest ache and her head pound. She never wanted to feel such agony again.

Melisande rounded a corner and mounted the stairs. Since Timothy, she'd had few suitors and none of them serious. Harold and Gertrude had probably long resigned themselves to her living with them for the rest of her natural life. She was grateful that they had never shown any aversion to her constant company. Unlike many spinsters, she'd not been made to feel a burden or out of place.

In the upper hall, her room was the first around a curve to the right. She shut the door, and Mouse, her little terrier, jumped onto the bed. He turned three times, then lay down on the counterpane and looked at her.

"An exhausting day for you as well, Sir Mouse?" Melisande inquired.

The dog tilted his head at her voice, his black bead eyes alert, his button ears—one white, the other brown— pricked forward. The fire was burning low in the grate, and she used a taper to light several candles around the small bedroom. The room was sparsely furnished, yet each piece was chosen carefully. The bed was narrow, but the delicately carved posts were a rich, golden brown. The counterpane was a plain white, but the sheets hidden underneath were made of the finest silk. There was only one chair in front of the fireplace, but the arms were gilt, the seat richly embroidered in gold and purple. This was her refuge from the world. The place where she could simply be herself.

Melisande went to her desk and contemplated the pile of papers there. She was nearly done with the fairy-tale translation, but—

A knock sounded at her door. Mouse sailed off the bed and barked wildly at the door as if marauders were without.

"Hush." Melisande toed him aside and opened the door.

A maid stood outside. She bobbed a curtsy. "Please, miss, might I have a word with you?"

Melisande raised her brows and nodded, stepping back from the door. The girl eyed Mouse, who was grumbling under his breath, and made a wide berth around the dog.

Shutting the door, Melisande looked at the maid. She was a pretty girl, with gold curls and fresh, pink cheeks, and she wore a rather elegant green printed calico gown. "Sally, isn't it?"

The maid bobbed again. "Yes, mum, Sally from downstairs. I heard . . ." She gulped, squeezed her eyes shut, and said very quickly, "I heard that you'll be marrying Lord Vale, ma'am, and if you do that, you'll be leaving this house and going to live with him, and then you'll be a viscountess, ma'am, and if you're a viscountess, ma'am, then you'll be needing a proper lady's maid, because viscountesses have to have their hair and clothes just so, and begging your pardon, ma'am, but they're not just so right now. Not"—her eyes widened, as if fearing she'd just insulted Melisande—"*not* that there's anything wrong with your clothes or hair right now, but they're not, not—"

"Exactly like that of a viscountess," Melisande said dryly.

"Well, no, ma'am, if you don't mind me saying so, ma'am. And what I wanted to ask—and I'll be ever so grateful if you let me, truly I will, you won't be a wit disappointed, ma'am—is if you'd take me with you as your lady's maid?"

Sally's flow of words stopped abruptly. She simply stared, eyes and mouth wide, as if Melisande's next words would decide her very fate.

Which well they might, since the difference in station between a downstairs maid and a lady's maid was considerable. Melisande nodded. "Yes."

Sally blinked. "Ma'am?"

"Yes. You may go with me as my lady's maid."

"Oh!" Sally's hands flew up and it seemed she might grasp Melisande's in gratitude, but then she must have thought better of it and merely waved them excitedly in the air. "Oh! Oh, thank you, ma'am! Oh, thank you! You'll not regret it, really you won't. I'll be the best lady's maid you ever did see, just you watch."

"I'm sure you will." Melisande opened the door again. "We can discuss your duties more thoroughly in the morning. Good night."

"Yes, ma'am. Thank you, ma'am. Good night, ma'am."

Sally bobbed into the hall, did a half-turn, bobbed again, and was still bobbing as Melisande shut the door.

"She seems a nice enough girl," she said to Mouse.

Mouse snorted and leaped back onto the bed.

Melisande tapped him on the nose, then crossed to her dresser. A plain tin snuffbox sat on top. She briefly brushed the battered surface with her fingertips before taking out the button from where she'd hidden it in her sleeve. The silver *V* winked in the candlelight as she contemplated it.

She'd loved Jasper Renshaw for six long, long years. It must've been shortly after he'd returned to England that she'd attended the party where she'd met him. He hadn't noticed her, of course. His blue-green eyes had drifted over her head as they were introduced, and shortly afterward, he'd excused himself to flirt with Mrs. Redd, a notorious and notoriously beautiful widow. Melisande had watched from the side of the ball, sitting next to a line of elderly ladies, as he'd thrown his head back and laughed with complete abandon. His neck had been strong, his mouth opened wide with mirth. He was a captivating sight, but she probably would've dismissed him after that as a silly, feckless aristocrat if not for what had happened several hours later.

It was after midnight, and she'd long since grown tired of the festivities. In fact, she would've gone home if it wouldn't have spoiled her friend Lady Emeline's pleasure. Emeline had bullied her into attending, for it had been over a year since the fiasco with Timothy, and Melisande's spirits were still low. But the noise, the heat and press of bodies, and the staring of strangers had become unbearable, and Melisande had drifted away from the ballroom. She thought she'd gone in the direction of the ladies' retiring room, until she'd heard male voices. She should've turned back then, crept away down the dark corridor, but one of the male voices had risen, had seemed to be *weeping,* in fact, and curiosity had gotten the better of her. She'd peered around a corner and had witnessed . . . well, a tableau.

A young man she'd never seen before leaned against a wall at the end of the corridor. He wore a white wig, beneath which was a pale and smoothly flawless complexion, save for the ruddy color in his cheeks. He was beautiful, but his head was flung back, his eyes closed, his face the picture of despair. In one hand, he grasped a bottle of wine. Next to him was Lord Vale, but a completely different Lord Vale than the man who'd spent three hours flirting and laughing in the ballroom. This Lord Vale was silent and still and listening.

Listening to the other man weep.

"They used to come to me only in my dreams, Vale," the young man cried. "Now they come even when I wake. I see a face in a crowd, and I imagine it a Frenchie or one of those savages, come to take my scalp. I know 'tisn't so, but I can't convince myself. Last sennight, I struck my valet and knocked him down just because he startled me. I don't know what to do. I don't know if it will end. I can't rest!"

"Hush," Vale murmured, almost as a mother would a child. His eyes were sad, his mouth twisted down. "Hush. It'll end. I promise you, it'll end."

"How do you know?"

"I was there, too, wasn't I?" Vale answered. With one hand, he took the bottle gently from the other man's hand. "I survived and so will you. You must be strong."

"But do you see the demons?" the young man whispered.

Vale closed his eyes as if in pain. "It's best to ignore them. Turn your mind to lighter, more wholesome images. Don't dwell on the morbid and hellish thoughts. They'll capture your mind if you do and will pull you down with them."

The other man sagged against the wall. He still looked unhappy, but his brow was clearing. "You understand me, Vale. No one else does."

A footman came from the other end of the hall and caught Lord Vale's eye. Lord Vale nodded.

"Your carriage is already waiting. This man will show you the way." Lord Vale placed his hand on the other man's shoulder. "Go home and rest. On the morrow, I shall call 'round, and we shall go riding in Hyde Park together, my friend."

The young man sighed and let himself be led away by the footman.

Lord Vale stared after them until they disappeared around the corner. Then he tilted his head back and drank a long swallow from the bottle of wine.

"Goddamn it," he muttered when he lowered the bottle, and his wide mouth twisted in pain or another less understandable emotion. "Goddamn it to hell."

And he turned and strode away.

A half hour later, she saw Lord Vale again. He was in the ballroom, slyly whispering in Mrs. Redd's ear, and Melisande would never have believed this careless rogue the same man who had comforted his friend, if she had not seen it herself. But she had seen it, and she'd known. Despite Timothy and the hard lessons learned about love, grief, and loss, she'd known. Here was a man who kept his secrets as close as she did her own. Here was a man she would fall helplessly—*hopelessly*—in love with.

For six years, she'd loved him, though she knew he did not know her. She'd stood and watched as Emeline became engaged to Lord Vale, and she hadn't turned a hair. After all, what use was mourning when the man would never be hers? She'd watched as he'd engaged himself again to the insipid Mary Templeton, and she'd been serene—at least on the outside. But when she'd realized in that church yesterday that Mary had actually thrown Lord Vale over, something wild and uncontrollable had risen up in her breast. *Why not?* it'd cried. *Why not try and claim him?*

And so she had.

Melisande tilted the button until the candlelight flashed off its polished surface. She would have to be very, very careful how she proceeded with Lord Vale. Love, as she so well knew, was her Achilles' heel. Not by word or deed must she let him know how she really felt. Melisande opened the snuffbox and placed the button carefully inside.

She undressed and extinguished the candles before climbing into bed. Holding the covers up, she let Mouse bustle underneath. The bed trembled as he turned around and then lay down, his smooth, warm back against her calves.

Melisande stared into the darkness. Soon she would be sharing her bed with more than little Mouse. Would she be able to lie with Jasper without revealing her terrible love? She shivered at the question and closed her eyes to sleep.

ONE WEEK LATER, Jasper drew his matched grays to a halt in front of Mr. Harold Fleming's town house and sprang down from his phaeton. His *new* phaeton. It was tall and elegant, had cost an extravagant amount of money, and the wheels were absolutely enormous. He was rather looking forward to driving Miss Fleming to an afternoon musicale. He wasn't looking forward to the musicale itself, of course, but he supposed one must end up somewhere when driving a phaeton.

Tilting his tricorne at a jaunty angle, he bounded up the steps and knocked. Ten minutes later, he was cooling his heels in a rather boring library while he waited for his fiancée to appear. He'd actually seen this library only four days before when he'd called upon Mr. Fleming to discuss the marriage settlement. *That* had been an entirely tedious three hours, brightened only by the fact that Miss Fleming had been quite right: She did indeed have an excellent dowry. Miss Fleming herself had not appeared once during his visit. Not that she was required for the business meeting—in fact, it was usual for the lady involved to be absent—but her presence would've been a welcome break.

Jasper strolled the library and inspected the shelves. The books seemed to be all in Latin, and he was just wondering if Mr. Fleming actually read everything in Latin or if he'd bought the books by the crate at a booksellers when Miss Fleming entered the room, drawing on her gloves. He hadn't seen her since that morning in the vestry, but she wore nearly the same expression: a look of mingled determination and faint disapproval. Oddly, he found the expression rather charming.

Jasper bowed with a flourish. "Ah, my dear, you are as winsome as the breeze on a sunny summer's day. That frock enshrines your beauty like gold does a ruby ring."

She tilted her head. "I believe your simile is not quite correct. My dress is not gold-colored, and I am not a ruby."

Jasper widened his smile, showing more teeth. "Ah, but I have no doubt that your virtue will prove you a ruby among women."

"I see." Her mouth twitched, whether in irritation or amusement it was hard to tell. "You know, I've never understood why there isn't a similar passage in the Bible instructing husbands."

He tsked. "Careful. You come perilously close to blasphemy. Besides, are not husbands universally virtuous?"

She humphed. "And how do you explain my dress that is not gold?"

"It may not be gold, but the color is, ah . . ." And here he rather unfortunately ran out of ideas, because, in fact, the frock Miss Fleming wore was the color of horse dung.

Miss Fleming slowly arched an eyebrow.

Jasper clasped her gloved hand and bent over it, inhaling the spicy orange scent of Neroli water as he thought for something to say. All he could think was that the sensuous Neroli scent was in sharp contrast to her plain gown.

It did stimulate his brain, however, because when he rose, he smiled charmingly and said, "The color of your frock reminds me of a wild and stormy cliff."

Miss Fleming's eyebrow remained arched skeptically. "Indeed?"

Damnable girl. He tucked her hand in his elbow. "Yes."

"How so?"

"It is an exotic and mysterious color."

"I thought it was plain brown."

"Nay." He widened his eyes in feigned shock. "Never say 'plain brown.' Ash or oak or tea or fawn or perhaps even squirrel-colored, but certainly not brown."

"Squirrel-colored?" She looked at him sideways as he led her down the steps. "Is that a compliment, my lord?"

"I believe so," he said. "I have certainly tried my best to make it so. But it might depend on how one feels about squirrels."

They had halted in front of his phaeton, and she was frowning up at the seat. "Squirrels are rather pretty sometimes."

"There, you see. Definitely a compliment."

"Silly man," she murmured, and gingerly placed a foot on the wooden steps set before the phaeton.

"Allow me." He grasped her elbow to steady her as she climbed into the carriage, conscious that he could wrap his fingers all the way about her arm—the bones beneath her flesh were delicate and thin. He felt her stiffen as she settled, and it occurred to him that she might be nervous sitting so high. "Hold on to the side. There's nothing to be worried about, and Lady Eddings's house isn't far."

That earned him a scowl. "I'm not afraid."

"Of course not," he called as he rounded the carriage and climbed in. He could feel her body, stiff and still beside him as he took the ribbons and started the horses. One of her hands lay limply in her lap, but the other grasped the carriage's side tightly. Whatever she might say, his fiancée was indeed wary of the carriage. He felt a twinge of tenderness for her. She was such a prickly thing, she must hate to show weakness.

"I think you are very fond of squirrels," he said to distract her.

A line knit itself between her brows. "Why do you say that?"

"Because you wear it so often—that squirrel color. I have deduced from your fondness for squirrel-colored gowns that you are fond of the animal itself. Perhaps you had a pet squirrel as a child, and it ran about the house, upsetting the maids and your nanny."

"What a flight of fancy," she said. "The color is brown, as you well know, and I don't know if I'm fond of brown, but I am used to it."

He snuck a look at her. She was frowning at his hands handling the ribbons. "They wear it so they can't be seen."

She tore her gaze from his hands and looked at him rather bemusedly. "You've lost me, my lord."

"The squirrels again, I'm afraid. I am sorry, but if you don't start another topic, I shall probably babble about them all the way to the musicale. Squirrels are squirrel-colored because squirrel color is hard to see in a forest. I wonder if that's why you wear it as well."

"So that I might hide in a forest?" Her smile was definite this time.

"Perhaps. Perhaps you want to flit from tree to tree in a shadowed forest, eluding both beast and poor, poor man. What do you think?"

"I think you don't know me very well."

And he turned and looked at her as she stared back at him, amused, but with her hand still tightly gripped on the carriage's side. "No, I suppose you're right."

He did want to know her, though, he realized, this vexing creature who refused to show fear.

"Are you happy with the arrangements your brother and I came to?" he asked. The first banns had been called yesterday, and they would be married in another three weeks. Many ladies would not like such a short engagement. "I must tell you that we tussled long and hard. At one point, I thought our men of business would come to fisticuffs. Fortunately, your brother averted the crisis with the quick application of tea and muffins."

"Oh, dear, poor Harold."

"Poor Harold indeed, but what about me?"

"You are obviously a saint among men."

"I am glad you realize it," he said. "And the arrangements?"

"I am content with them," she replied.

"Good." He cleared his throat. "I should tell you that I'll be leaving town tomorrow."

"Oh?" Her tone was still even, but the hand in her lap had fisted.

"Can't be helped, I'm afraid. I've been the recipient of letters from my land steward for weeks now. He informs me that my presence is desperately needed to settle some type of dispute. I can ignore them no longer. I suspect," he confided, "that Abbott, my neighbor, has again let his tenants build on my land. He does it every decade or so— tries to expand his border. The man's eighty if he's a day, and he's been doing it for half a century. Used to drive my pater mad."

There was a short pause as he guided the horses into a smaller street.

"Do you know when you shall return?" his fiancée inquired.

"A week, maybe two."

"I see."

He glanced at her. Her lips were thinned. Did she want him to stay? The woman was as inscrutable as the Sphinx. "But I shall certainly return by our wedding date."

"Naturally," she murmured.

He looked up and saw that they were already at Lady Eddings's town house. He drew the horses to a halt and threw the ribbons to a waiting boy before jumping from the carriage. Despite his swiftness, Miss Fleming was already standing when he rounded to her side, which rather irritated him.

He held out his hand. "Let me help you."

She stubbornly ignored his hand and, still gripping the carriage side, gingerly lowered a foot toward the steps set beside the carriage.

Jasper felt something snap. She could be as brave as she wanted, but she need not spurn his help. He reached up and wrapped his hands about her slender, warm waist. She gave a breathless squeak, and then he was letting her go in front of him. The scent of Neroli floated in the air.

"There was no need for that," she said, shaking out her skirts.

"Oh, yes, there was," he muttered before tucking her

hand safely into his elbow. He led her toward the imposing white doors of the Eddings town house. "Ah, a musicale. What a delightful way to spend an afternoon. I do hope there will be country ballads about damsels drowning themselves in wells, don't you?"

Miss Fleming shot a disbelieving glance at him, but a formidable butler was already opening the door. Jasper grinned at his fiancée and ushered her in. His blood was running high, and it wasn't at the prospect of an afternoon of screeching or even the company of Miss Fleming, interesting as she was. He hoped to see Matthew Horn here. Horn was a very old friend, a fellow veteran of His Majesty's army and, more to the point, one of the few men to survive Spinner's Falls.

MELISANDE SAT ON a narrow chair and tried to concentrate on the young girl singing. If she sat very still and closed her eyes, she knew the awful panic would recede eventually. The trouble was, she hadn't anticipated how much comment the news of their precipitous engagement would excite in the *ton*. The moment they'd stepped into Lady Eddings's town house, she and Jasper had been the center of all eyes—and Melisande had wanted to simply disappear. She *loathed* being the center of attention. It made her hot and sweaty. Her mouth went dry and her hands trembled. And worst of all, she always seemed to lose the power of intelligent speech. She'd just stared dumbly when that horrid Mrs. Pendleton had inferred that Lord Vale must be desperate to've made Melisande an offer. Tonight, a half-dozen biting repartee would come to her as she lay sleepless in her bed, but right now she might as well be a sheep. She hadn't anything more intelligent to say than *baaaaa*.

Next to her, Lord Vale leaned close and whispered hoarsely and none too quietly, "Do you think she's a shepherdess?"

Baaa? Melisande blinked up at him.

He rolled his eyes. *"Her."*

He tilted his head at the cleared space next to the harpsichord where Lady Eddings's youngest daughter stood. The girl actually sang rather well, but the poor thing wore enormous panniers and a floppy bonnet, and she carried a pail of all things.

"Surely she's not a chambermaid?" Lord Vale wondered. He'd taken their notoriety in stride, laughing loudly when he'd been cornered by several gentlemen before the musicale. Now he jiggled his left leg like a small boy forced to sit at church. "I'd think she'd be carrying a coal shuttle if she were a chambermaid. Though that might be rather heavy."

"She's a milkmaid," Melisande murmured.

"Really?" His shaggy eyebrows drew together. "Surely not with those panniers?"

"Shh!" someone hissed from behind them.

"I mean," Lord Vale whispered only a little lower, "wouldn't the cows trod on her skirts? Don't seem practical at all. Not that I know all that much about cows and milkmaids and such, but I do like cheese."

Melisande bit her lip, fighting down an unusual urge to giggle. How strange! She wasn't the giggling sort at all. She glanced at Lord Vale out of the corner of her eye only to see him watching her.

His wide mouth curved, and he leaned closer, his

breath brushing her cheek. "I adore cheese and grapes, the dark, round, red kind of grape that burst in one's mouth all sweet and juicy. Do you like grapes?"

Although the words were perfectly innocent, he said them with such a deep drawl, that she was hard pressed not to blush. And she suddenly realized that she'd seen him do this before: lean close to a lady and whisper wicked things in her ear. She'd watched him do it innumerable times over the years to innumerable ladies at innumerable parties. But this time was different.

This time he was flirting with *her*.

So she straightened her back and cast her eyes down demurely and said, "I do like grapes, but I think I prefer raspberries. The sweetness is not so cloying. And sometimes there's a tart one with a bit of a . . . bite."

When she raised her eyes and looked at him, he was staring back thoughtfully, as if he didn't know quite what to make of her. She held his gaze, whether in challenge or warning, she wasn't quite sure, until her breath began to grow short, and his cheeks darkened. He'd lost his habitual careless smile—he wasn't smiling at all, in fact—and something serious, something dark, was staring out of his eyes at her.

Then the audience burst into applause, and Melisande started at the crash of sound. Lord Vale looked away, and the moment was lost.

"Shall I bring you a glass of punch?" he asked.

"Yes." She swallowed. "Thank you."

And she watched him get up and saunter away, aware that the world had rushed back into her senses. Behind her, the young matron who had shushed them was gossiping with a friend. Melisande caught the word *enceinte* and tilted her head away so she could no longer overhear the murmurs. Lady Eddings's daughter was being congratulated on her performance. A spotty youth stood next to the girl loyally holding her pail. Melisande smoothed her skirts, glad that no one had bothered to come talk to her. If she were allowed to only sit and observe the people around her, she might enjoy events like this one.

She turned her head and located Lord Vale in the crowd around the refreshments table. He wasn't hard to find. He stood half a head taller than all the other gentlemen, and he was laughing in that open way he had, one arm thrown out, the glass of punch in his hand in danger of splashing in the wig of the gentleman next to him. Melisande smiled—it was hard not to when he was so boisterous— but then she saw his face change. It was a subtle thing, a mere narrowing of the eyes, his wide smile falling just slightly. Probably no one else in the room would notice it. But she had. Melisande followed his gaze. A gentleman in a white wig had just entered the room. He stood talking to their hostess, a polite smile on his face. He looked almost familiar, but she couldn't place him. He was of average height, his countenance open and fresh, his bearing military.

She looked back at Lord Vale. He'd started forward, the glass of punch still in his hand. The young man glanced up, saw Vale, and excused himself from Lady Eddings. He walked toward Vale, his hand extended in greeting, but his face was somber. Melisande watched as her fiancé took the other man's hand and drew him close to murmur something; then he glanced around the room and, inevitably, met her eyes. He'd lost his smile somewhere as he'd crossed the room, and now his face was quite expressionless. Deliberately, he turned his back to her, drawing the other man with him. Just then, the young man in the white wig looked over his shoulder, and Melisande inhaled, finally remembering where she'd seen him before.

He was the man she'd seen weeping six years before.

Chapter Three

After the last crumb of meat pie was eaten, the old man stood, and a very strange thing happened. His tattered clothes fell away, and suddenly there stood before Jack a young, handsome man in shining white garments.

"You have been kind to me," the angel said—for who else could he be but an angel of God? "And so I shall reward you."

The angel drew forth a little tin box and pressed it into Jack's palm. "Look inside for what you need, and it shall be there."

He turned and was gone.

Jack blinked for a moment before peering inside the box. And then he laughed, for there was nothing inside but a few leaves of snuff. Tucking the little tin snuffbox into his pack, he set off along the road again. . . .

—from LAUGHING JACK

Three weeks later, Melisande hid her trembling hands in the full skirts of her wedding dress. Behind her, Sally Suchlike, her new lady's maid, was doing some last-minute fussing with the skirts.

"Don't you just look a treat, miss," Suchlike said as she worked.

They stood in the enclosed church porch, just off the nave. The organ had already started inside, and soon Melisande would have to walk into the crowded church. She shivered with nerves. Even on such short notice, nearly all the pews were full.

"I thought gray was a bit dull when you picked it out," Suchlike chattered, "but now it almost shines like silver."

"It's not too much, is it?" Melisande looked down worriedly. The dress was more ornamented than she'd originally wished, with pale yellow ribbons tied in small bows all along the low round neckline. Her overskirt was pulled back to reveal the heavily embroidered underskirt of gray, red, and yellow.

"Oh, no. It's very sophisticated," the lady's maid replied. She came around to face Melisande and frowned, inspecting her rather like a cook examining a haunch of beef. Then she smiled. "Lord Vale will be that taken with you, I'm sure. After all, it's been ages since he last saw you."

Well, that wasn't quite true, Melisande reflected, but it *had* been several weeks since she'd seen the viscount. Lord Vale had left the day after Lady Eddings's musicale and had not returned to London until yesterday. She'd even begun to wonder if he was staying away to avoid her. He'd been rather distracted at the musicale after talking to his friend, and he'd never introduced her to the man.

Indeed, his friend had disappeared after talking to Lord Vale. But none of that mattered, she chided herself. After all, Lord Vale stood right now at the front of the church waiting for her appearance.

"Ready?" called Gertrude, who hurried in from the nave door and reached out to twitch at Melisande's skirts. "I never thought I'd see this day, my dear, never! Married, and to a viscount. The Renshaws are a very nice family— no hint of bad blood at all. Oh, Melisande!"

To her amazement, Melisande saw that phlegmatic Gertrude had tears in her eyes.

"I'm so happy for you." Gertrude gave her a stiff hug, pressing her cheek briefly to Melisande's. "Are you ready?"

Melisande straightened her back and drew in a steadying breath before answering. Even her trembling nerves couldn't keep the quiet joy from her voice. "Yes, I am."

JASPER LOOKED DOWN at the slice of roasted duck on his plate and thought how very odd the tradition of the wedding breakfast was. Here was a group of friends and family gathered to celebrate love when in reality it was fertility they should be feting. That was, after all, the desired point to a union such as this: the production of children.

Ah, well, he was finally married, and perhaps he should lay aside cynicism and look no further than that fact. Yesterday, whilst riding toward London, he'd begun to wonder if he'd left off returning for too long. What if Miss Fleming had grown weary of being ignored? What if she didn't even bother showing up at the church to give him his congé? He'd been detained in Oxfordshire far longer than he'd planned. There always seemed to be something more to delay his return there—another field his land steward wanted to show him, a road that badly needed repair, and, if he was honest with himself, the very steadiness of his fiancée's gaze. She seemed to see right through him with those tilted brown eyes, seemed to look beyond his surface laughter and saw what he hid in the depths of his soul. At Lady Eddings's musicale, when he'd turned and saw Melisande Fleming watching him and Matthew Horn, he'd had a moment of stark terror—fear that she knew what they talked about.

But she didn't know. Jasper took a swallow of ruby wine, reassured on that point. She didn't know what had happened at Spinner's Falls, and she would never know if, with God's grace, he could help it.

"Jolly good wedding, what?" an elderly gentleman leaned forward to shout down the table.

Jasper hadn't a notion who the gentleman was—must be a relative of his bride's—but he grinned and raised his wineglass to the fellow. "Thank you, sir. I rather enjoyed it myself."

The gentleman winked hideously. "Enjoy the wedding night more, what? I say, enjoy the wedding *night* more! Ha!"

He was so taken with his own wit that he nearly lost his gray wig laughing.

The elderly lady sitting across from the gentleman rolled her eyes and said, "That's quite enough, William."

Beside him, Jasper felt his bride still, and he cursed under his breath. Some of the color had finally returned to her cheeks. She'd gone quite white at the ceremony, and he'd prepared himself to catch her should she faint. But she hadn't. Instead, she'd stood like a soldier before a firing squad and grimly recited her marriage vows. Not quite the expression a bridegroom hoped for on his bride on her wedding day, but he'd learned not to be particular after the last fiasco.

Jasper raised his voice. "Will you tell us the story of your own wedding, sir? I feel we shall be quite entertained."

"He doesn't remember," the old lady said before her husband could recover enough to speak. "He was so drunk he fell asleep afore he even came to bed!"

The guests within earshot roared.

"Aw, Bess!" the elderly man shouted above the laughter. "You know I was plumb worn out from chasing you." He turned to the young lady beside him, eager to recount his memories. "Courted her for nigh on four years and . . ."

Jasper gently replaced his wineglass and glanced at his bride. Miss Fleming—*Melisande*—was pushing her food into neat piles on her plate.

"Eat some of that," he murmured. "The duck is not nearly as bad as it looks, and it'll make you feel better."

She didn't look at him, but her body stiffened. "I am fine."

Stubborn girl. "I'm sure you are," he replied easily. "But you were as white as a sheet in the church—for a while, you were even green. I can't tell you how it shattered my bridegroom's nerves. Indulge me now and have a bite."

Her mouth curved a little, and she ate a small piece of the duck. "Is everything you say in jest?"

"Nearly everything. I know it's tedious, but there it is." He motioned to a footman, and the man bent near. "Please refill the viscountess's wineglass."

"Thank you," she murmured when the man had poured more wine. "It's not, you know."

"What isn't?"

"Your jesting." She looked at him, her tilted eyes mysterious. "It isn't tedious. I like it, actually. I only hope you will be able to bear my own reticence."

"If you look at me like that, I shall bear it most admirably," he whispered.

She held his eyes as she sipped from her wineglass, and he could see her swallow, the hollow of her throat soft and vulnerable. He would bed this woman tonight—this woman he hardly knew. He'd cover her body and enter her soft, warm flesh, and he'd make her his wife.

The thought was strange at this highly civilized breakfast. Strange, and at the same time pleasantly arousing. What a very odd thing marriage was between people of his rank. Like breeding horses in many ways. One picked out the dam and the sire based on their bloodlines, put them in proximity to each other, and hoped nature took its course and produced more horses—or aristocrats, depending on the parties.

He smiled as he watched his new wife, wondering what she would say if he told her his thoughts about horses and aristocratic marriages. Alas, though, the topic was too risqué for virginal ears.

But others were not. "Is the wine to your liking, my lady?"

"It's acidic, tart, with just a tiny bit of sweetness from the grapes." She smiled slowly. "So, yes, it's to my liking."

"How delightful," Jasper murmured, his eyelids drooping lazily. "It is, of course, my duty as your husband to see that your every desire, no matter how small, is fulfilled."

"Indeed?"

"Oh, yes."

"Then what is my duty as your wife?"

To bear my heirs. The reply was too blunt to voice. This was a time for pretty flirtation and banter, not the cold realities of a marriage such as theirs. "My lady, you have no more onerous a duty than to be lovely and grace my home and heart."

"But I believe I may soon become bored by such light duties. I'd require additional tasks to fulfill than merely looking lovely." She sipped her wine and set the glass down; as she did so, her tongue darted out to slowly lick a droplet from her bottom lip. "Perhaps you can invent a more exacting duty?"

He inhaled, for his entire attention had become focused on her wet bottom lip. "My lady, my mind is awhirl with possibilities. It dances hither and yon, brushing many but alighting on none, though several tantalize. Have you no examples to give me of what a wife's duties should be?"

"Oh, examples abound." A smile was playing about her lips. "Should I not obey and honor you?"

"Ah, but those are light duties, and you specified an exacting one."

"Obeying you may not always be a light task," she murmured.

"With me it shall be. I will merely bid you to do such things as smile at me and make my day brighter. Will you obey me in this?"

"Yes."

"Then already I feel a surfeit of wifely honor. But I seem to remember another vow."

"To love you," she said. Her eyes dropped in maidenly modesty. He could no longer see her expression.

"Yes, only that," he said lightly. "To love me is, I fear, a much greater task than any other wifely duty—I am a very unlovable fellow at times—and I'll not blame you should you choose to forsake it. You may merely admire me instead, if it is more to your liking."

"But I am a woman of honor, and I have made a vow," she said.

He looked at her and tried to see which was the banter and which was her real feeling—if she had one. "Then you will love me?"

She shrugged. "Of course."

He raised his glass to her. "Count me, then, the most fortunate man alive."

But she merely smiled now, as if wearying of their wordplay.

He sipped his wine. Was she looking forward to this night or dreading it? Surely the latter rather than the former. Even at her age—older than many brides—she likely knew very little of the physical act between a man and a woman. Perhaps that fact accounted for some of the paleness in her face earlier. He must remind himself to go slowly tonight and not to do anything that might frighten or disgust her. Despite her lively repartee, she was by her own admission a reserved woman. Perhaps he ought to consider putting off the consummation for another day or so, in order that she grow more used to him. A depressing thought.

He shook his head and shoved all depressing thoughts

aside, then took another slice of roast duck. After all, it was his wedding day.

"OH, IT WAS a beautiful wedding, my lady," Suchlike said dreamily that night as she helped Melisande from her gown. "His lordship looked so handsome in his red embroidered coat, didn't he? So tall and with those lovely wide shoulders. I don't think he needs to use padding at all, do you?"

"Mmm," Melisande murmured. Lord Vale's shoulders were one of her favorite things about him, but her new husband's physique didn't seem quite the thing to discuss with her maid. She stepped out of her underskirts.

Suchlike draped the underskirts over a chair and began unlacing Melisande's stays. "And when Lord Vale threw those coins to the crowd! What a kind gentleman he is. Did you know, ma'am, that he gave a guinea to every servant in this house, even the little bootblack boy?"

"Really?" Melisande bit back a fond smile at this evidence of Lord Vale's sentimental nature. She wasn't surprised at all. She rubbed a sore spot under her arm where the stays had chafed a bit. Then, clad in her chemise, she sat at a dainty burlwood vanity and began taking down her stockings.

"Mrs. Cook says that Lord Vale is a very pleasant gentleman to work for. Pays a regular wage and doesn't shout at the maids as some gentlemen do." Suchlike shook out the stays and laid them carefully in the big carved wardrobe in the corner.

The viscountess's rooms in Renshaw House had been closed since Lord Vale's father had died and his mother had moved to the London dowager residence. But Mrs.

Moore, the housekeeper, was obviously a very competent woman. The rooms had been thoroughly cleaned. The bedroom's honey-colored woodwork was freshly waxed and shining dully, the dark blue and gold drapes had been aired and brushed, and even the carpets looked to have been taken out and beaten.

The bedroom was not overly large but was quite lovely. The walls were a soothing creamy white, the carpets dark blue with spots of gold and ruby patterning. The fireplace was a pretty little thing, tiled in cobalt blue and surrounded by a white woodwork mantel. There were two gilt-legged chairs in front of it with a low marble-topped table between them. On one wall was a door that led to the viscount's rooms—she looked quickly away from it—on the opposite wall, a door that led to her dressing room, and beyond, a private little sitting room. Now and again, a faint scratching came from the dressing room, but she ignored it. Overall, the rooms were very comfortable and pleasant.

"So, you've met the other servants?" Melisande asked to distract herself from staring at Lord Vale's connecting door like a lovesick ninny.

"Yes, my lady." Suchlike came over and began taking down her hair. "The butler, Mr. Oaks, is very stern, but he seems fair. Mrs. Moore says she respects his judgment wholeheartedly. There are six downstairs maids and five upper, and I don't know how many footmen."

"I counted seven," Melisande murmured. She'd been introduced to the household this afternoon, but it would take time to learn individual names and duties. "They were all kind to you, then?"

"Oh, yes, ma'am." Suchlike was silent a moment,

taking out the myriad of pins that had held her hair up. "Although . . ."

Melisande watched the little maid in the vanity's mirror. Suchlike's delicate brows were drawn together. "Yes?"

"Oh, it's nothing, ma'am," she said, then immediately added, "Only that man, Mr. Pynch. There I was being quite polite as Mr. Oaks introduced everyone, and that man Mr. Pynch looked down his nose at me—and a very big nose it is, too, ma'am. I don't think he should be so awfully proud of it. And he says, 'Rather young for a lady's maid, aren't you?' in this terribly stuffy voice. And what I want to know is, what business is it of his anyway?' "

Melisande blinked. She'd never seen Suchlike take offense at anyone or anything before. "Who is this Mr. Pynch?"

"He's his lordship's man," Suchlike said. She picked up the brush and ran it through Melisande's hair with vigorous strokes. "A big oaf of a man, no hair at all on top. Cook said he served with Lord Vale in the Colonies."

"Then he's been with Lord Vale for many years."

Suchlike braided her hair with quick, sure movements. "Well, I think he's gotten full of himself. A less likable, stuck-up, *nasty* man I've rarely met."

Melisande smiled, but then the smile faded and she looked up at a sound, her breath quickening.

The door connecting her rooms to the viscount's opened. Lord Vale stood in the doorway dressed in a scarlet banyan over breeches and a shirt. "Ah. I've arrived too early. Come back, shall I?"

"There's no need, my lord." Melisande struggled to keep her voice from quavering. She was having trouble not staring at him. His shirt was unbuttoned at the throat, and that small bit of intimate skin was having a devastating effect on her. "That will be all, Suchlike."

The maid bobbed a curtsy, suddenly tongue-tied in the presence of her new master. She trotted to the door and left.

Lord Vale looked after Suchlike. "I hope I haven't frightened your little maid."

"She's just nervous in a new house." Melisande watched him in the mirror as he roamed her room, an exotic male beast. She was his *wife*. She was hard-pressed not to laugh aloud at the thought.

He strolled to the little fireplace and peered at a china clock on the mantel. "I really didn't mean to disturb your evening toilet. I'm terrible about time. I can return in another half hour or so, if you'd prefer."

"No. I'm perfectly ready." She took a breath, stood, and turned.

He looked at her, his gaze trailing down over her lace-trimmed chemise. It was voluminous but nearly sheer, and she felt her belly tighten at the touch of his eyes.

Then he blinked and looked away. "Perhaps you would like some wine?"

A small twinge of disappointment went through her, but she didn't let it show. She inclined her head. "That would be nice."

"Excellent." He moved to a side table by the fireplace where a decanter stood and poured two glasses.

She came to the fireplace and was standing near him when he turned back around.

He held out a glass. "There you are."

"Thank you." She took the glass and sipped. Was he nervous? He was staring into the fire, so she sank into one of the gilt chairs and waved at the other. "Please. Won't you sit, my lord?"

"Yes. Quite." He sat and drained half his glass, then leaned forward suddenly, the glass dangling from his fingers between his legs. "Look here, I've been trying to figure out how to say this properly all day, and I've yet to find a way, so I'll just say it. We married rather rapidly, and I was away for most of our engagement, which was my own damned fault, and I'm sorry. But because of all that, we haven't had a chance to become properly acquainted and I was thinking, ah . . ."

"Yes?"

"Perhaps you'd rather wait." He finally raised his eyes to hers and watched her with something very much like pity. "It's your decision—I leave it completely up to you."

It came to her, in a blinding, terrible flash of light, that perhaps he didn't find her attractive enough to bed. Why should he, after all? She was tall and rather thin, her figure not particularly shapely. And her face had never been called pretty. He'd flirted with her, but then he flirted with *every* woman he met, high or low. It didn't mean anything. She looked at him mutely. What was she to do? What *could* she do? They'd married just this morning; it wasn't something that could be undone.

She didn't want it undone.

He'd continued speaking during her awful realization. ". . . and we could wait a bit, a month or two, or however long you wished because—"

"No."

He stopped. "I beg your pardon?"

If they waited, there was a chance the marriage would never be consummated. That was the last thing she wanted—the last thing *he'd* said he wanted. She couldn't let that happen.

She set her glass on the table in front of the fire. "I don't want to wait."

"I . . . see."

She stood and went to stand in front of him. He looked up at her, his eyes brilliantly blue.

He drained his wineglass, set it down, and stood as well, making her look up. "You're certain?"

She merely raised her brows. She would not beg.

He nodded, his lips firming, and took her hand, leading her to the bed. She was trembling already, just at the touch of his hand, and now she didn't bother trying to hide her reaction. He folded back the covers and indicated she should climb in. She lay down, still in her chemise, and watched as he took a small tin out of his banyan pocket and placed it on the bedside table. Then he took off his banyan and shoes.

The bed dipped beneath his weight when he climbed in beside her. He was warm and large, and she reached out to touch the sleeve of his shirt. Just that, because she thought her heart might beat itself to death if she touched any other part of him. He leaned over her and brushed his lips against hers; she closed her eyes in ecstasy. Oh, dear Lord, *finally*. She was now drinking sweet sherry after spending her entire life living in a dry, lonely desert. His mouth was soft but firm, the tart taste of wine on his lips. He laid his hand on her breast, large and warm through the thin cloth of the chemise, and she shuddered.

She opened her mouth in invitation, but he pulled his head back. He looked down, fumbling between their bodies.

"Vale," she whispered.

"Shh." He brushed a kiss over her forehead. "It'll soon be over." He reached for the tin on the table beside her bed and opened it. Inside was some type of unguent. He dipped a finger in, and his hand disappeared between them again.

She frowned. It being over soon wasn't exactly what she'd hoped for. "I—"

But he'd hiked up her chemise, baring her to the waist, and she was distracted by the feel of his hands on her hips. Perhaps if she stopped thinking so much and simply felt . . .

"Let me," he murmured.

He widened her legs and settled between them, and she realized that he'd opened the placket of his breeches. She could feel him, hot and hard, pressing against her thigh. All sound left her throat as she felt a spurt of excitement.

"This may seem rather odd, and it may hurt, but I won't be long," he muttered rapidly. "And it'll only hurt the first time. You can close your eyes if you wish."

What?

And he entered her.

Instead of closing her eyes, she widened them, staring up at him, wanting to experience every small part of this. His eyes were closed, his brow furrowed as if he were in pain. She wrapped her arms around him, feeling the width of his shoulders and how tensely he held them.

"Ahhh. That's . . ." He jerked against her. "Just hold still a moment."

He raised himself up on straight arms, and to her disappointment, knocked aside her arms. And then he thrust. Once, twice, a third time, heavy and hard. He grit his teeth and made a sort of choked coughing sound and slumped over her.

Soon indeed.

She shifted to wrap her arms about him again so that she might at least lie with him afterward, but he rolled to the side and off her. "I'm sorry. Didn't mean to crush you."

He turned his back and presumably put himself to rights. Melisande pulled her chemise slowly down over her thighs, fighting a feeling of chagrin. The bed bounced as he rolled off it. He yawned and bent to pick up his banyan and shoes, then leaned over her to buss her cheek.

"Not too bad, I hope?" His blue eyes were worried-looking. "Get some sleep and I'll make sure the footmen bring up a hot bath in the morning. That'll help."

"I'm—"

"Be sure to drink some more wine if you have any pain." He ran a hand through his hair and nearly dislodged his tie. "Good night, then."

And he left the room.

Melisande stared for a moment at the closed door, completely dumbfounded. The scratching came from her dressing room door again. She closed her eyes and tried to ignore the sound. She slid her hand up under her chemise. She was wet down there, slippery with his semen and her own fluids. She ran her fingers between her folds, concentrating, thinking how he'd felt inside of her, how very blue his eyes were. She brushed that bit of flesh at the top of her cleft. It was swollen, throbbing with frustrated need. She stroked, trying to relax, trying to remember . . .

The scratching came again.

She huffed and opened her eyes, staring at the silk canopy of her bed. It was blue and had a slight hole in the corner. "Damn."

The scratching was accompanied by a whine this time.

"Oh, have a little patience!"

She climbed from the big bed, annoyed, and felt semen slide down her inner thigh. A pitcher of water was on the dresser, and she poured a little out into the washbowl. Dipping a cloth into the cool water, she washed herself. Then she walked to the dressing room door and opened it.

Mouse sneezed indignantly and came bustling out. He jumped to the bed and turned around three times before settling on a pillow, his back pointedly toward her. He hated being locked away in the dressing room.

Melisande climbed back in the bed, feeling just as grumpy as the terrier. She lay for a moment staring at the silk canopy, wondering where, exactly, she'd gone wrong in that hasty exercise. She sighed and decided she could figure it all out in the morning. She snuffed the bedside candle and closed her eyes. As she drifted to sleep, she had one last coherent thought.

Thank goodness she hadn't been a virgin.

TONIGHT'S WORK HADN'T been his most sterling moment as a lover, Jasper reflected just a few minutes later. He sat in his own rooms, in a large chair before his fire. He hadn't shown Melisande true pleasure. The whole thing had been much too quick and hurried for that, he knew. He'd been fearful that if he'd drawn it out too much, he might forget himself and use her harder than he meant. So the experience hadn't been exciting for her. But on the other hand, he fancied he hadn't hurt her overmuch either. And that, after all, had been his main intention: not to frighten his virgin bride on her first night in his bed.

Or rather hers. He glanced at his own bed, huge, dark, and rather overwhelming. Just as well that he'd gone to her rooms instead of trying to bring her into his. His bed would frighten the most intrepid woman on her initiation into the pleasures of the flesh. Not to mention that afterward, he would've had to find a way to eject her from his rooms. He downed the last swallow of brandy in his glass. *That* would've been an awkward moment.

All in all, the act had gone as well as could be expected. Time enough later to show her how pleasurable the joining of a man's and a woman's bodies could be. Assuming, of course, that she wanted to linger in the connubial bed in the first place. Plenty of aristocratic ladies weren't very interested in making love with their husbands.

He frowned at the thought. He'd never before seen anything particularly wrong with fashionable marriages of that sort. The ones in which the interested parties produced an heir or two and then went their separate ways socially and sexually. It was the type of marriage that was almost usual in his tier of society. The type of marriage he himself had been expecting. Now, however, the thought of a marriage in which the man and wife were civil and nothing more seemed . . . cold. And rather unpleasant, actually.

Jasper shook his head. Perhaps matrimony was having a morbid effect on his brain. That might explain these odd thoughts. He stood and set the glass by the decanter on a side table. His rooms were more than twice as large as his new wife's. But that fact only made the space hard to adequately light at night. Shadows loomed in the corners near the wardrobe and around the big bed.

He disrobed and washed himself in the chilly water already in his rooms. He could've sent down for fresh, warm water, but he didn't like anyone entering his rooms after dark. Even Pynch's presence made him restless. He blew out all but one candle. Picking that up, he took it into his dressing room. Here there was a small bed such as a valet might use. Pynch, however, had other rooms, and this bed was never used. Beside the bed, in the corner against the far wall, was a rather wretched pallet.

Jasper set the candle on the floor near the pallet and checked, as he did every night, that everything was here. There was a bundled pack with a change of clothes, water in a tin canteen, and some bread. Pynch refreshed the loaf and water every couple of days or so, even though Jasper had never discussed his pack with his valet. Beside the pack was a small knife and a steel and flint. He knelt and wrapped the one blanket about his naked shoulders before lying down on the thin pallet, his back to the wall. He stared for a moment at the flickering shadows the candle cast against the ceiling, and then he closed his eyes.

Chapter Four

—≈—

*By and by, Jack came upon another old man in
tattered rags sitting by the side of the road.
"Have you aught to give me to eat?" the second
beggar called in a disagreeable voice.
Jack set down his pack and took out some cheese.
The old man snatched it from his hand and gobbled it
down. Jack brought out a loaf of bread. The old man
ate the entire loaf and then held out his hands for
more. Jack shook his head and dug to the very bottom
of his pack to find an apple.
The old man devoured the apple and said, "Is this
rubbish all that you can offer?"
And finally Jack's patience broke. "For pity's sake,
man! You've eaten the last of my food and not a word
of thanks in return. I'll be on my way and damn you
for my trouble!"*
—from LAUGHING JACK

Renshaw House was the grandest place Sally Suchlike had ever seen, and she was still a bit in awe. Cor! Pink and black marble floors, carved wood furniture so delicate the legs looked hardly more than toothpicks, and fancy embroidered silks and brocades and velvets everywhere, yards and yards of them, much more than was needed to cover a window or chair, all just draped for the finery of it. Oh, Mr. Fleming's house had been lovely, but *this*, this was like living in His Majesty's own palace; it was so beautiful. Indeed it was!

And wasn't it an amazing step up from the Seven Dials area where she'd been born and had lived? If you could call living working every day from sunup until sundown, picking up horseshit and dog shit and any other shit to be found and sold again for just a scrap of bread and a tiny piece of gristly meat if she and her pa were lucky. She'd stayed until the age of twelve, which was when her pa had talked about marrying her off to his friend Pinky, a large, stinking man with all his front teeth missing. She'd seen a life full of shit and sorrow if she married Pinky, stretching away until she died too young in the same neighborhood she'd been born in.

Sally had run away that very night to seek her fortune as a kitchen wench. She'd been clever and quick, and when the cook had found a better house—Mr. Fleming's—she'd taken Sally along with her. And Sally had worked—hard. She'd made sure not to find herself alone with any footman or butcher's boy. For the last thing she needed was to get herself with child. All along, she'd kept herself neat and her ears open. She'd listened to how the Flemings spoke, and at night in her narrow bed next to Alice, the downstairs maid, who snored like an old man, she'd whisper the words and the inflections over and over until her speech was nearly as good as Miss Fleming's.

When the time came—when Bob the footman had run into the kitchens, breathless with the news that Miss Fleming, who had such a plain, sad face, had somehow caught herself a viscount—Sally had been ready. She'd folded the mending she'd been doing and quietly crept from the kitchens to make her plea to Miss Fleming.

And here she was! The lady's maid of a viscountess! Now, if only she could learn all the passages and floors and doors in this great, grand house, everything would be perfect. Sally straightened her apron as she pushed open a door in the servant's passage. If she'd calculated correctly, she would enter into the hallway outside the master bedrooms. She peeked. The hall was large, with dark wood-paneled walls and a long red and black carpet. Unfortunately, it looked quite a bit like all the other halls in the house until she turned her head to the right and saw the scandalous little black marble statue of some ancient gentleman attacking a naked lady. She'd noticed the figures before—well, they *were* hard to miss—and she knew they stood outside the door of the viscount's room. Sally nodded and shut the concealed panel door behind her before pausing to examine the little statue.

Both figures were naked, and the lady didn't look all that worried. In fact, she had a dimpled arm thrown around the gentleman's neck. Sally cocked her head. The gentleman seemed to have furry goatlike flanks, and on his head were stumpy little horns. Actually, now that she peered closer, it occurred to her that the nasty stone man looked quite a bit like the viscount's man, Mr. Pynch—if Mr. Pynch had hair and horns and furry flanks. Which made her gaze drop lower on the statue gentleman and wonder if Mr. Pynch also had a long—

A man cleared his throat behind her.

Sally shrieked and spun around. Mr. Pynch stood directly behind her, as if summoned by her thoughts. He had one eyebrow raised, and his bald head shone dully in the dim hallway.

She could feel a hot flush rise up her neck. She planted both fists on her hips. "Cor! Was you trying to give me a start? Don't you know you can kill a person that way? I knew a lady once, got killed by a lad sneaking up behind her and yelling, 'Boo!' I might be lying stiff and dead on the carpet this very minute. And what would you say to my lord had you gone and killed me the day after his wedding, I'm wondering? Fine fix you'd be in then."

Mr. Pynch cleared his throat again, a sound like rocks being rolled around in a tin pail. "Perhaps if you had not been so engrossed in your examination of that statue, Miss Suchlike—"

Sally blew out a snort, which was quite unladylike but fitting at the moment. "Are you accusing me of staring at this statue, Mr. Pynch?"

Both of the valet's eyebrows rose. "I simply—"

"I'll have you know that I was merely checking for dust on that statue."

"Dust?"

"Dust." Sally jerked her head in a single sharp nod. "My lady can't abide dust."

"I see," Mr. Pynch said in lofty tones. "I shall keep that in mind."

"I should certainly hope you do," Sally replied. She tugged at her apron to straighten it and then looked at her mistress's door. It was already eight of the clock, late for the new Lady Vale to rise, but on the day after her wedding . . .

Mr. Pynch was still watching her. "I suggest you knock."

She rolled her eyes at him. "I know well enough how to wake my mistress."

"Then what's the problem?"

"Perhaps she's not alone." She felt her hot blush rise again. "You know. What if *he's* in there? Right fool I'd look if I go trotting in there and they're not . . . not . . . not"— Sally inhaled deeply, trying to get a grip on her runaway tongue—"*right*. I'd be most embarrassed."

"He isn't."

"Isn't what?"

"In there," Mr. Pynch said with utter certainty, and entered the room of their master.

Sally scowled after him. What a nasty man. She gave a last tug to her apron and rapped smartly on her mistress's door.

MELISANDE WAS SITTING at her desk, translating the last of the fairy tales when she heard a rap on her door. Mouse, who'd been lying at her feet, jumped up to growl at the door.

"Come," she called, and was unsurprised when Suchlike peeked in.

Melisande glanced at the china clock on her mantel. It was just after eight o'clock, but she'd been awake for over two hours. She rarely slept past sunrise. Suchlike knew her routine and usually came to dress her much earlier than this. The maid probably had been circumspect because of Melisande's newly wedded status. She felt a flash of mortification. Soon the entire household would know that she'd slept apart from her husband on their wedding night. Well, it couldn't be helped. She'd just have to get through it.

"Good morning, my lady." Suchlike eyed Mouse and edged around the terrier.

"Good morning. Come here, Mouse." Melisande snapped her fingers.

Mouse gave a last suspicious sniff at the maid and ran to sit under the desk next to Melisande's legs.

She'd already pulled back the drapes from the window over the desk, but Suchlike went now to open the other drapes as well. "It's a lovely day. Sunshine, not a cloud in the sky, and hardly any wind. What would you like to wear today, my lady?"

"I thought the gray," Melisande murmured absently.

She frowned over a German word in the story she was working on. The old book of fairy tales had belonged to her dearest friend Emeline, a memento from her childhood. It had apparently come from Emeline's Prussian nanny. Before she had left to sail to America with her new husband, Mr. Hartley, Emeline had given the book to Melisande so that she could translate its stories. When she'd accepted the task, she'd understood that it meant much more to both of them than a simple translation. Giving the cherished book to her was Emeline's way of promising that their friendship would endure this separation, and Melisande had been touched and grateful for the gesture.

She'd hoped to translate the book and then have the stories copied out and hand-bound to give to Emeline when next she visited England. Unfortunately, Melisande had run into a problem. The book consisted of four related fairy tales, each the story of a soldier returning from war. Three of these stories she'd translated handily enough, but the fourth . . . The fourth was proving to be a challenge.

"The gray, my lady?" Suchlike repeated doubtfully.

"Yes, the gray," Melisande said.

The problem was the dialect. And the fact that she was trying to translate the written word. She'd learned German from her mother but had mostly spoken the language, not read it, and the difference was proving to be key. Melisande stroked her finger across the brittle page. Working on the book reminded her of Emeline. She wished her friend could have been there for her wedding. And she wished even more that she was here right now. How comforting it would be to talk to Emeline about her marriage and the puzzle that was gentlemen in general. Why had her husband—

"*Which* gray?"

"What?" Melisande finally glanced at her maid and saw that Suchlike wore an exasperated frown.

"Which gray?" Suchlike opened wide the doors to the wardrobe, which, admittedly, was filled with a rather dull-colored collection of gowns.

"The bluish gray."

Suchlike took down the indicated gown, muttering under her breath. Melisande chose not to comment on the sound, instead rising and pouring out a basin of tepid water to wash her face and neck. Thus refreshed, she stood patiently while Suchlike dressed her.

Half an hour later, Melisande dismissed the maid and made her way to the lower hall, paneled in palest pink marble with gold and black accents. Here she hesitated.

Surely breakfast was served in one of the lower rooms. But there were so many doors to choose from, and yesterday, in all the excitement of meeting the staff and moving in, she'd not thought to ask.

Nearby, someone cleared his throat. Melisande turned to find the butler, Oaks, behind her. He was a short man with round shoulders and hands that were too big for his wrists. On his head he wore an extravagantly curled and powdered white wig.

"Might I help you, my lady?"

"Yes, thank you," Melisande said. "Could you have one of the footmen take my dog, Mouse, out into the garden? And please show me to the room where breakfast is served."

"My lady." Oaks snapped his fingers, and a lanky young footman sprang forward like an acolyte to a priest. The butler gestured to Mouse with a flick of his hand. The footman bent toward the dog and then froze as Mouse lifted a lip and snarled.

"Oh, Sir Mouse." Melisande bent, picked up the little dog, and deposited him, still growling, in the footman's arms.

The footman arched his head as far away from his own arms as possible.

Melisande tapped the dog on the nose with one finger. "Stop that."

Mouse ceased growling, but he still eyed his bearer with suspicion. The footman headed to the back of the house with Mouse held straight-armed before him.

"The breakfast room is through here," Oaks said.

He led the way through an elegant sitting room to a room that overlooked the town-house gardens. Melisande looked out the window and could see Mouse sprinkling every ornamental tree along the main path as the footman followed.

"This is the room the viscount uses to breakfast when he has guests," Oaks said. "Naturally, should you wish to make other arrangements, you need only inform me."

"No. This is quite nice. Thank you, Oaks." She smiled and sat in the chair he held for her at the long, polished wood table.

"Cook's coddled eggs are excellent," Oaks said. "But if you wish for herring or—"

"The eggs will be fine. I'd also like a sweet bun or two and some hot chocolate."

He bowed. "Then I shall have a maid bring them up directly."

Melisande cleared her throat. "Not yet, please. I'd like to wait for my husband."

Oaks blinked. "The viscount is a late riser—"

"Nevertheless, I shall wait."

"Yes, my lady." And Oaks eased out of the room.

Melisande watched Mouse finish his business, then come trotting to the house. In another few minutes, he appeared at the breakfast room door with the footman. Mouse's button ears pricked forward when he saw her, and he ran over to lick her hand and then settle beneath her chair with a groan.

"Thank you." Melisande smiled at the footman. He looked quite young, his face still spotty beneath his white wig. "What is your name?"

"Sprat, my lady." His cheeks reddened at her notice.

Good Lord, hopefully his parents hadn't christened him Jack. Melisande nodded. "Sprat, you shall be in charge of

Sir Mouse. He needs to visit the garden in the morning, again just after lunch, and before retiring for bed. Can you remember to see to him for me?"

"Yes, my lady." Sprat's head jerked down in a nervous bow. "Thank you, my lady."

Melisande repressed a smile. Sprat didn't look entirely sure if he should be grateful. From beneath her chair, Mouse gurgled a soft growl. "Thank you. That will be all."

Sprat backed out and Melisande was alone again. She sat for a minute until her nerves couldn't stand her inaction anymore; then she stood and paced to the windows. How to face her new husband? With wifely serenity, of course. But was there any way she could gently—*discreetly*—make it known that last night had been, well, a disappointment? Melisande winced. Probably not over the breakfast table. Gentlemen were notoriously sensitive in this area, and many were not at their most reasonable in the early morning. But she had to broach the subject sometime, somehow. The man was a famous lover, for goodness' sake! Unless every lady who'd been the object of his desire was lying, he was capable of doing *much* better than last night.

Somewhere a clock chimed the nine o'clock hour. Mouse stood and stretched, yawning until his pink tongue curled. With a twinge of disappointment, Melisande gave up waiting and went to the hall. Sprat was standing there, staring rather vacantly at the ceiling, although he brought his gaze hastily down when he saw her.

"Please bring me my breakfast," Melisande said, and went back to the breakfast room to wait. Had Vale already left the house, or did he always sleep this late?

After a solitary meal shared with Mouse, Melisande turned her mind to other matters. She sent for the cook and found an elegant yellow and white sitting room to plan the week's meals.

The cook was a small, wiry woman, her face thin and lined with concern, her graying black hair scraped back into a tight knot at the crown of her head. She perched on the edge of her seat, leaning forward and nodding rapidly as Melisande spoke to her. Cook didn't smile—her face didn't seem to know how—but the tight purse of her mouth relaxed as Melisande praised the tasty coddled eggs and hot chocolate. In fact, Melisande was just feeling that she'd established a nice understanding with the woman when a loud commotion interrupted their discussion. Both women looked up. Melisande realized that she could hear barking at the center of raised male voices.

Oh, dear. She smiled politely at the cook. "If you will excuse me?"

She rose and walked unhurriedly to the breakfast room where she found the makings of a pantomime drama. Sprat stood gaping, Oaks's beautiful white wig was askew, and he was talking rapidly, but unfortunately in a voice that couldn't be heard. Meanwhile, her husband of only one day was waving his arms and shouting as if impersonating a particularly angry windmill. The object of his ire stood resolute only inches from Lord Vale's toes, barking and growling.

"Where did this mongrel come from?" Vale was demanding. "Who let it in? Can't a man have breakfast without having to defend his bacon from vermin?"

"Mouse," Melisande said quietly, but it was loud enough

for the terrier. With one last triumphant *arf!* Mouse came trotting over to sit on her slippers and pant.

"Do you know this mongrel?" Lord Vale asked, wild-eyed. "Where did it come from?"

Oaks was straightening his wig, muttering under his breath, while Sprat stood on one leg.

Melisande's eyes narrowed. Really! After making her wait an hour. "Mouse is my dog."

Lord Vale blinked, and she couldn't help noticing that even confused and out of sorts, his blue eyes were startling in their beauty. *He lay on me last night,* she thought, feeling the heat pool low in her belly. *His body became one with mine. He is my husband at last.*

"But it ate my bacon."

Melisande looked down at Mouse, who panted up at her adoringly, his mouth curved as if in a grin. "He."

Lord Vale ran a hand through his hair, dislodging his tie. "What?"

"He," Melisande enunciated clearly, then smiled. "Sir Mouse is a gentleman dog. And he's particularly found of bacon, so really you ought not to tempt him with it."

She snapped her fingers and sailed from the breakfast room, Mouse on her heels.

"GENTLEMAN DOG?" JASPER stared at the door where his new wife had just swanned from the room. She'd looked remarkably elegant for a woman being followed by a foul little beast. "Gentleman dog? Have you ever heard of a gentleman dog?" he appealed to the males remaining in the room.

His footman—a tall, lanky fellow with a name like a nursery rhyme that Jasper couldn't remember at the moment—scratched under his wig. "My lady seemed right fond of that dog."

Oaks had put himself together by now, and he cast a rather fishy eye on his master. "The viscountess had specific instructions for the animal when she broke her fast an hour ago, my lord."

Which was when it finally dawned on Jasper that he might've been an ass. He winced. To be fair, he'd never been particularly quick in the morning. But even for him, shouting at his new wife on the day after their marriage was a bit beyond the pale.

"I shall instruct Cook to make another breakfast for you, my lord," Oaks said.

"No." Jasper sighed. "I'm no longer hungry." He stared meditatively at the door a minute more before deciding that he hadn't the eloquence at the moment to apologize to his wife. Some might call him a coward, but discretion was the better part of valor when it came to women. "Have my horse brought 'round."

"My lord." Oaks bowed and whispered from the room. Amazing how lightly the man moved on his feet.

The young footman still stood in the breakfast room. He looked as if he wanted to say something.

Jasper sighed. He hadn't even had his tea before the dog had spoiled his meal. "Yes?"

"Should I tell her ladyship that you're off?" the fellow asked, and Jasper felt like a cad. Even the footman knew better than he how to behave with a wife.

"Yes, do." And then he avoided his footman's eyes and strode from the room.

A little more than half an hour later, Jasper was riding through the crowded streets of London, headed to a town house in Lincoln Inns Fields. The sun was out again, and the populace seemed determined to enjoy the fair weather, even at this early hour. Street venders were stationed at strategic corners, bawling their wares, fashionable ladies strolled arm in arm, and carriages lumbered by like ships in full sail.

Six months ago, when he and Sam Hartley had questioned survivors of the Spinner's Falls massacre, they hadn't been able to contact every soldier. Many had gone missing. Many were old men, crippled and reduced to begging and thieving. They lived their lives on the edge—the possibility that they might fall off and disappear at any moment was a real one. Or perhaps the danger was simply fading into oblivion, not so much dying as ceasing to live. In any case, many had been impossible to locate.

Then there were the survivors like Sir Alistair Munroe. Munroe hadn't actually been a soldier in the 28th but a naturalist attached to the regiment and charged with discovering and recording the animal and plant life for His Majesty. Of course, when the regiment had been attacked at Spinner's Falls, the hostile Indians hadn't made a distinction between soldier and civilian. Munroe had been in the group captured with Jasper and suffered the same fate as those who'd been eventually ransomed. Jasper shuddered at the thought as he halted his mare, letting a team of shouting sedan-chair bearers past. Not everyone who had been captured and force-marched through the dark and mosquito-infested woods of America had come back alive. And those who had survived were not the same men as they'd been before. Sometimes Jasper thought he'd left a piece of his soul in those dark woods. . . .

He shook the thought away and guided Belle into the

wide, fashionable square of Lincoln Inns Field. The house he rode to was a tall elegant redbrick with white trim around the windows and door. He dismounted and handed the reins to a waiting boy before mounting the steps and knocking. A few minutes later, the butler showed him into a study.

"Vale!" Matthew Horn rose from behind a large desk and held out his hand. " 'Tis the day after your wedding. I hadn't thought to see you so soon."

Jasper took the other man's hand. Horn wore a white wig and had the pale skin of a redheaded man. His cheeks often had reddened patches from the wind or his razor, and no doubt he'd be ruddy by the time he was fifty. His jaw and cheekbones were heavy and angular as if to balance his pretty complexion. In contrast, his eyes were light blue and warm, with laugh lines crinkling the corners, though he hadn't yet seen his thirtieth birthday.

"I am a blackguard to leave my lady wife so soon." Jasper dropped Horn's hand and stepped back. "But the matter is pressing, I fear."

"Please. Sit."

Jasper flicked the skirts of his coat aside and lowered himself into the chair opposite Horn's desk. "How is your mother?"

Horn cast his eyes to the ceiling as if he could see into his mother's bedroom in the floor above. "She is bedridden, I fear, but her spirits are bright. I take tea with her every afternoon if I can, and she always wants to know the latest gossip."

Jasper smiled.

"You mentioned Spinner's Falls at the Eddings musicale," Horn said.

"Yes. Do you remember Sam Hartley? Corporal Hartley? He was a Colonial attached to our regiment to guide us to Fort Edward."

"Yes?"

"He came to London last September."

"When I was touring Italy." Horn leaned back in his chair to pull a bell cord. "I'm sorry to've missed him."

Jasper nodded. "He came to see me. He showed me a letter that had come into his hands."

"What sort of letter?"

"It detailed the march of the 28th Regiment of Foot from Quebec to Fort Edward, including the route we would take and the exact time we'd be at Spinner's Falls."

"What?" Horn's eyes had narrowed, and suddenly Jasper could see that this man was no longer a boy. Had not been a boy for some time.

Jasper leaned forward. "We were betrayed, our position given to the French and their Indian allies. The regiment walked into a trap and was slaughtered at Spinner's Falls."

The door to Horn's study opened, and the butler entered, a tall, thin fellow. "Sir?"

Horn blinked. "Ah . . . yes. Have Cook send up some tea."

The butler bowed and retreated.

Horn waited until the door closed before speaking. "But who could've done this? The only ones who knew of our route were the guides and the officers." He tapped his fingers on his desk. "You're sure? Did you see this letter Hartley had? Perhaps he mistook it."

But Jasper was already shaking his head. "I saw the

letter; there is no mistake. We were betrayed. Hartley and I thought it was Dick Thornton."

"You said that you'd talked to him before he was hung."

"Yes."

"And?"

Jasper inhaled deeply. "Thornton swore he wasn't the traitor. He insinuated it was one of the men captured by the Indians."

For a moment, Horn stared at him, his eyes widening; then abruptly he shook his head and laughed. "Why would you believe a murderer like Thornton?"

Jasper glanced at his hands, clasped together between his spread knees. He'd asked himself the same question many times. "Thornton knew he was going to die. He had no reason to lie to me."

"Except the reason of a madman."

Jasper nodded. "Even so . . . Thornton was a prisoner in chains when we marched. He was at the back of the line. I think he may've seen things, heard things the rest of us missed because we were busy leading the regiment."

"And if you accept Thornton's accusations as truth, where does that take you?"

Jasper watched him, not moving.

Horn spread his hands. "What? Do you think I betrayed us, Vale? Do you think I asked to be tortured until my voice was hoarse from screaming? You know the nightmares I suffered from. You know—"

"Hush," Jasper said. "Stop. Of course I don't think you—"

"Then who?" Horn looked at him, his eyes blazing through his tears. "Who among us would betray the entire regiment? Nate Growe? They cut off half his fingers. Munroe? They cut out only his eye; that's little enough for what must've been a grand payment."

"Matthew—"

"Then St. Aubyn? Oh, but he's dead. Perhaps he miscalculated and got himself burned at the stake for his troubles. Or—"

"Shut it, damn you!" Jasper's voice was low, but it was harsh enough to cut through Horn's awful recitation. "I know. I know all that, damn it."

Horn closed his eyes and said quietly, "Then you know none of us could have done it."

"Someone did. Someone set a trap and walked four hundred men into an abattoir."

Horn grimaced. "Shit."

A maid entered then, bearing a laden tea tray. Both men were silent while she set it up on a corner of the desk. The door closed gently behind her when she left.

Jasper looked at his old friend, his comrade in arms so long ago.

Horn pushed a pile of papers to the side of his desk. "What do you want me to do?"

"I want you to help me find who betrayed us," Jasper said. "And then help me kill him."

IT WAS WELL past the dinner hour when Lord Vale finally returned home. Melisande knew this because the large sitting room at the front of the house had a terribly ugly clock on the mantelpiece. Fat pink nymphs cavorted about the clock face in a manner that was no doubt meant to be erotic. Melisande snorted. How little the man who had designed that clock knew of true eroticism. At her feet,

Mouse had sat up at the sound of Lord Vale's arrival. Now he trotted to the door to sniff at the crack.

She pulled a silk thread carefully through her embroidery hoop, leaving behind a perfect French knot on the right side of the fabric. She was pleased at how steady her fingers were. Maybe with continued proximity to Vale, she'd overcome her terrible sensitivity to him. Lord knew that the anger that had built during the hours she had waited for him certainly helped in that regard. Oh, she still felt his presence, still longed for his company, but those feelings were presently masked with exasperation. She hadn't seen him since breakfast, hadn't received word that he wouldn't be home for supper. Theirs might be a marriage of convenience, but that didn't mean that simple courtesy must be thrown out the window.

She could hear her husband talking in the hallway with the butler and footmen. Not for the first time that evening, she wondered if he'd entirely forgotten that he had a wife. Oaks seemed like a capable man. Perhaps he'd remind his master of her existence.

The ugly clock on the mantel chimed the quarter hour, the tones tinny and flat. Melisande frowned and placed another stitch. The smaller yellow and white sitting room at the back of the house was much prettier. The only reason she'd chosen this sitting room was because of its proximity to the front hall. Vale would have to walk past to go to his rooms.

The sitting room door opened, startling Mouse, who jumped back and then, as if realizing he'd been caught in retreat, leapt forward to bark at Lord Vale's ankles. Lord Vale gazed down at Mouse. Melisande had the distinct impression that he wouldn't mind kicking her dog.

"Sir Mouse," she called to prevent any tragedy.

Mouse gave one last bark, trotted over to her, and jumped up on the settee beside her.

Lord Vale closed the door and advanced into the room, making a bow to her. "Good evening, madam wife. I apologize for my absence at dinner."

Humph. Melisande inclined her head and gestured to the chair opposite her. "I am sure the business that detained you was most important, my lord."

Lord Vale leaned back in his chair and laid one ankle over the opposite knee. "Pressing, yes, but whether important or not, I don't know. It seemed so at the time." He flicked a finger against the skirts of his coat.

She set another stitch. He seemed somehow downcast this evening, as if his usual joie de vivre had deserted him. Her outrage deflated as she wondered what had made him somber.

Lord Vale frowned at her and Mouse. "That settee is covered in satin."

Mouse laid his head on her lap. Melisande stroked his nose. "Yes. I know."

Lord Vale opened his mouth and then closed it. His gaze roamed the room, and she could almost feel his need to jump up and pace. Instead, he drummed his long fingers against the arm of his chair. He looked tired and, with the humor in his eyes gone, older.

She hated to see him down. It made her heart ache. "Would you care for a brandy? Or something from the kitchen? I'm sure Cook has some kidney pie left over from dinner."

He shook his head.

She watched him a moment, perplexed. She'd loved this

man for years, but in many ways, she didn't know him. She didn't know what to *do* for him when he was weary and sad. She looked down, her brows knit, and snipped off the end of her thread. From her basket, she selected a silk the exact shade of ripe raspberries.

Lord Vale stopped drumming. "Your design looks like a lion."

"That's because it is a lion," she murmured as she placed the first stitch in the lion's lolling tongue.

"Isn't that unusual?"

She glanced at him beneath lowered brows.

A small amount of amusement crept into his face. "Not that it's not a fine piece of embroidery. Very, ah, pretty."

"Thank you."

He drummed some more.

She outlined the lion's tongue and began to fill it in with smooth satin stitches. It was nice to sit here together even if they both didn't know quite what to do. She silently sighed. Perhaps that wisdom would come with time.

Lord Vale stopped drumming. "Almost forgot. Got you something whilst I was out." He fished in his coat pocket.

Melisande laid aside her embroidery hoop to accept a small box.

"A token apology for shouting at you this morning," Lord Vale said. "I was a cad and a blackguard and the worst of husbands."

A corner of her mouth tilted up. "You weren't quite that bad."

He shook his head. "It's not the thing, to yell like a madman at one's lady wife, and I won't do it as a rule, I assure you. At least not after I've had my morning tea, in any case."

She opened the box to find small garnet-drop earrings. "How lovely."

"You like them?"

"Yes, thank you."

Across from her, he nodded and leapt to his feet. "Excellent. I'll bid you a good night, then."

She felt the brush of his lips against her hair, and then he was at the door. He touched the doorknob and then half turned toward her. "I say, no need to wait up for me tonight."

She arched an eyebrow.

He grimaced. "That is, I shan't be coming to your rooms. Too soon after our wedding night, what? I just thought you should know so you wouldn't be worried. Sleep well, my heart."

She inclined her head, biting her lip to keep back the tears, but he was already out the door.

Melisande blinked rapidly, then looked back to the little box with the garnet earrings. They were quite lovely, but she never wore earrings. Her ears weren't pierced. She touched one of the garnets with a fingertip and wondered if he'd ever looked—really looked—at her at all.

She closed the box gently and put it in her embroidery bag. Then she gathered her things and left the room, Mouse trailing behind.

Chapter Five

*The second beggar stood, and all his rags fell away,
revealing a horrible thing, half beast, half man, and
entirely covered with black and rotting scales.
"Damn me, will you?" rasped the demon, for such
it obviously was. "I will see you damned
in my stead!"
Jack began to shrink, his legs and arms growing
shorter, until he stood only the height of a child. At
the same time, his nose grew and hooked down until it
nearly met his chin, which had elongated and
curved up.
The demon roared with laughter and vanished in
a sulfurous cloud of smoke. And then Jack stood all
alone in the road, the sleeves of his soldier's uniform
trailing in the dust. . . .*
—from LAUGHING JACK

"Ah, lovely," Jasper said over dinner three days later.
"Beef and gravy with Yorkshire pudding, the very epitome

of an English supper." Could he sound any more of an ass if he tried?

He sipped from his wineglass and watched over the rim to see if his new wife would agree with his self-assessment of assedness, but as usual, the dratted woman wore a polite mask.

"Cook does make a pleasant Yorkshire pudding," she murmured.

He'd hardly seen her in the last few days, and this was the first supper they'd shared together. Yet she didn't scold or fret or indeed show any emotion at all. He set his wineglass down and tried to pinpoint the source of his discontent. This was what he'd wanted, surely? To have a complacent wife, one who didn't make scenes or cause a fuss? He'd thought—when he'd thought ahead at all—that he'd see her now and again, escort her to the odd ball, and when she'd become safely pregnant, discreetly take a mistress. He was well on the way to achieving that goal.

And yet the reality was oddly dissatisfying.

"We've invitations to Lady Graham's annual masked ball, I noticed," he said as he cut his beef. "Rather a tedious event, of course, what with the need to wear masks. Mine always makes me hot and gives me a terrible urge to sneeze. But I thought you might like to come?"

She winced slightly as she raised her glass of wine. "Thank you for asking, but I don't think so."

"Ah." He applied himself to his meat, feeling a twinge of disappointment. "If a mask is the problem, I can have one made in a trice. Perhaps a gilt one with feathers and little jewels about the eyes?"

She smiled at that. "I should look like a crow in a peacock's finery. Thank you, but no."

"Of course."

"I trust you'll attend, however," she said. "I wouldn't wish to spoil your enjoyment."

He thought of the endless damnable night hours and how he tried to fill them with the company of drunken strangers. "Most kind. I'm afraid I can't withstand the temptation of a masquerade ball. Perhaps it's the pleasure of watching otherwise dignified gentlemen and ladies prance about in dominoes and masks. Childish, I know, but there it is."

She didn't comment but merely watched him as she sipped from her wineglass. A single line had incised itself between her brows. Perhaps he'd revealed too much.

"You look lovely tonight," he said to change the subject. "The candlelight becomes you."

"I'm disappointed." She shook her head sadly. "I sit with one of London's most famous lovers, and he tells me the candlelight becomes me."

His mouth twitched. "I am chastised, madam. Then shall I compliment your eyes?"

She widened them. "Are they liquid pools that doth reflect my soul?"

A surprised laugh burst from his lips. "Lady, you are a hard critic. Shall I tell you of your wondrous smile?"

"You may, but I may yawn."

"I can shower praises on your figure."

She arched a mocking brow.

"Then I shall expound upon your sweet soul."

"But you don't know my soul, sweet or otherwise," she said. "You don't know me."

"So you've said before." He sat back in his chair and examined her. She looked away from his gaze as if regretting her challenge. Which only piqued his interest more. "But you haven't offered any insight into who you are either."

She shrugged. One hand was pressed to her belly; the other idly twirled her glass stem.

"Perhaps I should go exploring into my lady wife's mind. I shall begin simply," he said gently. "What do you like to eat?"

She nodded to the cooling beef and Yorkshire pudding on her plate. "This is nice."

"You don't make this easy." He cocked his head. Most ladies of his acquaintance loved to talk about themselves—it was their favorite subject, in fact. Why not his wife? "I mean, what do you like to eat most of all?"

"Roast chicken is nice. We can have that tomorrow night, if it's agreeable to you."

He placed his arms on the table and leaned toward her. "Melisande. What is your favorite food in all the world?"

She finally looked up at him. "I don't believe I have a favorite food in all the world."

Which nearly drove him over the edge of reason. "How can you not have a favorite food? Everyone has a favorite food."

She shrugged. "I've never thought about it."

He sat back in exasperation. "Gammon steak? Biscuits with butter? Ripe grapes? Seed cake? Syllabub?"

"Syllabub?"

"You must have something you like. No. Something you *adore*. Something you crave in the dark of night. Something you dream about at afternoon teas when you should be listening to the old lady sitting next to you, droning on about cats."

"You yourself must have a favorite dish, if your theory holds true."

He smiled. A feeble attack. "Pigeon pie, gammon steak, raspberry tart, ripe fresh pears, a good beef steak, biscuits hot from the oven, roasted goose, and any kind of cheese."

She touched her wineglass to her lips but did not sip. "You've listed many foods, instead of one favorite."

"At least I have a list."

"Perhaps your mind cannot settle on one favorite." Her lips tilted at one corner, and he noticed for the first time that although they weren't lush and full, her lips were elegantly curved and rather lovely. "Or perhaps, having none to raise above the others, they are all equally mundane to you."

He sat up in his chair and cocked his head. "Are you calling me frivolous, madam?"

Her smile widened. "If the shoe fits . . ."

An affronted laugh puffed from his mouth. "I am insulted at my own table and by my own wife! Come, I will kindly give you a chance to retract your statement."

"And yet I cannot in all conscience do so," she replied at once. That smile still played about her mouth, and he wanted to reach across the table and touch it with his thumb. To physically feel her amusement. "What would you call a man who has so many favorite foods he can't choose amongst them? Who gains and loses two fiancées in the course of less than a year?"

"Oh, a low blow!" he protested, laughing.

"Who I have never seen wear the same coat twice."

"Ah—"

"And who is the friend of every man he meets, yet has not a favorite friend himself?"

Her smile had died, and he had stopped laughing. He'd had a favorite friend once. Reynaud St. Aubyn. But Reynaud had died in the bloody aftermath of Spinner's Falls. Now he spent his nights among strangers. She was right, his damnable wife; he was the acquaintance of many and the soul mate of none.

Jasper swallowed and said low, "Tell me, madam, why having a plethora of likes is worse than being too fearful to pick one at all?"

She set her wineglass on the table. "I don't like this conversation anymore."

Silence hung between them for several heartbeats.

He sighed and pushed back from the table. "If you'll excuse me?"

She nodded and he strode from the room, feeling as if he were admitting defeat. No, this wasn't defeat; this was a short retreat to regroup his forces. Nothing shameful in that. Many of the best generals considered falling back much preferable to an all-out rout.

SHE'D COME CLOSE to revealing too much about herself this evening. Too much about her feelings for Vale.

Melisande pressed a hand to her lower belly as Such-like pulled a brush through her hair. To have anyone, but especially Vale, be that interested in discovering her inner soul was seductive. His entire attention had been focused on her tonight. That kind of total concentration might very well become addictive if she wasn't careful. She'd let her emotions take hold of her once before with Timothy, her fiancé, and it had nearly destroyed her. Her love had been deep and single-minded. To love like that was not a blessing. It was a curse. To be capable of—to *endure*—that unnaturally strong emotion was a kind of mental deformity. It had taken her years to recover from losing Timothy. She kept the reminder of that hurt close, a warning of what might happen if she let her emotions gain control of her person. Her very sanity depended on her strict constraint.

She shivered on the thought, and another pain hit her. The ache was low and dull in her belly, like a knot drawn tight there. Melisande swallowed and gripped the edge of her dresser. She'd been enduring this monthly pain for fifteen years, and there was no point in making a fuss over it.

"Your hair's so pretty when it's down, my lady," Suchlike said from behind her. "So long and fine."

"Fine brown, I'm afraid," Melisande said.

"Well, yes," Suchlike conceded. "But it's a pretty brown. Like the color oak wood turns when it ages. Sort of a soft blondy brown."

Melisande stared skeptically at her maid in the mirror. "There's no need to flatter."

Suchlike met her gaze in the glass and seemed genuinely startled. "It's not flattery, my lady, if it's true. And it is. True, that is. I like the way your hair waves a bit about your face, if you don't mind me saying so. Pity you can't wear it down always."

"A fine sight that'd be," Melisande said. "Me looking like a sad dryad."

"I don't know about them things, my lady, but—"

Melisande closed her eyes as another pain squeezed her belly.

"Are you hurt, my lady?"

"No," Melisande lied. "Don't fuss."

The lady's maid looked uncertain. Naturally she must be aware of what the problem was since she took care of Melisande's linens. But Melisande hated having anyone, even someone as innocuous as Suchlike, know such an intimate thing.

"Shall I fetch a heated brick, my lady?" Suchlike asked tentatively.

Melisande almost snapped at the maid, but then another pain hit her, and she nodded mutely. A wrapped hot brick might very well help.

Suchlike hurried from the room, and Melisande made her way to the bed. She crawled underneath the covers, feeling the ache reach long tentacles into her hips and thighs. Mouse hopped on the bed and crept over to lay his head on her shoulder.

"Oh, Sir Mouse," she murmured to the dog. She stroked the tip of his nose, and his tongue darted out to lick her fingers. "You are my most loyal cavalier."

Suchlike returned, carrying the hot brick wrapped in flannel. "There, my lady," she said, shoving the brick beneath the bedcovers. "See if that helps at all."

"Thank you." Melisande hugged the brick against her belly. Another wave crested and she bit her lip.

"Can I get you something else?" Suchlike still stood beside the bed, her eyes worried, her hands twisted together. "Some hot tea and honey? Or another blanket?"

"No." Melisande softened her voice. The little maid really was a dear. "Thank you. That will be all."

Suchlike bobbed a curtsy and shut the door quietly.

Melisande closed her eyes, trying to ignore the pains. Behind her, she felt Mouse creep beneath the covers and settle his warm little body against her hips. He sighed and then there was silence in the room. Her mind drifted a bit, and she shifted a little, groaning under her breath as her belly fisted.

A knock came on the connecting door and then it opened. Lord Vale strolled in.

For a second, Melisande closed her eyes. Why had he chosen tonight to resume his marital duties? He'd kept his distance since their wedding night, presumably to let her heal, and now here he came when she was entirely unable to entertain him. And how exactly was she to tell him that without sinking through the floor in mortification?

"Ah, already abed?" he started to say.

But he was interrupted by Mouse bursting from the covers, leaping atop her hip and barking furiously.

Lord Vale started back, Mouse lost his balance and skidded off her hip, and Melisande groaned as she was jostled by the terrier.

"Has he hurt you?" Lord Vale came toward her, his brows knit, which caused Mouse to bark so hard that all four paws left the bed at once.

"Hush, Mouse," Melisande moaned.

Lord Vale looked at Mouse with cold blue eyes. Then, in a move so sudden and fast she didn't have time to protest, he grabbed the dog by its ruff, picked him up off the bed, and tossed him into the dressing room. He shut the door firmly and returned to the bed to frown down at her.

"What is the matter?"

She swallowed, a bit put out that he'd taken Mouse away. "Nothing."

Her answer caused him to frown more sternly. "Do

not lie to me. Your dog has hurt you somehow. Now tell me—"

"It wasn't Mouse." She closed her eyes, because she couldn't look at him and say this. "I have my . . . my courses."

The room was so quiet, she wondered if he was holding his breath. She opened her eyes.

Lord Vale was staring at her as if she'd metamorphosed into a salted herring. "Your . . . ah . . . quite."

He glanced about the room as if for inspiration.

Melisande wished she could vanish. Simply disappear into the air.

"Do you . . . ah." Lord Vale cleared his throat. "Do you require anything?"

"Nothing. Thank you." She tucked the comforter under her nose.

"Good. Well, then—"

"Actually—"

Her words collided with his. He stopped and looked at her, then gracefully waved a large-knuckled hand for her to speak.

Melisande cleared her throat. "Actually, could you let Mouse out again?"

"Yes, of course." He strode to the dressing room door and cracked it open.

Mouse immediately darted out, scrambled onto the bed, and resumed barking at Lord Vale as if the intervening session in the dressing room hadn't happened at all. Her husband grimaced and came to the bed, looking down at her pet. Mouse had his stumpy little legs braced and was growling.

Lord Vale arched an eyebrow at Melisande. "Your pardon, but it's best if we work this out now."

Once again he moved with startling speed, but this time he reached out and closed his hand about the dog's muzzle. Mouse must've been surprised as well, for he squeaked.

Melisande opened her mouth in instinctive protest, but Vale shot her a glance, and she closed it again. It was his house, and he was her husband, after all.

Still holding Mouse's muzzle, Lord Vale leaned down and looked the dog in the eye. *"No."*

Man and dog stared a moment more, and man gave the dog a firm shake. Then he released him. Mouse sat down against Melisande and licked his muzzle.

Lord Vale's gaze returned to her. "Good night."

"Good night," she murmured.

And he left the room.

Mouse came and pressed his nose against her cheek.

She stroked his head. "Well, you really did deserve that, you know."

Mouse exhaled gustily and then pawed the edge of the coverlet. She held it up so he could creep beneath and resume his place against her back.

Then she closed her eyes. *Men.* How was it possible that Vale had had a parade of paramours in the last several years and still didn't seem to know what to do with his own wife? Even insulated as she was by society, she'd heard whispers each time he'd taken a new mistress or formed a liaison. Each time it was like a tiny bit of glass pressed into the softness of her heart, grinding, grinding, oh so silently, until she no longer noticed when she bled. And now she had him—finally had him—all to herself, and it turned out that he had the sensitivity of . . . an *ox.*

Melisande turned and thumped her pillow, causing Mouse to grumble as he resettled himself. Oh, this was a great cosmic joke! To have the man of her dreams and find he was made of lead. But he couldn't be a universally bad lover and have the reputation he had with the ladies of the *ton*. Some of them had stayed with him for months, and most were sophisticated creatures, the type who could have their pick of paramours. The type who had dozens of men.

She stilled at the thought. Her husband was used to experienced lovers. Perhaps he simply did not know what to do with a wife. Or—terrible thought!—perhaps he intended to keep his passion for a mistress and use his wife merely to mother his children. In that case, he might feel that there was no need to expend extra energy in seeing that she enjoyed the marriage bed.

Melisande scowled into the darkness of her lonely room. If they continued on their present course, she would have a loveless *and* sexless marriage. The love she could do without—*had* to do without, if she were to maintain her sanity. She no more wanted Vale to find out her true feelings for him than she wanted to jump from the roof of a building. But that didn't mean she had to do without passion as well. If she was very careful, she might seduce her husband into a satisfying marriage bed without him ever discovering her pathetic love for him.

EVERY TIME HE looked at Matthew Horn, he felt guilt, Jasper reflected the next afternoon. They were riding side by side in Hyde Park. Jasper thought of his thin pallet and wondered if Matthew had a secret badge of shame as well. They all seemed to, in one way or another, the ones who had survived. He patted Belle's neck and pushed the thought aside. Those demons were for the night.

"I forgot to offer felicitations on your marriage the other morning," Horn said. "I had thought not to see the day."

"You and many others," Jasper replied.

Melisande had still not risen when he'd left the house, and he supposed his wife might spend the day abed. He wasn't very well versed in these feminine matters; he'd known many women, but the subject had not arisen when the ladies in question had been paramours. This marriage business took more work than it first appeared.

"Did you tie a blindfold around the poor lady's eyes to get her to the altar?" Horn asked.

"She came most willingly, I'll have you know." Jasper glanced at the other man. "She wanted a small wedding; otherwise, you would've been invited."

Horn grinned. "Quite all right. Weddings tend to be dull affairs for all but the principals. No offense meant."

Jasper inclined his head. "None taken."

They guided their horses around a stopped carriage. A scrawny fellow was sitting, scratching his head under his wig as his female companion leaned down to gossip with two lady pedestrians. He and Horn doffed their hats as they passed. The gentleman nodded absently; the ladies curtsied and then bent their heads together to whisper furiously.

"Have you any aspirations in that direction yourself?" Jasper asked.

Horn turned to look a question at him.

Jasper nodded to the various knots of vibrant colors

that marked the presence of the female sex in the park. "Marriage?"

Horn grinned. "Thus it begins."

"What?"

"Every newly married man must needs lure his fellows into the trap."

Jasper arched an eyebrow repressively.

Not that it did any good. Horn shook his head. "Next you'll be introducing me to a whey-faced creature with a squint and informing me how vastly improved my lot will be once I tie myself to her forever."

"Actually," Jasper murmured, "I do have a maiden cousin. She's nearing her fourth decade, but her estate is quite large and of course her connections good."

Horn turned a face full of mute horror.

Jasper grinned.

"Oh, mock me if you will, but I had a very similar offer just last month." Horn shuddered.

"Is this unnatural aversion to the fairer sex your reason for spending so much time on the continent?"

"No, indeed." Horn bowed to a carriage of elderly ladies. "I traveled Italy and Greece to view the ruins and collect statuary."

Jasper raised his eyebrows. "I had not realized you were a connoisseur of art."

Horn shrugged.

Jasper looked ahead. They'd nearly reached the far end of the park. "Did you find Nate Growe?"

"No." Horn shook his head. "When I went to the coffeehouse I thought I'd seen him at, they had no knowledge of him. It may not even have been Growe in the first place. It was months ago now. I'm sorry, Vale."

"Don't be. You tried."

"Who does that leave us with?"

"Not many. There were eight captured: You, me, Alistair Munroe, Maddock, Sergeant Coleman, John Cooper, and Growe." Jasper frowned. "Who am I missing?"

"Captain St. Aubyn."

Jasper swallowed, remembering Reynaud's sharp black eyes and sudden wide grin. "Of course. Captain St. Aubyn. Cooper was killed on the march. Coleman died from what the Indians did to him when we made the camp, as did St. Aubyn, and Maddock died in the camp as well, from his battle wounds festering. Who does that leave alive?"

"You, me, Munroe, and Growe," Horn said. "That's it. We've hit a dead end. Munroe won't talk to you, and Growe has disappeared."

"Hell." Jasper stared at the dirt track, trying to think. There had to be something he'd missed.

Horn sighed. "You said yourself that Thornton was probably lying. I think you have to give it up, Vale."

"I can't."

He had to find out the truth—who had betrayed them and how. There'd been too many men lost, *his* men, at Spinner's Falls for it all to be simply forgotten. He could never forget, God knew. He glanced around. People strolled and rode and gossiped. What did these gentle people in their silks and velvets, their slow paces, their elegant bows and curtsies know about a forest half a world away? A place where the trees blocked out the light and the silence of the forest swallowed the panting of terrified men? Sometimes, late at night, he wondered if the whole thing had been a nightmarish fever dream, a vision he'd had many years ago that he was unable to escape even now. Had he really seen his regiment slaughtered, his men killed like cattle, his commanding officer pulled from his horse and nearly beheaded? Had Reynaud St. Aubyn really been stripped and crucified? Tied to a stake and set alight? Sometimes at night, the dreams and the reality seemed to merge so that he couldn't tell what was real and what was false.

"Vale—"

"You said yourself that it was the officers who knew our route," Jasper said.

Horn looked at him patiently. "Yes?"

"So, let us concentrate on the officers."

"They're all dead, save me and you."

"Perhaps if we talked to their survivors—friends or relatives. Perhaps something was mentioned in a letter."

Horn was looking at him with something close to pity. "Sergeant Coleman was near to illiterate. I doubt he wrote any letters home."

"Then what about Maddock?"

Horn heaved a sigh. "I don't know. His brother is Lord Hasselthorpe, so—"

Jasper's head whipped around. "What?"

"Lord Hasselthorpe," Horn said slowly. "Didn't you know?"

"No." Jasper shook his head. He'd been a guest of Hasselthorpe just last fall and had never known the man was related to Maddock. "I must talk to him."

"I don't see how he'll know anything," Horn said. "Hasselthorpe was in the Colonies as well, or so I've heard, but he was in an entirely different regiment."

"Even so. I must try and talk to him."

"Very well." They'd come to the end of the track and the entrance to Hyde Park, and Horn pulled his horse to a halt. He looked worriedly at Jasper. "Good luck, Vale. Let me know if there is anything I can do."

Jasper nodded and shook hands with Horn before they parted. The mare shifted beneath him and mouthed her bit as he watched Horn ride off. Jasper turned her head toward his town house, trying to dispel the awful images still in his mind's eye. Maybe Melisande would be up by now, and he could sit with her a while and spar. Bantering with his new wife was proving to be a surprisingly entertaining sport.

But when he entered his home and inquired of Oaks, he was informed that his wife had gone out. Jasper nodded to the butler and gave him his tricorne before mounting the stairs to the upper story.

Strange. She'd only lived here less than a week, and already her presence was imprinted on the house. She hadn't redecorated the rooms or replaced all the servants, but she'd made the house hers nevertheless. It was in the little things. The elusive scent of her Neroli perfume in the small sitting room, the fire that was always laid there, the thread of yellow silk he'd found on the carpet the other day. It was almost like living with a ghost. He reached the upper hall and turned toward his rooms but hesitated as he passed her door. His fingers touched the doorknob, and then he was inside her rooms before he could rethink the impulse.

The room was so neat it might not've been inhabited at all. The hangings were freshly washed, of course, in preparation for a new viscountess. She had the same tall, dark wood wardrobe his mother had used, a dressing table and chair, and several low chairs by the fireplace. For the first time, it occurred to him that she'd not brought any of her own furniture when she'd come to live here.

He wandered to the wardrobe and opened it, seeing rows and rows of dull-colored dresses. Her bed was neatly made, no lace pillow or sachet to give it her own touch. The bedside table held only a candlestick, no pins or a book she might read late at night. He crossed to the dressing table. A gilt and mother-of-pearl brush lay on the surface. He ran his fingers through the bristles but couldn't find any hairs. She had a small china dish to hold her hairpins and next to it, a pretty ivory box. Inside was her jewelry—a few pins, a string of pearls, and the garnet earrings he'd given her. He closed the box. There was a single drawer in the dressing table, which he pulled open but found only ribbons and lace and more pins. He shut it gently and looked around the room. She must have something of her own, some possession that had special value to her.

If she did, she kept it well hidden. He crossed to the chest of drawers and pulled out the top, finding linens neatly folded. The scent of oranges rose as he fingered them. The next drawer held the same, and the third as well, but underneath the linens in the bottom drawer he finally found something. He sat on his heels to examine it: an old tin snuffbox, no bigger than the length of his thumb. He turned it over in his palm. Where had she gotten such a thing? Surely her father and brothers, if they took snuff, owned much fancier boxes?

He pulled back the little hinged lid. Inside was a silver button, a tiny china dog, and a pressed violet. He stared at the button, then picked it up. It must be his own—the monogrammed *V* proclaimed it, but he didn't remember losing it. He placed it back in the little tin box. He hadn't a clue what it or the other items signified to her, why she saved them, if they even were important to her or perhaps only placed there on a whim. She was right: he didn't know her, his wife.

Jasper closed the tin snuffbox and replaced it under the linens in the bottom drawer. Then he stood and looked around the room. He wouldn't find her here. The only way to learn Melisande would be to study the lady herself.

He nodded to himself, decision made, and left the room.

Chapter Six

Well, this was a terrible thing, but what could Jack do but continue on his way? After walking for another day, he came to a magnificent city. When he entered the gates, people stared and laughed, and a little crowd of boys followed him, jeering at his long nose and curving chin.

Jack threw down his pack, placed tiny hands on hips, and yelled, "D'you think me a figure of fun?"

And then behind him came another laugh, but this one was soft and sweet. When Jack turned, he beheld the most beautiful woman he'd ever seen, with rich golden hair and rosy cheeks.

She bent down and said to him, "I think you the funniest little man I've ever seen. Will you come and be my fool?"

And that was how Jack became fool to the daughter of the king. . . .

—from LAUGHING JACK

Melisande was enjoying her usual coddled eggs and buns the next morning at the usual time—half past eight o'clock—when something *un*usual happened. Her husband entered the breakfast room.

Melisande paused with her cup halfway to her lips and darted a quick glance at the china clock that stood on the side table. She hadn't mistaken the time. The clock read 8:32.

She took a sip of her chocolate and set the cup precisely back down on the saucer, glad that her hands didn't tremble at his presence. "Good morning, my lord."

Lord Vale smiled, those lines beside his mouth deepening in a way she'd always found devastatingly charming. "Good morning, my dearest wife."

Mouse came out from under her skirts, and for a moment, man and dog eyed each other. Then Mouse wisely conceded the moment and retreated to his lair.

Her husband strolled to the sideboard and frowned. "There isn't any bacon."

"I know. I don't usually eat it." Melisande beckoned to the footman, standing by the door. "Have Cook prepare some bacon, eggs, a few buttered kidneys, toast, and a fresh pot of tea for Lord Vale. Oh, and make sure that Cook includes some of her good marmalade."

The footman bowed and left the room.

Vale came to sit opposite her. "I am enchanted. You know what I like to eat in the morning."

"Of course." She'd been studying him for years, after all. "That is one of a wife's responsibilities."

"Responsibility," he murmured as he slouched in his chair. His lips twisted a little as if he found the word distasteful. "And is it the *responsibility* of a husband to know what his wife eats?"

She frowned, but as she'd just put a forkful of egg into her mouth, she couldn't reply.

He nodded. "I think it must be, so I shall take note. Soft coddled eggs, buttered buns, and hot chocolate. No jam or honey for your buns, I see."

She swallowed. "No. Unlike you, I don't much care for jam."

He slouched farther into the chair, his turquoise eyes lazy. "I admit I have a sweet tooth. Jam and honey and even treacle syrup. Spread it on anything and I just might lick it off."

"Would you?" She could feel her belly heat at just his words, wicked, wicked man.

"I would indeed. Would you like me to list the possible things I could spread treacle on?" he asked innocently.

"Not at the moment, thank you."

"Pity."

She eyed him. She was terribly pleased that he'd joined her, but what an odd mood he seemed to be in. He sat watching her, a smile playing about his wide sensuous lips. "Have you an appointment this morning?"

"No."

"I've never known you to rise before eleven of the clock."

"True, but you've only been married to me less than a week. Perhaps I habitually rise before nine or even five, like a crowing cock."

She felt a blush begin to heat her cheeks. "Do you?"

"No."

"Then why are you up so early?"

"Perhaps I was hungry for my marmalade jam."

She looked at him from under her brows.

He stared back, his look rather disconcerting. "Or perhaps I fancied my lovely wife's company for breakfast."

Her eyes widened. She wasn't sure whether to be intrigued or alarmed at his sudden interest. "Why would—?"

Two maids entered, bearing his breakfast, and she swallowed the question. They were both silent as the maids arranged the dishes and looked to her for approval. Melisande nodded and the servants left.

"Why—?"

But he spoke at the same time. They both stopped, and he gestured for her to speak.

Melisande said, "No, I beg your pardon. Please continue."

"I merely wish to inquire about your plans for the day."

She reached across the table and poured him some tea. "I hope to call on my great-aunt, Miss Rockwell."

He looked up from buttering his toast. "On your mother's side?"

"No. My father's mother's sister. She's quite elderly now, and I heard that she took a fall last week."

"A shame. I'll come with you."

She blinked. "What?"

He took a huge bite of toast and crunched it, holding up a finger to indicate she should wait. She stared as he masticated and then gulped down half his tea.

"Ouch. Hot," he muttered. "Think I've burned my tongue."

"You cannot mean to accompany me on a visit to my aunt," Melisande burst out.

"Actually, I do."

"My *elderly* aunt, who—"

"I've always had a terrible fondness for elderly ladies. It's a weakness of mine, if you must know."

"But you'll expire from boredom."

"Oh, no, not whilst in your company, sweet wife," he said softly. "Unless, of course, you don't wish me to accompany you?"

She looked at him. He lounged in his chair like a big tomcat, his expression relaxed as he ate his bacon. But his greenish-blue eyes had a spark in them. Why did she feel as if she'd just walked straight into a trap? What possible motive could he have to want to visit her great-aunt, of all people? If he were the cat, did that make her the little brown mouse? And why did the thought of playing mouse to his cat make her so very, very warm?

Oh, she was an idiot. "I'd be most pleased to have you accompany me," she murmured, the only answer she could possibly make to his question.

He grinned. "Excellent. We'll take my phaeton." And he crunched into a fresh slice of toast.

Melisande's eyes narrowed. She was sure of it now. Her husband was up to something.

IT COULD'VE BEEN worse, Jasper thought cheerfully as he handled the ribbons of his phaeton. She could've been going to see . . . hmm. Actually, there really weren't too many things worse than an elderly maiden aunt. But it didn't matter. He'd sent Pynch off this morning to learn if Lord Hasselthorpe was in town and, if so, where Jasper might find him. In the meantime, Jasper had no pressing business. The day was fine, he was driving his new phaeton, and his lovely wife sat beside him unable to escape. Sooner or later, she would have to talk to him too.

He glanced sideways at her. She sat ramrod straight in the phaeton seat, her back not even touching the crimson leather seat. Her expression was serene, but she clutched at the carriage side. At least her eyes no longer held that edge of pain he'd seen two nights before. He looked away. He'd rarely felt as useless as he had the other night, seeing her in pain but unable to do anything about it. How did other men deal with this part of marriage? Did they have some secret remedy for a wife's womanly ills, or did they simply pretend nothing was wrong?

He slowed the phaeton as a gaggle of ladies crossed the street in front of them. "You seem better this morning."

Her back stiffened even more. He knew at once that it was not the right thing to say. "I don't know what you mean."

"You know." He gave her a look.

"I'm perfectly fine."

A perverse part of him couldn't let it go. "You weren't perfectly fine two nights ago, and I only saw you in passing yesterday."

Her lips pressed together.

He frowned. "Is it always like this? I mean, I know it happens monthly, but is it always so painful? How long does it last?" A sudden thought struck him. "I say, you don't think it's because we—"

"Oh, dear Lord," she muttered. Then rapidly, in a low voice he had to bend his head to hear, "I'm perfectly fine.

Yes, this happens every month, but only for a few days and the . . . the pain is usually over after the first day or two."

"Really?"

"Yes."

"How many days, exactly?"

She shot him a look of pure exasperation. "Whyever would you wish to know that?"

"Because, sweetest wife," he said, "if I know when your flow ceases, then I will know when I may visit your rooms again."

That made her quiet for a few minutes, and then she said softly, "Usually five."

His brows drew together. This was the third day. If she was "usual," then he might bed her again in three nights. He was rather looking forward to the prospect, actually. The first time was never very good for the lady—or so he'd heard. He wanted to show her how lovely it could be. He had a sudden vision of cracking that mask she wore, making her head arch back in ecstasy, her eyes opened wide, her mouth soft and vulnerable.

He shifted uncomfortably at the thought. Several days of waiting yet. "Thank you for telling me. Still. Rotten luck, that. Does it happen with every lady?"

She turned her head to stare at him. "What?"

He shrugged. "You know. Does every lady have this much pain, or do—"

"I can't believe this," she muttered, either to herself or to the horses; there wasn't anyone else within earshot. "I know you weren't born under a rock. Why are you asking these questions?"

"You're my wife now. I'm sure every man wants to know these things about his wife."

"I very much doubt it," she muttered.

"*I* at least want to know these things." He felt his lips curve. Theirs might be an unorthodox conversation, but he was enjoying it nevertheless.

"Why?"

"Because you're my wife," he said, and knew suddenly that it was true, deep in his soul. "My wife to hold, my wife to protect and shield. If there is something hurting you, I want—no, I *need*— to know it."

"But this isn't something you can do anything about."

He shrugged. "I still need to know. Don't ever keep this or any other pain from me."

"I don't think I'll ever understand men," she said under her breath.

"We're a rummy lot, it's true," he said cheerfully. "But it's good of you to put up with us."

She rolled her eyes at that and then leaned forward, unconsciously placing her hand on his arm. "Turn the corner here. My aunt's house is down this lane."

"As my lady wife wishes." He guided the horses as directed, all the while aware of her hand on his arm. She let it drop a minute later, and he wished he could have it back.

"Here it is," she said, and he halted the horses in front of a modest town house.

He tied the reins off and jumped from the phaeton. Even with his haste, by the time he rounded the carriage, she had stood and was about to get down from the high seat by herself.

He gripped her about the waist and looked her in the eye. "Permit me."

He hadn't made it a question, but she inclined her head

anyway. She was a tall woman, but fine boned. His hands nearly met around her waist. He lifted her easily and felt a kind of thrill go through his body. Held above his head, she was helpless and in his power.

She looked down at him and arched an awful eyebrow, despite the fact that he could feel her trembling beneath his hands. "Might you set me on the ground now?"

He grinned. "Of course."

He lowered her slowly, relishing the feel of control. He knew it wouldn't become an everyday occurrence with her. As soon as her toes touched the road, she stepped back and shook out her skirts.

She gave him a repressive look from under her brows. "My aunt is rather hard of hearing, and she doesn't like gentlemen much."

"Oh, good." He held his arm for her. "This should be interesting."

"Humph." She placed her fingertips on his sleeve, and again he felt that thrill. Perhaps he'd had too much tea at breakfast.

They mounted the steps, and he let the tarnished brass knocker fall against the door. Then there was a rather extended wait.

Jasper glanced at his bride. "You said she was deaf, but are her servants deaf as well?"

She pursed her lips, which had the contrary effect of making him want to kiss her. "They're not deaf, but they are rather old and—"

The door creaked open, and a rheumy eye peered out at them. "Aye?"

"Lord and Lady Vale to see Miss . . ." He turned to Melisande and whispered, "What was her name again?"

"Miss Rockwell." She shook her head and addressed the aged butler. "We're here to see my aunt."

"Ah, Miss Fleming," the old man wheezed. "Come in, come in."

"It's Lady Vale," Jasper said loudly.

"Eh?" The butler cupped a hand behind his ear.

"Lady Vale," Jasper bawled. "My wife."

"Yes, sir, indeed, sir." The man turned and tottered down the hall.

"I don't think he understood me," Jasper said.

"Oh, good Lord." Melisande tugged at his sleeve, and they entered the house.

Her aunt must either have a dislike of using candles or be able to see in the dark, for the hallway was very nearly black.

Jasper squinted. "Where'd he go?"

"This way." Melisande marched forward as if she knew exactly where to go.

And she did, for after a series of turns and a flight of stairs, they were presented with a door and a room with a light.

"Who's there?" a querulous voice asked from beyond the door.

"Miss Fleming an' a gentleman, mum," the old butler replied.

"Lady Vale," Jasper shouted as they entered the room.

"What?" A petite elderly lady sat upright in a daybed, surrounded by white lace and ribbons and bows. She held a long brass horn to her ear, which she swiveled in their direction. "What?"

Jasper bent and spoke into the ear horn. "She's Lady Vale now."

"Who?" Miss Rockwell lowered the ear horn in evident exasperation. "Melisande, dear, it's so nice to see you, but who is this gentleman? He says he's a lady. That can't be right."

Jasper felt a tremble go through Melisande's slight frame, and then she was still again. He had a violent urge to kiss her, but he suppressed it with effort.

"This is my husband, Lord Vale," Melisande said.

"Is he indeed?" The lady didn't look particularly pleased at the news. "Well, why've you brought him 'round here?"

"I wanted to meet you," Jasper said, tiring of being talked about as if he weren't there.

"What?"

"I heard you had the best cakes," he bawled.

"Cheek!" The old lady's head reared back, making the ribbons on her cap tremble. "Who told you that?"

"Oh, everyone," Jasper said. He sat in a settee and pulled his wife down to sit beside him. "Isn't it true?"

The old lady pursed her lips in a manner he'd grown to recognize from Melisande. "My cook does make rather good cakes."

She nodded at the butler, who looked somewhat surprised to be sent from the room.

"Splendid!" Jasper crossed one ankle over the opposite knee. "Now, I'm hoping you know what kind of mischief my wife used to get up to as a child."

"Lord Vale!" Melisande exclaimed.

He looked at her. Her cheeks were pink, and her eyes were wide in irritation. She was quite lovely, in fact.

He tilted his head toward her. "Jasper."

She pursed her lips.

His eyes dropped to her mouth and then rose again to meet her own. "Jasper."

Her mouth opened, vulnerable and a little tremulous, and he thanked God that the skirts of his coat covered his groin.

"Jasper," she whispered.

And at that moment, he knew he was lost. Lost and blind and going down for the third time without any hope of salvation, and he didn't give a damn. He would give anything to unravel this woman. He wanted to search out her innermost secrets and bare her soul. And when he knew her secrets, knew what she kept hidden away in her heart, he would guard it and her with his life.

She was his, to protect and to hold.

It was well past midnight by the time Melisande heard Vale return home that night. She'd been dozing in her own room, but the muted voices in the hall brought her to full wakefulness. After all, she'd been waiting for his return. She sat up in excited anticipation, and Mouse stuck his black nose out from under the covers. He yawned, his pink tongue curling up.

She tapped his nose. "Stay."

She rose and reached for the wrapper laid out in the chair beside her bed. It was a deep violet color, shaped almost like a man's banyan and without the usual feminine frills and ribbons. Melisande pulled it on over her fine lawn chemise and shivered from the sensuous weight. It was of heavy satin, overembroidered in fine crimson thread. As she moved, the fabric subtly changed color from violet to crimson and back again. She crossed to her dresser and dabbed scent at her throat, trembling as the cold liquid slid between her breasts. The scent of bitter oranges rose in the air.

Thus armored, she went to the connecting door and pulled it open. The rooms beyond were Vale's, and she'd never ventured into his domain. She looked about curiously. The first thing she saw was the enormous black wood bed, draped in linens of such a dark red it was almost black. The second thing she noticed was Mr. Pynch. Vale's man had straightened away from the banyan he'd laid on the bed and now stood, huge and immobile, in the middle of the room.

Melisande had never actually spoken to the valet. She leveled her chin and looked him in the eye. "That will be all."

The valet didn't move. "My lord will need me to undress him."

"No," she said softly. "He won't."

The valet's eyes sparked with something that might've been amusement. Then he bowed and glided from the room.

Melisande felt a knot between her shoulder blades loosen in relief. The first obstacle passed. Vale may've surprised her this morning, but tonight she planned to turn the tables on him.

She glanced around the room, noting the fire blazing in the hearth and the abundance of lit candles. The room was almost as bright as day. Her brows rose a little at the expense, and she strolled the room, pinching out a few of the tapers until only a soft glow lit the room. The scent of candle wax and smoke drifted in the air, but under them was another, more exciting scent. Melisande closed her eyes and inhaled. *Vale.* Whether she imagined it or not, the scent of her husband was in the room: sandalwood and lemons, brandy and smoke.

She was trying to calm her nerves when the door opened. Vale walked in, already shrugging out of his coat.

"Have you sent for hot water?" he asked, throwing the coat into a chair.

"Yes."

He whirled at the sound of her voice, his face oddly expressionless, his eyes narrowed. If she were not a very, very brave woman, she would've stepped back from him. He was so large and stood so still and grim, staring at her.

But then he smiled. "My lady wife. Forgive me, but I didn't expect you here."

She nodded mutely, not trusting her voice. A queer shivering excitement gripped her, and she knew she must control herself so that her emotions might not burst forth.

He crossed to the dressing room and glanced in. "Is Pynch here?"

"No."

He nodded, then closed the dressing room door.

Sprat entered the open door, carrying a large steaming pitcher. He was trailed by a maid bearing a silver tray of bread, cheese, and fruit.

The servants set down their burdens, and Sprat looked at Melisande. "My lady?"

She nodded. "That will be all."

They trooped from the room, and then there was silence.

Vale looked from the tray of food to her. "How did you know?"

She'd found out easily enough from the servants that

he habitually ate a light snack when he returned in the evenings. She shrugged and glided to him. "I do not mean to disturb your schedule."

He blinked. "That's, ah . . ."

He seemed to lose his train of thought, possibly because she'd started unbuttoning his waistcoat. She concentrated on the brass buttons and the slitted holes, aware that her breathing had quickened with the temptation of his proximity. This close she could feel his warmth through the layers of his clothes. An awful thought intruded: how many other women had had the privilege of undressing him?

She looked up, meeting his turquoise blue eyes. "Yes?"

He cleared his throat. "Uh, kind of you."

"Is it?" She raised her brows and returned her gaze to the buttons. Had he been with another woman tonight? He was a man of known appetites, and she was unable to fulfill them at the moment. Was it enough to make him look elsewhere? She slipped the last one through the hole and glanced up. "Please."

He raised his arms, allowing her to slide the garment from his shoulders. She was aware of his intent gaze as she untied his neck cloth. His breath stirred her hair, and she could smell wine. She had no idea where he went in the evenings. Presumably he was out doing gentlemanly things—gambling, drinking, and perhaps wenching. Her fingers fumbled on that last thought, and she finally identified the emotion flooding her brain: jealousy. She was completely unprepared for it. She'd known before they'd married who he was—*what* he was. She had believed she would be content with whatever small part of himself he could share with her. The other women, when they came, she would simply ignore.

But now she found she couldn't. She wanted him. All of him.

She laid aside his neck cloth and started unbuttoning his shirt. The warmth of his skin seeped through the thin cloth and surrounded her fingers. The scent of his skin was hot and masculine. She breathed in through her nose, discreetly sniffing. He smelled of sandalwood and lemon soap.

Above her, his voice rumbled. "You don't have to—"

"I know."

With the last button unfastened, he bowed and she pulled the shirt over his shoulders and head. He straightened and for a moment, she forgot how to breathe. He was a tall man—even at her height, her head came only to his chin—and his chest and shoulders were in proportion to his height. Broad and almost bony. With his shirt on, one might think him skinny. With it off, it was impossible to make that mistake. Long, lean muscle corded his arms and shoulders. She knew he rode almost every day, and she must approve of the exercise, if this was the result. He had a light sprinkling of body hair on his upper chest that broke over his abdomen and started again low on his belly. That thin line of hair leading from his navel was the most erotic thing she'd ever seen. She had a desperate urge to touch it, to trail her fingers down that line until it disappeared into his breeches.

She pulled her gaze away and glanced up. He was watching her, his cheeks lined and hollowed. So often his face seemed almost comical, but right now there was no trace of laughter. His lips had a cruel edge.

She inhaled and gestured to the chair behind him. "Please. Sit."

His eyebrows shot up, and he looked from the pitcher of hot water to her as he sat. "Do you mean to play barber as well?"

She soaked a cloth in the hot water. "Do you trust me?"

He eyed her, and she had to master the twitch of her lips as she laid the cloth against his jaw. She'd found out from Sprat that Vale liked to shave and bathe in the evenings. It was perhaps too soon to help him with his bath, but shaving she could do. When her father had been bedridden in his final illness, she was the only one he'd let near with the razor. Odd, since he'd never been particularly affectionate with her.

She went to the chest of drawers where Pynch had laid out the shaving implements and picked up the razor. She tested the edge with her thumb. "You seemed quite entertained by my aunt's stories about me this afternoon."

She watched him as she strolled back to his chair, the razor held casually in her fingers. His eyes glinted with amusement over the white cloth.

He peeled the cloth from his face and tossed it to the table. "I particularly enjoyed the story of how you cut off all your hair at the age of four."

"Did you?" She set the razor on the table and picked up a small cloth. She dipped it in a pot of soft soap and began rubbing it on his face, working up a lather. The scent of lemons and sandalwood filled the room.

"Mmm." He closed his eyes and tilted back his head like a great cat being stroked. "And the one about the ink."

She'd drawn pictures on her arms with ink and had looked tattooed for a month.

"I'm so glad to have provided a source of amusement," she said sweetly.

One bright blue eye opened warily.

She smiled and laid the razor against his neck. She raised her eyes to meet his. "I've often wondered where you go in the evenings."

He opened his lips. "I—"

She touched his lips with her finger, feeling his breath against her skin. "Ah. Ah. You don't want me to cut you, do you?"

He closed his mouth, his eyes narrowed.

She made the first careful stroke. The rasp was loud in the room. She flicked the lather from the blade with a practiced movement and reapplied the razor. "I've wondered if you see females when you go out."

He started to answer, but she gently tilted his head back and stroked along his jaw. She could see him swallow, his Adam's apple dipping in his strong neck, but the look in his eyes told her he wasn't afraid. Far from it.

"I don't go anywhere special," he drawled as she wiped the blade. "Balls, soirees, various events. You could accompany me, you know. I believe I asked to escort you to Lady Graham's masked ball tomorrow night."

"Hmm." His reply gave a little relief to the burning jealousy in her breast. She concentrated on his chin. So many indentations just waiting to be nicked. She had a dislike of social events where one was expected to make small talk. To smile and flirt and always have a witty reply on the tip of one's tongue. That kind of light discourse had never been her forte, and she was resigned to the fact that it never would be. When he'd mentioned the ball, she hadn't even thought before making an excuse not to attend.

"You could come with me at night," he murmured. "Attend some of the social events."

She looked down at her hands. "Or you could stay here with me at home."

"No." The corner of his mouth curved in a sad, self-mocking smile. "I fear I am too capricious a creature to be amused for long by evenings by the fire at home. I need chatter and people and loud laughter."

Everything she hated, in fact. She swished the razor in the hot water.

He cleared his throat. "But I don't see other women when I go out at night, sweet wife."

"No?" She met his eyes as she stroked the razor delicately down his cheek.

"No." He held her gaze. It was strong and steady.

She swallowed and lifted the razor. His cheeks were perfectly smooth now. Only a thin line of soap lingered by the corner of his mouth. She carefully smudged it away with her thumb.

"I'm glad," she said, her voice husky. She leaned close, her lips hovering over his wide mouth. "Good night."

Her lips met his in a whispered kiss. She felt his arms rise to grasp her, but she'd already slipped away.

Chapter Seven

Now, the princess of this wonderful city was named Surcease, and while Princess Surcease was beautiful beyond a man's dreams, with eyes as bright as stars and skin as smooth as silk, she was a haughty woman and had not found a man she would consent to marry. One man was too old, another too young. Some talked too loudly, and quite a few chewed with their mouths agape. As the princess neared her twenty-first birthday, the king, her father, lost patience. So he proclaimed that there would be a series of trials held in honor of the princess's natal day and that the man who won them would also win her hand in marriage. . . .

—from LAUGHING JACK

After the scene the night before, Melisande had been rather disappointed this morning when she'd breakfasted alone. Vale had already left the house on some vague male business, and she'd resigned herself to go about her own affairs and not see him again until nightfall.

And so she had. She'd conferred with both the house-keeper and Cook, had partaken of a light luncheon and done a little bit of shopping, and then she'd arrived at her mother-in-law's garden party. Where all her expectations had been overthrown.

"I don't believe my son has ever attended one of my afternoon salons," the dowager Viscountess of Vale mused now. "I can't help but think that it is your influence that has drawn him here. Did you know he would attend this afternoon?"

Melisande shook her head. Her mind was still assimilating the fact that her husband had come to a sedate and boring garden party. This simply couldn't be one of his usual rounds, and that thought had her rather breathless with anticipation, though she was doing her best to keep a calm face.

She and her mother-in-law sat in the dowager's large town garden, which was in its full midsummer glory. The elder Lady Vale had had small tables and numerous chairs scattered about on her slate terrace so that her guests could enjoy the summer day. They sat or strolled in small groups, the majority of them well into their sixth decade or older.

Vale stood across the terrace with a group of three older gentlemen. Melisande watched as her husband threw his head back and laughed at something one of the gentlemen said. His throat was strong and corded, and something in her heart clenched at the sight. In a thousand years, she would never grow bored of watching him when he laughed so uninhibitedly.

She hastily glanced away so she wouldn't be caught making cow's eyes at him. "Your garden is lovely, my lady."

"Thank you," the other woman said. "It should be, considering the army of gardeners I employ."

Melisande hid a smile behind her teacup. She'd found before her marriage that she greatly liked Vale's mother. The dowager countess was a petite lady. Her son looked like a giant when he stood next to her. Nonetheless, she seemed to have no problem in setting him or any other gentleman down with merely a pointed stare. Lady Vale wore her softly graying hair pulled into a simple knot at the crown of her head. Her face was round and feminine and not at all like her son's, until one came to her eyes—they were a sparkling turquoise. She'd been a beauty in her youth and still had the confidence of a very handsome woman.

Lady Vale eyed the pretty pink and white pastries that sat on a dainty plate on the table between them. She leaned a little forward, and Melisande thought she might take a cake, but then the elder lady looked away.

"I was so glad when Jasper chose to marry you instead of Miss Templeton," Lady Vale said. "The girl was pretty but overly flighty. She hadn't the temper to keep my son in hand. He would've been bored with her within the month." The dowager countess lowered her voice confidentially. "I think he was enamored of her bosom."

Melisande checked an impulse to glance at her own small chest.

Lady Vale patted her hand and said somewhat obscurely, "Don't let it worry you. Bosoms never last. Intelligent conversation does, though the majority of gentlemen don't seem to realize it."

Melisande blinked, trying to think of a reply. Although perhaps one wasn't needed.

Lady Vale reached for a cake and then seemed to change

her mind again, picking up her teacup instead. "Did you know that Miss Templeton's father has given his permission for her to marry that curate?"

Melisande shook her head. "I hadn't heard."

The dowager countess set her teacup down without sipping from it. "Poor man. She'll ruin his life."

"Surely not." Melisande was distracted by Vale taking leave of the group of gentlemen and sauntering in their direction.

"Mark my words, she will." The countess suddenly darted out a hand and snatched a pink cake from the plate. She set it on her dish and glared at it a moment before looking at Melisande. "My son needs warmth, but not gentleness. He hasn't been the same since he returned from the Colonies."

Melisande had only a moment to register these words before Vale was upon them.

"Lady wife and lady mother, good afternoon." He bowed with a flourish and addressed his mother. "Might I steal my wife for a stroll about your lovely gardens? I had a mind to show her the irises."

"I don't know why since the irises have stopped blooming," his mother replied tartly. She inclined her head. "But go. I think I'll ask Lord Kensington what he knows about the palace scandal."

"You are kindness personified, ma'am." Vale proffered his elbow to Melisande.

She rose as her mother-in-law muttered, "Oh, pish" behind them.

Melisande's lips curved as Vale guided them toward a pea-gravel path. "Your mother thinks I've saved you from a terrible fate in a marriage to Miss Templeton."

"I bow to my mater's wonderful common sense," Vale said cheerfully. "Can't think what I saw in Miss Templeton in the first place."

"Your mother says it may've been the lady's bosom."

"Ah." She felt him look at her, though she kept her gaze on the path ahead. "We men are pitiful creatures made of clay, I'm afraid, easily distracted and led astray. A lush bosom may have indeed fogged my innate intelligence."

"Hmm." She remembered the parade of women who had been his lovers. Had they all had lush bosoms as well?

He leaned toward her, his breath brushing her ear, making her shiver. "I would not be the first to mistake quantity for quality and reach for a large, sugary cake, when a neat, small bun was in reality more to my taste."

She tilted her head to glance at him. His eyes were sparkling, and a smile played around his mobile lips. She had trouble maintaining a stern expression. "Did you just compare my form to a baked good?"

"A neat and delectable baked good," he reminded her. "You should take it as a compliment."

She turned her face away to hide her smile. "I'll consider it."

They turned a corner, and he abruptly pulled her to a stop in front of a clump of greenery. "Behold. My mother's irises, no longer in bloom."

She looked at the plant's lobed leaves. "That's a peony. Those"—she pointed to some plants with sword-shaped leaves farther down the path—"are irises."

"Really? Are you sure? How can you tell without the flowers?"

"By the shape of the leaves."

"Amazing. It's almost like divination." He stared first

at the peony and then the irises. "Don't look like much without the flowers, do they?"

"Your mother did say they weren't in bloom."

"True," he murmured, and turned them down a new path. "What other talents have you hidden from me? Do you sing like a lark? I've always wanted to marry a girl who could sing."

"Then you should've asked about it before we wed," she said practically. "My voice is only fair."

"A disappointment I shall have to bear with fortitude."

She glanced at him and wondered what he was about. He sought her out, almost as if he were courting her. The thought was disconcerting. Why court a wife? Perhaps she was seeing more than was there, and the possibility frightened her. If she hoped, if she let herself believe he actually might want her, then the fall when he turned away again would be even more terrible.

"Perhaps you can dance," he was saying. "Can you dance?"

"Naturally."

"I am reassured. What about the pianoforte? Can you play?"

"Not very well, I'm afraid."

"My dreams of evening musicales by the fireplace are crushed. I've seen your embroidery, and that's quite fine. Do you draw?"

"A little."

"And paint?"

"Yes."

They'd come to a bench at a turn in the path, and he carefully dusted the seat with a cloth from his pocket before gesturing for her to sit.

She sat slowly, marshalling her defenses. A rose arbor shielded the seat, and she watched as he broke off a blossom.

"Ouch." He'd pricked himself on a thorn and stuck his thumb in his mouth.

She looked away from the sight of his lips around the digit and swallowed. "Serves you right for mangling your mother's roses."

"It's worth it," he said, too close. He'd braced a hand on the seat and leaned down to her. She caught the scent of sandalwood. "The prick of the thorns only makes attaining the rose that much more gratifying."

She turned and his face was only inches from hers, his eyes a strange tropical color that never occurred naturally in England. She thought she saw sadness lurking in their depths. "Why are you doing this?"

"What?" he asked idly. He brushed the rose against her cheek, the softness of the petals sending a shudder down her spine.

She caught his hand, hard and warm beneath her fingertips. "This. You act as if you're wooing me."

"Do I?" He was very still, his lips only inches from hers.

"I'm already your wife. There's no need to woo me," she whispered, and couldn't keep the plea from her voice.

He moved his hand easily, though she still had her fingers wrapped about his. The rose drifted across her parted lips.

"Oh, I think there's every need," he said.

HER MOUTH WAS the exact same shade as the rose.

Jasper watched as the petals brushed against her lips.

So soft, so sweet. He wanted to feel that mouth beneath his own again. Wanted to part it and invade it, marking it as his own. Five days, she'd said, which left another still to go. He'd have to practice patience.

Her cheeks were flushed a delicate pink, her eyes wide above the rose, but as he watched, they lost focus, and her lids began to drift down. She was so sensitive, so responsive to the smallest of stimuli. He wondered if he could make her come simply by kissing her. The thought quickened his breath. Last night had been a revelation to him. The luscious creature who'd invaded his room and taken charge was every man's erotic dream. Where had she learned such sensuous wiles? She'd been like quicksilver—mysterious, exotic, slipping away from him when he'd tried to grasp her.

Yet he'd never noticed her before that day in the vestry. He was a stupid, blind fool, and he thanked God for it. Because if he was a fool, then so were all the other men who'd passed her by at innumerable balls and soirees and never taken the time to look. None of them had noticed her either, and now she was his.

His alone to bed.

He had to fight to keep his smile from turning wolfish. Who would've thought chasing one's own wife would be so arousing? "I have every right to woo you, to court you. After all, we had no time before we were married. Why not do it now?"

"Why bother at all?" she asked. Her voice sounded dazed.

"Why not?" He teased her mouth again with the rose, watching as the flower pulled down her lower lip, revealing the moist inner skin. His groin tightened at the sight.

"Should not a husband know his wife, cherish and possess her?"

Her eyes flickered up at the word *possess*. "Do you possess me?"

"I do legally," he said softly. "But I don't know if I do spiritually. What do you think?"

"I think you don't." He pulled back the flower to let her speak, and her tongue touched her bottom lip where it had been. "I don't know if you ever will."

Her frank gaze was a challenge.

He nodded. "Perhaps not, but that won't stop me from trying."

She frowned. "I don't—"

He placed his thumb across her mouth. "What other talents have you not told me of, my fair wife? What secrets do you keep hidden from me?"

"I have no secrets." Her lips brushed his thumb like a kiss as she spoke. "If you look, you'll not find any."

"You lie," he said gently. "And I wonder why."

Her eyelids dropped, veiling her gaze. He felt the moist heat of her tongue against his thumb.

He caught his breath. "Were you found, fully formed, in some ancient spot? I fancy you as one of the fey, strange and wild, and completely enticing to a human male."

"My father was a simple Englishman. He would've scoffed at the thought of fairies."

"And your mother?"

"She was from Prussia and even more pragmatic than he." She sighed softly, her breath brushing his flesh. "I am no romantic maiden. Just a plain Englishwoman."

He very much doubted that.

He took his hand away, caressing her cheek as it left. "Did you grow up in London or in the country?"

"The country, mostly, though we came to London to visit at least yearly."

"And did you have playmates? Sweet girls to whisper and giggle with?"

"Emeline." Her eyes met his, and there was a vulnerability there.

Emeline lived in the American Colonies now. "You miss her."

"Yes."

He brought the rose up to absently brush her bare neck as he tried to remember details of Emeline's childhood. "But you did not know her until you were nearly out of the schoolroom, yes? My family estates adjoin hers, and I have known both her and her brother, Reynaud, since the nursery. I would've remembered you had you been with Emeline then."

"Would you?" Her eyes flashed with anger, but she continued before he could make a defense. "I met Emeline when I came to visit a friend in the area. I was fourteen or fifteen."

"And before that? Who did you play with? Your brothers?" He watched as the rose brushed her collarbone, then moved lower.

She shrugged. The rose must tickle, but she didn't bat it away. "My brothers are older than I. They were both away at school when I was in the nursery."

"Then you were alone." He held her gaze as the rose dipped between the upper curve of her breasts.

She bit her lip. "I had a nanny."

"Not the same as a playmate," he murmured.

"Perhaps not," she conceded.

When she inhaled, her breasts pressed a little against the rose. O, fortunate flower!

"You were a quiet child," he said, because he knew it must be true.

Even with the stories he'd heard yesterday from her aunt, he knew in the main that she would've been a quiet child. A nearly silent child. She held herself contained. Her limbs under strict control, her body small and neat, even though she wasn't a little woman. Her voice was always well modulated, and she stayed at the back of gatherings. What childhood had made her so determined not to be noticed?

He leaned closer to her, and even though the sweet scent of roses surrounded them, he smelled spicy oranges. Her scent. "You were a child who kept her inner thoughts secret from the world."

"You don't know that. You don't know me."

"No," he conceded. "But I want to know you. I want to learn you until the workings of your mind are as familiar to me as I am to myself."

She drew in her breath, pulling back almost as if in fear. "I will not become—"

But he laid a finger against her lips and then quickly straightened away again. He could hear voices on the path they'd just come from. A moment more and another couple rounded the corner.

"Pardon," the gentleman said, and at the same time Jasper realized it was Matthew Horn. "Vale. I had not thought to meet you here."

Jasper bowed with irony. "I have always found it instructive to walk my mother's gardens. Just this afternoon,

I have been able to teach my wife the difference between a peony plant and an iris."

A sound that might have been a muffled snort came from behind him.

Matthew's eyes widened. "Is this your wife, then?"

"Indeed." Jasper turned and met Melisande's secretive brown eyes. "My heart, may I present Mr. Matthew Horn, a former officer in the 28th Regiment like myself. Horn, my wife, Lady Vale."

Melisande held out her hand, and Matthew took it and bent over it. All quite proper, of course, but Jasper still felt an instinctive need to lay his hand on Melisande's shoulder as if to claim ownership.

Matthew stepped back. "May I present Miss Beatrice Corning. Miss Corning, Lord and Lady Vale."

Jasper bent over the pretty chit's hand, suppressing a smile. Matthew's presence at the salon was explained, and his motives were similar to Jasper's. He was in pursuit of the lady.

"Do you make your home in London, Miss Corning?" he asked.

"No, my lord," the girl said. "I usually live in the country with my uncle. I think you must know him, for we are neighbors of yours, I believe. He is the Earl of Blanchard."

The girl said something else, but Jasper lost it. Blanchard had been Reynaud's title, the one he should've inherited on his father's death. Except Reynaud had been dead by then. Captured and killed by the Indians after Spinner's Falls.

Jasper focused on the girl's face, really looking at her for the first time. She was chatting with Melisande, her countenance open and frank. She had a fresh, country appearance, her hair the color of ripened wheat, her eyes a contented gray. Tiny sandy freckles dotted her upper cheeks. She had no title herself, but Matthew was still reaching high if he thought to court the niece of an earl. The Horns were an old family but not titled. Whereas the Blanchard name went back centuries, and the earldom's seat was a sprawling feudal mansion. The girl had said she lived in that mansion.

In Reynaud's home.

Jasper felt his chest tighten, and he looked away from Miss Corning's expressive face. No use to blame this girl. She would've been in the schoolroom six years ago when Reynaud died on a fiery cross. It wasn't her fault that her uncle had inherited the title. Or that she now lived on the estate that had been Reynaud's birthright. Still, he could not bear to look her in the face.

He held out his arm to Melisande and interrupted the conversation. "Come. We have an afternoon engagement, I believe."

He bowed to Matthew and Miss Corning as they made their farewells. He didn't look at Melisande, but he was aware that she watched him curiously, even as she laid her hand on his arm. She knew there was no afternoon engagement. It occurred to him—finally, belatedly—that in searching out her secrets, he ran the risk of revealing his own, far darker ones. That, simply, must never happen.

Jasper covered her hand with his. It was a gesture that appeared husbandly, when in reality it was instinctive. An urge to capture and keep her from fleeing. He couldn't tell her about Reynaud and what had happened in the dark woods of America, couldn't tell her how his soul had been fractured there, couldn't tell her of his greatest failure and his greatest grief. But he could hold her and keep her.

And he would.

". . . AND DIDN'T HE look right gormless, his arse hangin' out for all to see?" Mrs. Moore, Lord Vale's housekeeper, finished her tale by slapping the kitchen table with a loud *thump*.

The three upstairs maids collapsed together in a heap of giggles, the two footmen at the end of the table nudged each other, Mr. Oaks gave a deep bass chuckle, and even Cook, whose face normally wore a pinched expression, let a smile show.

Sally Suchlike grinned. Lord Vale's household was a real change from Mr. Fleming's. There were more than twice as many servants, but under the guidance of Mr. Oaks and Mrs. Moore, they were more friendly, almost like a family. Within a couple of days of starting here, Sally had made friends with both Mrs. Moore and Cook—who was a shy woman under that stern demeanor—and her fears of not being liked, not being accepted, were put to rest.

Sally leaned over her cooling tea. Lord and Lady Vale had already taken their dinner, and it was the servants' dinnertime now. "An' what happened then, Mrs. Moore, if you don't mind me asking?"

"Well," that lady began, obviously quite pleased to be asked to continue her ribald tale.

But she was interrupted by the entrance of Mr. Pynch. Immediately, Mr. Oaks sobered, the footmen straightened in their seats, one of the upstairs maids giggled nervously—a sound shushed by her neighbor—and Mrs. Moore blushed. Sally let out a sigh of frustration. Mr.

Pynch was like a bucket of muddy Thames river water thrown over everyone: cold and unpleasant.

"May I help you, Mr. Pynch?" the butler asked.

"Thank you, no," Mr. Pynch said. "I've come for Miss Suchlike. She's wanted by the mistress."

His wooden tones produced another giggle from the upstairs maid. Her name was Gussy, and she was the sort to giggle at nearly anything. Her little giggle stopped on a gasp, though, when Mr. Pynch turned his cold green gaze on her.

Bully, Sally thought. She pushed back from the long kitchen table and rose. "Well, I thank you, Mrs. Moore, for a most delightful story."

Mrs. Moore blinked and a pleased flush lit her cheeks.

Sally smiled at the people around the table before hurrying in Mr. Pynch's footsteps. He, of course, hadn't waited for her leave-taking.

She caught up with him on a turn on the back stairs. "Why do you have to be so nasty?"

He didn't even pause in his climb. "I don't know what you refer to, Miss Suchlike."

She rolled her eyes as she panted in his wake. "You hardly ever eat with the rest of the servants, and when you do make an appearance, you flatten the talk like a horse sitting on a cat."

They'd reached a landing, and he stopped so suddenly that she ran into his back and nearly lost her balance on the stairs.

He turned and grasped her arm without any sign of confusion. "You have a colorful turn of phrase, Miss Suchlike, but I believe it is you who are overly familiar with the other servants."

He let go of her arm and continued his climb.

Sally had to suppress an urge to stick out her tongue at his broad back. Sadly, Mr. Pynch was correct. As a lady's maid, she should be placing herself above all the other servants save Mr. Oaks and Mrs. Moore. Probably she, too, should disdain their jolly meals and turn up her nose at their laughter. Except that would leave her with hardly anyone to talk to below stairs. Mr. Pynch might be content to lead the life of a hermit, but *she* wasn't.

"Wouldn't hurt you to be friendly at least," she muttered as they reached the hallway outside the master bedrooms.

He sighed. "Miss Suchlike, a young girl like yourself can hardly—"

"I'm not so young as all that," she said.

He stopped again, and she saw amusement on his face. Considering how wooden he usually looked, he might as well be laughing at her.

She set her hands on her hips. "I'll have you know I'll be twenty next birthday."

His lips twitched.

She scowled. "And how old are you, Grandfather?"

He arched an eyebrow, which was a very irritating thing to do. "Two and thirty."

She staggered back, pretending shock. "Oh, my goodness! It's a wonder you're still standing, a man your age."

He merely shook his head at her antics. "See to your mistress, little girl."

She gave up suppressing the urge and stuck out her tongue before fleeing into Lady Vale's bedroom.

*   *   *

MELISANDE HID HER trembling hands in the fullness of her skirts as she entered Lady Graham's masked ball that night. It had taken all her courage to come. As it was, the decision to attend had been last minute—if she'd thought of it longer, she would've talked herself out of it. She loathed these types of entertainments. They were filled with tight knots of people, gossiping and staring, and always seeming to exclude her. But this was Vale's own ground. She needed to confront him in just such a venue as this if she was to show him that she could be a fitting replacement for his parade of paramours.

She rubbed her skirt between nervous fingers and tried to steady her breathing. She was a little helped by the fact that it was a masquerade ball. She wore a velvet demi-mask that was so purple it was nearly black. It didn't hide her identity—that wasn't its purpose, after all—but it still gave her a small measure of confidence. Melisande took a fortifying breath and looked about. Around her, masked ladies and gentlemen laughed and shouted, all of them confident in the knowledge that they were here to see and be seen. Some wore dominoes, but many ladies had decided to wear colorful ball gowns and rely only on a demi-mask for their disguise.

She was enveloped in a domino of purple silk, and she drew the folds around herself as she moved through the crowds, looking for Vale. She hadn't seen him since the garden party that afternoon. They'd parted ways when they'd left the party—he on his horse, she in the carriage. From subtle questioning of Mr. Pynch, she knew her husband was wearing a black domino, but then so were half the men in the room. A lady moved past her, jostling her shoulder. The other woman glanced back at her dismissively.

For a moment, Melisande fought down an urge to flee. To abandon the room and this night's purpose and seek the shelter of her waiting carriage. But if Vale could brave a crowd of elderly ladies to stalk her at a garden party in the afternoon, then by God she could brave the terrors of a ballroom to hunt him by night.

She heard his laugh then. Turning, she saw him. Vale stood nearly a head taller than those around him. He was surrounded by smiling men and one or two giggling ladies. They were all beautiful, all entirely sure of themselves and their place in the world. Who was she to try inserting herself in this group? Would they not take one look at her and laugh?

She was on the point of turning away and seeking the sanctuary of the waiting carriage when the lady to Vale's left, a beautiful yellow-haired woman with rouged cheeks and a large bosom, laid a hand on his sleeve. It was Mrs. Redd, Jasper's onetime mistress.

This was her husband, her *love*. Melisande folded her fingers into a fist and sailed toward the group.

When she was still several yards away, Vale looked in her direction and stilled. She met his eyes, gleaming blue behind a black satin demi-mask, and held his gaze as she walked toward him. The people around them seemed to step back, parting as she approached, until she stood directly in front of him.

"Is this not your dance?" she asked, her voice husky from nervousness.

"My lady wife." He bowed. "Your pardon for my unforgivable forgetfulness."

She took the arm he offered her, triumphant that he'd left the other woman so easily. He led her silently through the throng. She felt his muscles shift beneath the fabric of coat and domino, and her breath came short. Then they were on the dance floor and taking their respective places. He bowed. She curtsied. They paced toward each other and then apart, his eyes never leaving her face.

When the movement next brought them close, he murmured, "I had not hoped to see you here."

"No?" She raised her eyebrows behind her mask.

"You seem to favor the day."

"Do I?"

The dance took them apart while she thought on that odd statement. When they drew close again, she laid her palm against his as they paced in a semicircle. "Perhaps you mistake habit for love."

His eyes seemed to spark behind his mask. "Explain."

She shrugged. "My usual social rounds are in the day; yours are in the night—but this does not mean that you love the night and I the day."

A line appeared between his brows.

"Perhaps," she whispered as they moved apart again, "you play in the night because that is what you're used to. Perhaps you actually prefer the day."

He tilted his head in query as they paced together. "And you, my sweet wife?"

"Perhaps my domain is really the night."

They parted and glided away. She moved through the figures of the dance until they came together again, the touch of his hand on hers sending a thrill through her.

He smiled as if he knew what his touch did to her. "What would you do with me, then, my mistress of the night?" They paced around each other, only the fingertips of their hands touching. "Will you lead me? Taunt me? Teach me about the night?"

They separated and dipped. She watched him the entire time. His eyes glinted with green and blue lights. They advanced, and he bent his head to her ear, their bodies not touching at all. "Tell me, madam, will you dare to seduce a sinner such as I?"

Her breath was coming fast, her heart fluttering in her chest, alive with excitement, but her face was serene. "Is that really the question?"

"What question do you prefer?"

"Will you allow yourself to be seduced by me?"

They halted as the dance concluded and the music died away. Her eyes on his, Melisande sank into a curtsy. She rose, her gaze still locked with her husband's.

He took her hand and bent over the knuckles, murmuring as he kissed her hand, "Oh, yes."

He guided her from the dance floor, and they were immediately surrounded.

A gentleman in a scarlet domino pressed into Melisande's side. "Who is this delectable creature, Vale?"

"My wife," Vale said lightly as he adroitly maneuvered Melisande to his other side, "and I'll thank you not to forget it, Fowler."

Fowler laughed drunkenly, and someone else shouted a quip that Vale responded to easily, but Melisande couldn't hear the words. She was too conscious of the press of hot bodies, of the leer of unkind eyes. Mrs. Redd had disappeared—for good, she hoped. She'd found Vale and danced with him, and now only wished to go home.

But he was guiding her farther into the crowd, his hand firm and strong on her elbow.

"Where are we going, my lord?" Melisande asked.

"I thought . . ." He glanced at her distractedly. "Lord Hasselthorpe just came in, and I had some business to discuss with him. You don't mind, do you?"

"No, of course not."

They'd reached the knot of gentlemen standing by the entrance to the ballroom. They were a noticeably more somber group than the one Vale had been with earlier.

"Hasselthorpe! How fortuitous to meet you here," Vale called.

Lord Hasselthorpe turned, and even Melisande could see his confusion. But Vale held out his hand, and the other man was forced to take it, eyeing him warily. Hasselthorpe was a nondescript man of medium height with heavy-lidded eyes and deep lines incising his cheeks about his mouth. His habitual expression was grave as befitted a leading member of Parliament. Beside him was the Duke of Lister, a tall, heavyset man in a gray wig. Hovering several paces away was a beautiful blond woman, Lister's longtime mistress, Mrs. Fitzwilliam. She didn't look to be enjoying the ball, standing all by herself.

"Vale," Hasselthorpe said slowly. "And is this your lovely wife?"

"Indeed," Vale said. "I believe you met my viscountess at your house party last fall?"

Hasselthorpe murmured an assent as he bowed over Melisande's hand. He hadn't taken his eyes from Vale's face, and indeed she might not've been there at all. She looked at Vale as well and saw that he wasn't smiling. There was an undercurrent of something here that she couldn't quite place, but she knew one thing—it was masculine business.

Melisande smiled and placed her hand on Vale's sleeve. "I fear I've grown weary, my lord. Will you be terribly disappointed if I retire home early?"

He turned and she could see the conflict in his face, but then he darted a look at Lord Hasselthorpe and his expression smoothed. He bowed over her hand. "Terribly, terribly disappointed, my heart, but I shall not detain you."

"Good night, then, my lord." She curtsied to the gentlemen. "Your grace. My lord."

The gentlemen bowed, murmuring their farewells.

She stood on tiptoe and whispered in Vale's ear, "Remember, my lord: one more night."

Then she turned away. But as she made her way through the crowd, she heard two words from the group of huddled men behind her.

Spinner's Falls.

Chapter Eight

❧

Well, you can imagine what happened upon the king's proclamation. Suitors began arriving in the little kingdom, traveling from the four corners of the world. Some were princes, high and low, with caravans of guards and courtiers and lackeys. Some were dispossessed knights, seeking their fortune, their armor battered from many tournaments. And a few even traveled on foot, beggars and thieves without much hope. But they all had one thing in common: they each believed they were the one who would win the trials and marry a beautiful princess royal. . . .
—from LAUGHING JACK

For a mistress of the night, his wife certainly rose early in the morning. Standing outside the newly appointed breakfast room, Jasper tried to shake the sleep from his frame. She'd left the ball early the night before, but it'd still been nearly an hour past midnight. How, then, could she be awake and, from the sound of it, already breaking her fast? He, in contrast, had stayed another hour or so, futilely trying to get Lord Hasselthorpe to listen. Hasselthorpe had found the whole idea of his brother's regiment being betrayed by a French spy preposterous, and he'd been loud in his denial. Jasper had decided to wait several days before attempting to talk to the man again.

Now he widened his eyes in a last desperate attempt at seeming awake and entered the breakfast room. There she sat, her back ramrod straight, every hair carefully controlled into a simple knot at the crown of her head, her light brown eyes cool and composed.

He bowed. "Good morning, my lady wife."

Watching her this morning, one would never guess at the mysterious woman in the purple domino from the night before. Perhaps he'd dreamed that seductive vision. How else to explain the dichotomy of the two women living in one body?

She glanced at him, and he thought he saw a fleeting glimpse of his midnight mistress, lurking somewhere behind her serene gaze. She nodded. "Good morning."

Her little dog came out from beneath her skirts to cast a jaundiced eye on him. Jasper stared the animal down, and it retreated again under her chair. The dog obviously loathed him, but at least they'd established which of them was master in this house.

"Did you sleep well?" Jasper asked as he strolled to the side table.

"Yes," she replied from behind him. "And you?"

He stared blindly at the plate of fish staring blindly back at him and thought of his rude little pallet on the floor of his dressing room. "Like the dead."

Which was correct, assuming the dead slept with a knife

under their pillow and tossed all night long. He stabbed a fish and transferred it to the dish in his hand.

He smiled at Melisande as he neared the table. "Do you have plans for the day?"

Her eyes narrowed at him. "Yes, but none that would interest you."

This statement had the natural effect of piquing his interest. He sat opposite her. "Oh, indeed?"

She nodded as she poured him a cup of tea. "Some shopping with my maid."

"Splendid!"

She peered at him skeptically. Perhaps his enthusiasm was overdone.

"You don't mean to accompany me." It was a statement, her lips pressed together primly.

What would she say if she knew her censorious face only aroused him? She'd be appalled, surely. But then Jasper recalled the seductive woman from the night before, the one who'd whispered a bold challenge with unflinching eyes, and he wondered. Which was his true wife? The prim lady of the day or the adventuress of the night?

But she waited for his reply. He grinned. "I can think of nothing more enjoyable than a morning of shopping."

"I can't think of any other man who would say the same."

"Then you're lucky to be married to me, are you not?"

She didn't answer that but merely poured herself another cup of chocolate.

He broke open a bun and buttered a piece. "It was a delight to see you at the ball last night."

She stiffened almost imperceptibly. Was he not supposed to mention her nocturnal actions?

"I had not met your friend Matthew Horn until yesterday," she said. "Are you close?"

Ah, then this was how it would be played. She would try to ignore her own nightly mechanisms. Interesting.

"I knew Horn when I was in the army," he said. "He was a good friend back then. We've grown apart since."

"You never speak of your time in the army."

He shrugged. "It was six years ago."

Her eyes narrowed. "How long were you commissioned?"

"Seven years."

"And you held the rank of captain?"

"Indeed."

"You saw action."

It wasn't a question, and he didn't know if he should bother to answer. *Action.* Such a small word for the blood and sweat and screaming. The thundering of the cannons, the smoke and ashes, the corpses littering the field afterward. Action. Oh, yes, he'd seen *action.*

He sipped his tea to wash the taste of acid from his mouth. "I was at Quebec when we took the city. A tale I hope to someday tell our grandchildren."

She looked away. "But that's not where Lord St. Aubyn died."

"No." He smiled grimly. "Think you this is a pleasant conversation for the breakfast table?"

She didn't back down from him. "Should not a wife know about her husband?"

"My time in the army is not everything I am."

"No, but I think it is a fair part of you."

And what could he say to that? She was right. Somehow she knew, though he didn't think he'd given any sign. She knew he was changed, forever scarred and diminished, by what had happened in the north woods of America. Did he wear it like a badge of the devil? Could she see what he was? Did she know somehow of his deepest shame?

No, she must not. If she knew, her face would hold contempt. He looked down as he broke apart the rest of his bun.

"Perhaps you no longer want to accompany me this morning?" his wife asked softly.

He looked up at that. Sly creature. "I don't scare that easily."

Her eyes widened a bit. Perhaps his smile had shown too much teeth. Perhaps she'd seen the thing that lurked beneath. But she was brave, his wife.

"Then tell me," she said, "about the army."

"There's not much to tell," he lied. "I was a captain in the 28th."

"That was Lord St. Aubyn's rank as well," Melisande said. "You bought your commissions together?"

"Yes." So young, so thickheaded. He'd been mostly interested in the dashing uniform.

"I never knew Emeline's brother," Melisande said. "Not well, at least. I only saw him once or twice. What was he like?"

He swallowed the last of his bun, trying to buy time. He thought of Reynaud's crooked grin, his dark laughing eyes. "Reynaud always knew he would someday inherit the earldom, and he spent his life rehearsing for that day."

"What do you mean?"

He shrugged. "As a boy, he was too serious. That burden of responsibility marks a man, even when he's but a child. Richard was the same way."

"Your elder brother," she murmured.

"Yes. He and Reynaud were more alike." His mouth twisted at the old realization. "Reynaud should've chosen him as a friend, not me."

"But perhaps Reynaud saw in you something that he himself lacked."

He cocked his head and smiled. The idea that he should possess a feature that Richard, his perfect elder brother, lacked seemed comical. "What?"

She raised her eyebrows. "Your joy of life?"

He stared at her. Did she really see joy of life in the shell that was all that remained of him? "Perhaps."

"I think so. You were a friend full of delight and mischief," she said, and then, almost to herself, "How could he resist you?"

"You don't know that." His teeth scraped together. "You don't know me."

"Don't I?" She rose from the table. "I think you'd be surprised how much I know you. Ten minutes, then?"

"What?" He was caught flat-footed and blinking up at his wife like a fool.

She smiled. Maybe she had a love of fools. "I'll be ready to go shopping in ten minutes."

And she slipped from the breakfast room, leaving him confused and intrigued.

MELISANDE WAS STANDING by the carriage consulting with Suchlike when Vale emerged from the town house a short time later. He ran down the front steps and sauntered over.

"Are you ready?" Melisande asked.

He spread his arms. "I am at your disposal, my lady wife." He nodded to Suchlike. "You may go."

The little maid flushed and looked worriedly at Melisande. Suchlike usually came on these outings to consult with wardrobe selections and to carry packages. Vale was watching her, too, waiting to see if she'd object.

Melisande smiled tightly and nodded at the maid. "Perhaps you can do that mending."

Suchlike bobbed a curtsy and went into the town house.

When Melisande turned back to Vale, he was eyeing Mouse, who was standing against her skirts.

She spoke before he could dismiss her dog as well. "Sir Mouse always accompanies me."

"Ah."

She nodded, glad that at least that was established, and mounted the steps to the carriage. She settled on the plush seat that faced the front, and Mouse hopped up beside her. Vale sat facing her, his long legs stretched diagonally across the floor. It had seemed like a large—even huge—vehicle until he entered, and then the space was filled with male elbows and knees.

He knocked on the roof and looked across at her, catching her frowning at his legs. "Anything wrong?"

"Not at all."

She glanced out the window. It seemed strange to be confined with him in such a small space. Too intimate somehow. And that was an odd thought. She'd had sexual congress with this man, had danced with him only the night before, and had had the audacity to strip off his shirt and shave him. Yet those things had been done in the night, lit only by candlelight. Somehow she found it easier to be relaxed at night. The shadows made her brave. Perhaps she really was the mistress of the night, as he called her. And if so, did that make him master of the day?

She watched him, struck by the thought. He sought her out mainly during the daylight hours. Stalked her in the sunlight. He might like to go to balls and gaming hells at night, but it was during the day that he sought to discover her secrets. Was it because he sensed that she felt more weak exposed to sunlight? Or because he was stronger in the day?

Or maybe both?

"Do you take it everywhere?"

She glanced at him, her thoughts scattered. "What?"

"Your dog." He pointed his chin at Mouse, curled on the seat beside her. "Does it go everywhere with you?"

"Sir Mouse is a *him,* not an *it*," she said firmly. "And, yes, I do like taking him places that he might enjoy."

Vale's eyebrows shot up. "The dog enjoys shopping?"

"He likes carriage rides." She stroked Mouse's soft nose. "Haven't you ever had any pets?"

"No. Well, there was a cat when I was a boy, but it never came when I called it and had a habit of scratching when displeased. It was often displeased, I'm afraid."

"What was its name?"

"Cat."

She looked at him. His face was solemn, but there was a diabolical gleam in his blue eyes.

"And you?" he asked. "Did you have pets as a child, my fair wife?"

"No." She looked out the window again, not wishing to revisit her lonely childhood.

He seemed to sense her aversion to talking about that time and for once did not press. He was silent a moment before saying softly, "Actually, the cat was Richard's."

She looked at him, curious.

His wide lips curved into a lopsided smile as if he mocked himself. "Mother doesn't particularly like cats, but Richard was sickly as a child, and when he took a liking to a kitten in the stables"—he shrugged—"I suppose she made an exception."

"How much older than you was your brother?" she asked softly.

"Two years."

"And when he died?"

"Not yet thirty years." He no longer smiled. "He'd always been weak—he was thin and often had trouble catching his breath—but he took the ague while I was in the Colonies and never quite recovered. Mother didn't smile for a year after I came home."

"I'm sorry."

He turned his palm upward. "It was long ago."

"And your father was already dead, wasn't he?"

"Yes."

She looked at him, lounging so carelessly in the carriage as he talked about the premature death of his brother and father. "You must have found that hard."

"I never thought I'd be the viscount even though Richard was always so ill. Somehow everyone in my family thought he would live to beget an heir." He suddenly looked at her, the corner of his mouth cocked. "He might have been weak of body, but my brother had a strong spirit. He carried himself like a viscount. He could command men."

"As do you," she reminded him gently.

He shook his head. "Not as he did. Nor as Reynaud did, for that matter. They were both better leaders than I."

She found that hard to believe. Vale might mock himself, might like to tell jokes and sometimes play the fool, but other men listened to him. When he entered a room, the very air sizzled. Both men and women were drawn to him like a miniature sun. She wanted to tell him this, wanted to tell him how much she herself admired him, but the fear that she might reveal too much of her own emotions held her back.

The carriage slowed, and she looked out the window to find that they were on Bond Street.

The door opened and Vale jumped to the ground before turning and offering his hand in assistance. She rose and placed her hand in his, feeling the strength of his fingers. She climbed down from the carriage, and Mouse hopped down as well. The street was lined with fashionable shops, and both ladies and gentlemen strolled by the display windows.

"Which way do you fancy, my sweet wife?" Vale asked, holding out his arm. "You shall lead and I will follow."

"Down here a bit, I think," Melisande replied. "I want to visit a tobacconist first, to purchase some snuff."

She felt him glance at her. "Are you a fashionable snuff-taker, like our queen?"

"Oh, no." She wrinkled her nose at the thought before she recalled herself and smoothed out her expression. "It's for Harold. I always give him a box of his favorite snuff on his birthday."

"Ah. Lucky Harold, then."

She glanced up at him. "Do you like snuff?"

"No." His turquoise eyes were warm as he smiled down at her. "I referred to his fortune in having such a caring sister. If I'd known—"

But his words were cut off by a sharp bark from Mouse. Melisande looked around in time to see the terrier bound from her side and tear across the crowded street.

"Mouse!" She started forward, her eyes on the dog.

"Wait!" Vale grabbed her arm, holding her back.

She pulled her arm. "Let me go! He'll be hurt."

Vale yanked her back from the road, just as a big brewer's cart rumbled by. "Better him than you."

She could hear shouting across the street, a series of growls, and Mouse barking hysterically.

She turned and placed her palm on Vale's chest, trying to convey her desperation. "But Mouse—"

Her husband muttered something, then said, "I'll get the little beast for you, never fear."

He let a cart pass and then darted into the road. Melisande could now see Mouse across the street, and her heart seized with fear. The terrier was in battle with a huge mastiff at least four times his size. As she watched, the mastiff shook off Mouse and snapped. Mouse skittered away, missing the gaping jaws by inches. Then he charged forward again, fearless as ever. Several boys and men had stopped to watch the fight, some yelling encouragement to the mastiff.

"Mouse!" She looked this time for carriages, horses, and carts as she dashed across the street after Vale. "Mouse!"

Vale reached the dogs just as the mastiff gripped Mouse in its huge jaws. The mastiff lifted Mouse and began shaking him. Melisande felt a scream build in her throat, but strangely no sound came. The bigger dog would break Mouse's neck if he kept shaking him.

And then Vale brought both fists down on the mastiff's snout. The big dog backed up a step but didn't release his prize.

"Oy!" Vale yelled. "Drop it, you devil spawn!"

He hit the dog again just as Mouse twisted wildly in the bigger dog's grasp. This must've been too much, for the mastiff finally dropped Mouse. For a moment, it looked like the massive animal might attack Vale, but her husband aimed a kick at the animal's flank, and that decided the matter. The bigger dog took off running, much to the crowd's disappointment. Mouse leapt forward to continue the chase, but Vale grabbed him by the scruff of the neck.

"Oh, no, you don't, you little idiot."

To Melisande's horror, Mouse twisted in Vale's hold and sank his teeth into his hand.

"No, Mouse!" She reached for her pet.

But Vale held her off with his other arm. "Don't. He's mad with temper and might bite you as well."

"But—"

He turned, one hand still holding the dog that was biting him, and looked at her. His eyes were a deep blue now and held only a certainty of purpose; his face was more stern than she'd ever seen it, dark and lined and with no trace of amusement. It came to her that this must be what he looked like when he'd ridden into battle.

His voice was as cold as the North Sea. "Listen to me. You are my wife, and I'll not see you hurt, even if it makes me your enemy. There can be no compromise in this matter."

She swallowed and nodded.

He eyed her a moment more, seemingly oblivious to

the blood dripping from his hand. Then he jerked a nod. "Good. Stand back and don't interfere in what I do."

She grasped her hands in front of herself so that she might not be tempted to snatch at Mouse. She adored the dog, even knowing he was an ill-tempered animal that no one else liked. Mouse was *hers,* and he returned her adoration. But Vale was her husband, and she could not contradict his authority—even if it meant sacrificing Mouse.

Vale shook the dog in his hand. Mouse growled and held on. Vale calmly thrust his free thumb down Mouse's throat. The dog gagged and let go. In a flash, Vale wrapped his hand around the dog's snout.

"Come on," he said to her, holding the dog in both hands. The crowd had scattered when the prospect of blood had disappeared. Now Vale led her back to their carriage.

One of the footmen saw them coming and started forward. "Are you hurt, my lord?"

"It's nothing," Vale said. "Is there a box or bag in the carriage?"

"There's a basket under the coachman's seat."

"Does it have a lid?"

"Yes, sir, a sturdy one too."

"Fetch it, please."

The footman ran back to the carriage.

"What will you do?" Melisande asked.

Vale glanced at her. "Nothing terrible. He needs to be contained until he calms down a bit."

Mouse had stopped growling. Every now and then, he gave a violent wriggle in a bid for freedom, but Vale held fast.

The footman had the basket out and open when they reached the carriage.

"Close it as soon as I put him in." Vale eyed the man. "Ready?"

"Yes, my lord."

The action was done in a flash, the footman wide-eyed, Mouse struggling desperately, and Vale grim. And then her pet was confined in a basket that rocked violently in the footman's hands.

"Put it back under the seat," Vale said to the footman. He took Melisande's arm. "Let's return home."

HE MAY HAVE alienated her, perhaps made her hate him, but it couldn't be helped. Jasper watched his wife as she sat opposite him in the carriage. She held herself rigidly erect, her back and shoulders straight, her head tilted down just a little as she stared at her lap. Her expression was veiled. She wasn't a beautiful woman—a part of him was coldly aware of that fact. She dressed in demure, forgettable clothes, didn't do anything, in fact, to make herself known. He'd engaged—bedded—women far more beautiful. She was an ordinary, plain woman.

And still, his mind furiously worked as he sat, planning his next assault against the fortress of her soul. Perhaps this was a kind of madness, for he was as fascinated by her as if she were a magical fairy come to lure him into another world.

"What are you thinking?" she asked, her voice dropping into his thoughts like a pebble into a pond.

"I'm wondering if you're a fairy," he replied.

Her eyebrows arched delicately upward. "You're bamming me."

"Alas, no, my heart."

She looked at him, her light brown eyes unfathomable. Then her gaze lowered to his hand. He'd wrapped a handkerchief around the bite as soon as they'd entered the carriage.

She bit her lip. "Does it still hurt?"

He shook his head, even though his hand had begun to throb. "Not at all, I assure you."

She still frowned down at his hand. "I should like Mr. Pynch to bandage it properly when we return. Dog bites can be ugly. Do make sure he washes it properly, please."

"As you wish."

She looked out the window and clasped her hands tightly together in her lap. "I'm so sorry Mouse bit you."

"Has he ever done it to you?"

She stared at him, puzzled.

"Has the dog ever bitten you, my lady wife?" If the animal had, Jasper would have it put down.

Her eyes widened. "No. Oh, no. Mouse is terribly affectionate with me. In fact, he's never bitten anyone else at all."

Jasper smiled wryly. "Then I suppose I should be honored to be the first."

"What will you do with him?"

"Merely let him stew for a bit."

Her face was once again expressionless. He knew how much the mongrel meant to her; she'd all but confessed that it was her only friend in the world.

He shifted on the seat. "Where did you get him?"

She was quiet so long that he thought she might not answer.

Then she sighed. "He was one of a litter of puppies found in my brother's stables. The head groom wanted them drowned—he said they already had enough ratters about. He'd put the puppies into a sack while a stable boy went to fetch a bucket of water. I came into the stable yard just as the puppies escaped the sack. They scattered and all the men were running about and yelling, trying to catch the poor things. Mouse ran to me and immediately caught the hem of my dress between his teeth."

"So you saved him," Jasper said.

She shrugged. "It seemed the thing to do. I'm afraid Harold was not best pleased."

No, he doubted her stodgy brother would've been happy with a mongrel in his house. But Melisande would've ignored any complaints and simply done as she pleased, and poor Harold would've had to eventually give up. Jasper was learning that his wife was almost terrifyingly determined when she set her mind to something.

"We're here," she murmured.

He looked up to find they were drawn up in front of his town house.

"I'll have the footman bring Mouse inside." He caught her gaze to impress upon her his inflexibility in this matter. "Don't let him out or touch him until I say you may."

She nodded, her face as serene and regal as a queen. Then she turned and descended the carriage without waiting for his help. She walked to the town house steps and climbed them unhurriedly. Her head was erect, her shoulders level, and her back straight. Jasper found that back oddly provoking.

He frowned, cursed under his breath, and followed in his wife's wake. He may've won that round, but in some ways he felt as if he'd been ignominiously routed.

Chapter Nine

*Princess Surcease stood high on the battlements of
the castle and watched as her suitors arrived below.
Beside her was Jack the Fool. She'd become quite
fond of him, and he accompanied her everywhere.
He stood now on an overturned piece of masonry,
the better to see over the wall, since he was
only half her height.*

"Ah, me!" sighed the princess.

*"What troubles you, o fair and gusty maid?" Jack
asked.*

*"Oh, Fool, I wish my father would let me choose
a husband of my own liking," the princess said. "But
that will never happen, will it?"*

*"More likely that a fool marry a beautiful princess
royal," Jack replied. . . .*

—from LAUGHING JACK

Mouse was barking.

Melisande winced as Suchlike set a pin in her hair. The

sound was muffled, true, because it came from three floors below. Vale'd had the dog locked in a little stone storage room off the cellar. Mouse had begun barking shortly after he'd been locked in. Probably when he realized that he wasn't going to be let out again right away. Since that time—late this morning—he'd barked steadily. It was evening now. Once in a while, he'd stop as if listening for a rescue, but when none came, he'd start up again. And each time the barking seemed louder than before.

"Loud little dog, isn't he?" Suchlike said. She didn't sound particularly put out by the racket.

Maybe the household wasn't as affected as Melisande thought. "He's never been locked up before."

"Do him good, then." Suchlike set another pin and then stepped back to eye her handiwork critically. "Mr. Pynch says he'll go stark raving mad soon."

Her lady's maid sounded as if she'd relish the valet's insanity.

Melisande arched an eyebrow. "Has Lord Vale returned?"

"Yes, my lady. A half hour or so ago." Suchlike began to tidy the dressing table.

Melisande stood and wandered across the room. Mouse's barking stopped suddenly, and she held her breath.

Then he began again.

Vale had forbade her from going to the dog, but if this lasted much longer, she didn't know if she could stay away. Mouse's distress was terribly hard for her to bear.

A knock sounded on her door.

She turned and stared. "Come."

Vale opened the door. He may not've been home

long, but from the dampness of his hair, he'd had time to wash and change his clothes. "Good evening, my lady wife. Would you care to accompany me on a visit to the prisoner?"

She smoothed down her skirts and nodded. "Yes, please."

He stood aside, and she led the way down the stairs, the barking becoming clearer the nearer they got.

"I've a boon to ask, my lady," Vale said.

"What is it?"

"I'd like you to stand back and let me handle the dog."

She pressed her lips together. Mouse had only ever responded to her. What if the terrier tried to bite Vale again? Her husband seemed a gentle man, but she sensed that the gentleness was but a surface layer.

"Melisande?"

She turned. He had stopped on the stairs, waiting for her answer. His turquoise eyes seemed to gleam in the shadows.

She nodded jerkily. "As you wish."

He descended the last steps and took her hand, leading her back to the kitchens.

The hallway became more dim as they entered the servants' domain until they reached the kitchen. The room was huge, dominated by a large arched brick fireplace at one end. Two windows at the back of the house let in light, making it a bright room during the day. At the moment, candles supplemented the fading light from outside.

The cook, three scullery maids, several footmen, and the butler were all in the midst of dinner preparations. At their entrance, the cook dropped her spoon into a pot of simmering soup, and everyone else stilled. Mouse's barking echoed from below.

"My lord," Oaks began.

"Please. I don't wish to interrupt your work," Vale said. "I've just come to deal with my lady's dog. Ah, Pynch."

The valet had risen from a chair by the fireplace.

"Did you find a scrap of meat?" Vale asked.

"Yes, my lord," Mr. Pynch said. "Cook has most kindly given me some of the beef from last night's supper." He proffered a lumpy folded handkerchief.

Melisande cleared her throat. "Actually . . ."

Vale looked down at her. "My heart?"

"If it's for Mouse, he loves cheese," she said apologetically.

"I bow to your superior knowledge." Vale turned to the cook, who was hovering near her soup. "Have you a bit of cheese?"

Cook curtsied. "Aye, my lord. Annie, fetch that round of cheese from the pantry."

A scullery maid scurried into a room off the kitchen and reappeared with a wheel of cheese nearly as large as her head. She set it on the kitchen table and carefully unwrapped the cloth about it.

Cook took a sharp knife and cut off a slice. "Will this do, my lord?"

"Perfect, Mrs. Cook." Vale grinned at the woman, making her thin cheeks tinge a light pink. "I am forever in your debt. Now if you will show me your cellar, Mr. Oaks?"

The butler led the way through the pantry and to a door that opened to a short flight of stairs leading into the partially underground cellar.

"Mind your head," Vale admonished Melisande. He

had to bend nearly double to descend the stairs. "Thank you, Oaks. You may leave us."

The butler looked greatly relieved. The cellar was lined in cold, damp stone, the walls stacked with shelves holding all matter of food and wine. In one corner was a little wooden door, behind which Mouse had been imprisoned. He'd stopped barking at the sound of their footsteps on the stairs, and Melisande could imagine him behind the door standing with his head cocked to the side.

Vale looked at Melisande and put his finger to his lips.

She nodded, pressing her lips together.

He grinned and cracked the cellar door. Immediately a small black nose peeped through the opening. Vale squatted and pinched off a bite of cheese.

"Now, then, Sir Mouse," he murmured as he held out the cheese in long, strong fingers. "Have you thought over your sins?"

The nose twitched, and then Mouse took the cheese very carefully from Vale's hand and disappeared.

Melisande expected Vale to push into the little cellar room, but he simply waited, still squatting on the stone floor as if he had all the time in the world.

A few seconds more and the black, twitching nose reappeared. This time Vale held the cheese just out of the dog's reach.

Melisande waited, holding her breath. Mouse could be terribly stubborn. On the other hand, he did adore cheese. The dog nudged the door open with his nose. Dog and man eyed each other a moment, until Mouse trotted out and took the second piece of cheese from Vale. He immediately retreated a few steps, turned his back, and gobbled down the cheese. This time Vale held the cheese in his open palm on his knee. Mouse crept forward and hesitantly took the cheese.

When he came back for another bite, Vale ran his hand gently over the dog's head as he ate. Mouse didn't seem to mind or even notice the touch. Vale took a long, thin leather cord from his pocket. One end had been made into a loop. When Mouse came back for his next bite of cheese, Vale deftly slipped the loop over the dog's neck, where it hung loosely. Then he fed Mouse more cheese.

By the time he'd consumed the entire slice of cheese, Mouse was letting Vale rub him all over his little body. Vale stood and tapped his thigh. "Come on, then."

He turned and left the cellar. Mouse shot a puzzled glance at Melisande, but since he was on the other end of the lead, he was compelled to follow.

Melisande shook her head with wonder and trailed behind. Vale continued through the kitchen and out the back door, where he played out the lead enough to let Mouse do his business.

Then he reeled in the leash and smiled at Melisande. "Shall we partake of supper?"

She could only nod. Gratitude was welling in her chest. Vale had tamed Mouse, proved his mastery over the dog, and all without hurting him. She knew of very few men who would bother to do the same, let alone without beating an animal. What he had done had taken intelligence and patience and not a little compassion. Compassion for a dog that had bitten him only that morning. If she didn't already love him, she would love him now.

MOUSE LAY UNDER the table at Jasper's feet. The leash was wrapped about his wrist, and he'd felt the tug when the animal had made a couple of abortive attempts to go to his mistress. Now, the animal simply lay, head between his paws, and gave a theatrical sigh every now and again. Jasper felt a smile curve his lips. He could see why Melisande was fond of the little beast. Mouse had an outsized presence.

"Do you intend to go out again tonight?" Melisande asked from across the table.

She was watching him over the rim of her wineglass, her eyes shadowed and mysterious.

He shrugged. "Perhaps."

He looked down as he sawed at the roast beef on his plate. Did she wonder why he was always going out, why many nights he stayed away until the wee hours of the morn? Or did she simply think him a mindlessly drunken wastrel? What a lowering thought. Especially since he didn't particularly like the gaming hells and balls he attended every night. He simply hated the hours of black night more.

"You could stay in," Melisande said.

He looked at her. Her expression was bland, her movements unhurried as she broke a roll and buttered it.

"Would you like me to?" he asked.

She raised her brows, her gaze still on her roll. "Perhaps."

He felt his belly tighten at the single, subtly taunting word. "And what would we do, sweet wife, if I did stay here with you?"

She shrugged. "Oh, there're many things we could do."

"Such as?"

"We could play cards."

"With only two players? Not a very interesting game."

"Checkers or chess?"

He arched a brow.

"We could talk," she said quietly.

He took a sip of wine. He chased her during the day, but for some reason the idea of simply spending the evening talking with her made him uneasy. His ghosts were most ferocious at night. "What would you like to discuss?"

A footman brought in a tray of cheeses and fresh strawberries and set it between them. Melisande didn't move—her back, as always, was militarily straight—but Jasper thought she leaned a little forward. "You could tell me about your youth."

"Alas, a rather boring subject"—he idly fingered the wineglass—"except for the time Reynaud and I nearly drowned in the St. Aubyn pond."

"I'd like to hear about that." She still hadn't taken a strawberry.

"We were in a perilous time of life," Jasper began. "Eleven, to be exact. The summer before we were sent away to school."

"Oh?" She selected one strawberry and transferred it to her plate. It was neither the biggest nor the smallest berry, but it was perfectly red and ripe. She stroked it with her forefinger as if savoring the anticipation of eating it.

Jasper swallowed some wine. His throat had gone suddenly dry. "I'm afraid I'd escaped from my tutor that afternoon."

"Escaped?" She turned the strawberry on the plate.

He watched her fingers on the fruit and imagined them somewhere else entirely. "My tutor was a rather elderly man, and if I had a bit of a head start, I could outrun him easily."

"Poor man," she said, and bit into the strawberry.

For a moment, his breath caught and all coherent thought fled his mind. Then he cleared his throat, though his voice still emerged hoarse. "Yes, well, and what was worse, Reynaud had slipped his traces as well."

She swallowed. "And?"

"Unfortunately, we chose to meet up by the pond."

"Unfortunately?"

He winced, remembering. "Somehow we got the notion to build a raft."

Her eyebrows lifted, delicate light brown wings.

He skewered a bit of cheese on his knife and ate it. "As it turns out, building a raft from fallen branches and bits of twine is actually much harder than one would at first think. Especially if one is an eleven-year-old boy."

"I sense a tragedy in the making." Her face was grave, but somehow her eyes laughed at him.

"Indeed." He took a strawberry and twirled the stem between his fingers. "By afternoon, we were covered in mud, sweaty and panting, and we'd somehow constructed a contraption about three feet square, although square it certainly was not."

She bit her lip as if to keep from laughing. "And?"

He set his elbows on the table, still holding the strawberry, and assumed a solemn expression. "In retrospect, I very much doubt that the thing we'd assembled could float on the water by itself. Naturally, the notion of trying it out on the water *before* actually trying to sail on it never occurred to us."

She was smiling now, no longer holding back the

laughter, and he felt a thrill of gladness. To make this woman lose composure, to make her express joy, was no mean feat. And the wonder of it was the pleasure he took in making her smile.

"The outcome was inevitable, I fear." He reached across the table and pressed the strawberry he held against that smiling mouth. She parted her pale pink lips and bit into the fruit. His groin tightened, and he stared at her mouth as she chewed. "We came a cropper almost immediately, the very instability of the raft saving us."

She swallowed. "How so?"

He tossed aside the strawberry stem and folded his arms on the table. "We got only about a yard from shore before we sank. We landed in the weeds, the water only to our waists."

"That's all?"

He felt the corner of his mouth kick up. "Well, it would've been all had not Reynaud managed to land almost on top of a goose nest."

She winced. "Oh, dear."

He nodded. "Oh, dear, indeed. The gander took exception to us invading his pond-side cottage. Chased us nearly back to Vale Manor. And there, my tutor finally caught up with us and gave me such a caning I could hardly sit for a week. Haven't really cared for roast goose since."

For a moment, he held her laughing brown eyes, the room quiet, the servants somewhere out in the hall. Jasper could feel each inhale, feel time seem to pause as he looked into his wife's eyes. He was on the precipice of something—a turning point in his life, a new way of feeling or thinking—he wasn't sure, but it was right beneath his feet. All he had to do was take the step.

But it was Melisande who moved. She shoved back her chair and rose.

"I thank you, my lord, for a very amusing tale." And she walked to the dining room door.

Jasper blinked. "Are you leaving me so soon?"

She paused, her ramrod-straight back still toward him. "I hoped you would accompany me upstairs." She looked over her shoulder at him, her eyes grave, mysterious, and just a little teasing. "My courses are over."

She closed the door very quietly behind her.

MELISANDE HEARD A muttered curse followed by a sharp bark as she left the dining room. She smiled. No doubt Vale had forgotten Mouse's leash tied to his wrist. She mounted the stairs quickly, not looking back. She could feel the beat of her pulse, was aware that he would be following her. The thought sped her feet as she reached the upper hallway.

Heavy footsteps sounded behind her on the stairs, drawing swiftly closer. He must be taking the treads two at a time. She reached her bedroom door, her breath coming in short pants of excitement. She pushed through the door into the empty room and ran to the fireplace, where she whirled around.

Vale prowled into the room a moment later.

"What did you do with Mouse?" She struggled to keep her voice even.

"Gave him to a footman." He locked the door.

"I see."

He turned back to her and halted, his head cocked. He seemed to be waiting for her move.

Melisande inhaled and glided forward. "He sleeps with me usually, you know."

She grasped the edges of his coat and drew them apart, urging it from his arms.

"In this room?"

"In my bed." She laid his coat carefully on a chair.

"Ah. Indeed." His eyebrows were drawn together as if he were puzzling something out.

"Indeed," she repeated softly. She pulled loose his neck cloth and laid it on the coat. Her hands shook as if she had a palsy.

"In the bed."

"Yes." She unbuttoned his waistcoat.

He shrugged out of it and dropped it to the floor. She glanced at it and decided to leave it. She began working on his shirt.

"I would think . . ." He trailed away, seeming to lose his train of thought.

She drew his shirt off over his head and looked at him. "Yes?"

He cleared his throat. "Perhaps we should sit down."

"Why?" She wasn't about to let this go the way of their wedding night. She laid her fingertips on his chest and traced down lightly over his stomach, reveling in the freedom to touch his bare skin.

He sucked in his belly in reaction. "Ah . . ."

She reached his breeches and found the buttons.

"Slow."

"You think we should slow down?" she asked gently. She slipped buttons through their holes.

"Well . . ."

"Yes?" The flap of his breeches sagged open.

"Ah . . ."

"Or no?" She slid her hand into his smallclothes and found him hard and heavy, waiting just for her. Warmth pooled at her center in anticipation. She'd have him tonight—have him the way *she* wanted.

He closed his eyes as if in agony and said quite distinctly, "No."

"Oh, good," she murmured. "I concur."

And she slipped her other hand into his breeches to cradle him.

He swayed a little before planting his feet.

She was caught in discovery. Oddly, her hands had stopped shaking, finally, now that she touched the most intimate portion of his anatomy. She could feel the crisp hair brushing the back of her fingers, and her palms were filled with hot flesh. She wrapped her left hand about his width and explored him with her right. Soft skin, granite-hard muscle beneath. The slight bumps of veins, a wide flanged head. She ran her fingertips across that head, sensitive skin to sensitive skin, and felt the tiny slit. The moisture that seeped from that slit. She rubbed the moisture in little circles and at the same time squeezed with her left hand.

"Oh, God," Vale implored. "You make me weak, my lady wife."

She smiled, a secret, feminine smile of triumph, and stood on tiptoe, his cock still in her hands. "Kiss me, please."

His eyes opened, and he looked at her almost wildly. Then he grasped her arms and bent his head to kiss her. His mouth was open, wet, a little desperate—exactly the way she wanted it. She made a humming sound of pleasure in her throat and stroked him firmly. He groaned and thrust his tongue into her mouth, his cock into her hands. She captured his tongue and sucked. His big hands dropped to her bottom, squeezing. A thrill of pure pleasure rushed through her center.

He pulled back suddenly, gasping. "Sweet my heart, maybe we should . . ."

No. She shoved his breeches down, off his hips. She examined his beautiful, bared cock and felt her internal muscles squeeze at the sight.

"Melisande . . ."

His penis was a dark red, proud and erect, his balls drawn up tight and hard beneath. She placed her thumb under the head, in that small, sensitive indent on the underside. "What?"

"Don't you . . . ?"

She glanced back up at him. Her husband looked a little dazed.

"No," she said quite firmly, and leaned forward to lick his left nipple.

He jerked in reaction and pulled her toward him, smashing her hands between them.

She relinquished her prize and, placing her palms on his chest, pushed him backward to a chair. He stumbled a step before bending impatiently and stripping off his breeches and smallclothes, followed by hose and shoes. He sat splendidly naked in the chair and then seemed to realize she was still dressed.

"But—"

"Shh." She laid a fingertip across his mouth, feeling the humid brush of his breath, the smooth satin of his lips. ·

He closed his mouth, and she stepped back. Her hands

went to the laces of her bodice, and he watched intently as she took off her clothes. The room was hushed, save for the pop of the fire and the sound of his breathing. The firelight highlighted his big body. His broad shoulders more than spanned the chair back. His long fingers gripped the arms of the chair tightly, as if he held himself in check. The muscles in his upper arms swelled with the tension. And below . . .

She caught her breath as she stepped from her skirts. His hard thighs braced his erection, which pointed aggressively up. The sight made her legs tremble, made her core heat and liquefy. She met his gaze, and he no longer looked dazed. He stared at her, intent, focused, no trace of a smile on his wide, expressive mouth.

She took a steadying breath and let her stays drop to the floor. She wore only a silk chemise now, fine as a dragonfly wing. As she stepped toward him, he started to rise from the chair. But she put a hand on his shoulder and placed one knee by his hip in the chair.

"Do you mind?" she asked.

She was gratified that he had to clear his throat. "Not at all."

She nodded and raised the hem of her chemise to her hips before climbing into the chair. She straddled his lap carefully and let the chemise fall. Then she sat. For a moment, all she could do was savor the heat of his thighs against her bottom. She could feel his body hair tickling her most intimate parts.

Then she smiled and wove her arms about his neck. "Will you kiss me?"

"God, yes," he growled.

He pulled her tightly against his chest, his arms strong

around her back. She almost giggled; it was so wonderful to finally be held by him like this. But then he brought his mouth to hers and all laughter fled. He kissed her as if he were a starving man, and she was the first bite of bread he'd seen in weeks. His mouth was wide, moving over hers, gasping for breath, nipping at her lips. His hands were hard on her, and she wondered if she'd have bruises in the morning.

She lifted a little, bringing herself closer to his cock. He froze, his mouth still on hers, as if waiting to see what she would do. She scooted forward in his lap until his penis lay beneath her, trapped firmly between their bodies. Then she slowly rubbed herself against him. The head of his cock parted her folds, and she ground her secret flesh against him. Her eyes fluttered closed at the exquisite feeling.

He broke their kiss and tried to reach between them.

"No." She opened her eyes and gazed at him sternly. Then she ground against him again.

His face was flushed, his lips wet. The long vertical lines about his mouth had deepened until his face looked saturnine.

She ground against him, the heat building, her folds slippery now. She still held his eyes, defying him to stop her.

Instead, he brought both hands between them and covered her breasts. "Do it now."

She raised up on her knees and pushed against his cock. She was panting now. He watched her and brought his thumbs and forefingers together, pinching her nipples. She gasped and arched her back, but his cock slid to one side. Frantically, she reached between them to hold his slippery length steady. She ground against him. She could feel her folds, swollen beneath her fingers. She imagined her sex, crimson and wet, flowering against his cock. She rubbed the head of his penis against her clitoris, biting her lips, striving, struggling toward that goal.

Then he leaned forward and sucked a nipple into his hot, humid mouth, and she went over the cliff. Rushing, panting, she shattered in space. Her chemise collapsed like tissue beneath his tongue, and he sucked hard on her nipple. She watched him through slitted eyes, her head thrown back in pleasure. *Vale.* She was shuddering against him, trembling, still between heaven and earth, not wanting to return.

His hands were soothing now instead of hard, running up and down her back. She quivered in his arms, her breathing beginning to subside, even as her need to have him inside her grew urgent. He shifted and wrapped his hands about her waist, lifting her without any show of effort. His cock was suddenly lower, at her entrance. She lifted her head, and her eyes met his implacable ones. He held her gaze and pushed against her, into her, stretching her passage, making her shudder with renewed pleasure. She tilted her pelvis and bore down, taking his entire length, seating herself firmly on his penis. Female to male. Wife to husband.

Their eyes were still locked, and she wondered what he thought—if he was surprised or pleased or displeased. Or perhaps he didn't have any such coherent thoughts at all. His wide mouth was stretched, almost frowning, and his eyes were narrowed. A bead of sweat ran down his jaw. Perhaps he didn't need to think. Perhaps he only felt.

And so would she. She leaned forward and licked the

bead of sweat, tasting salt and man—her man now. She took his face between her hands and bit his lower lip. He grunted, tightening his hands and lifting her, sliding his cock from her sheath, and then letting her body drop on his again.

She wanted to laugh, wanted to sing. She was flying and free—finally free—making love to the man she loved. She swiveled her hips the next time he brought her down, and he pulled his lip from between her teeth and muttered a curse. Then he was moving beneath her, surging up like a wave, roughly pushing his flesh into her as if he wanted to mark her.

She grabbed his broad shoulders and hung on. Her legs were wide, her breasts jiggling, and her mouth was open against his face, kissing, licking, biting. And all the while, his cock plundered her. Leaping. Demanding. Plunging.

Until all his muscles tightened at once. He shook his head, his teeth clenched, his body rigid, and she felt the hot wash of his seed into her body. He jerked once. Again. Then exhaled as if all the air was leaving his body at once.

She trailed kisses down his face and over his jaw, watching him, her husband, as he relaxed from their lovemaking. Gradually his muscles loosened. His hands fell from her waist. His head lolled against the chair back. And still she kissed him. On his neck, his ear, his shoulder. Light, soft kisses. *Vale. Vale. Vale.* She couldn't say aloud what her heart sang, but she could worship him with her mouth. His body was hot, his chest damp beneath her palms. She could smell the musk of their bodies, intimate in sex. This was right in a way it never had been before. All the various pieces of her life—her world—were in their correct places, all aligned in harmony. At peace.

She could stay here forever.

But he shifted beneath her and withdrew his flesh from hers. She bit back the cry of loss, because he was lifting her and carrying her to the bed. He lay her down and bent over her to kiss her gently on the lips. Then he turned away and left the room through the connecting door.

He never even saw the arms she held out to him.

Chapter Ten

❧❧

*On the day that the trials were to begin, hundreds,
perhaps thousands, of hopeful men stood outside the
castle walls. A tall platform was built for the king to
stand on so that all the suitors could hear. And from
this platform, the king explained what was to happen.
There would be three trials in all, in order that the
man who would win the princess be thoroughly
tested. The first test was to find and bring back a
ring of bronze. This ring lay at the bottom of a deep
and chilly lake. And in this lake there lived a giant
serpent. . . .*
—from LAUGHING JACK

Melisande awoke to a solitary bed. Suchlike must've let
Mouse into the room during the night, for the dog was
curled in a tight ball at the foot of her bed. She lay for
a moment, staring at the silk canopy overhead, sorting
through her emotions. Their lovemaking last night had
been wonderful—or at least she had thought so. Had Jas-

per left afterward because he was repulsed by her boldness? Or because it was simply a physical act for him and therefore he felt no need to stay and lay with her? Wasn't that what she wanted in the first place? To share with Vale the physical part of marriage without engaging her unnaturally intense emotions? Melisande blew out a frustrated breath. She didn't know anymore what she wanted, it seemed.

At the foot of the bed, Mouse uncurled himself and stretched, rump in the air. Then he padded softly toward her and nudged her hand.

"And what do you think, Sir Mouse?" Melisande inquired as she stroked his soft ears. "Has he quite tamed you?"

Mouse shook himself all over, then jumped from the bed and trotted to the door. He made his purpose known by scratching at the wood with a paw.

Melisande sighed and flung back the covers. "Very well, then. I suppose I won't answer my questions lying abed anyway."

She rang for Suchlike, and while she waited for the maid, she washed with the pitcher of rather chilly water on the dresser. Then, with the maid's help, she dressed quickly and was soon pattering down the stairs with Mouse. She handed over the dog's care to Sprat before making her way to the breakfast room, bracing herself to see Vale.

But the breakfast room was empty. Melisande hovered on the threshold for a moment before entering. The table had been cleared and cleaned, of course, but a few leftover crumbs made the case for her husband already having come and gone. She bit her lip. Why hadn't he waited?

"Shall I bring some chocolate, my lady?" Sprat asked from behind her. He'd returned with Mouse.

"Yes, please," she murmured automatically. Then she whirled, startling the footman. "No. Have the carriage brought 'round instead, will you?"

Sprat looked confused. "Yes, my lady."

"And tell Suchlike to meet me in the hall."

The footman bowed and left the room. Melisande went to the sideboard where a selection of buns and meats were already laid out. She wrapped several buns in a cloth and headed to the hall, Mouse at her heels.

Suchlike was already waiting in the hallway. She looked up as Melisande entered. "Are we going somewhere, my lady?"

"I thought a walk in the park would be nice," Melisande said briskly. She glanced at Mouse, sitting sedately by her feet. He gazed back at her innocently. "Sprat, I believe we will need Mouse's leash as well."

The footman hurried back to the kitchens to fetch the leash, and soon dog and women were in the carriage, headed west toward Hyde Park.

"It's a lovely day, isn't it, my lady?" Suchlike commented. "Blue sky and sunshine. 'Course, Mr. Pynch says we should enjoy it while we can, because soon it'll rain." The maid's brows lowered. "He's always predicting bad weather, Mr. Pynch is."

Melisande looked at her maid, amused. "A dour sort, is he?"

"Dour?"

"Dark and scowling."

"Oh." The maid's brow cleared. "Well, he is dark, but

not so much scowling as always looking down his nose at people, if you know what I mean."

"Ah." Melisande nodded. "A superior sort, then."

"Aye, my lady, that's it exactly," Suchlike exclaimed. "He acts like other people aren't quite as bright as he. Or just because a person is younger than him, she might not know as much."

Suchlike brooded for a bit on the superior valet. Melisande watched her with interest. Suchlike was usually a very cheerful sort of girl. She had never seen her in a glum frame of mind—and over a bald valet a dozen years her senior at that.

"Here's Hyde Park, my lady," Suchlike said.

Melisande glanced up and saw they'd entered the park. It was early still, and the park was not yet crowded with the fashionable carriages that would later parade. Right now, there were only a few riders, a carriage or two, and several figures strolling in the distance.

The carriage rolled to a stop. The door opened and a footman peered in. "Is this spot good, my lady?"

They were near a small duck pond. Melisande nodded. "Very nice. Tell the coachman to wait here while we stroll."

"Yes, my lady." The footman helped Melisande down first and then Suchlike. Mouse scampered to the ground and immediately lifted his leg against a bush.

Melisande cleared her throat. "Shall we make for the duck pond?"

"Wherever you'd like to go, my lady." Suchlike fell into step several paces behind Melisande.

She sighed. It was most proper for the lady's maid to follow her instead of walking by her side, but it did preclude any kind of intimate conversation. But the day was indeed fine, and she set out determinedly. Why wait at home for a husband who had a life of his own? No, she would enjoy the day, enjoy this walk, and *not* think about Vale and why he'd not waited to have breakfast with her.

However, Melisande found that it was somewhat hard to achieve a serene state of mind whilst out walking Mouse. The terrier strained against the leash, his sturdy legs digging into the ground as if he fought for each footstep. Indeed, he strained so mightily against the loop of leather that he was half strangling himself.

"What do you think you're doing, you silly, silly animal?" Melisande muttered as the dog choked and coughed dramatically. "If you simply stopped pulling, you'd be fine."

Mouse didn't even turn at the sound of her voice, intent on his struggle with the braided leather lead.

Melisande sighed. The portion of the park they were walking in was nearly deserted. In fact, the only people in sight were a woman and two children by the duck pond, still ahead. And Mouse had always loved children. She bent and slipped the loop off Mouse's head.

The dog immediately put his nose to the ground and began running in circles.

"Mouse," Melisande called.

He stopped and looked at her with ears pricked.

She smiled. "Very well."

The dog wagged his tail and scampered to investigate the base of a tree.

"He does seem to like a ramble, doesn't he, my lady?" Suchlike called from behind her.

"Yes, and he hasn't had one in quite a while."

Melisande walked more easily now that Mouse was no longer pulling against her. She unwrapped the cloth and took out the buns, offering one to Suchlike.

"Thank you, my lady."

Melisande strolled and munched. Mouse came running back and took a bite of bun from her hand before exploring again. She could hear the laughter of the children in the distance now, as well as the lower tones of the woman with them. The children were crouched near the pond's edge, the woman a little farther off but still near. One child had a long stick and was poking it about in the mud while the other watched.

Mouse saw a duck and drake waddling on the bank, and giving a joyful bark, he rushed at them. The ducks took flight. The silly terrier flung himself into the air, teeth snapping, as if he could actually catch a flying duck.

The children looked up and one shouted something. Mouse took this as an invitation and trotted over to make friends. As Melisande strolled closer, she could see that Mouse's new acquaintances were a boy and a girl. The boy looked about five or six, while the girl was perhaps eight. The boy was wearing a lovely suit but now had his arms wrapped about Mouse's neck. Melisande winced to think what mud was being transferred from dog to boy. The girl was less enthusiastic, which was fortunate since she wore a pristine white gown.

"Ma'am! Ma'am, what's his name?" the boy called when he saw her. "He's a grand dog."

"You shouldn't shout," his sister said in a repressive tone.

Melisande smiled at the girl. "His name is Mouse, and he is a grand dog indeed."

Mouse seemed to grin before putting his nose into the mud near the edge of the pond. Boy and dog went back to investigating the water.

Melisande paused. She hadn't much experience talking with children, but surely some things were universal? She nodded at the girl. "And what is your name?"

The child blushed and looked down. "Abigail Fitzwilliam," she whispered to her toes.

"Ah." Melisande's mind worked as she looked from the child to her mother, whom she'd seen just the other night at the masked ball. Helen Fitzwilliam was the Duke of Lister's mistress. The duke was a powerful man, but no matter how powerful the man in such situations, the woman was still considered beyond the pale. She smiled at Helen Fitzwilliam's daughter. "I am Lady Vale. How do you do?"

The girl still stared at her toes.

"Abigail," a low feminine voice said. "Curtsy to the lady, please."

The girl dropped a wobbly but pretty curtsy even as Melisande looked up. The woman who had spoken was beautiful—shining golden hair, wide blue eyes, and a perfect cupid's-bow mouth. She must be a little older than Melisande, but she would outshine women both younger and older than herself. But then it wasn't surprising that the Duke of Lister would choose a blindingly beautiful woman as his mistress.

She should walk away, not acknowledge the courtesan by either look or word. By the set of Mrs. Fitzwilliam's shoulders, that was exactly what the other woman expected. Melisande's gaze dropped to the little girl, her eyes still firmly fixed on the ground. How many times had she seen her mother cut dead?

Melisande inclined her head. "How do you do? I am Melisande Renshaw, Viscountess Vale."

She saw the flash first of surprise, then gratitude, on Mrs. Fitzwilliam's face before the woman sank into a curtsy. "Oh! It's an honor to meet you, my lady. I am Helen Fitzwilliam."

Melisande returned the curtsy, and when she rose, found the little girl looking at her. She smiled. "And what is your brother's name?"

The girl glanced over her shoulder to where her brother was squatting by the water, poking at something with a stick. Mouse was sniffing at whatever they'd found, and Melisande hoped he wouldn't take it into his head to roll in something noxious.

"That's Jamie," Abigail said. "He likes stinky things."

"Mmm," Melisande concurred. "So does Mouse."

"May I go see, Mother?" the girl asked.

"Yes, but do try not to paint yourself with the mud like your brother," Mrs. Fitzwilliam said.

Abigail looked insulted. "Of course not."

She walked carefully over to where the boy and dog were playing.

"She's a pretty child," Melisande commented. Usually she disliked trying to make conversation with strangers, but she knew that if she was quiet, the other woman would take it as a snub.

"She is, isn't she?" Mrs. Fitzwilliam said. "I know a mother isn't supposed to notice, but I've always thought her rather lovely. They're the light of my life, you know."

Melisande nodded. She wasn't sure how long Mrs. Fitzwilliam had been Lister's mistress, but the children were almost certainly his. What a strange half-life it must be to be a man's concubine. Lister had a legitimate family with his wife—some half-dozen sons and daughters already grown. Did he even acknowledge Jamie and Abigail as his own children?

"They love the park," Mrs. Fitzwilliam continued. "I come here with them as often as I can, which, I'm afraid, isn't often enough. I don't like coming when there are too many other people about."

She said it matter-of-factly, without any self-pity.

"Why do you suppose little boys and dogs love the mud so much?" Melisande mused. Abigail was keeping her distance, but Jamie had stood and stomped at something in the muck. Mud flew up in great lumps. Mouse barked.

"The stench?" Mrs. Fitzwilliam guessed.

"The mess?"

Abigail shrieked and leaped back as her brother stomped in the mud again.

"The fact that it disgusts little girls?"

Melisande smiled. "That certainly explains Jamie's fascination, but not Mouse's."

She found herself wishing she could ask the other woman to tea. Mrs. Fitzwilliam wasn't what she'd expected at all. She didn't ask for sympathy, didn't seem distressed at her lot in life, and she had a sense of humor. She might make a very good friend.

But, alas, it would never do to invite a cyprian to tea.

"I understand that you are newly wed," Mrs. Fitzwilliam said. "May I offer my felicitations?"

"Thank you," Melisande murmured. Her brow wrinkled as she was reminded of how Jasper had left her the night before.

"I've often thought that it must be hard to actually live with a man," Mrs. Fitzwilliam mused.

Melisande darted a glance at her.

Mrs. Fitzwilliam's cheeks reddened. "I hope I haven't offended you."

"Oh, no."

"It's just that a man can be so distant sometimes," the other lady said quietly. "As if one is intruding on his life. But perhaps not all men are like that?"

"I don't know," Melisande said. "I've only the one husband."

"Of course." Mrs. Fitzwilliam looked down at the ground. "I wonder, though, if it is even possible for a man and a woman to be truly close. In a spiritual sense, I mean. The sexes are so far apart, aren't they?"

Melisande clasped her hands together. Mrs. Fitzwilliam's view of marriage was rather cynical, and a part of her—the sensible, pragmatic part—urged her to agree. But another part of her disagreed violently. "I don't think that always has to be the case, surely? I have seen couples very much in love with each other, so close that they seem to understand each other's thoughts."

"And do you have such a bond with your husband?" Mrs. Fitzwilliam asked. The question would've been rude coming from any other lady, but Mrs. Fitzwilliam seemed honestly curious.

"No," Melisande answered. "Lord Vale and I don't have that type of marriage."

And that was what she wanted, wasn't it? She'd loved once before and had been wounded to her very soul. She simply couldn't endure that kind of pain again. Melisande felt a shrinking, a sadness, infuse her being as she acknowledged this fact. She would never have one of those glorious marriages based on love and mutual understanding.

"Ah," Mrs. Fitzwilliam said, and then they stood together silently and watched the children and Mouse.

Finally, Mrs. Fitzwilliam turned to her and smiled, a wonderfully beautiful smile that simply took Melisande's breath away. "Thank you for letting them play with your dog."

As Melisande opened her mouth to answer, she heard a shout from behind her. "My lady wife! What a joy to find you here."

And she turned to see Vale riding toward them with another man.

MELISANDE HAD BEEN so deeply in conversation with the other woman that she didn't even notice Jasper until he hailed her. As he and Lord Hasselthorpe rode closer, the other woman turned and strolled unhurriedly away. Jasper recognized the woman. She called herself Mrs. Fitzwilliam, and she'd been the Duke of Lister's mistress for almost a decade.

What had Melisande been doing, talking to a demimondaine?

"Your wife keeps fast company," Lord Hasselthorpe said. "Sometimes young matrons get the idea in their head that they can become fashionable by skirting the edges of respectability. Best warn her, Vale."

A biting retort was on Jasper's lips, but he swallowed it. He'd just spent the prior half hour ingratiating himself to Hasselthorpe.

He grit his teeth and said, "I'll keep it in mind, sir."

"Do," Hasselthorpe replied, pulling his horse to a stop before they'd reached Melisande. "No doubt you wish to discuss matters with your lady wife, so I'll part ways with you here. You've given me much to think about."

"Does that mean you'll help us find the traitor?" Jasper pressed.

Hasselthorpe hesitated. "Your theories seem sound, Vale, but I dislike rushing into things. If my brother Thomas was indeed killed because of some cowardly traitor, you will have my help. But I would like to contemplate the matter further."

"Very well," Jasper said. "May I call on you tomorrow?"

"Best make it the day after," Hasselthorpe said.

Jasper nodded, though he hated the delay. He shook hands with the other man and then rode toward Melisande. She had turned to watch him approach, her hands folded at her waist, her back as usual impossibly straight. She didn't look at all like the woman who'd seduced him so expertly the night before. For a moment, he wanted to take her by the shoulders and shake her, make her lose her impenetrable poise, make her back bend.

He did no such thing, of course; one didn't accost one's wife in a public park in the middle of the morning even if she had just been conversing with persons of low repute.

Instead, he smiled and hailed her again. "Out for a walk, my heart?"

Mouse caught sight of him and, abandoning a small, muddy boy, raced toward Vale's horse, barking frantically. The dog really did have the brains of a peahen. Fortunately, Belle merely snorted at the terrier dancing at her hooves.

"Mouse," Jasper said sternly. "Sit down."

Miraculously, the dog planted its arse in the grass.

Jasper swung down from the bay and looked at Mouse. Mouse wagged his tail. Jasper continued to stare until Mouse lowered his head, his tail still wagging so vigorously that the dog's rear half wriggled as well. Mouse laid his head almost on the ground and crept toward Jasper on his elbows, his mouth drawn back in a grimace of submission.

"Oh, for God's sake," Jasper muttered. One would think from the dog's behavior that he'd beaten the animal.

Mouse took his words as permission to jump up, trot toward him, and sit expectantly at Jasper's feet. He stared down at the dog, nonplussed.

He heard a muffled giggle. Cocking an eye at Melisande, he saw that she now had one hand over her mouth. "I think he likes you."

"Yes, but do I like him?"

"It doesn't matter whether or not you like him." She strolled closer. "He likes you and that's that."

"Hmm." Jasper looked back at the dog. Mouse had his head tilted to the side as if awaiting instructions. "Go on, then."

The dog gave one bark and ran in a wide circle around Jasper, Melisande, and the horse.

"You'd think he'd dislike me after I shut him in the cellar," Jasper muttered.

Melisande gave an elegant shrug. "Dogs are funny that way." She bent and picked up a stick between forefinger and thumb. "Here."

Jasper eyed the stick. It was muddy. "I'm overwhelmed by your thoughtfulness, my lady."

She rolled her eyes. "It's not for you, silly. Throw it for Mouse."

"Why?"

"Because he likes to fetch sticks," she said patiently, as if talking to a very slow child.

"Huh." He took the stick, and Mouse immediately stopped running and looked up. Jasper flung the stick as far as he could, absurdly aware that he was showing off.

Mouse raced after the stick, pounced on it, and shook it vigorously. Then he trotted off around the pond.

Jasper frowned. "I thought he was supposed to bring it back to me?"

"I never said he was very good at playing fetch."

Jasper looked down at his wife. The morning air had pinkened her normally pale cheeks; her eyes were sparkling at having winged him, and she looked . . . lovely. Quite, quite lovely.

He had to swallow before he could speak. "Are you informing me that I've lost a perfectly good stick?"

There was a muted *snap!* from across the little pond as Mouse chewed through the stick.

Melisande winced. "I'm not sure you'd want it back now anyway."

"He won't eat it, will he?"

"He never has before."

"Ah." And then he wasn't quite sure what to say—a circumstance that happened very rarely in his life. He wanted to ask her what she'd been talking about with Mrs. Fitzwilliam, but for the life of him, he wasn't exactly sure how to phrase the question. *Have you been taking lessons in seduction from a courtesan?* didn't seem quite the thing.

He noticed that Mrs. Fitzwilliam and her children seemed to have left the park. They were no longer in sight.

"Why did you not wait for me at breakfast?" she asked into the silence.

They had begun to stroll about the pond, Jasper leading his horse. "I don't know exactly. I thought after last night . . ."

What? That she would want some time alone? No, that wasn't quite true. Perhaps he was the one who needed the solitude. And what did that say about him?

"Did I disgust you?" she asked.

And he was so startled that he halted and looked at her. Why ever would she think he was disgusted by her? To even ask revealed a tender spot in her soul. "No. No, my heart. You could never disgust me if you tried for a thousand years."

Her eyebrows were slightly knit as she searched his face. She seemed to be watching to see if he lied.

He bent toward her and murmured, "You intrigue me, you tempt me, you inflame me, but disgust? Never, sweet wife, never."

She caught her breath, and when she spoke, her voice was low. "It wasn't what you expected, though."

He thought of her assured and controlled as she'd taken his cock into her hand last night. The feel of her cool fingers, the sight of her intent face, had nearly made him spill right then and there.

"No," he said, just a little hoarsely. "Not what I expected. Melisande—"

A shot blasted from across the park. Jasper instinctively pulled Melisande into his arms. Mouse began barking hysterically. They could hear shouting and the high whinnying of a horse, but whatever was happening was hidden by a copse of trees.

"What is it?" Melisande asked.

"I don't know," Jasper muttered.

A hatless gentleman on a big black horse galloped into view, coming from the sounds of the commotion.

Jasper put Melisande behind him. "Oy! You there! What's happened?"

The man yanked on his horse, pulling it into a half rear. "I'm after a doctor. I haven't the time."

"Is someone shot?"

"A murder attempt," the man cried as he spurred his horse. "Someone's tried to kill Lord Hasselthorpe!"

"BUT WHY WOULD someone shoot at Lord Hasselthorpe?" Melisande asked later that night. Vale had bundled her into the carriage and ordered her home before going to the scene of the assassination attempt. He'd been away until after dinner, and this was the first she'd been able to question him.

"I don't know," he answered. He had come to her rooms, but now he paced as if he'd been caged. "Perhaps it was some kind of accident. An idiot practice shooting without a proper straw target to catch the bullet."

"In Hyde Park?"

"I don't know!" Vale's voice was overloud, and he looked at her in apology. "Forgive me, my lady wife. But if it was an assassin, he was a damn bad shot. Hasselthorpe was merely winged on the arm. He should make a full recovery. I saw plenty of similar wounds in the war, and they were hardly worth noting as long as infection didn't set in."

"I'm glad the hurt is so slight, then," Melisande said. She sat on one of the low armchairs before the fire—the one they'd made love in the night before, in fact—and watched him. "You hardly ever talk about the war."

"Don't I?" he replied vaguely. He was standing by her dresser, poking his finger in a bowl of hairpins. He wore a red and black banyan over his breeches and shirt. "Not much to tell, really."

"No? You were in the army for six years, though, weren't you?"

"Seven years," he muttered. He moved to her wardrobe, which he flung open and peered at as if he'd find the hidden secrets of the cosmos amongst her gowns.

"Why did you join?"

He turned and stared at her blindly for a moment.

Then he blinked and laughed. "I joined the army to learn how to be a man. Or at least that was my father's purpose. He thought me too lazy, too effete. And since there wasn't any use for me at home"—he shrugged carelessly—"why not buy a commission for me?"

"And your best friend, Reynaud St. Aubyn, bought a commission at the same time?"

"Oh, yes. We were terribly excited to join the 28th Regiment of Foot. May it rest in peace." He closed the wardrobe doors and went to brood at the window.

Perhaps she should leave it be. Stop poking at him, let his secrets lie buried. But some part of her wouldn't let go. Every bit of his life was fascinating to her, and this bit that he kept hidden even more so than the others. Sighing, she rose from the armchair. She wore a heavy satin wrap over her chemise, and she slipped out of the wrap now, carefully laying it on the chair.

"Did you like army life?" she asked quietly.

She could see his reflection watching her in the black glass of the window. "Some of it. Men complain of the ghastly food, the marches, the living in tents. But it can be a lark at times. Sitting by a campfire, trying to eat boiled peasemeal and bacon."

She drew off her chemise as she listened, and he abruptly stopped talking. Nude, she walked toward him and laid her hands on his back. His muscles were rock-hard, as if he'd turned to granite.

"And the battles?"

"Like being in hell," he whispered.

She smoothed her hands down his broad back, feeling the valley of his spine, the muscles on either side. *Like being in hell.* She ached for the part of him that had been in hell. "Were you in many battles?"

"A few." He sighed and lowered his head as she dug her thumbs into the muscles above his hips.

She tapped his shoulder. "Take this off."

He shrugged out of his banyan and shirt, but when he made to turn around, she firmly pushed him back. She pressed her thumbs in hard, small circles on either side of his spine. He groaned and his head fell forward again as he braced his hands on either side of the windowsill.

"You were at Quebec," she said softly.

"That was the only real battle. The rest were skirmishes. Some lasted only minutes."

"And Spinner's Falls?"

His shoulders hunched as if she'd hit him, but he didn't say a word. She knew that Spinner's Falls had been a massacre. She'd comforted Emeline when word finally came back that Reynaud had not survived his capture there. She should push—this was obviously his weak point. But she couldn't be so ruthless. She hated the thought of hurting him anew.

Instead, she took his hand and led him to her bed. He stood silently, passively, as she stripped him of his remaining clothes—although his cock was far from passive. Then she pushed him onto the bed and climbed in beside him. She propped herself up on an elbow next to him and drew her free hand down over his chest. She felt grateful that she had this man, at least for this time, for herself. Here, now, she could do with him as she wished.

It was a gift. A glorious gift.

So she leaned down and trailed soft, wet kisses along his side, licking the ridge of his ribs, nipping at the jut of his hip bone. Above her, he rumbled something, a warning perhaps, or maybe encouragement. She wasn't sure, and she didn't care. In front of her was her goal: his penis, bold and thick and hard. She touched it with just a fingertip, running along its length. Then she leaned down and softly, gently, kissed him on the weeping eye.

His hips arched, and he grabbed her hair, pulling her face up. "Don't. You don't have to. I don't deserve it."

There were beads of sweat on his upper lip, and his eyes were wild and sorrowful.

Deserve was an interesting choice of word, and she stored it away so that she could bring it out and examine it later.

Right now, though, she deliberately licked her lips, tasting his seed, and said, "I want to." She wanted to bring him peace if she could.

His grip relaxed, perhaps in surprise, but she took advantage by dipping her head and taking his cock into her mouth. Then his hands tightened again, but she hardly thought it was to stop her now.

She sucked on the tip, a salty plum in her mouth, and ran her hand dreamily down the length. She hadn't a lot of practice at this, and if there was a proper way of doing it, she wasn't aware, but he didn't seem to mind. He muttered something unintelligible and bucked his hips. She smiled secretly and let his cock pull out of her mouth with a soft *pop*. She tested her teeth against the meaty head, stroking faster below. There was no give in his shaft. He was hard and ready and—

He jackknifed up and flipped her beneath him. And then he was looming large and menacing over her, his face dark as he growled, "Do you think me a plaything, my lady?"

She opened her legs wide, planted her feet, and arched her hips off the bed. She rubbed her sex against his length, watching as his eyelids fell in reaction.

"Perhaps I do," she whispered. "Perhaps your cock is my favorite toy. Perhaps I want my toy in my—"

But he thrust fast and hard, making her lose her words on a gasp of pleasure.

"Wanton," he gritted. "*My* wanton."

And she could only laugh in sheer erotic frenzy. She bucked her hips up, making him thrust harder just to stay on top. She laughed aloud as she rotated and ground against him, the sweat from his exertions dripping onto her bare breasts. He gripped her hips and held her firmly still as he thudded into her, galloping at an impossible pace. Stars lit behind her open eyes, and she threw her head back and gasped in ecstasy. She held on to his slippery shoulders, feeling the heat spread from her center, conscious dimly that she still laughed aloud even as she crested in glory.

It wasn't until he shuddered in her arms, swearing steadily under his breath, that her vision cleared and she saw that above her his face was a mask of tragedy.

Chapter Eleven

*All of the suitors set off after the ring of bronze, and
  Princess Surcease sighed and went back into the
  castle. But Jack found a quiet corner and opened
his little tin snuffbox. And what should be inside but
    exactly what he needed: a suit of armor made of
night and wind and the sharpest sword in the world.
Jack put the suit on his stumpy body and grasped the
sword. Then whoosh! Whist! he stood before a lake.
Jack was just wondering if this was the right lake,
when an enormous serpent rose up out of the water.
What a mighty battle commenced! The serpent was
very large and Jack very small, but he did have the
sharpest sword in the world, and that suit certainly
helped. In the end, the serpent lay dead and the ring
           lay in Jack's hand. . . .
        —from LAUGHING JACK*

He'd apparently married a wanton, Jasper reflected late
the next morning. A shameless, sensual wanton, and he

couldn't believe his luck. While sitting in that church vestry, listening to her proposal with his head ringing from a hangover, he'd never once thought that the marriage bed would be so wonderfully intense with her.

Of course, all that wonderfulness didn't quite explain why he was riding *away* from his town house this morning, having once again eaten breakfast without his wife. This came perilously close to cowardice. But while his body was enthralled by her sensuality, his intellect coldly wondered where she'd gained her knowledge. She must've had at least one lover—possibly more—and he wasn't sure he wanted to examine that thought too closely. The image of another man teaching her. Showing her how to take a cock into her sweet, warm mouth . . .

He growled. A passing chimney sweep shot him a startled glance and shied away.

Jasper pushed the thought from his mind. He hunched his shoulders and drew up his collar against the misty drizzle. The good weather had finally broken, and London was a gray, gloomy world this morning. His mind drifted back to last night. He remembered his wife reflected in the black window as she drew her chemise from her tall, slender body. She'd looked pale and otherworldly, her light brown hair swirling about her hips.

She probably thought him a coward or, worse, an imbecile. He'd left her after they'd made love, without so much as a good night, and spent the night on his pallet. He was an ass. But those eyes, watching him as she kissed his chest, watching him as she asked about Spinner's Falls. God. She'd had no idea what she'd married. Perhaps it was best that he'd left so ungraciously. Better not to give her hope of something more when he didn't have it in him to *be* anything more.

And now he didn't even make sense in his own mind. He looked up to see Matthew Horn's town house, glad that he could escape these maudlin musings.

Jasper dismounted Belle and handed the reins to a boy, then leapt up the front steps. A minute later, he was prowling Horn's library, waiting for him to come down from wherever he was.

He'd just bent to peer at a large and dusty volume when Horn's voice came from the door. "Looking for some light reading?"

"Just wondering why anyone would want a history of copper mining." Jasper straightened and grinned.

Horn made a wry face. "My pater's. Not that it did him any good. The mine he picked to invest in failed." He strolled into the room and flung himself into a large chair, looping his leg over the arm. "The Horns are not exactly known for their financial sense."

Jasper grimaced sympathetically. "Bad luck, that."

Horn shrugged. "Want some tea? Seems early for whiskey."

"No. Thank you." Jasper wandered to a framed map of the world and tried to make out where Italy was.

"Come about Spinner's Falls again, have you?" Horn asked.

"Mmm-hmm," Jasper agreed without turning. Was it possible Italy wasn't on the map at all? "Have you heard about what happened to Hasselthorpe?"

"Shot in Hyde Park. They're calling it an assassination attempt."

"Yes. And right after Hasselthorpe agreed to think about helping me."

There was a brief silence, broken by Horn's incredulous laugh. "You can't think the two are related?"

Jasper shrugged. He wasn't sure, of course, but the whole thing was a very strange coincidence.

"I still think you ought let Spinner's Falls go," Horn said quietly.

Jasper didn't reply. If he was capable of letting this go, he would.

Horn sighed. "Well, I've been thinking about it."

Jasper turned and glanced at Horn. "Have you?"

Horn waved a vague hand. "Here and there. What I don't understand is why someone would betray the regiment. What would be the point? Especially if it was one of us who was captured. Seems like a good way to get yourself killed."

Jasper blew out a breath. "Don't think he meant to be captured—the traitor, that is. Probably thought to lie low and avoid the fighting."

"Every one of us that was captured fought and fought well."

"Aye, you're right." Jasper turned back to the map.

"Then what possible reason to betray the regiment and get us all killed? I think you've got hold of the wrong end of the stick, old man. There wasn't any traitor. Spinner's Falls was just bad luck, plain and simple."

"Perhaps." Jasper leaned so close to the map that his nose nearly touched the parchment. "But I can think of one very good reason someone might betray us."

"What?"

"Money." Jasper gave up on the map entirely. "The

French had made it known that they'd pay good money for information."

"A spy?" Matthew's dark eyebrows shot up. He didn't look particularly convinced.

"Why not?"

"Because I and anyone else who was there would tear the bloody bastard limb from limb, that's why," Matthew replied. He jumped up from his chair as if he couldn't stay still anymore.

"All the more reason to make sure no one found out," Jasper said softly.

Matthew was looking out the window now and merely shrugged.

"Look, I have no more love of the idea than you," Jasper said. "But if we were betrayed, if they all died from one man's greed, if we marched through that forest and endured . . ." He stopped, unable to say the rest.

Jasper closed his eyes, but in the blackness, he still saw the glowing stick pressing into flesh, still smelled the stench of burned human skin. He opened his eyes. Matthew was watching him without expression.

"We need—*I* need—to find him and bring him to justice. Make him pay for his sins," Jasper said.

"What about Hasselthorpe? Have you seen him since the shooting?"

"He refuses to see me. I sent a message this morning asking for an interview, and he sent it back saying he intends to retire to his country estate to recover."

"Damn."

"Quite." Jasper brooded over the map again.

"You need to speak to Alistair Munroe," Horn said from behind him.

Jasper turned. "You think he's the traitor?"

"No." Matthew shook his head. "But he was there. He might remember something we haven't."

"I've tried writing him." Jasper grimaced in frustration. "He doesn't write back."

Matthew looked at him steadily. "Then you'll just have to travel to Scotland, won't you?"

MELISANDE SAW HER husband for the first time that day at dinner. She'd actually begun to wonder if he was avoiding her, if something was the matter, but he seemed perfectly normal now as he forked up peas and joked with the footmen.

"How was your day?" Vale asked her carelessly.

Really, he could be a most aggravating man at times. "I took luncheon with your mother."

"Did you?" He gestured to the footman for more wine.

"Mmm-hmm. She served stuffed artichokes and cold sliced ham."

He shuddered. "Artichokes. I never know how to eat them."

"You scrape the leaf against your teeth. Quite easy."

"And leaves. Who thinks to eat leaves?" he asked, apparently rhetorically. "I wouldn't. Probably some woman discovered artichokes."

"The Romans ate them."

"A *Roman* woman, then. She probably served up a plate of leaves to her husband and said, 'Here you are, dear, eat hearty.'"

Melisande found herself smiling at Vale's depiction of the fictional Roman wife and her unfortunate husband.

"In any case, the artichokes your mother served were very good."

"Huh." Vale grunted skeptically. "I expect she told you all about my misspent youth."

Melisande ate a pea. "You expect correctly."

He winced. "Anything particularly egregious?"

"Apparently you spat up a lot as a baby."

"At least I'm over that," he muttered.

"And you had a flirtation with a milkmaid at the age of sixteen."

"I'd forgotten that," Vale exclaimed. "Lovely girl. Agnes, or was it Alice? Perhaps Arabella—"

"I doubt Arabella," Melisande murmured.

He ignored her. "She had lovely peaches-and-cream skin and the biggest . . ." He suddenly coughed.

"Feet?" Melisande asked sweetly.

"Amazing, really. Her feet." His eyes gleamed wickedly at her.

"Humph," Melisande said, but she had to repress a smile. "And what about your day?"

"Ah. Well." Jasper stuck a large piece of beef in his mouth and chewed vigorously before swallowing. "I went 'round to Matthew Horn's house. Remember him? Fellow from my mother's garden party?"

"Yes."

"You won't believe it, but he has a map of the world that doesn't have Italy on it."

"Perhaps you weren't looking in the right spot," she said kindly.

"No. No." He shook his head and drank some wine. "It's this side of Russia and above Africa. I'm pretty sure I'd've noticed it."

"Perhaps the map was made by someone who disliked Rome."

"Do you think?" He seemed much struck by the thought. "Just decided to do away with Italy altogether?"

She shrugged.

"What an idea! I wouldn't have had to study Latin all those years if Italy had disappeared."

"But now you already have, and I'm sure you're a better man for it."

"Huh." Jasper sounded unsure.

Melisande ate some boiled carrots. They were quite good. Cook had added something sweet—honey, perhaps. She'd have to remember to compliment the little woman. "And did you discuss anything more with Mr. Horn besides his defective map?"

"Yes, we talked about a fellow we know in Scotland."

"Oh?" Vale was drinking more wine, and it was hard to read his expression. Melisande's interest sharpened. "What is his name?"

"Sir Alistair Munroe. He was attached to my regiment, but he wasn't a soldier. He was sent by the crown to record animals and plants in America."

"Really? He sounds like a fascinating man."

Vale frowned. "He is if you like talking about ferns for hours at a time."

Melisande sipped her wine. "I quite like ferns."

Vale frowned harder. "In any case, I'm thinking of making a trip up to jolly old Scotland to see him."

There was a silence as Melisande contemplated her cooling peas and carrots. Was he running from her? She'd so enjoyed living in his house and knowing he was nearby. Even if he was away for large parts of the day or stayed out until all hours of the night, she knew he'd come home eventually. Just being in the same house as he soothed her soul. Now she wouldn't have even that.

Vale cleared his throat. "Thing is, he lives north of Edinburgh. It's a ways away, a trip of a week or more on bad roads in a carriage. There'll be drafty inns and bad food and the possibility of highwaymen—probably be an awful trip altogether."

He had transferred his scowl to his plate. He jabbed at his beef with the tines of his fork.

Melisande was silent, no longer eating because her throat seemed to have closed. He was going to see a man, whom, by his own admission, he didn't particularly like or know well. Why?

"But, despite all that, I wonder if you'd like to accompany me, my lady wife."

She was so wrapped up in her own thoughts that for a minute his words didn't make sense. She looked at him to find that he was watching her intently, his eyes bright blue-green. A blessed relief began spreading through her chest.

"When will you leave?" she asked.

"Tomorrow."

Her eyes widened. "So soon?"

"I have something important to discuss with Munroe. Something that can't wait." He leaned forward. "You can take Mouse. We'll have to bring his leash, of course, and make sure he doesn't scare the horses at inns. It really won't be comfortable, and you might be terribly bored, but—"

"Yes."

He blinked. "What?"

"Yes." Melisande smiled and resumed eating. "I'd like to come with you."

"THEY'RE TRAVELING TO Scotland," Bernie the footman said as he brought the dish of peas back into the kitchen.

Sally Suchlike nearly dropped her spoon into her bowl of soup. *Scotland?* That heathen land? They said the men grew beards so fierce you could hardly see their eyes. And it was a well-known fact that the Scots didn't bathe.

Cook was obviously having similar thoughts. "And them only newly married," she lamented as she set dishes of lemon curd tart on a tray. "It's a pity, truly it is."

She gestured for Bernie to take the tray in and then stopped him with a hand on his arm. "Have they said how long they'll be gone?"

"He's only now told my lady, but it'd have to be weeks, won't it?" The footman shrugged, nearly upsetting the tray on his shoulder. "Months, even. An' they leave right away. Tomorrow."

One of the scullery maids burst into tears as Bernie left the kitchen.

Sally tried to swallow, but there didn't seem to be any spit left in her mouth. She'd have to travel with Lady Vale to Scotland. That was what lady's maids did. Suddenly her new position, with the lovely increase in wages—enough even to set some by—didn't seem so grand. Sally shuddered. Scotland was the edge of the world.

"Here now, there's no need to carry on like this." Mr. Pynch's deep voice came from beside the fireplace where he was smoking his nightly pipe.

At first Sally thought he was admonishing her, but he was clearly addressing Bitsy, the scullery maid.

"Scotland isn't as bad as all that," the valet said.

"Have you been to Scotland, then, Mr. Pynch?" Sally asked. Perhaps if he'd journeyed there and back and survived, it wouldn't be so terrible.

"No," Mr. Pynch said, dashing her hopes. "But I've known Scotsmen in the army, and they're just the same as us, saving for the fact that they speak funny."

"Oh."

Sally looked down at her beef soup, made from the bones left over from the roast Cook had prepared for their master and mistress. It was a very good soup. Sally had been enjoying it until just a couple of minutes ago. But now her stomach made a little unpleasant turn at the sight of the grease floating on top. Knowing a Scotsman and traveling to Scotland were two entirely different things, and Sally was almost angry with Mr. Pynch for not knowing the difference. His Scotsmen were probably tamed from their time in the army. There was no way to know what a Scotsman was like on his home ground, so to speak. Perhaps they had a liking for short blond girls from London. Perhaps she'd be kidnapped from her bed and used in horrible ways—or worse.

"Now, see here, my girl." Mr. Pynch's voice was very near.

Sally looked up to find that the valet had taken the seat opposite her at the table. The kitchen servants had gone back to work while she brooded. Bitsy was snuffling over the pan of dishes she washed. No one paid any mind to the valet and the lady's maid at the far end of the long kitchen table.

Mr. Pynch's eyes were bright and intent on her. Sally

had never noticed before what a lovely shade of green they were.

The valet put his elbows on the table, his long, white clay pipe in one hand. "There's nothing to fear in Scotland. It's just a place like any other."

Sally stirred her spoon about in her bowl of cooling soup. "I've never been farther than Greenwich in my life."

"No? Where were you born then?"

"Seven Dials," she said, and then peered up at him to see if he'd sneer at the knowledge she'd been raised in such a hellhole.

But he merely nodded his head and sucked on the end of his pipe, blowing fragrant smoke to the side so it wouldn't get in her eyes. "And do you have family there still?"

"Just my pa." She wrinkled her nose and confessed, "Leastwise, he used to live there. I haven't seen him in years, so that might not be true anymore."

"Bad sort was your pa?"

"Not too bad." She traced the rim of her soup bowl with a finger. "He didn't beat me much, and he fed me when he could. But I had to get out of there. It was like I couldn't breathe."

She looked at him to see if he understood.

He nodded, pulling on his pipe again. "And your mam?"

"Died when I was born." The soup smelled good again, and she took a spoonful. "No brothers or sisters either. Leastwise none that I know of."

He nodded and seemed quite content to watch her eat the soup as he smoked his pipe. Around them, the kitchen and downstairs servants scurried about, doing their jobs, but this was a time of rest for Sally and Mr. Pynch.

She ate half her soup and then looked up at him. "Where are you from, then, Mr. Pynch?"

"Oh, a ways off. I was born in Cornwall."

"Really?" She stared curiously at him. Cornwall seemed nearly as foreign as Scotland. "But you don't have an accent."

He shrugged. "My people are fisher folk. I got the wandering urge, and when the army men came to town with their drums and ribbons and flash uniforms, I took the king's shilling fast enough." One corner of his mouth curved in a funny sort of half-smile. "Didn't take me long to find out there's more to His Majesty's army than pretty uniforms."

"How old were you?"

"Fifteen."

Sally looked down at her soup, trying to imagine big, bald Mr. Pynch as a lanky fifteen-year-old. She couldn't do it. He was too much a man now to have ever been a child. "Do you still have family in Cornwall?"

He nodded. "My mother and a half-dozen brothers and sisters. My father died when I was in the Colonies. Didn't know about it until I returned to England two years later. Mam said she paid for a letter to be written and sent to me, but I never got one."

"That must've been sad, coming home to find your father dead for two years."

He shrugged. "That's the way of the world, lass. Nothing a man can do but go on."

"I suppose so." She frowned a little, thinking of wild highland Scotsmen with beards that covered their faces.

"Lass." Mr. Pynch had stretched out his arm and tapped her hand with one large, blunt-nailed finger. "There won't be anything to fear in Scotland. But if there is, I'll keep you safe."

And Sally could only stare dumbly into Mr. Pynch's steady green eyes, the thought of him keeping her safe warming her belly.

WHEN HE STILL hadn't come to her rooms by midnight, Melisande went looking for Vale. Perhaps he'd simply gone to his own bed, not deigning to visit her that night, but she didn't think so. She hadn't heard any voices from his room next door. How the man got enough sleep when he stayed up until all hours and then left the house before she rose was a curiosity. Perhaps he didn't need sleep at all.

In any case, she was tired of waiting for him to come to her. So she left her room—still in a shambles from Suchlike's hurried packing—and went out in the hall to search for Jasper. He wasn't in the library or any of the sitting rooms, and finally she was forced to inquire of Oaks if he knew where her husband was. Then she hoped that her cheeks didn't flame in embarrassment when she learned that he'd gone out without a word to her.

She felt like kicking something, but since gentlewomen did no such thing, she merely thanked Oaks and ascended the stairs again. Why was he doing this? Asking her to accompany him to Scotland, then avoiding her? Had he even thought about a days-long carriage ride with her? Or would he spend the journey atop the carriage with the luggage? It was so strange. First he would pursue her for days, and then he would suddenly disappear, just when she thought they were drawing closer.

Melisande exhaled heavily as she came to her own bedroom door, but then she hesitated. Vale's door was right next to hers. Really, the temptation was too great. She strode to her husband's door and opened it. The room was empty, although Mr. Pynch's work was obvious: Rows of shirts, waistcoats, and neck clothes were laid out on the bed in preparation for packing. Melisande shut the door gently behind her.

She wandered to the bed and touched a fingertip to the dark red coverlet. He would sprawl here at night, his long limbs spread wide. Did he sleep on his back, or on his belly, his tousled head half shoved beneath a pillow? Somehow she imagined him sleeping in the nude, although for all she knew, he had a drawerful of nightshirts. It was such an intimate thing, sleeping with another person. One's shields were all thrown down in sleep, leaving one vulnerable, almost childlike. She wished desperately that he would share her bed. Stay the night and let himself be at his most vulnerable with her.

She sighed and turned from the bed. On his dresser he had a framed miniature portrait of his mother. A few brown hairs were caught in the bristles of his brush. One was almost red. She took her handkerchief from her sleeve and carefully folded the hairs inside before tucking it away again.

She went to the bedside table and glanced at the book sitting there—a history of the English kings—then went to the window and looked out. His view was nearly the same as hers: the back of the garden. She glanced around the room, frustrated. There were far more things lying about—clothing, books, odd bits of string, a pinecone, broken pens, a penknife, and ink—but nothing that told her very much about her husband. How silly to sneak in here, thinking she might find out more about Jasper. She shook her head at her own folly, and then her gaze fell on the dressing room door. A dressing room would hardly hold more intimate stuff than what she'd seen, but she'd already come this far.

Melisande turned the handle of the door. Inside was another dresser, various racks for holding clothes, a narrow cot, and in the corner, against the wall, a thin pallet and blanket. Melisande cocked her head. Odd. Why both a cot and a pallet? Mr. Pynch needed only one, surely. And why a pallet? Vale struck her as a generous employer. Why such a mean bed for his faithful valet?

She stepped into the narrow room, went around the cot, and bent to look at the pallet. A single candle stood nearby in a holder very much covered in old, burnt wax, and a book lay half under the carelessly tossed blanket. She looked from the pallet to the cot. Actually, the cot didn't look as if anyone slept there at all—the mattress was bare. Melisande pulled the blanket back from the pallet to read the title of the book. It was a book of poems by John Donne. She stared at it a moment, thinking what an odd choice of reading matter for a valet, when she noticed the hair on the pillow. It was dark brown, almost red.

Behind her, someone cleared his throat.

Melisande whirled and saw Mr. Pynch, his eyebrows raised. "May I help you find something, my lady?"

"No." Melisande hid trembling hands in her skirts, very glad that it wasn't Vale who'd discovered her. Although being caught by the valet rummaging through her husband's things was embarrassing enough. She tilted her chin and sailed to the door of the bedroom.

But then she hesitated and looked back at the valet. "You've served my husband for many years, haven't you, Mr. Pynch?"

"Aye, my lady."

"Has he always slept so little?"

The big bald man picked up one of the neck cloths from the bed and carefully refolded it. "Aye, since I've known him, my lady."

"Do you know why?"

"Some men don't need as much sleep," the valet said.

She only looked at him.

He replaced the neck cloth and finally looked at her. He sighed as if she'd pressed him. "Some soldiers don't sleep as well as they ought. Lord Vale . . . well, he likes company. Especially during the hours it's dark."

"He's afraid of the dark?"

He straightened and his frown was quite ferocious. "I received a ball to the leg in the war."

Melisande blinked, startled at the change of subject. "I'm sorry."

The valet waved away her sympathy. "It's nothing. Only bothers me when it rains sometimes. But when I got it, that ball took me down. We were in battle, and I was lying there, with a Frenchie standing over me about to stick me with his bayonet when Lord Vale came charging. There was a stand of Frenchies with rifles raised between him and me, but that didn't stop him. They fired on him, and how he didn't fall, I don't know, but he wore a grin the entire time. Cut them down, too, my lady. Wasn't one standing when he was done."

Melisande drew a shuddering breath. "I see."

"I decided right then and there, my lady," Mr. Pynch said, "that I'd follow Lord Vale into hell itself, should he tell me to."

"Thank you for telling me this, Mr. Pynch," Melisande said. She opened the door. "Please inform Lord Vale that I shall be ready to travel at eight o'clock in the morning."

Mr. Pynch bowed. "Yes, my lady."

Melisande nodded and left, but she couldn't help a lingering thought. The entire time Mr. Pynch had told her his story, he'd stood as if guarding the little dressing room.

Chapter Twelve

Now, when Jack got back to the castle, he did a very strange thing. He donned once again his fool's rags and went down to the castle's kitchens. The royal supper was being prepared, and there was a great deal of activity. The head cook shouted, the footmen ran back and forth, the scullery maids scrubbed dishes, and all the minor cooks chopped and stirred and baked. No one noticed as Jack crept to where a small boy stirred a soup pot over the fire.

"Hist," said Jack to the boy. "I'll give you a silver coin if you'll let me stir the princess's soup."

Well, the boy liked this exchange very much. The minute his back was turned, Jack dropped the bronze ring into the soup. . . .

—from LAUGHING JACK

The carriage bumped over a great rut in the road and swayed. Melisande swayed with it, having learned on the first day of their journey that it was far easier to let herself move with the carriage rather than hold herself stiff against it. It was now the third day, and she was quite used to swaying. Her shoulder bumped gently against Suchlike, curled next to her and dozing. Mouse was on the seat on her other side, also asleep. Every once in a while, the dog let out a little snore.

Melisande looked out the window. They appeared to be in the middle of nowhere. Blue-green hills rolled away into the distance, demarcated by hedges and drystone walls. The light was beginning to fade.

"Shouldn't we have stopped by now?" she asked her husband.

Vale lounged on the opposite seat, his legs canted diagonally across the carriage so that his feet were almost touching hers. His eyes were shut, but he answered her immediately, confirming her suspicion that he hadn't been asleep at all.

"You're correct. We should've stopped in Birkham, but the coachman says the inn was closed. He's taken us off the main road to find the next inn, but I suspect he may've lost his way."

Vale opened one eye and peered out the window, not looking at all anxious that dark was falling and they appeared to be lost.

"Definitely gone off the main way," he said. "Unless the inn's in the middle of a cow pasture."

Melisande heaved a sigh and began to put away the fairy tale she'd been translating. She was almost done now, the strange fairy tale unfolding beneath her pen. It was about a soldier who'd been turned into a funny little man. A funny little man who was nevertheless very brave. He didn't seem a normal hero for a fairy tale, but then again, none

of the fairy-tale heroes in Emeline's book were exactly
normal. The translation would have to wait for tomorrow
in any case. It was too dark to see properly now.

"Can't we turn back?" she asked Vale as she closed her
writing case. "A derelict inn is better shelter than aban-
doned hills."

"An excellent point, dear wife, but I'm afraid it will be
dark before we can return to Birkham anyway. Better to
press on."

He closed his eyes again, which was very frustrating.

Melisande gazed out the window for a bit, worrying her
lip. She glanced at her still-sleeping maid and lowered her
voice. "I promised Suchlike we wouldn't travel after dark.
She's never left London before, you know."

"Then she'll learn lots on this trip," her husband said
without opening his eyes. "Never fear. The coachman and
footmen are armed."

"Humph." Melisande folded her arms. "How well do
you know Mr. Munroe?"

She'd already spent the previous two days trying to find
out what Vale needed to speak to the man about. He merely
changed the subject when she asked him questions. Now
she tried a different tack.

"Sir Alistair Munroe," he murmured.

He must've felt her exasperated look, because although
his eyes never opened, he smiled. "Knighted for service to
the crown. He wrote a book describing the plants and animals of the New World. More than plants and animals, actually. Fishes and birds and insects as well. It's a massive,
portfolio-sized thing, but the engravings are quite lovely.
Hand-colored and based on his own sketches. It impressed

King George enough that he had Munroe to tea—or so I've heard."

Melisande thought about this naturalist who'd been to tea with the king. "He must've spent many years in the Colonies to have enough material to write a book. Was he with your regiment the entire time?"

"No. He moved around from regiment to regiment, according to where they were marching. He was only with the 28th three months or so," Vale said. "He joined us just before we marched to Quebec."

He sounded sleepy, which made Melisande suspicious. Twice now he'd conveniently fallen asleep when she was questioning him.

"Did you talk to him when he was with your regiment? What is he like?"

Vale switched his crossed legs without opening his eyes. "Oh, very Scots. Taciturn and not much for long speeches. He had a wicked sense of humor, though. I do remember that. Very dry."

He was silent a bit, and Melisande watched the hills turn purple in the fading light.

Vale finally said dreamily, "I remember he had a big trunk, leather-bound with brass. He'd had it specially made. Inside were dozens of compartments, all lined in felt, very clever. He had boxes and glass vials for various specimens, and different-sized presses for preserving leaves and flowers. He took it apart once, and you should've seen the hardened soldiers, some who'd been in the army decades and didn't turn a hair at anything, standing and gawking at his trunk like little boys at the fair."

"That must've been nice," Melisande said softly.

"It was. It was." He sounded far away in the gathering darkness.

"Perhaps he will show it to me when we visit."

"He can't," he said from the gloom on the other side of the carriage. "It was destroyed when we were attacked by the Indians. Smashed to bits, all his specimens dragged out and scattered, completely ruined."

"How awful! Poor man. It must've been terrible when he saw what had been done to his collection."

There was silence from the other side of the carriage.

"Jasper?" She wished she could see his face.

"He never saw." Vale's voice came abruptly from the darkness. "His wounds . . . He never made it back to the scene of the massacre. I didn't either. I only heard what had happened to his trunk months later."

"I'm sorry." Melisande gazed blindly out the black window. She wasn't quite sure what she apologized for—the broken trunk, the lost artifacts, the massacre itself, or the fact that neither man survived entirely the same as before. "What's he look like, Sir Alistair? Is he young? Old?"

"A bit older than me, perhaps." Vale hesitated. "You should know—"

But she interrupted him, leaning forward. "Look." She'd thought she'd seen movement outside the window.

A shot sounded, crashingly loud in the night air. Melisande flinched. Suchlike woke with a little scream, and Mouse jumped to his feet and barked.

A loud, hoarse voice came from without. "Stand and deliver!"

The carriage shuddered to a halt.

"Shit," Vale said.

*   *   *

JASPER HAD BEEN worried about this very thing since night had begun to fall. They were in prime territory for a highway robbery. He didn't much mind the loss of his purse, but he was damned if he'd let anyone touch Melisande.

"What—?" she began, but he reached across and laid his hand gently over her mouth. She was a smart woman. She immediately held still. She drew Mouse into her lap and wrapped her hand around his muzzle.

The little lady's maid had her fist stuffed into her mouth, her eyes wide and round. She didn't make a sound, but Jasper pressed a finger across his own lips. Although he had no idea if the women could see him adequately in the dark carriage.

Why hadn't the coachman tried to make a run for it? The answer came to Jasper even as he ran through his options. The coachman had already admitted he didn't know the terrain well. He'd probably been afraid of overturning the carriage in the dark and killing them all.

"Come out o' there," a second man called.

So there were at least two, probably more. He had two footmen and two coachmen, along with two men on horses, one of them Pynch. Six men in all. But how many robbers?

"D'you hear me? Get out o' there!" the second voice shouted. One would be holding a gun on the coachman to keep him from moving the carriage. Another would be covering the outriders. A third would be in charge of relieving them of any valuables—that is, if there were only three. If there were more—

"Dammit! Come out or I'm coming in, and I'll be shooting when I do!"

Melisande's maid moaned, low and fearful, Mouse

struggled, but his dear wife held him firmly and was silent. A smart robber would start killing the servants outside one by one to force them to emerge. But this highwayman might just be stupid enough to—

The carriage door was flung open, and a man holding a pistol leaned into the carriage. Jasper grabbed his gun arm and pulled hard. The gun went off, shattering the opposite carriage window. The maid screamed. The robber half fell into the carriage. Jasper twisted the pistol away from him.

"Don't look," he said to Melisande, and slammed the pistol grip down on the man's temple, shattering the bone. He did it quickly again, three more times, vicious and hard, just to make sure the man was dead, then dropped the pistol. He hated handling guns.

From outside came a shout and then a gunshot.

"Damn. Get down," he ordered Melisande and the girl. A bullet could blow right through the wood of the carriage. She didn't protest and lay across her seat with the maid and the dog.

Running footsteps came nearer, and Jasper moved in front of the women, bracing himself.

"My lord!" Pynch's broad face peered into the carriage door. "Are you safe, my lord? Are the women—?"

"Yes, I think so." Jasper turned to Melisande, running his hands over her face and hair in the dark. "Are you all right, my dearest love?"

"Y-yes." She straightened immediately, her back as straight as ever, and a pang tore at his heart. If ever she were hurt, if ever he could not protect her . . .

The maid was trembling violently. Melisande let go of the dog and pulled the girl into her arms, patting her back comfortingly. "It's all right. Lord Vale and Mr. Pynch have kept us safe."

Mouse jumped to the floor of the carriage and growled at the dead robber.

Pynch cleared his throat. "We've captured one of the highwaymen, my lord. The other galloped away."

Jasper looked at him. Gunpowder blackened half of Pynch's face. Jasper grinned. His valet had always been an excellent shot.

"Help me get this one out of the carriage," he told Pynch. "Melisande, please stay here until we are sure it's safe."

She nodded bravely, her chin up. "Of course."

And even though Pynch and the maid were watching, Jasper couldn't help leaning over to kiss her hard. It had all happened so fast. If things had turned out a little differently, he might've lost her.

Jasper scrambled from the carriage, eager to meet the man who'd put his sweet wife in danger. First, though, he helped Pynch pull the dead robber out of the carriage. He hoped Melisande hadn't looked too closely. He'd crushed the robber's cheekbone and temple.

Mouse jumped down from the carriage.

Jasper straightened. "Where is he?"

"Over here, my lord." Pynch gestured to a tree by the side of the road where several footmen stood over a recumbent figure. Mouse trailed behind them, sniffing the ground.

Jasper nodded and asked as they walked to the group, "Anyone shot?"

"Bob the footman has a graze on his arm," Pynch reported. "No one else was hit."

"You've checked?" In the dark, with all the excitement, sometimes a man could be shot and not even know it.

But Pynch had been in the army as well. "Yes, my lord."

Jasper nodded. "Good man. Have a footman light some more lanterns. Light drives away all manner of vermin."

"Yes, my lord." Pynch headed back to the carriage.

"And what have we here?" Jasper asked as he came on the group of footmen.

"One of the robbers, my lord," Bob said.

He held a cloth against his upper right arm, but the pistol in his hand was steady and pointed at their prisoner. Pynch arrived with a lantern, and they all looked down at the robber. He wasn't much more than a child, a boy not yet twenty, his chest bleeding profusely. Mouse sniffed the boy, then lost interest and urinated on the tree.

"He's still alive?" Jasper asked.

"Just barely," Pynch said impassively. It must've been his shot that had brought the boy off his horse, but Pynch didn't show any pity.

Then again, this boy had held a gun on them. He could've shot Melisande. A horrible image of Melisande lying where the boy was rose up in Jasper's mind. Melisande with her chest blown open. Melisande struggling to draw air into shattered lungs.

Jasper turned away. "Leave him."

"No."

He looked up and saw Melisande, standing outside the carriage despite his explicit orders to stay inside.

"Madam?"

She didn't back down, though his tone was chilly. "Have him brought with us, Jasper."

He stared at her, illuminated by lantern light, looking ethereal and fragile. Too fragile. He said gently, "He could've killed you, my heart."

"But he didn't."

She might look fragile, but her core was made of iron.

He nodded, his gaze still fixed on her. "Wrap him in a blanket, Pynch, and take him up on your horse with you."

Melisande frowned. "The carriage—"

"I won't have him near you."

She looked at him and must've seen she wasn't getting her way in this. She nodded.

Jasper glanced at Pynch. "You can bandage his wound when we get to the inn. I don't like lingering in this spot any longer than we have to."

"Yes, my lord," Pynch said.

Then Jasper walked to his lady wife and took her arm, warm and alive beneath his fingers. He bent his head and murmured in her ear, "I do this for you, my heart. Only for you."

She looked up at him, her face a pale moon in the darkness. "You do it for yourself as well. It's not right to let him die alone, no matter what he did."

He didn't bother arguing. Let her think he worried about such matters if she wished. He led her to their carriage and bundled her inside, closing the door. Even if the highwayman lived a few hours more, he could no longer hurt Melisande, and that was all that mattered in the end.

MELISANDE SIGHED WHEN the door closed to her inn room later that evening. Vale always acquired two rooms at the inns they stayed in, and tonight was no different. Despite the excitement of the near robbery, despite the dying robber—who'd been carried into a back room—despite the fact that the little inn was nearly full, Melisande still found herself in a solitary room.

She wandered to the little fireplace, piled high with coal, thanks to a generous tip to the innkeeper's wife. The flames danced, but her fingers remained cold. Did the servants talk about their mistress and master taking separate rooms so soon after their marriage? Melisande felt vaguely ashamed, as if she'd failed in some way as a wife. Mouse leapt onto the foot of the bed and turned about three times before lying down. He sighed.

At least Suchlike never mentioned the sleeping arrangements. The little maid dressed and undressed her with unfailing cheerfulness. Although she'd been hard-pressed to smile this evening after their near robbery. She'd still been shaking from the shock, and she'd lost all her merry chatter. Melisande had taken pity on the girl and sent her down early to eat her supper.

Which left Melisande all alone. She hadn't much appetite for the dinner the round innkeeper's wife had served. The boiled chicken had looked delicious enough, but it was hard to eat knowing a young boy was dying in the back of the inn. She'd excused herself early and come upstairs instead. Now she wished she'd stayed in the dining room Vale had reserved for them. She shook her head. No use remaining awake. She couldn't go back down now that she'd undressed, and that was that. Melisande pulled back the bedclothes from the sturdy inn bed, relieved to see they looked clean, and climbed in. She pulled the sheets to her nose and snuffed out the light. Then she watched the firelight flicker on the ceiling until her eyelids grew heavy.

Her thoughts floated and drifted. Vale's bright eyes and

the look in them when he'd savagely pulled the first high-wayman into the carriage. Boiled chicken and the dumplings Cook had made when she was a child. How many more days they'd spend traveling rutted roads in the swaying carriage. When they might cross into Scotland. Her thoughts scattered, and she began to sink into sleep.

Then she was conscious of a warmth against her back. Of strong arms and the brush of lips that tasted of whiskey.

"Jasper?" she mumbled, still half dreaming.

"Hush," he whispered.

His mouth opened over hers, and he kissed her deeply, his tongue penetrating her mouth. She thought she tasted salt. She moaned, caught between waking and sleeping, all her defenses down and in shambles. She felt him lift her chemise and pull it from her body. His hands explored her breasts, stroking tenderly, then pinched her nipples almost to the point of pain.

"Jasper," she moaned.

She ran her palms over his back. He was nude, his skin so hot it almost burned. His muscles shifted under her hands as he lay atop her, his weight settling between her spread thighs.

"Hush," he whispered again.

She felt the nudge as he found her center and thrust inside.

Her body was soft, yielding from sleep and his hands, but she wasn't quite ready. He shifted back and rocked slowly, gently, each small thrust stretching her and pushing him deeper inside. He hooked his hands under her knees and lifted them up so he was cradled between her thighs. And then he kissed her, brushing his palms lightly over her exposed nipples. Tantalizing her and tormenting her at the same time.

She tried to arch up, to make him touch her more firmly, but she hadn't the leverage or the strength. He was in control, and he would make love to her in the manner that he desired. All she could do was submit.

So she tangled her hands in his hair and hung on, kissing him back, moving her mouth lushly, submissively under his.

He groaned. His hips worked a little faster now, his cock crammed all the way inside of her. She felt each thrust, each stretch of her feminine flesh as she received him again and again.

He broke the kiss and lifted his head away from her, his breath coming in loud, harsh pants. She didn't open her eyes; she didn't want to disrupt her dreamy state. Then she felt his fingers sliding down her side, twisting between their bodies. He searched and found her, his fingers strong and knowing. He pressed his thumb down on her clitoris.

"Come with me," he whispered, his voice a rasp of desire. "Come with me."

She opened her eyes at last. He must've brought a candle into the room, for muted light played along his side. His shoulders were wide and bunched with muscle, strands of hair clinging damply to his face, and his wild turquoise eyes stared into hers, compelling her.

"Come with me," he whispered again.

His thumb circled her, pressing with exquisite accuracy as his cock filled her. She was splayed before him, a prize all his own, and he kept whispering, "Come with me."

How could she deny him? The pleasure was building inside, and she wanted to hide her face. He was in control in ways she hadn't let him be before. He would watch. He would know the secrets she kept hidden from him.

"Come with me." He bent his head to lick her nipple.

She arched her head and wailed. He caught the sound in his mouth. Licked it up and swallowed it, a prize of this battle. He pressed down on her and held her as she came, jolting with each bolt of pleasure. He held her down with mouth and hips and that thumb, brushing lightly, sweetly, madly now. She'd never experienced an orgasm like this one, nearly painful in its intensity. She opened her eyes, gasping, and saw he wasn't done. She'd been reduced to shivering pleasure, and he'd only started. He propped himself up on straight arms and watched her as he surged into her, hot and heavy and without mercy. His mouth was twisted, his eyes mad with lust and something else.

"God," he ground out. "God. God. *God!*"

He threw back his head, arching convulsively, and she saw him bare his teeth as his body jerked into hers. His seed flooded her, warm and alive. She felt a joy such as she'd never felt before. She'd given and she'd received from him.

It was nearly holy.

His head was tilted back above her, his arms still straight. She couldn't see his face because of his hair. A single drop of liquid fell to her left breast.

"Jasper," she whispered, and cradled his wet face. "Jasper."

He pulled out of her, the loss of his flesh almost a painful wrench, and climbed from the bed. He bent and scooped up his banyan and flung it on. "The robber boy died."

He left the room.

Chapter Thirteen

*That night, the royal court was abuzz with rumor.
The serpent was dead and the bronze ring gone, but
no one had come forward with the ring. Who was the
brave man who had captured the ring?*

*Jack, as usual, stood beside the princess's chair at
supper, and she gave him a very strange look when
she sat down.*

*"Why, Jack," she cried, "where have you been?
Your hair is quite wet."*

*"I have been to visit a wee silver fishy," Jack said,
and turned a silly somersault.*

*The princess smiled and ate her soup, but what a
surprise awaited her at the bottom of the bowl! There
lay the bronze ring.*

*Well! That caused quite a stir, and the head cook
was summoned at once. But although the poor man
was questioned before the entire court, he had no
knowledge of how the ring had got in Princess
Surcease's soup. At last the king was forced to dismiss
the cook, no wiser than before. . . .*

—from LAUGHING JACK

She must think him a ravening beast after the night before. It was not a happy thought to have over breakfast, and Jasper scowled at the eggs and bread the innkeeper's wife had provided. They were rather tasty, but the tea was weak and not of the best quality; besides, he would take the smallest reason to feel out of sorts this morning.

He peered over his teacup at his lady wife. She didn't look like a woman who had been ravished in the night. On the contrary, she appeared fresh and rested and with every hair in place, which for some reason irked him even more.

"Did you sleep well?" he asked, possibly the most mundane of conversational openings.

"Yes, thank you." She fed a bit of bun to Mouse, who sat beneath the table. He knew this, although she neither moved nor changed expression. Indeed she continued to gaze steadily at him. It was something in the very steadiness of her gaze that let him know what she did.

"We shall enter Scotland today," he said. "We should be in Edinburgh by tomorrow."

"Oh?"

He nodded and buttered a bun, his third. "I have an aunt in Edinburgh."

"You do? You never said." She took a sip of tea.

"Yes, well, I do."

"Is she a Scot?"

"No. Her first husband was a Scot. I believe she is on husband number three at the moment." He laid his butter knife down on the plate. "Her name is Mrs. Esther Whippering, and we will spend a night with her."

"Very well."

"She's getting on in years but sharp as a tack. Used to twist my ear rather painfully as a boy."

She paused over her teacup. "Why? What had you done?"

"Nothing at all. She said it was good for me."

"No doubt it was."

He opened his mouth, about to defend his youthful honor, when he felt something cold and wet on the hand in his lap.

He'd been reaching for the butter knife with his other hand, and he nearly dropped it again. "My God, what is that?"

"I expect it's only Mouse," Melisande said serenely.

He peered under the table and saw two eyes gleaming back. They looked a little devilish in the dark. "What does he want?"

"Your bun."

Jasper looked at his wife, outraged. "He shan't have it."

She shrugged. "He'll only bother you until you give him some."

"That's no reason to reward bad behavior."

"Mmm. Shall we have the innkeeper's wife pack a luncheon for us? She seems to be a good cook."

He felt another nudge against his leg. A warm weight settled on his foot. "An excellent idea. We may not be near an inn at luncheon time."

She nodded and went to the door of the little private dining room to make arrangements.

Jasper shoved a piece of egg under the table when her back was turned. A wet tongue licked it from his fingers.

Melisande came back in the room and eyed him suspiciously but did not say a word.

Half an hour later, the horses were hitched, the lady's maid was perched beside the coachman for a change, Melisande and Mouse were in the carriage waiting, and Jasper was having a last conversation with the innkeeper. He thanked the man and leapt up the steps to his carriage, then knocked on the roof and sat.

Melisande looked up from her embroidery as the carriage jolted forward. "What did you say to him?"

He glanced outside the window. Fog was rolling down the hills. "Who?"

"The innkeeper."

"I thanked him for a perfectly lovely night without fleas."

She simply looked at him.

He sighed. "I gave him enough money to pay to bury the boy. And a bit more for his trouble. I thought you'd want me to."

"Thank you."

He slumped in his seat and canted his legs to the side. "You have a soft heart, my lady wife."

She shook her head decisively. "No, I have a just one."

"A just heart that gives succor to a boy who would've shot you without a qualm."

"You don't know that."

He watched the hills. "I know he set off last night with older men and a loaded gun. If he did not mean to use it, he should never have loaded it."

He felt her gaze. "Why didn't you shoot last night?"

He shrugged. "The highwayman's pistol went off and used the shot."

"Mr. Pynch told me this morning that there are pistols beneath the seat."

Damn Pynch and his loose tongue. He glanced at Melisande. Her expression was curious rather than condemning.

He sighed. "I suppose I should show you so you can use them if need be. But for God's sake don't take one up unless you intend to use it, and always keep it pointed at the ground."

She raised her brows but didn't comment.

He moved across to her seat and pulled up the thin cushion from his own. Underneath was a compartment with a hinged lid. He lifted the lid to reveal a pair of pistols. "There."

She peered at them and Mouse jumped from the seat where he'd been dozing to take a look as well.

"Very nice," Melisande said. She looked at him frankly. "Why didn't you take them out last night?"

Jasper shoved the dog gently aside before closing the compartment lid, replacing the cushion and sitting back down again. "I didn't take them out because I have an unreasoning dislike of guns, if you must know."

She raised her brows. "That must've been a handicap during the war."

"Oh, I shot a pistol or a rifle often enough when I was in the army. I'm not a bad shot either. Or at least I wasn't—haven't picked up a pistol since I returned to England."

"Then why do you hate guns now?"

He used his left thumb to rub hard at the palm of his right hand. "I don't like the feel—the weight maybe—of a pistol in my hand." He looked across at her. "I would've gotten them out, though, if there was no other way. I wouldn't've risked your life, my heart."

She nodded. "I know."

And that simple sentence filled him with a feeling he hadn't felt in some time—happiness. He stared at her, so sure of his competence, so sure of his courage, and he thought, *Please, Lord, let her never find out the truth.*

SHE WISHED SHE could simply tell Vale that she didn't want to sleep apart from him, Melisande thought later that night. She stood in the courtyard of another inn—this one fairly big—and watched as the hostlers unhitched the horses and Vale talked to the innkeeper. He was procuring a room for the night.

Her room.

It seemed the inn was nearly full, and there was only one room left, but instead of sharing it with her, Vale intended to sleep in the common room. Lord only knew what the innkeeper made of that. She sighed and looked to where a footman was leading Mouse on a leash. Or, rather, Mouse was leading the footman, straining forward on the leash. He dragged the poor man to a hitching post, lifted his leg against it, and began dragging to the next post.

"Ready, my sweet?"

Melisande looked up to find that while she had been puzzling out their marriage, Vale had finished his transaction with the innkeeper.

She nodded and took his arm. "Yes."

"Mouse is going to wear out that footman's arm," Vale commented as they strode inside. "Do you know that they toss dice to see who will take him for his nightly walks?"

"The winner walks him?" she asked as they entered the inn's main building.

"No, the loser," he replied, then frowned.

A shout of boisterous laughter had come from the common room. The inn was ancient, with huge blackened beams holding the low ceiling aloft. To the left was the big common room with battered round tables and a roaring fire, though it was the height of summer. Every table was crowded with travelers—mostly men—drinking ale and eating their suppers.

"Through here," Vale said, and guided her to the right into a small back room. This was their private dining room, already laid with sturdy earthenware dishes and a loaf of what looked like fresh brown bread.

"Thank you," Melisande murmured as he held a chair for her. She sat just as the footman brought in Mouse. The terrier immediately trotted over and stood against her for a pat. "And how are you, Sir Mouse? Did you have a nice constitutional?"

"Nearly got a rat, 'e did, my lady," the footman said. "In the stables. Fast little dog."

Melisande smiled at the terrier and ruffled his ears. "Well done."

The innkeeper hurried in with a bottle of wine, a girl followed behind with a mutton stew, and all was chaos in the little dining room for a bit. Five minutes passed before Vale and she were alone again.

"Tomorrow," he began to say, but was interrupted by a particularly loud yell from the common room.

Vale frowned at the door. They were sheltered in their private room, but the constant buzz of noise could still be heard.

He looked across the table at her, his brows drawn over his blue-green eyes. "You must lock the door and stay in your room tonight. I don't like this crowd."

Melisande nodded. She always locked the door if she could or stood a chair against it. Anyway, Vale was usually right in the room next door.

"Your room wasn't locked last night."

She wondered if he was remembering their heated lovemaking. "There wasn't a lock on the door."

"I'll have one of the footmen sleep outside your room tonight."

They finished the meal in companionable silence after that. It was well past ten by the time Melisande got to her room with Mouse. She found Suchlike yawning as she laid out a fresh chemise. The room was small but neat, with a bed, a table, and some chairs by the fireplace. Someone had even hung two tiny paintings of horses on the wall by the door.

"How was your dinner?" Melisande asked the maid. She went to the window and found her room overlooked the stable yard.

"It was very good, my lady," Suchlike replied. "Although I've never liked mutton much."

"No?" Melisande began picking at the laces of her gown.

"Let me do that, my lady," Suchlike said, and bustled over. "No, give me a nice bit o' beef if it's good, and I'm quite happy. Now, Mr. Pynch declares that fish is his favorite thing to eat. Can you fancy that?"

"I suppose there are many people who like fish," Melisande said diplomatically. She shrugged off the bodice.

Suchlike looked skeptical. "Yes, my lady. Mr. Pynch says it's on account of him being born by the sea, liking fish, that is."

"Mr. Pynch was born by the sea?"

"Yes, my lady. In Cornwall. Such a long ways away and him not even talking strange like."

Melisande studied her lady's maid as she removed the rest of her clothing. She would've thought the valet too old and dour for Suchlike, but the maid seemed to like chattering about him. She only hoped Mr. Pynch wasn't trifling with her maid's affections. She made a mental note to speak about the matter with Vale in the morning.

"There, my lady," Suchlike exclaimed as she flung the chemise over Melisande's head. "You look very pretty in that. The lace becomes you. Now, I've put a warming pan in the bed and brought up a pitcher of water. There's some wine on the table and glasses, too, should you care for a drink before bed. Will you want your hair braided tonight?"

"No, it's fine," Melisande said. "I'll brush it out myself. Thank you."

The maid bobbed a curtsy and went to the door.

Melisande remembered something. "Oh, and Suchlike?"

"My lady?"

"Be sure that you sleep where our men can hear you. Lord Vale doesn't like the crowd in the common room."

"Mr. Pynch didn't like their looks either," the maid replied. "He said he'd keep a sharp eye on me tonight."

Melisande's heart warmed toward the stoic valet. At least he was protective of Suchlike. "I'm glad to hear it. Good night."

"'Night, my lady. Sleep well." And Suchlike left the room.

Melisande poured herself a little wine from the decanter on the table and took a sip. It certainly wasn't of the quality that Vale kept in his cellars, but it was pleasantly tart. She took the pins from her hair and laid them neatly on the table.

She let down her hair and combed it out. Suddenly, there was a crash from below. She went to the door to listen, her brush still in her hand, but after a minute of raised voices, everything seemed to settle back down. Melisande finished brushing her hair, drank the wine in her glass, and climbed into bed.

She lay thinking for a bit on whether Vale would come to her rooms tonight. He'd have to ask the innkeeper for the key to her room. She'd been sure to lock the door tonight after Suchlike took her leave.

She must've slept then, because she dreamed of Jasper in battle, cannon fire all around him, while he laughed and refused to take up his gun. In her dream, she called to him, imploring him to defend himself. Tears ran down her face. Then she woke to the sound of shouting and blows against her door. She sat up just as her door burst open and four drunken louts spilled into the room.

Melisande stared in shocked horror. Mouse leapt from her bed and began barking.

"She's a pretty bit o' rough," one said, and then a whirlwind caught him from behind.

Vale was on the man, hitting him savagely and silently. He was barefoot and wearing only his breeches. He took the man by the hair and slammed his face into the floorboards. Blood splattered.

Two of the drunkards blinked at the sudden violence, but the third swung forward. Before he could reach Vale, he was grabbed from behind by Mr. Pynch and hauled into the hallway. A thud shook the wall, and one of the small horse paintings fell. Vale rose from the still man on the floor and advanced on the other two men. Melisande bit back a cry. They might be drunk, but it was two against one. Mr. Pynch still fought the other man in the hall.

One tried to smile. "Jess a bit o' fun."

Vale hit him in the face. The man spun from the force of the blow and went down like a felled tree. Turning to the last man, who was trying to back away, Vale took him by the coat, turned him about, and ran him headfirst into the wall. The other horse painting fell. Mouse attacked the frame.

Mr. Pynch appeared in the doorway.

Vale looked up from where he stood panting over the last fallen man. "Everything settled out there?"

Mr. Pynch nodded. His left eye was reddened and beginning to swell. "I've roused the footmen. They'll spend the rest of the night in the corridor to prevent further incidents."

"What about Bob?" Vale demanded. "He was supposed to be outside my wife's door."

"I'll find out what happened," Mr. Pynch said.

"See that you do," Vale snapped. "Tell the others to get this rubbish out of here."

"My lord." Pynch disappeared back into the hallway.

Vale finally looked at Melisande. His face was savage, a cut on his cheek leaking blood. "Are you all right, my lady wife?"

She nodded.

But he turned and slammed his fist into the wall. "I promised you this wouldn't happen."

"Jasper—"

"Goddamnit!" He kicked one of the fallen louts.

"Jasper—"

Mr. Pynch returned at that moment with the other men-servants. They dragged the louts from the room, none of the men daring to even glance at her. Melisande still sat up in her bed, the sheets drawn to her chin. Bob appeared, white-faced and stricken and trying to explain that he'd been ill. Vale turned his back on the footman and clenched his fists. She saw Mr. Pynch jerk his chin to the footman, silently telling him to leave the room. Poor Bob slunk away again.

And then her room was clear. The servants left and only Vale remained, pacing the room like a caged lion. Mouse gave a last bark at the door and jumped on the bed to receive his praise. Melisande stroked his soft, smooth ears as she watched her husband shove a chair against the door. The frame was splintered near the lock and wouldn't close properly.

Melisande watched him for a moment, then sighed and climbed from the bed. She padded barefoot to the table, poured a glass of wine, and held it out to him.

He came and took the glass from her hand without a word and tossed back half the wine.

She wanted to tell him it wasn't his fault. That he'd had the foresight to post a guard and when that had failed, he'd arrived in time. But she knew that nothing she said would stop him from berating himself. Perhaps in the morning she could talk about it, but not now.

After a while, he swallowed the rest of the wine and put

the glass carefully down as if it might shatter. "Go back to bed, dearest heart. I'll stay here with you the remainder of the night."

He settled in one of the chairs by the fire as she got back into bed. It was only a straight-backed wooden chair, which couldn't be terribly comfortable, but he stretched out his long legs and folded his arms across his chest.

Melisande watched him sadly for a while, wishing he would sleep with her, and then she closed her eyes. She knew she wouldn't sleep again tonight, but if she lay awake, it would worry him, so she feigned slumber. After a bit, she heard a low murmur at the door and the scrape of a chair. Vale moved about nearly silently, and then all was quiet again.

Melisande cracked her eyelids. Her husband lay in a corner on a kind of pallet. Very similar, in fact, to the one that had been in his dressing room. He was on his side, his back to the wall. She watched him for a bit until his breathing grew slow and even. Then she waited some more.

When she could wait no longer, she crept from the bed and tiptoed to the pallet. She stood for a moment, watching him sleep on his crude bed; then she stepped over him. She'd meant to squeeze by him and ease down between him and the wall, but the moment she set her foot by him, his hand shot out and grabbed her ankle.

Vale looked up at her, his blue-green eyes nearly black in the darkness. "Go back to bed."

Very carefully, she knelt beside him. "No."

He released her ankle. "Melisande—"

She ignored his pleading tone, lifting the blanket covering him and lying down behind his back.

"Dammit," he muttered.

"Hush." She lay facing his strong, broad back. Slowly she smoothed her hand over his rigid side and inched forward until she hugged against him. She inhaled his scent, rising with the heat of his body. He was warm and comforting, and she gave a little sigh, her face nuzzling his wide shoulders. He'd been stiff at first, but now he relaxed, as if conceding the moment to her. She smiled. All her life she'd slept alone. Now she did not.

Finally, she was home.

JASPER WOKE TO feminine hands sliding down his back, and his first emotion was shame. Shame that she knew he slept on the floor like a beggar. Shame that he couldn't sleep in a bed like other men. Shame that she knew his secret. Then her hands moved lower, and lust uncurled in his belly.

He opened his eyes and found it still dark, the fire having died down. Normally he would light a candle, but at the moment, the dark didn't bother him. Her hand crept around his side to clasp his cock, and he groaned. To feel those cool, slim fingers curiously exploring his heat was the stuff that men dreamed about late at night when they were far from home. She fingered the head of his cock and then wrapped her hand about the shaft, slowly sliding up and down. His balls were drawn up hard and tight; he could feel the press of her small, lovely breasts against his back, and it was more than he could take this early in the morning.

He turned over. "Climb atop me."

Her hair was down, waving about her face, and in the dim glow of the fireplace, she looked like some fey creature come to lure him away from his mortal existence. She sat up and swung a long slender leg over his hips. Then she sat straight and tall and so prim on top of his throbbing prick.

"Take me inside, my lady wife," he whispered. "Put me in your pretty cunny."

He thought he saw her frown in the dark, as if disapproving of an inappropriate subject at tea. She might look prim and proper when at tea in the afternoon, but at night and with him she was a wanton creature.

"Ride me, my heart," he urged. "Ride me until you weep on my prick. Ride me until I fill you with my seed."

She gasped then and rose. He could feel her hands about him as she sank down, and it was all he could do not to cry out. Tight wet feminine heat. Holding him. Yielding to him. He arched up and at the same time grabbed her buttocks to pull her firmly against him.

She placed her hands on his chest and slid against him, her back straight, her long hair brushing his face. She rode him, biting her lip, grinding her pelvis against his. He waited, holding back, watching her expression. Her eyes were closed, her lovely face tipped back. He moved his hand to palm her breast, and she arched her back. He pinched that pretty little nipple, torturing that bit of flesh until she gasped. And then he flicked it lightly.

"Jasper," she panted. "Jasper . . ."

"Yes, my love?"

"Touch me."

"I am," he said lightly, innocently, though his face shone with sweat.

She jolted against him, swiveling her hips to punish him, and for a moment he lost all coherent thought.

Then she said, "Not like that. You know."

He shook his head gently and flicked her nipple again. "You'll have to say it, my heart."

She sobbed.

He should've taken pity, but alas he was a wicked carnal man, and he wanted to hear those sweet, prim lips utter the words. "Say it."

"Oh, God, touch my pussy!"

And he felt the first spurt, just at the words. He gasped and thumbed her wildly rocking cunny, feeling his hard flesh working in and out of hers, and it was too much.

He arched up off the floor and caught her mouth to his to muffle his yell. And he came, exploding into her, showering her with his soul.

Chapter Fourteen

> *The next day, the king announced the second trial:*
> *to bring back a silver ring that was hidden atop a*
> *mountain, which was guarded by a troll. Once again,*
> *Jack waited until everyone left, and then he opened*
> *his little tin snuffbox. Out came the suit of night and*
> *wind and the sharpest sword in the world. Jack put*
> *on the suit and took up the sword and then* whoosh!
> Whist! *there he was, quick as you please, in front of*
> *the nasty troll and his blade. Well, this battle took a*
> *little longer than the first, but in the end, the result*
> *was the same. Jack had the silver ring. . . .*
> —from LAUGHING JACK

When Melisande awoke the next morning, Vale was already gone from the room. She brushed her hand over his pillow. It was still warm, and she could see the indent where his head had been. She was alone, just like all the other mornings of her short marriage, but this time it was different. She'd lain in his arms last night. She'd listened to his breathing, heard the slow thump of his heartbeat, been warmed by his hot, bare skin.

She lay a moment smiling before rising and calling for Suchlike. Half an hour later, she was downstairs, ready for breakfast, but her husband was not to be found.

"Lord Vale went riding, my lady," a sheepish footman said. "He said he'd be back when 'twas time to leave."

"Thank you," Melisande said, and went into the little dining room to break her fast. It was no good chasing him. Besides, he'd have to come back eventually.

But Vale chose to ride his horse beside the carriage that day, and she swayed inside with just Suchlike for company.

They made Edinburgh by late afternoon and pulled up beside Vale's aunt's stylish town house just after five in the evening. Vale opened the door to the carriage, and Melisande only had time to place her hand in his before his aunt was welcoming them. Mrs. Whippering was a small, stout lady wearing a sunny yellow dress. She had rosy cheeks, a perpetual smile, and a rather loud voice, which she kept constantly in use.

"This is Melisande, my lady wife," Vale said to his aunt when she paused for breath in her effusive welcome.

"So happy to meet you, my dear," Mrs. Whippering yodeled. "*Do* call me Aunt Esther."

So Melisande did.

Aunt Esther led them into her house, which had apparently been redecorated on the occasion of her marrying her third husband. "New man, new house," she said merrily to Melisande.

Jasper just grinned.

It was a lovely house. High on one of Edinburgh's many

hills, it was of Whitestone and had clean, classical lines. Inside, Aunt Esther favored white marble and a checkered black and white floor.

"In here," she called, bustling down the hall. "Mr. Whippering is *so* looking forward to meeting both of you."

She led them to a red sitting room with paintings of enormous baskets of fruit bracketing a black enamel and gilt fireplace. A man so tall and thin he looked like a knobby walking stick sat on a settee. He had a muffin halfway to his mouth when they walked in.

Aunt Esther flew at him in a flurry of flapping yellow skirts. "*Not* the muffins, Mr. Whippering! You know they are not good for your digestion."

The poor man gave up his muffin and stood to be introduced. He was even taller than Vale, his coat hanging on him in folds. But he had a very sweet smile as he peered at them over half-moon glasses.

"This is Mr. Horatio Whippering, my husband," Aunt Esther announced proudly.

Mr. Whippering bowed to Vale and took Melisande's hand, twinkling up at her roguishly.

The introductions made, Aunt Esther plopped herself down on the settee. "Sit down, sit down, and tell me all about your trip."

"We were attacked by highwaymen," Vale said obligingly.

Melisande arched an eyebrow at him and he winked.

"No!" Aunt Esther's eyes rounded, and she turned to her spouse. "Did you hear that, Mr. Whippering? Highwaymen attacking my nephew and his wife. I never heard the like." She shook her head and poured tea. "Well, I expect you frightened them off."

"All by myself." Vale smiled modestly.

"You're lucky to have such a strong, brave husband," Aunt Esther told Melisande.

Melisande smiled and avoided Jasper's gaze for fear she might laugh.

"I think they should be hung, really I do," the little woman continued. She passed a cup of tea to Vale and Melisande and one to her husband, admonishing him, "Mind you don't add cream. Remember what it does to your digestion, dear." Then she sat back with a plate full of muffins on her lap and announced, "I must take issue with you, dear nephew."

"And why is that, dear aunt?" Vale asked. He'd chosen the largest muffin, and now he bit into it, spilling crumbs down his shirt.

"Why, this hasty marriage. There's no reason for such haste unless"—she peered at them sharply—"there *is* a reason?"

Melisande blinked and shook her head.

"No? Well, then, why the rush? Why, I'd hardly got the announcement that you had changed fiancées and in the very next post—it was the very next post, wasn't it, Mr. Whippering?" she appealed to her spouse. He nodded, obviously well used to his part in her monologues. "I thought so," Aunt Esther continued. "As I say, the *very next post,* a letter came from your mother writing that you'd already married. Why, I hadn't even time to think of a suitable wedding present, let alone make plans to travel to London, and what I want to know is why marry so fast? Mr. Whippering courted me for three years, did you not, Mr. Whippering?"

A dutiful nod.

"And even then I made him wait nine months for a proper engagement before we were wed. I can't think why you should marry in such a hurry." She stopped to inhale and drink some tea, frowning ferociously at her nephew.

"But, Aunt Esther, I had to wed Melisande as soon as humanly possible," Vale said, all wounded innocence. "I was afraid she might call it off. She was surrounded by suitors, and I had to beat them off with a stick. Once I had her pledge, I got her to the altar as swiftly as possible."

He finished this outrageous pack of lies by smiling innocently at his aunt.

The lady clapped her hands delightedly. "And so you should've! Well done! I'm glad you caught such a fine lady to make your wife. She looks like she has a level head on her shoulders—that should balance your foolery."

Vale clasped his chest and swooned in his chair dramatically. "You wound me, dear lady."

"Pish," said his aunt. "You are a silly fool, but then most men are when it comes to women, even my dear Mr. Whippering."

They all looked at Mr. Whippering, who tried his best to appear suitably scampish. He was somewhat hampered by the teacup balanced on his knobby knees.

"Well, I wish you both a long and happy marriage," Aunt Esther declared, popping a bite of muffin into her mouth. "*And* a fruitful one."

Melisande swallowed at the allusion to babies and looked blindly down at her cup of tea. The thought of holding a small bit of her and Jasper, of stroking baby-fine reddish brown hair, sent a bolt of painful yearning through her. Oh, how wonderful it would be to have a baby!

"Thank you, Aunt," Vale was saying gravely. "I shall endeavor to father at least a dozen or so offspring."

"I know you jest with me, but family is most important. *Most* important. Mr. Whippering and I have discussed this on numerous occasions, and we both agree that children settle a young man. And you, dear nephew, could do with a bit of settling. Why, I remember the time—" Aunt Esther cut herself off with a start and a squeak as she stared at the mantel clock. "Mr. Whippering! Look at the time. Look at the time! Why didn't you tell me it was so late, you horrid man?"

Mr. Whippering looked startled.

Aunt Esther rocked violently, trying to get up from the settee. She was hampered by her voluminous skirts, her teacup, and her plate of muffins. "We have guests for supper tonight, and I must get ready. Oh, do help me!"

Mr. Whippering stood and pulled his wife from the settee.

She bounced up and ran to ring for the maid. "We're to have Sir Angus, and he's a terrible stickler, but don't let that bother you," she confided to Melisande. "He tells the most delicious stories after he's had his second glass of wine. Now, I'll have Meg show you to your room and let you wash up, if you desire, but be sure to come down by seven o'clock, for Sir Angus is sure to be on the doorstep at exactly that time. Then we shall have to somehow make conversation with him while we wait for everyone else to arrive. Oh, I've invited some lovely people."

She clapped her hands like an excited little girl, and Mr. Whippering beamed down at her fondly. Melisande set aside her plate and rose, but Aunt Esther was listing her guests on her fingers.

"Mr. and Mrs. Flowers—I've seated you next to Mr. Flowers because he's always quite kind and knows when to agree with a lady. Miss Charlotte Stewart, who has the best gossip. Captain Pickering and his wife—he used to be in the navy, you know, and has seen the strangest things, and—oh! Here's Meg."

A maid, presumably Meg, had entered the room and curtsied.

Aunt Esther flew to her. "Show my nephew and his wife to their room—the blue room, *not* the green. The green might be bigger, but the blue is ever so much more warm. There's a draft in the green," she confided to Melisande. "Now don't forget: seven of the clock."

Vale, who had been sitting all this while, complacently munching muffins, finally rose. "Don't you worry, Aunt. We'll be down precisely at seven and with our best bows and buttons."

"Lovely!" his aunt exclaimed.

Melisande smiled, for it seemed quite useless to try and say anything, and began to follow the maid from the room.

"Oh, and I forgot," Aunt Esther called. "One other couple will be there as well."

Both Melisande and Vale turned politely to hear the name of these new guests.

"Mr. Timothy Holden and his wife, Lady Caroline." Aunt Esther beamed. "They used to live in London before they moved to Edinburgh, and I thought they might be a treat for the both of you. Mr. Holden is quite a dashing gentleman. Maybe you even know him?"

And for the life of her, Melisande didn't know what to say.

*   *   *

SOMETHING WAS WRONG with Melisande, Jasper thought later that night. She sat on the farther end of the long supper table from him, between the kind Mr. Flowers and the punctilious Sir Angus, the latter already on his third glass of tongue-loosening wine. Melisande wore a deep brown dress with small green flowers and leaves embroidered down the bodice and around the sleeves. She looked quite lovely, her pale oval face serene, her light brown hair softly pulled back. Jasper doubted anyone else in the room noted her unease save he.

He sipped his wine and considered his lady wife, smiling vaguely at something Mrs. Flowers leaned close to say. Perhaps the company of newly met people intimidated Melisande. He knew she was a shy creature, as all the fey were wont to be. She didn't like crowds, didn't like long social events. It was opposite to Jasper's own nature, but he understood this about her, even if he could never feel that way himself. He was used to her stiff reticence when they went out.

But this unease was more than that. Something was wrong, and it bothered him that he didn't know what.

It was a pleasant gathering. Aunt Esther's cook was very good, and the supper was plain but enjoyable. The narrow dining room was intimately lit. The footmen were generous with the wine bottles. Miss Stewart was to his right. She was a woman of mature years, with powdered and rouged cheeks and an enormous gray-powdered wig. She leaned toward Jasper, and he caught the strong scent of patchouli.

"I hear you've just come from London, what?" the lady said.

"Indeed, ma'am," Jasper replied. "Over hill and over dale we've ridden, just to visit sunny Edinburgh."

"Well, at least you didn't come in winter," she retorted somewhat obscurely. "Travel's dreadful after the first snowfall, though the city's pretty enough—all the snow cloaking the dirt and soot. Have you seen the castle?"

"Alas, no."

"You should, you should." Miss Stewart nodded vigorously, making the wattles beneath her chin shake. "Magnificent. Not many English appreciate the beauty of Scotland."

She fixed him with a gimlet eye.

Jasper hastily swallowed a bite of the very fine lamb his aunt had served. "Oh, quite. My lady wife and I have been stunned by the countryside thus far."

"And so you should be in my opinion." She sawed at her lamb. "Now, the Holdens moved here from London some eight or ten years ago, and they haven't regretted it for a day. Have you, Mr. Holden?" she appealed to the gentleman sitting across the table from her.

Timothy Holden was strikingly handsome if one liked men with soft cheeks and red lips, which apparently most women did, judging from the feminine glances aimed his way. He wore a snowy white wig and a red velvet coat, worked in gold and green embroidery at the sleeves.

At Miss Stewart's question, Holden inclined his head and said, "My wife and I enjoy Edinburgh."

He glanced down the table, but oddly it wasn't his own wife he looked at but rather Jasper's.

Jasper sipped his wine, his eyes narrowed.

"The society here is quite superior," Lady Caroline chimed in.

She looked to be a good deal older than her handsome husband and was titled to boot. There must lie a tale. She had blond hair so light it was nearly white, and pale pinkish skin that made her as nearly monochromatic as paper. Only her light blue eyes gave her any color, poor woman, and they looked rimmed in red against her colorless skin, giving her the appearance of a white rabbit.

"The garden is lovely this time of year," she said. "Perhaps you and Lady Vale will honor us by coming to tea during your visit?"

Out of the corner of his eye, Jasper saw Melisande go still. She was so motionless he wondered if she breathed.

He smiled politely. "I'm devastated to decline your kind offer. I'm afraid we stay only the night in Edinburgh. I have business with a friend who lives north of here."

"Oh, yes? Who is that?" Miss Stewart inquired.

Melisande had relaxed again, so Jasper turned his attention to his neighbor. "Sir Alistair Munroe. Do you know him?"

Miss Stewart shook her head decisively. "Know *of* him, of course, but never met the man, more's the pity."

"A wonderful book he's written," Sir Angus rumbled from the far end of the table. "Simply marvelous. Filled with all manner of birds, animals, fishes, and insects. Most instructional."

"But have you ever met the man?" Aunt Esther demanded from the foot of the table.

"Can't say that I have."

"There!" Mrs. Whippering sat back triumphantly. "And I don't know a single person who has—save for you, dear nephew, and I don't think you've seen him in years, have you?"

Jasper shook his head somberly. It was his turn to stare at the table and twist his wineglass.

"Well, how do we know he's even still alive?" Aunt Esther asked.

"I've heard he sends letters to the university," Mrs. Flowers ventured from his left. "I have an uncle who lectures there, and he says Sir Alistair is very well respected."

"Munroe is one of Scotland's great intellectuals," Sir Angus said.

"Be that as it may," Aunt Esther said, "I don't know why he doesn't show his face here in town. I know that people have invited him to dinners and balls, and he always declines. What is he hiding, I ask you?"

"Scars," Sir Angus rumbled.

"Oh, but surely that's just a rumor," Lady Caroline said.

Mrs. Flowers leaned forward, putting her ample bosom perilously near the gravy on her plate. "I've heard his face is so terribly scarred from the war in America that he has to wear a mask so that people don't faint in horror."

"Poppycock!" Miss Stewart snorted.

"It's true," Mrs. Flowers defended herself. "My sister's neighbor's daughter caught a glimpse of Sir Alistair leaving the theater two years ago and swooned. Afterward she took to bed with a delirious fever and wasn't well for months."

"She sounds a very silly girl," Miss Stewart retorted, "and I'm not sure I believe a word of it."

Mrs. Flowers drew herself up, obviously offended.

Aunt Esther intervened. "Well, my nephew ought to know whether or not Sir Alistair is horribly scarred. He served with the man, after all. Jasper?"

Jasper felt his fingers begin to shake—an awful physical symptom of the rotting malaise within himself. He let go of his wineglass before he knocked it over and hastily hid his hand beneath the tablecloth.

"Jasper?" his aunt repeated.

Damn it, they were all looking at him now. His throat was dry, but he couldn't raise his glass of wine.

"Yes," he finally said. "Yes, it's true. Sir Alistair Munroe is scarred."

BY THE TIME Jasper helped see off his aunt's guests, he was bone-tired. Melisande had excused herself from the company shortly after supper. He paused outside the door to the bedroom Aunt Esther had given them. Melisande was probably abed. He twisted the doorknob gently so as to not awaken her. But when he entered the room, he saw that she wasn't asleep. Instead, she was making a pallet on the floor against the far wall. He halted because he didn't know whether to laugh or swear.

She looked up and saw him. "Can you hand me the blanket from the bed?"

He nodded, not trusting his voice, and went to the bed to pull off the blanket. What must she think of him? He crossed to the fire and handed the blanket to her.

"Thank you." She bent and began tucking it about a pile of linens to make a rough mattress.

Did she worry that she'd married a madman? He looked away. The room wasn't big, but it was cozy. The walls were a gray-blue, the floor covered by a faded brown and rose patterned rug. He went to the window and pulled back the curtain to look out, but the night was so dark, he couldn't pick anything out. He let the curtain fall. Suchlike must have been and gone. Melisande had already undressed. She wore a pretty lace-trimmed shift and her wrapper.

He took off his coat and began unbuttoning his waist-coat. "Lovely dinner."

"Yes, it was."

"Lady Charlotte was most amusing."

"Mmm."

He pulled off his neck cloth and then held the strip of material in his fingers, staring down at it blindly. "It's because of the army, I think."

She stilled. "What?"

"That." He tilted his chin toward the pallet, not meeting her eyes. "We all have quirks, the men who came back from war. Some start violently at loud noises. Some can't stand the sight of blood. Some have nightmares that wake them in the dark of night. And some"—he took a deep breath, closing his eyes—"some cannot bear to sleep in the open. Some fear attack in the night when they sleep and cannot . . . cannot help themselves. They must sleep with their back against the wall and with a lit candle so that they can see the attackers when they come."

He opened his eyes and said, "It's a compulsion, I'm afraid. They simply cannot help themselves."

"I understand," she said.

Her eyes were gentle, as if she hadn't just heard that her husband was a lunatic. She bent and continued putting together the pallet. She seemed as if she really did understand. But how could she? How could she accept that her husband was only half a man? He couldn't accept it himself.

He poured some wine from a decanter on a table. He stood drinking it and gazing sightlessly into the fire for some time before he remembered what he'd been thinking about when he came to their room.

Jasper set his empty wineglass down and began unbuttoning his waistcoat. "You'll think me fanciful, but for a moment when we were first introduced to the Holdens, I thought Timothy Holden looked like he recognized you."

She didn't reply.

He tossed his waistcoat to a chair and looked over at Melisande. She was plumping the bedding rather overhard. "My lady wife?"

She straightened and looked at him, her chin up, her back stiff, as if she faced a firing squad. "I was engaged to him."

He simply looked at her. He'd known there was something—*someone*—but she'd never mentioned an engagement before. Stupid, of him, really. And now that he knew . . . He realized he felt a rising swell of jealousy. She'd set out to marry another man—Timothy Holden— once upon a time. Had she loved pretty Timothy Holden with his red lips?

"Did you love him?" he asked.

She looked at him a moment, then bent to finish putting together the pallet. "It was over ten years ago. I was only eighteen."

He cocked his head. She hadn't answered the question. "Where did you meet?"

"At a dinner party like tonight's." She picked up a pillow and smoothed the cover. "He sat beside me and was so kind. He didn't turn away, as most gentlemen did back then, when I didn't immediately fall into conversation with him."

Jasper pulled his shirt over his head. He had been one of those ungallant gentlemen, no doubt.

Melisande laid the pillow down on the pallet. "He took me for rides in the park, danced with me at balls, all the things a gentleman does when he courts a lady. He wooed me for several months, and then he asked my father for my hand in marriage. Naturally, Father said yes."

He sat to shed his hose and shoes. "Then why aren't you married to him?"

She shrugged. "He proposed in October, and we planned to be married in June."

Jasper winced. They had been married in June. He went to her and gently helped her out of her wrapper. Then he took her hand and lay down on the pallet with her. She shifted until her head was on his shoulder. He stroked his fingers idly through her long hair. Funny how much more comfortable a pallet could be with her in it.

"I had shopped for a trousseau," she said quietly, her breath brushing his bare chest. "Sent out invitations, planned the wedding day. Then one day, Timothy came to me and told me he loved another lady. Naturally, I let him go."

"Naturally," Jasper growled.

Holden was a filthy ass. To lead on a young, gentle girl and then leave her nearly at the altar was the work of a swine. He stroked his sweet wife's hair as if soothing her for hurts over a decade old and thought about their marriage and their marriage bed.

At last he sighed. "He was your lover."

He didn't bother phrasing it as a question. Still, he was almost surprised when she didn't deny it.

"Yes, for a while."

He frowned. Her tone was too flat. He stirred uneasily. "He didn't force you, did he?"

"No."

"Or threaten you in any way?"

"No. He was gentle."

Jasper closed his eyes. God, he hated this. His hand had stopped moving in her hair, and he was conscious that he was gripping a lock.

He exhaled and carefully unfisted his hand. "Then what is it? There's something more that you're not telling me, my heart."

She was silent so long that he began to think he'd imagined it in a jealous haze. Perhaps there was nothing else.

But in the end, she sighed, a lost, lonely sound, and said, "I found out I was increasing, shortly after he broke the engagement."

Chapter Fifteen

When Jack returned with the silver ring, he paused
only to change into his rags, and then he nipped down
to the royal kitchens. The same small boy was stirring
the princess's soup. Jack once again asked him if he
might buy a turn at the spoon. Plop! went the silver
ring, and Jack was away before the head cook could
spy him. He hurried up the stairs and to his
princess's side.

"Why, where have you been all day, Jack?"
Princess Surcease asked when she saw him.

"Here and there, thither and yon, beautiful lady."

"And what have you done to your poor arm?"

Jack looked down and saw that he had a cut
from the troll's blade. "Oh, Princess, I did wrestle a
monstrous pill bug in your honor today."

And Jack capered about until the entire court
roared with laughter. . . .

—from LAUGHING JACK

Melisande felt Vale's fingers pause in her hair. Would he repudiate her now? Get up and walk away? Or would he simply pretend he hadn't heard her self-damning words and never speak of it again? She held her breath, waiting.

But he merely ran his fingers through her hair and said, "Tell me."

So she closed her eyes and did, remembering that time so long ago now, and the pain that had nearly stopped her heart in her breast. "I knew at once what it was when I became sick in the mornings. I've heard of ladies being confused and waiting months to tell because they were not sure, but I knew."

"Were you frightened?" His deep voice was even, and it was hard to tell what he was feeling.

"No. Well," she amended, "perhaps when I first realized my condition. But very soon after that, I knew that I wanted my baby. That no matter what, he would be a joy to me."

She couldn't see his face, but she watched his chest rise and fall beneath her hand. There were curling hairs in the hollow of his breastbone. She threaded her forefinger idly through them and let herself remember a bit of that joy. So strong. So fleeting.

"Did you tell your family?"

"No, I told no one, not even Emeline. I think I was afraid of what they would make me do. That they would take the baby from me." She took a steadying breath, determined to tell him all now, in case she couldn't work up the courage to talk about this again. "I had a plan, you see. I would go to live with my elder brother, Ernest, until I'd begun to show, and then I would retire to a cottage in the country with my old nanny. I would have the baby, and we would raise him together, my nanny and I. It was a silly, childish plan, but at the time I thought it might work. Or maybe it was simply my desperate wishful thinking."

She felt the slide of hot tears and knew he must feel their dampness on his chest. Her voice was growing choked. But still he stroked her hair gently, and she found his hand soothing.

She swallowed and finished her sad story. "But I hadn't been long with my brother Ernest when I woke in the middle of the night with blood on my thighs. I bled for five days, very heavily, and after that it was gone. My baby was dead."

Melisande stopped because her throat had swelled with emotions and she could no longer talk. She closed her eyes and let the tears overflow, running down her temple and onto his chest. She sobbed once and then no more. She simply lay there and trembled with her grief. This was an old wound, but one that appeared fresh and new at odd moments, catching her off guard with its sharp pain. She'd held the possibility of life once, but that life had been taken away.

"I'm sorry," Vale rumbled beneath her. "I'm so sorry you lost your baby."

She couldn't speak. She could only nod.

He tilted her head up so he could see her face. His turquoise eyes were intense. "I will give you a baby, my dearest heart. As many babies as you wish, I swear it on my honor."

She stared at him in wonder. She wasn't ashamed of what had happened—of who she was—but she'd expected anger, not sympathy, from him.

He kissed her, his lips moving gently over hers, and it

was like a pledge between them, sacred and right. Vale pulled the coverlet over them, carefully tucking it along her side, and hugged her closer. "Go to sleep, my lady wife."

His gruff words and tender hands comforted her. Melisande closed her eyes, the last of her tears finally stopping, and listened to the beat of Jasper's heart under her ear. It was steady and strong, and she drifted into sleep on its rhythm.

THE NEXT MORNING dawned sullenly, the skies gray with a drizzling rain. Aunt Esther sent them off with a hearty breakfast and much calling and waving good-bye. When at last they turned a corner and Aunt Esther's town house was out of sight, Melisande turned from the window and looked at Vale.

"When will we arrive at Sir Alistair's house?"

"Today, I think, if we travel well," Vale replied.

His legs were canted across the carriage floor as usual, and his body lounged bonelessly on the seat, but his wide mouth was turned down at one corner in a small frown. What did he think of her? He hadn't treated her any differently this morning as they'd risen, dressed, and eaten, but her confession last night must've come as a shock. A man didn't expect his maiden bride to have taken a lover once upon a time and, what's more, to have been impregnated by that lover.

Melisande glanced away from Vale and stared blindly out the window. Vale had received the revelation well enough, but when he had time to think about it, would it bother him? Would the knowledge that she hadn't been a virgin on their wedding night begin to fester within him?

Would he turn against her? She didn't know, and with a troubled mind, she watched the highland hills roll by.

They stopped for a late luncheon by a wide, clear stream and ate the cold ham, bread, cheese, and wine that Aunt Esther's cook had packed for them. Mouse ran about and barked at some nearby highland cows—shaggy things with hair in their eyes—until Vale shouted at him to stop. Then the terrier came over and lay down to gnaw on a ham bone.

They traveled all that afternoon, and by the time night began to fall, Melisande could see that Vale was restless.

"Have we lost our way?" she asked him.

"The coachman assured me he knew where we were when last we stopped," Vale replied.

"You've never been to see Sir Alistair before?"

"No."

They rode another half hour or so, Suchlike dozing beside Melisande. The road was obviously rutted and poorly maintained, for the carriage rocked and jounced. Finally, just as the last light faded, they heard a shout from one of the men. Melisande peered out the window and thought she saw the dim outlines of a huge building.

"Does your friend live in a castle?"

Vale was peering now too. "It would appear so."

The carriage slowly turned into a narrow drive, and then they were bouncing toward the manor. Suchlike woke with a gasp. Melisande couldn't see a light in the building anywhere.

"Sir Alistair does know we're coming, doesn't he?"

"I wrote him," Vale said.

Melisande stared suspiciously at her husband. "Did he reply?"

But Vale pretended not to hear her, and then they'd rolled to a stop in front of the massive building. There was a shout outside and some scrambling, and after a pause, the carriage door opened.

Mr. Pynch held a lantern high, the light casting ominous shadows across his gloomy face. "No one answers the door, my lord."

"Then we shall just have to knock louder," Vale said.

He jumped from the carriage and turned to help Melisande out. Suchlike climbed carefully down, and Mouse scrambled out and ran to some bushes to relieve himself. The night was very dark indeed, and a cold wind was whistling across the drive, causing Melisande to shiver.

"Here." Vale reached back inside the carriage and took out a cloak from under her seat. He wrapped it around her shoulders and then offered her his arm. "Shall we, my lady wife?"

She took his arm and leaned close to whisper, "Jasper, what shall we do if Sir Alistair isn't at home?"

"Oh, someone will be about, never fear."

He led her up wide, stone steps so old they had a worn dip in the middle where countless feet had trod before. The door was a massive thing at least ten feet high and bound with great iron hinges.

Vale pounded his fist on the door. "Oy! Open up! There's travelers without who want a hot fire and a soft bed. Oy! Munroe! Come and let us in!"

He kept up this racket for a good five minutes or more and then suddenly stopped, his fist still raised in midair.

Melisande looked at him. "What—?"

"Shh."

And then she heard. From deep inside the house there came a dull scraping, as if some subterranean creature had stirred.

Vale slammed his fist into the door, making Melisande start. "*Oy!* Come and let us in!"

A bolt shot back with a *thump,* and the door slowly creaked open. A short little man stood in the doorway. He was rather stout, and his graying ginger hair sprang out on either side of his head like the down on a dandelion. The top of his head was completely bald. He wore a long nightshirt and boots, and he scowled up at them.

"Wot?"

Vale smiled charmingly. "I am Viscount Vale, and this is my lady wife. We've come to stay with your master."

"No, you ain't," the creature said, and began to swing shut the door.

Vale put out a hand and stopped the door. "Yes, we are."

The little man strained against the door, trying to close it, but it wouldn't budge. "No one's tol' me about no visitors. We ain't got the rooms cleaned nor victuals stocked in. You'll just have to go away again."

By this time, Vale had lost his smile. "Let us in and we'll settle the accommodations later."

The little man opened his mouth, obviously quite prepared to do further battle, but at that moment, Mouse finally rejoined them. The terrier took one look a Sir Alistair's servant and decided he was the enemy. He barked at the man so vigorously that all four legs bounced off the ground. The ginger-haired little man gave a high-pitched squeal and jumped back. That was all Vale needed. He slammed open the door and crowded in with Mr. Pynch by his side.

"Stay by the carriage until we're ready," Melisande instructed Suchlike, and then she entered the castle more sedately behind the men.

"You can't! You can't! You can't!" the little man was shrieking.

"Where is Sir Alistair?" Vale demanded.

"Out! He's gone out riding and might not be back for hours."

"He rides in the dark?" Melisande asked, startled. The countryside they'd been driving through was rugged, rocky, and hilly. She wouldn't have thought it safe to ride about alone and at night.

But the little man was scurrying ahead of them, down a wide hallway. They followed and stopped when he flung open a door. "You can wait in here, if you like. It makes no difference to me."

He turned to leave, but Vale caught him by the collar. "Wait." Vale looked at Melisande. "Can you stay here with Mouse while Pynch and I find bedrooms and some food?"

The room was dark and not at all welcoming, but Melisande lifted her chin. "Certainly."

"Brave, my sweet wife." Jasper brushed his lips across her cheek. "Pynch, light some candles for her ladyship, and then we'll have this fine fellow give us a tour."

"Yes, my lord." Mr. Pynch lit four candles—all the room held—from his lantern and the men left.

Melisande listened to their retreating footsteps and then shivered and looked around her. She was in a kind of sitting room, but it wasn't very pleasant. Here and there were groupings of chairs—very old and very ugly. The carved wood ceiling was terribly high, and the candlelight didn't entirely pierce the dark overhead. Melisande thought she saw wisps of old spiderwebs hanging down. The walls were also of dark, carved wood and had been decorated by stuffed animal heads—several moth-eaten deer, a badger, and a fox. Their glass eyes were eerie in the gloom.

Shaking herself, she walked determinedly to the great gray stone fireplace at the room's far end. It was obviously very old—probably older than all the carved wood paneling—and entirely black inside. She found a box by the side containing a few sticks and one log, which she carefully placed inside the fireplace, trying not to think of spiders. Mouse came over to see what she was about, but he soon wandered off again to investigate the shadows.

Melisande stood and brushed off her hands. She searched the mantelpiece and finally found a jar of dusty tapers. She lit one from a candle and held it to the sticks, but the sticks wouldn't catch, and the taper soon burned down. Melisande reached for another taper and was just about to light it when Mouse barked.

She started and turned. A man stood behind her, tall and dark and lean, his shoulder-length hair hanging tangled about his face. He was looking at Mouse, standing at his feet, but at Melisande's movement, he turned his head to her. The left side of his face was twisted with scars, lit awfully by the flickering candles, and the eye socket on that side was sunken and empty.

Melisande dropped the taper.

MUNROE'S MANSERVANT WAS telling them that he hadn't any clean linens in the entire manor, and Jasper was about to shake the man in frustration when he heard Mouse bark. He looked at Pynch, and without a word, they turned and ran back down the dark, twisting stairs. Jasper cursed. He should never have left Melisande alone.

Outside the sitting room, Jasper paused to approach silently. Mouse hadn't barked again since that first time. Jasper peered in the room. Melisande stood at the far end, her back to the fireplace. Mouse was in front of her, legs stiff, but he was silent. And facing both of them was a big man in leather gaiters and an old hunting coat.

Jasper stiffened.

Munroe turned and Jasper couldn't help but flinch. When last he'd seen the man, his wounds were raw and bleeding. Time had healed the wounds that covered the left side of his face, scarred them over, but it hadn't made them any prettier.

"Renshaw," Munroe rasped. His voice had always been husky, but after Spinner's Falls, it had taken on a broken quality, as if damaged by his screams. "But you're Vale now, aren't you? Lord Vale."

"Yes." Jasper moved into the room. "This is my lady wife, Melisande."

Munroe nodded, though he didn't turn back around to acknowledge her. "I believe I wrote you not to come."

"I received no missive," Jasper said honestly.

"Some might take that as an unwelcoming sign," Munroe said dryly.

"Would they?" Jasper took a deep breath to control the anger surging in his breast. He owed Munroe much—things he could never repay—but this involved Munroe too. "But, then, the matter I come on is most pressing. We need to talk about Spinner's Falls."

Munroe's head reared back as if he'd been hit in the face. He stared at Jasper, his light hazel eye hooded and unreadable.

Finally he nodded once. "Very well. But it's late, and your lady is no doubt tired. Wiggins will show you some rooms. I do not promise comfort, but they can be made warm. In the morning we will talk. Then you can leave."

"I have your word?" Jasper asked. He wouldn't put it past Munroe to simply disappear and stay away until they were gone.

The side of Munroe's mouth kicked up. "My word. I will talk to you on the morrow."

Jasper nodded. "I am grateful."

Munroe shrugged and walked out of the room. The little red-haired man—presumably Wiggins—had been lurking about the doorway, and now he said grudgingly, "I 'spose I can make th' fire in your rooms."

He turned and left without another word.

Jasper blew out a breath and looked at Pynch. "Can you look to settling the other servants? See if there's anything to eat in the kitchens and find them rooms."

"Yes, my lord," Pynch said, and departed.

And that left Jasper with his lady wife. He turned reluctantly to look at her. She still stood in front of the fireplace. Any other woman might be in hysterics by now. Not Melisande.

She stared back at him levelly and said, "What happened at Spinner's Falls?"

SALLY SUCHLIKE CAREFULLY spread the hot coals with a poker and then hung a kettle from the big hook in the fireplace. It was a huge fireplace, the biggest Sally had ever seen. Big enough for a grown man to walk into and stand upright. What anyone wanted with such a big fireplace, she didn't know. It was harder to work with than a nice, normal-sized one.

The water in her kettle soon began to steam, and she dropped in the jointed rabbit Mr. Pynch had found in the pantry. A lady's maid was a superior servant, and it wasn't part of her duties to cook, but there wasn't anyone else about to prepare their supper. No doubt Mr. Pynch knew how to make a rabbit stew—and a better one than she was attempting—but he was busy finding rooms for their mistress and master.

Sally threw some chopped carrots into the kettle. They were a little withered, but they'd have to do. She added some little round onions and stirred the whole thing. It looked a bit of a mess at the moment, but maybe it'd perk up once it had stewed a bit. She sighed and sat in a nearby chair, wrapping her shawl tightly about her shoulders. The fact was, she didn't know much about cooking. When she'd been a scullery maid, she'd mostly washed dishes and cleaned. Mr. Pynch had given her the rabbit, carrots, and onions and told her to boil them, so she did. They'd had no help from that nasty red-haired man, Wiggins. He reminded Sally of a troll from a fairy tale, he did. And he'd disappeared the minute Mr. Pynch's back was turned, leaving the Renshaw servants to stumble about in an unfamiliar house.

Sally got up and peered into the simmering pot. Perhaps she ought to add something else. Salt! That was it. Mr. Pynch would think her a ninny if she didn't know enough to salt a stew. She went to a big cupboard standing in the corner and began to rummage. It was nearly empty, but she did manage to find the salt and some flour.

Ten minutes later, she was trying to knead a bowl of flour, salt, butter, and water, when Mr. Pynch walked into the kitchens. He set down his lantern and came to where she was battling the dough, then stood silently at her elbow looking into the bowl.

She glared up at him. "It's dumplings for the stew. I tried to do it like I've seen Cook do, but I don't know if I have, and for all I know, it may taste just like glue. I'm not a cook, you know. I'm a lady's maid, and I'm not expected to know how to cook. You'll just have to be content with what I can make, and if it turns out terrible, I don't want to hear about it."

"I'm not complaining," Mr. Pynch said mildly.

"Well, don't."

"And I like dumplings."

Sally blew a lock of hair out of her eyes, feeling suddenly shy. "You do?"

He nodded. "Yes, and those look perfectly fine. Shall I carry the bowl to the hearth so you can drop them into the stew?"

Sally straightened her shoulders and nodded. She rubbed her hands to get most of the dough off, and Mr. Pynch picked up the big crockery bowl. Together they went to the fireplace, where he held the bowl while she carefully dropped spoonfuls of dough into the stew. She covered the kettle with an iron lid so the dumplings would steam and turned to Mr. Pynch. She was conscious that her face was sweaty from the heat of the fire. Strands of her hair had come down and were sticking to her face, but she looked him in the eye and said, "There. How's that?"

Mr. Pynch leaned close and said, "Perfect."

And then he kissed her.

MELISANDE PILED BLANKETS on the floor and watched her husband pace the room. He was agitated tonight, as if at any moment his control would break and he'd leave the room and run. Was that what Sir Alistair had been doing, riding so late and in the dark? Was he trying to outrun demons as well?

Yet Vale stayed, and she was grateful for that. He hadn't answered her question about Spinner's Falls yet. He drank from a glass of whiskey and paced the room, but he stayed with her. There had to be some comfort in that.

"It was after Quebec, you see," he said suddenly. Facing the window, he might not have even been talking to her, save for the fact that she was the only other person in the room. "It was September, and we'd been ordered to Fort Edward to spend the winter. We'd already lost over one hundred men in the battle and left another three dozen behind because they were too wounded to march. We were decimated but thought the worst was over. We'd won the battle —Quebec had fallen to us—and it was only a matter of time before the French would be forced to surrender entirely and the war would be ours. The tide had turned."

He paused to gulp from the whiskey and said softly, "We were so hopeful. If the war ended soon, we could go home. That's all we wanted: to go home to our families. To rest a bit after battle."

Melisande tucked a sheet about the blankets. It was a bit musty from the press where it'd been stored, but it would have to do. As she worked, she thought of a younger Jasper, marching with his men through an autumn forest half a world away. He would've been elated after a battle won. Happy at the prospect of going home soon.

"We were marching down a narrow trail, with rugged hills on one side and a river on the other that ran along a cliff face. The men were only two abreast. Reynaud had just ridden up to me and said he thought we were too strung out; the tail of the marching column was half a mile back. We decided to inform Colonel Darby, to request that we slow the head to let the tail catch up, when they struck."

His tone was flat, and Melisande sat back on her heels to watch him as he spoke. He still faced the window, his back broad and straight. She wished she could go to him, wrap her arms about him and hold him close, but it might interrupt the flow of his words. And she sensed that, like lancing an infected wound, he needed to let the festering corruption drain away.

"You can't think in battle," he said, his tone almost musing. "Instinct and emotion take over. Horror at seeing Johnny Smith shot with an arrow. Rage at the Indians screaming and running at your men. Killing your men. Fear when your horse is shot from beneath you. The surge of panic when you know you must jump clear or be trapped underneath the beast, helpless to a war axe."

He sipped at his drink while Melisande tried to understand his words. They made her heart beat faster, as if she felt the same urgent panic he had experienced so long ago.

"We fought well, I think," Vale said. "At least others have told me so. I can't evaluate the battle. There's only the men around you, the little piece of soil that you defend. Lieutenant Clemmons fell and Lieutenant Knight, but it wasn't until I saw Darby, our commander, dragged from his horse that it occurred to me that we were losing. That we would all be killed."

He chuckled, but the sound was dry and brittle, not at all like his usual laugh. "That was when I should've felt fear, but oddly I didn't. I stood in a sea of fallen bodies and swung my sword. And I killed a few of those savage warriors; yes, I did, but not enough. Not enough."

Melisande felt tears prick her eyes at the sad weariness of his voice.

"In the end, my last man fell and they overwhelmed me. I went down with a blow to the head. Fell on top of Tommy Pace's body, in fact." He turned from the window and crossed to a table where the decanter of whiskey stood. He filled his glass and drank. "I don't know why they didn't kill me. They should've; they'd killed nearly everyone else. But when my wits returned to me, I was roped by the neck to Matthew Horn and Nate Growe. I looked around and saw that Reynaud was part of their booty as well. You won't believe how relieved I was. Reynaud at least had lived."

"What happened?" Melisande whispered.

He looked at her, and she wondered if he'd forgotten she was in the room. "They marched us through the woods for days. Days and days with little water and no food, and some of us were wounded. Matthew Horn had taken a ball to the fleshy part of his upper arm during the battle. When John Cooper could no longer walk because of his wounds, they led him into the woods and killed him. After that, whenever Matthew stumbled, I leaned my shoulder into his back, urging him on. I couldn't afford to lose another soldier. Couldn't afford to lose another man."

She gasped at the horror. "Were you wounded?"

"No." He wore a horrible half-smile on his face. "Save for that bump on the head, I was perfectly fine. We marched until we reached an Indian village in French-held territory."

He drank more of his whiskey, nearly emptying the glass, and closed his eyes.

Melisande knew, though, that this wasn't the end of the tale. Something had caused the horrific scars on Sir Alistair's face. She took a deep breath, bracing herself, and said, "What happened at the camp?"

"They have a thing called a *gauntlet,* a pretty way to welcome captives of war to the camp. The Indians line up, men and women, in two long lines. They run the prisoners, one by one, between the lines. As the prisoners run, the Indians hit them with heavy sticks and kick them too. If the man falls, he is sometimes beaten to death. But none of us fell."

"Thank God," she breathed.

"We did at the time. Now I'm not so sure."

He shrugged and drank more whiskey. He sat slumped into a chair, his words slurring a bit now.

"Jasper?" Perhaps it would be best to go no further. Melisande was afraid of what would come next. He'd already endured so much, and it was late and he was tired. "Jasper?"

But he didn't seem to hear her. He stared into his whiskey glass, as if bemused. "And then came their real fun. They took away Reynaud, and they tied Munroe and Horn to stakes. They took burning sticks and they . . . they . . ."

He was breathing hard. He closed his eyes and swallowed, and still he couldn't seem to get the words out.

"Don't, oh, don't," Melisande whispered. "You don't have to tell me, you don't."

He looked at her, puzzled and sad and tragic. "They tortured them. Burned them. The sticks were red-hot, and the women wielded them—the women! And then Munroe's eye. God! That was the worst. I screamed at them to stop, and they spit at me and cut off the men's fingers. I knew then to be silent, no matter what they did, because crying out, showing any emotion, only made it worse. And I tried, Melisande, I tried, but the screams and the blood . . ."

"Oh, my dear, oh, my dear." Melisande had moved to him. She bent and held him in her arms, his face against her breast. And she couldn't hold back her tears now. She sobbed for him.

"The second day, they brought us to the other side of the camp," Vale whispered against her breast. "They were burning Reynaud there. He was crucified and on fire. I think he was dead already, because he didn't move, and I thanked God again. I thanked God that my dearest friend was dead and could no longer feel the pain."

"Shh," Melisande whispered. "Shh."

But he didn't stop. "And when the fire had died out, they took us back to the other side of camp and went on with it. Munroe's face and Horn's chest. On and on and on."

"But you were saved in the end, weren't you?" she asked desperately. He had to leave these dreadful images and go on to the hopeful part. He'd survived. He had lived.

"After two weeks. I'm told Corporal Hartley led back a rescue party and ransomed us, but I don't really remember. I was in a daze."

"You were in despair and wounded." Melisande tried to comfort him. "It's understandable."

He pulled violently out of her arms. "No! No, I was perfectly well, entirely intact."

She stared. "But the torture . . . ?"

He ripped open his shirt and revealed his broad chest. "You've seen me, my sweet wife. Is there a scar on any part of my body?"

Her eyes dropped, puzzled, to his unmarked chest. "No—"

"Because they didn't touch me. In all those days of torturing the others, they never laid a hand on me."

Dear God. Melisande stared at his chest. For a man like Vale, being the one left unscarred would be worse than bearing the wounds.

She took a deep breath and asked the question he so obviously expected. "But why?"

"Because I was the witness, the most senior officer after they'd killed Reynaud, the only other captain. They made me watch, and if I so much as flinched at what they did, they cut deeper, dug the burning brand in harder."

He looked at her and smiled awfully, the demons shining from his eyes. "Don't you see? They tortured the others while I sat and watched."

Chapter Sixteen

> Princess Surcease ate her soup, and what should be
> at the bottom of the bowl but the silver ring? Well, the
> king roared for the head cook, and the poor man was
> again dragged before the court. But no matter how
> they questioned him, he swore up, down, and sideways
> that he did not know how the ring had come to be in
> the princess's soup. In the end, the king had to send
> him back to the kitchens again. All the people of the
> court leaned their heads close and wondered who had
> won the silver ring.
> But Princess Surcease was silent. She merely
> stared thoughtfully at her fool. . . .
> —from LAUGHING JACK

Melisande woke the next morning to the sound of Mouse
scratching at the door. She turned and looked at Vale. He
lay with one arm flung over his head, the covers half off
his long form. In the last couple nights, she'd discovered
that he was a restless sleeper. He often draped an arm or

leg over her in his sleep, and sometimes she would wake with his face buried in her neck. More than once he'd rolled over, taking all the covers with him. She didn't mind. It was well worth the cost of lost blankets to sleep with him.

But after last night's harrowing confession, he needed more rest. Melisande carefully slipped from the covers and got up. She found a simple bodice and skirt to put on, wrapped a cloak about herself, and left the room quietly with Mouse. They pattered down the stairs and made their way through the dark hallways to the kitchens.

Melisande paused. The kitchen had a vast, wide-arched ceiling, plastered and painted with flaking whitewash. It looked terribly old. In the corner, she saw that two pallets had been laid out. Suchlike was fast asleep on one, and Mr. Pynch raised his head from the other. Melisande nodded silently at the valet before slipping out the kitchen door.

Outside, Mouse ran delightedly in circles before stopping to do his business. There was a long, sloping lawn here, uncut and wild, and farther on, terraced gardens that must once have been magnificent. Melisande began strolling in that direction. It was a lovely day, the bright morning sun just beginning to blow off the low mist from green hills. Melisande stopped and looked back at the castle. In the daylight, it wasn't so frightening. Of weathered pale pink stone, it rose up to crumbling stepped gables, and chimneys stuck out here and there. Round turreted towers projected from all four corners, making the whole look solid and ancient. She couldn't help but think the castle must be cold in winter.

"She's half a millennium old," a deep rasping voice came from behind her.

Melisande looked around just as Mouse raced up and began barking.

Sir Alistair stood with a dog so tall its head was above his waist. The animal's fur was a shaggy gray. Mouse stood in front of it and barked frantically. The big dog didn't move. It simply looked down its long nose at Mouse as if wondering what manner of dog this little yapping thing was.

Sir Alistair frowned at the terrier a moment. This morning, his hair was brushed and clubbed back, and he'd covered his damaged eye with a black eye patch.

"Whisht, laddie," he drawled in a broad Scots brogue, "dinna fasht yourself."

He hunkered down and held out his fist to Mouse, who trotted over and sniffed. Melisande saw with a little tremor of horror that Sir Alistair's right hand was missing the forefinger and little finger.

"He's a brave wee lad," Sir Alistair said. "What do you call him?"

"Mouse."

He nodded and stood, looking away, down the sloping lawn. His big dog sighed and lay down by his feet. "I didn't mean to frighten you last night, ma'am."

She looked at him. From this side, with his scars nearly concealed, he could've been handsome. His nose was straight and arrogant, his chin firm and not a little stubborn. "You didn't. I was merely startled at your sudden appearance."

He turned his face fully toward her as if daring her to flinch. "I'm sure you were."

She tilted her chin up, refusing to give ground. "Jasper thinks you blame him for those scars. Do you?"

She held her breath at her own bluntness. She'd never have been able to confront him if it had been only for herself. But she needed to know if this man was going to hurt Jasper more.

He held her gaze, perhaps startled himself at her candor. She'd wager that not many dared mention his scars to him.

Finally he looked away again, to the broken, ruined gardens. "If you wish, I'll talk to your husband about my scars, my lady."

Jasper awoke alone, his arms empty. After only a few nights, it was already a strange feeling. A wrong feeling. He should have his sweet wife by his side, her soft curves next to his harder body, the scent of her hair and her skin surrounding him. Sleeping with her was like a reviving elixir—he no longer tossed and turned the night away. Dammit! Where had she got to?

He got up and dressed hurriedly, swearing over the buttons on his shirt. He left off a neck cloth altogether and threw on a coat before leaving the room.

"Melisande!" he called like a lack-wit in the hall. The castle was so big, she wouldn't hear him unless she was nearby. He called anyway. "Melisande!"

Downstairs, he made his way to the kitchen. Pynch was there, stirring the fire. Behind him, Melisande's little maid slept on a pallet. Jasper raised his brows. There were two pallets, but still. Pynch merely nodded silently at the back door.

Jasper went outside and had to squint against the sunshine. Then he saw Melisande. She was standing talking to Munroe, and just the sight gave him a twinge of jealousy. Munroe might be a scarred recluse, but he used to have a way with women. And Melisande was standing too close to the man.

Jasper strode toward them. Mouse caught sight of him and announced his presence by barking once and running toward him.

Munroe turned. "Up at last, Renshaw?"

"It's Vale now," Jasper growled. He put his arm around Melisande's waist.

Munroe followed the movement, and his brow arched over his eye patch. "Of course."

"Have you broken your fast, my lady wife?" Jasper bent toward Melisande.

"Not yet, my lord. Shall I see what there is in the kitchens?"

"I sent Wiggins to a nearby farm for some bread and eggs this morning," Munroe muttered. His cheeks were a little red, as if his lack of hospitality might finally be embarrassing him. He said gruffly, "After breakfast, I can show you both the top of the tower. The view is marvelous from there."

Jasper felt a shudder run through his wife's frame and remembered how she clutched the side of his tall phaeton. "Perhaps another time."

Melisande cleared her throat and pulled gently away from Jasper. "If you gentlemen will excuse me, I'd like to see if there are any scraps for Mouse in the kitchen."

Jasper had no choice but to bow as his lady wife nodded and walked toward the castle.

Munroe stared after her thoughtfully. "Your wife is a charming lady. Intelligent too."

"Mmm-hmm," Jasper concurred. "She does not like heights."

"Ah." Munroe turned to look at Jasper speculatively. "I wouldn't have thought her your type."

Jasper scowled. "You have no notion of my type."

"Indeed I do. Six years ago, it ran to big-titted females of low intelligence and lower morals."

"That was six years ago. Many things have changed since then."

"That they have," Munroe said. He began strolling toward some overgrown terraces, and Jasper fell in beside him. "You've become a viscount, St. Aubyn is dead, and I have lost half my face, which, by the way, I don't blame you for."

Jasper stopped. "What?"

Munroe halted as well and turned to face him. He gestured toward the eye patch. "This. I don't blame you for it, never have."

Jasper looked away. "How can you not blame me? They cut your eye out when I broke." When he'd groaned in horror at what was being done to his fellow captives.

Munroe was silent for a moment. Jasper couldn't bear to look at him. The Scot had been a handsome man once. And though taciturn, he'd never before been a recluse. He used to sit by the fire with the other men and laugh at their coarse jokes. Did Munroe even smile anymore?

Finally, the other man spoke. "We were in hell then, weren't we?"

Jasper clenched his jaw and nodded.

"But they were human, you know, not demons."

"What?"

Munroe's head was back, his one good eye closed. He looked like he was enjoying the breeze. "The Wyandot Indians who tortured us. They were human. Not animals, not savages, just humans. And it was their choice to put out my eye, not yours."

"If I hadn't groaned—"

Munroe sighed. "If you hadn't made a sound, they would've put it out anyway."

Jasper stared.

The other man nodded. "Yes. I've studied it since. It's their way of dealing with prisoners of war. They torture them." The unscarred corner of his mouth twisted up, though he looked far from amused. "Just as we hang small boys by the neck for picking a grown man's pocket. It's simply their way."

"I don't see how you can look at it so dispassionately," Jasper said. "Don't you feel anger?"

Munroe shrugged. "I've been trained to observe. In any case, I do not blame you. Your wife was quite adamant that I should tell you."

"Thank you."

"I think we must add *loyal* and *fierce* to your wife's list of virtues. Can't think how you found her."

Jasper grunted.

"A rake like you doesn't deserve her, you know."

"Just because I don't deserve her doesn't mean I won't fight to keep her."

Munroe nodded. "Wise of you."

As one, they began walking again. There was a bit of silence that Jasper found oddly companionable. Munroe had never exactly been a friend—their interests were too different; their personalities tended to clash. But he'd been there. He'd known the men who were now dead, he'd marched through those hellish woods with a rope about his neck, and he'd been the one tortured at the hands of their enemy. There was nothing to explain to him, nothing to hide. He had been there and he knew.

They reached the terrace's second level, where Munroe stopped and stared at the view. In the distance was a river, to the right a copse. It was beautiful country. The deer-hound that had been following them sighed and lay down beside Munroe.

"Was that what you came for?" Munroe asked idly. "To seek my forgiveness?"

"No," Jasper said, then hesitated, thinking about his confession to Melisande last night. "Well, perhaps. But it isn't the only reason."

Munroe looked at him. "Oh?"

So Jasper told him. About Samuel Hartley and the damning letter. About Dick Thornton laughing in Newgate Prison. About Thornton's accusation that the traitor was one of the men captured. And finally about Lord Hasselthorpe's near assassination just after Jasper had talked to him.

Munroe listened to the whole story silently and attentively, and at the end, he shook his head and said, "Pure nonsense."

"You don't believe that there was a traitor and that we were betrayed?"

"Oh, that I believe readily enough. How else to explain why such a large party of Wyandot Indian warriors were waiting to ambush us on that trail? No, what I don't believe is that the traitor was one of the men captured. Which of us could do that? Do you think it was me?"

"No," Jasper said, and it was true. He'd never thought that Munroe was the traitor.

"That leaves you, Horn, and Growe, unless you think one of the dead men did it. Can you imagine any of them, dead or alive, betraying us?"

"No. But dammit." Jasper tilted his face toward the sun. "Someone betrayed us. Someone told the French and their Indian allies that we would be there."

"Agreed, but you only have the word of a half-mad murderer that it was one of the captives. Give it up, man. Thornton was toying with you."

"I can't give it up," Jasper said. "Can't give it up, can't forget it."

Munroe sighed. "Look at it from another angle. Why would any of us do such a thing?"

"Betray us all, you mean?"

"Aye, that. There must be a reason. Sympathy for the French cause?"

Jasper shook his head.

"Reynaud St. Aubyn did have a French mother," Munroe said dispassionately.

"Don't be an idiot. Reynaud's dead. He was killed almost as soon as we made that wretched village. Besides, he was a loyal Englishman and the best man I ever knew."

Munroe held up a hand. "You're the one pursuing this, not I."

"Yes, I am and I can think of another reason for betrayal—money." Jasper turned and looked significantly at the castle. He didn't truly think Munroe a traitor, but the allegation against Reynaud had irked him.

Munroe followed his gaze and laughed, his voice rusty with disuse. "Think you if I'd sold us all to the French that my castle would be in such disrepair?"

"You might have the money tucked away."

"What money I have I've inherited or made. It's my own. If someone did it for money, they were probably in debt or richer for it now. How are your finances? You used to like the cards."

"I told Hartley and I'll tell you—I paid off the gambling debts I had back then long ago."

"With what?"

"My inheritance. And my lawyers have the papers to prove it, if you must know."

Munroe shrugged and began walking again. "Have you looked into Horn's finances?"

Jasper fell in beside him. "He lives with his mother in a town house."

"There were rumors that his father had lost money in a stock scheme."

"Really?" Jasper looked at the other man. "The town house is in Lincoln Inns Field."

"An expensive part of London for a man with no inheritance."

"He has the money to tour Italy and Greece," Jasper mused.

"And France."

"What?" Jasper stopped.

It took a moment for Munroe to realize he'd paused. He turned from several paces ahead. "Matthew Horn was in Paris this last fall."

"How can you know this?"

Munroe cocked his head, turning his good eye toward

Jasper. "I may be a recluse, but I'm in correspondence with naturalists in England and the Continent. I received a letter from a French botanist this winter. In it he described a dinner party he went to in Paris. It was attended by a young Englishman called Horn who had been in the Colonies. I think this must be our Matthew Horn, don't you?"

"It's possible." Jasper shook his head. "What would he be doing in Paris?"

"Seeing the sights?"

Jasper arched a brow. "When we are enemies with the French?"

Munroe shrugged. "Some would see my correspondence with my French colleague as subversive."

Jasper sighed, feeling weary. "It's a mare's nest. I know I'm chasing possibilities that are vague at best, but I can't forget the massacre. Can you?"

Munroe smiled bitterly. "With the memories engraved on my face? No, I can never forget."

Jasper tilted his face to the breeze. "Why don't you come visit us, my lady wife and me, in London?"

"Children cry when they see me, Vale." Munroe stated it as an unemotional fact.

"Do you even go to Edinburgh now?"

"No. I go nowhere."

"You've imprisoned yourself in your castle."

"You make it sound like a tragedy on the stage." Munroe's mouth twisted. "It's not. I've accepted my fate. I have my books, my studies, and my writing. I am . . . content."

Jasper looked at the other man skeptically. Content to live in a big drafty castle with only a dog and a surly manservant for company?

Munroe must've known that Jasper would argue the

point. He turned back toward the mansion. "Come. We haven't broken our fast, and no doubt your wife waits for you inside."

He strode ahead.

Jasper cursed and followed. Munroe wasn't ready to leave his safe nest, and until the stubborn Scot was ready, there was no use arguing. Jasper only hoped that Munroe would budge in this lifetime.

"THAT MAN IS sorely in need of a housekeeper," Melisande said as their carriage drove away from Sir Alistair's castle. Suchlike's head was already nodding in the corner.

Vale shot an amused look at her. "You didn't approve of his linens, my heart?"

She pinched her lips together. "The musty linens, the dust on every surface, the nearly empty larder, and that horrible, horrible manservant. No, I certainly did not approve."

Vale laughed. "Well, we'll stay on clean sheets tonight. Aunt Esther said she was eager to see us on our return trip. I think she wants to hear gossip about Munroe."

"No doubt."

Melisande took out her embroidery and sorted through her silks, looking for a shade of lemon yellow. She thought she must have a few strands left, and it was the perfect shade to highlight the lion's mane.

She glanced at Suchlike to make sure the maid was asleep. "Did Sir Alistair tell you what you wanted to know?"

"In a way." He stared out the window, and she waited, carefully threading her needle. "Someone betrayed us at Spinner's Falls, and I've been trying to discover the man."

She frowned a little as she placed the first stitch—no small feat in a bumping carriage. "Did you think Sir Alistair was the man?"

"No, but I thought he might help me figure out who was."

"And did he?"

"I don't know."

The words should've held disappointment, but Jasper seemed cheerful enough. Melisande smiled to herself as she worked the lion's mane. Perhaps Sir Alistair had given him some peace.

"Blancmange," she said a few minutes later.

He looked at her. "What?"

"You once asked me what my favorite food is. Do you remember?"

He nodded.

"Well, it's blancmange. We had it every year at Christmas when I was a girl. Cook colored it pink and decorated it with almonds. I was the youngest, so I had the smallest dish, but it was wonderfully creamy and delicious. I looked forward to it every year."

"We can have pink blancmange every night for supper," Vale said.

Melisande shook her head, trying not to smile at his impulsive offer. "No, that would spoil the specialness of it. Only at Christmas."

A happy thrill went through her to be planning a Christmas with him. There would be many Christmases with him, she thought. She couldn't think of a more wonderful prospect.

"Only at Christmas, then," Vale was saying across from her. He was solemn, as if settling a business contract. "But I insist that you have an entire bowl for yourself."

She snorted and found herself smiling. "What would I do with a whole bowl of blancmange?"

"You could make a pig of yourself," he said, perfectly seriously. "Eat the entire thing at once if you like. Or you can hoard it, just looking at it and thinking how good it will be, how creamy and sweet—"

"Nonsense."

"Or you can eat but one spoonful every evening. One spoonful, and me sitting across the table looking on with envy."

"Won't you have your own bowl of blancmange as well?"

"No. That's why yours will be so special." He leaned back in his seat and folded his arms across his chest, looking well pleased with himself. "Yes, indeed. I pledge an entire bowl of pink blancmange to you every Christmas. Never let it be said that I am not a generous husband."

Melisande rolled her eyes at his foolery, but she smiled as well. She was looking forward to her first Christmas with Jasper.

They made good time that day and were at Aunt Esther's house well before supper time.

In fact, as their carriage rolled to a stop in front of the Edinburgh town house, Aunt Esther was seeing off another couple she'd no doubt had for tea. It took a moment to recognize Timothy and his wife. Melisande watched him, her first love. There had been a time when the mere sight of his handsome face had made her catch her breath. It had taken her years to recover from losing Timothy. Now the pain of his loss was muted and somehow apart from her, as if the broken engagement had happened to some other young, naive girl. She looked at him, and all she could think was, *Thank goodness*. Thank goodness she'd escaped marrying him.

Beside her, Vale muttered something under his breath, and then he was bounding from the carriage.

"Aunt Esther!" he cried, seemingly oblivious to the other couple. He strode toward her, and somehow, someway, bumped against Timothy Holden. The shorter man staggered, and Vale went to help him. But Vale must've knocked against Timothy again, because he landed on his rear in the muddy street.

"Oh, dear," Melisande muttered to no one in particular, and scrambled from the carriage before her husband killed her former lover with his "kindness." Mouse jumped down as well and ran to bark at the fallen man.

Before she could get there, Vale had offered his hand to help Timothy up. Timothy, the blind idiot, took it, and Melisande nearly covered her eyes. Vale pulled a trifle too hard, and Timothy popped off the ground like a cork and staggered against Vale. Vale leaned his head close to the other man, and Timothy's face suddenly went an ashy gray. He leapt back from Vale and, declining any further help, hurried his wife into their carriage.

Mouse gave one last self-satisfied bark, happy to have chased him off.

Vale bent and petted the dog, muttering something to Mouse that made his tail wag.

Melisande breathed a sigh of relief and strolled to the two males. "What did you say to Timothy?"

Vale straightened and turned entirely too-innocent eyes on her. "What?"

"Jasper!"

"Oh, all right, but it wasn't much. I requested that he not visit my aunt."

"Requested?"

A satisfied smile was playing about his mouth. "I don't think we'll be seeing Mr. Timothy Holden or his wife here again."

She sighed, secretly pleased at his concern for her feelings. "Was that entirely necessary?"

He took her arm and replied softly, "Oh, yes, my heart, oh, yes."

Then he was leading her toward Aunt Esther and calling, "We have returned, Aunt, and we bring news of the reclusive Sir Alistair!"

Chapter Seventeen

The next day, the king announced a final trial. A golden ring was hidden in a cavern deep underground and guarded by a fire-breathing dragon. Well, Jack put on his suit of night and wind and took up the sharpest sword in the world, and soon enough he stood at the entrance to the cavern. The dragon came roaring out, and Jack had quite a battle, I can tell you, for the dragon was very big. Back and forth they fought, all through the day. It was almost nightfall when the dragon finally lay dead and Jack held the golden ring in his hand. . . .
—from LAUGHING JACK

A week later, Melisande walked in Hyde Park with Mouse. They'd arrived back in London only the night before. The journey from Scotland had been uneventful—saving for a horrible meal of cabbage and beef on the third day. Last night, Melisande had made a pallet in a corner of her room, and Vale had slept with her there all night. It was an odd arrangement, she knew, but she was so glad to have him with her, sleeping next to her, that she didn't care. If she had to make her bed on the floor for the rest of her life, it would be fine with her. Suchlike had given the pallet a curious glance but hadn't said anything. Perhaps Mr. Pynch had informed her of Lord Vale's strange sleeping habits.

The wind fluttered her skirts as she walked. Vale had gone to speak with Mr. Horn this morning, probably about Spinner's Falls. Melisande frowned a little at the thought. She'd hoped that after talking to Sir Alistair, he'd give up the chase, perhaps find some peace. But he was just as intent as ever. Most of the ride back to London he'd theorized and plotted and told and retold her his ideas of who the traitor might be. Melisande had sat and worked her embroidery, but inside, her heart was sinking. What was the likelihood that Vale could discover the man after all these years? And if he couldn't find the traitor, what then? Would he spend the rest of his life in a fruitless search?

A shout interrupted her gloomy thoughts. She looked up in time to see Mrs. Fitzwilliam's little boy, Jamie, embracing Mouse. The dog licked the child's face enthusiastically. Evidently he remembered Jamie. His sister carefully bent to pat Mouse's head as well.

"Good day," Mrs. Fitzwilliam called. She had been standing a little apart from her children. Now she strolled over. "It's a lovely day, isn't it?"

Melisande smiled. "Yes, it is."

They stood side by side, watching the children and the dog for a bit.

Mrs. Fitzwilliam heaved a sigh. "I ought to get Jamie a dog. He begs for one most piteously. But His Grace can't abide animals. They make him sneeze, and he says they're dirty."

Melisande was a little surprised at the casual mention of the other woman's protector, but she tried to hide it. "Dogs are rather dirty sometimes."

"Mmm. I expect so, but then so are boys." Mrs. Fitzwilliam wrinkled her nose, which only made her lovely face more adorable. "And, really, it's not as if he visits us very much anymore. Hardly once a month in the last year. I expect he has gotten himself another woman, like an Ottoman sultan. They keep ladies like sheep in a herd—the Ottomans, I mean. I believe they call it a *harem.*"

Melisande could feel herself blushing, and she looked down at her toes.

"Oh, I'm so sorry," Mrs. Fitzwilliam said. "I've embarrassed you, haven't I? I'm always saying the wrong thing, especially when I'm nervous. His Grace used to say that I should always keep my lips firmly together, because it spoiled the illusion when I opened them."

"What illusion?"

"Of perfection."

Melisande blinked. "What an awful thing to say."

Mrs. Fitzwilliam cocked her head to the side, as if considering. "It is, isn't it? I didn't realize it at the time, I think. I was very much in awe of him when we first met. But then I was very young too. Only seventeen."

Melisande truly wished she could ask the other woman how she had become the Duke of Lister's mistress, but she was afraid of the answer.

Instead, she said, "Did you love him?"

Mrs. Fitzwilliam laughed. She had a lovely, light laugh, but it was tinged with sadness. "Does one love the sun?

It's there, and it provides us with heat and light, but can one truly love it?"

Melisande was silent because any answer she gave would only add to the other woman's sadness.

"I think one must be equals to love," Mrs. Fitzwilliam mused. "Equal on some fundamental level. I don't mean in wealth or even status. I know of women who truly love their protectors and men who love the women they keep. But they are equal on a . . . a spiritual level, if you see what I mean."

"I think I do," Melisande said slowly. "If the man or the woman holds all the emotional power, then they cannot truly love. I suppose one must lay oneself open to love. Let oneself be vulnerable."

"I hadn't thought of that, but I think you must be right. Love is essentially a surrender." She shook her head. "It would take courage to surrender like that."

Melisande nodded, looking at the ground.

"I'm not a very courageous woman," Mrs. Fitzwilliam said softly. "In a way, every choice I've made in life has been out of fear."

Melisande looked at her curiously. "Some would say that the life you've chosen takes a great deal of courage."

"They don't know me." Mrs. Fitzwilliam shook her head. "To be guided by fear isn't the life that I wished."

"I'm sorry."

Mrs. Fitzwilliam nodded. "I wish I was able to change."

As do I, Melisande thought. For a moment, they shared an odd rapport, just the two of them, respectable lady and kept mistress.

Then Jamie gave a shout, and they both looked over. He appeared to have fallen in some mud.

"Oh, dear," Mrs. Fitzwilliam murmured. "I had better take him home. I don't know what my maid will say when she sees his clothes."

She clapped her hands and called briskly to the children. They looked disappointed but began slowly walking over.

"Thank you," Mrs. Fitzwilliam said.

Melisande raised her eyebrows. "For what?"

"For talking with me. I enjoyed our conversation."

Melisande suddenly wondered how often Mrs. Fitzwilliam got to talk with other ladies. She was a kept woman and therefore beyond the pale with respectable ladies, but she was also the mistress of a duke, which would place her far above most anyone else. She stood in a rarefied and lonely sphere.

"I enjoyed it too," Melisande said impulsively. "I wish we might talk more."

Mrs. Fitzwilliam smiled tremulously. "Perhaps we shall."

Then she was gathering her children and bidding farewell, and Melisande was left with Mouse. She turned back the way she'd come. A carriage waited for her, and a footman trailed her discreetly behind. She thought about what she'd said to Mrs. Fitzwilliam, that true love demanded vulnerability. And she wondered if she had the courage to make herself that vulnerable once again.

"WAS MUNROE ABLE to provide you with any new ideas of who the traitor could be?" Matthew Horn asked Jasper later that afternoon.

Jasper shrugged. They were riding through Hyde Park again, and he was restless. He wanted to nudge Belle into a gallop, ride until both he and the mare were sweating. He felt near the breaking point. As if he couldn't push forward with his life until he found the traitor and moved on. God, how he wanted to move on.

Perhaps that was why his voice was sharp when he said, "Munroe said I should look at the money."

"What?"

"The man who betrayed us was probably working for the French. Either he did so for political reasons or he was paid. Munroe pointed out I should look into the finances of the men who were captured."

"Who would take money and then go through the hell of being captured?"

Jasper shrugged. "Maybe he didn't intend to get caught. Maybe something went wrong with his plan."

"No." Horn shook his head. "No. This is ridiculous. If there was a French traitor, he'd make sure he wasn't near Spinner's Falls when the Indians ambushed us. He'd pretend illness or fall behind or simply desert."

"What if he couldn't? What if he was an officer? See here, only the officers knew where we marched—"

Horn snorted. "There were rumors among the men. You know how well secrets are kept in the army."

"Granted," Jasper said. "But if he was an officer, he would've had a hard time getting away. We'd already been decimated at Quebec, remember. Officers were in short supply."

Horn pulled his horse to a halt. "So you will investigate the finances of every man who was there?"

"No, I—"

"Or will you just investigate the finances of the captives?"

Jasper looked at Horn. "Munroe told me something else as well."

Horn blinked. "What?"

"He also said you were in Paris."

"What?"

"He said he has a French friend who wrote that he met a man named Horn at a dinner party in Paris."

"That's preposterous," Matthew exclaimed. His face had reddened, and his mouth was a grim horizontal line. "Horn is not such an uncommon name. It was another man."

"Then you weren't in Paris this last fall?"

"No." Horn's nostrils flared. "No, I was not in Paris. I toured Italy and Greece, as I've already told you."

Jasper was silent.

Horn gripped his reins and leaned forward in the saddle, his body stiff with anger. "Are you questioning my honor, my very loyalty to my country? How dare you, sir? How dare you? Were you any other man, I would call you out this very minute."

"Matthew . . . ," Jasper began, but Horn wheeled his horse and cantered off.

Jasper watched him go. He'd insulted a man he'd considered a friend. Jasper rode back to his town house, grimly pondering what made him insult a man who'd never done him any harm. Horn was right: Munroe's friend could very well be mistaken as to who he'd seen in Paris.

He reached home, his thoughts conflicted, and found that Melisande was still out, a fact that turned his mood even more black. He'd been looking forward to seeing her, he realized, and discussing the disastrous ride with Matthew Horn. He bit back a curse and stalked to his study.

He'd only time to pour himself a splash of brandy before Pynch knocked on the door and entered.

Jasper turned and scowled at his valet. "Did you find your man?"

"Aye, my lord," Pynch said as he advanced into the room. "Mr. Horn's butler was indeed the brother of a fellow soldier I served with."

"Did he talk?"

"He did, my lord. Today is his half day off, and I met him in a tavern. I stood him several drinks as we reminisced about his brother. The man died at Quebec."

Jasper nodded. Many had died at Quebec.

"After the fourth drink, Mr. Horn's butler became loquacious, my lord, and I was able to turn the conversation to his master."

Jasper gulped the brandy, no longer sure he wanted to hear what Pynch had to say. But he'd started these events in motion, had sent Pynch on the hunt as soon as they'd returned to London. It seemed cowardly to balk now.

He looked at Pynch, his loyal servant who'd nursed him through the worst of the drunken stupors and nightmares. Pynch had always served him well. He was a good man.

"What did he say?"

His valet looked at him, his green eyes steady and a little sad. "The butler said the Horn finances were quite distressed on Mr. Matthew Horn's father's death. His mother was forced to relieve most of the servants. There were whispers that she'd have to sell the town house. And then Mr. Horn returned from the war in the Colonies. The servants were rehired, a new carriage was bought, and Mrs. Horn wore new gowns—the first in six years."

Jasper stared blindly into his empty glass. This wasn't what he wanted. This wasn't the relief he'd sought. "When did Mr. Horn's father die?"

"The summer of 1758," Pynch said.

The summer before Quebec fell. The summer before Spinner's Falls.

"Thank you," Jasper said.

Pynch hesitated. "There is always the possibility of an inheritance or some other perfectly innocent source of money."

Jasper arched a skeptical eyebrow. "An inheritance the servants never heard about?" That was very unlikely. "Thank you."

Pynch bowed and left the room.

Jasper topped off his glass of brandy and went to stare into the fire. Was this what he wanted? If Horn was the traitor, could he really turn him in to the authorities? He closed his eyes and sipped the brandy. He'd put these events in motion, and he was no longer sure he had any control over them.

When he looked up again, Melisande was standing in the doorway.

Jasper drained his glass. "My lovely wife. Where have you been?"

"I took a walk in Hyde Park."

"Did you?" He crossed to the decanter and poured himself more brandy. "Out meeting demimondaines again?"

Melisande's face grew cool. "Perhaps I should leave you by yourself."

"No. No." He smiled at her and raised his glass. "You

know how I hate being alone. Besides, we must celebrate. I am close to accusing an old friend of treason."

"You don't sound pleased."

"Au contraire. I am ecstatic."

"Jasper . . ." She looked at her hands, clasped at her waist, as she gathered her words. "You seem obsessed with this hunt. With what happened at Spinner's Falls. I worry that the hunt is harming you. Would it not be better to . . . to leave it be?"

He sipped the brandy, watching her. "Why would I do that? You know what happened at Spinner's Falls. You know what this means to me."

"I know that you seem caught by what happened, unable to move beyond it."

"I watched my best friend die."

She nodded. "I know. And perhaps now you should let your best friend go."

"If it were me, if I'd been the one to die there, Reynaud would never rest until he found the traitor."

She watched him silently, her tilted cat eyes mysterious, unfathomable.

His lip curled as he drank the rest of the brandy. "Reynaud wouldn't give up."

"Reynaud is dead."

His entire body stilled, and he slowly raised his eyes.

Her chin was tilted up, her mouth firm and almost stern. She looked as if she could face down an entire hoard of screaming Indians.

"Reynaud is dead," she repeated. "And besides, you are not him."

*   *   *

MELISANDE BRUSHED OUT her hair that night and thought about her husband. Vale had left his study without another word this afternoon after they'd argued. She stood up from her dressing table and roamed the room. The pallet was ready for their bed, and the decanter of wine on the side table had been newly filled. All was in readiness for her husband. Yet he wasn't here.

It was past ten o'clock, and he wasn't here.

He'd shared supper with her. Surely he hadn't gone out again afterward without telling her? That had been his habit in the first days of their marriage, but things had changed since then. Hadn't they?

Melisande drew her wrap about herself and made up her mind. If he wouldn't come to her, then she'd go to him. She crossed with determined steps to the door leading into his rooms and twisted the handle.

Nothing happened.

Melisande stared at the door handle dumbly for a moment, not quite believing what she'd felt. The door was locked. She blinked, but then pulled herself together. Perhaps it had been mistakenly locked. After all, she didn't usually go from her rooms to his. Normally it was the other way around. Melisande went out into the hall and walked to Vale's door. She tried the handle and found that it, too, was locked. Well, this was silly. She rapped on the door and waited. And waited. Then rapped again.

It was perhaps five minutes before the truth dawned on her: he wasn't going to let her in.

Chapter Eighteen

*It was late by the time Jack hurried back to the castle.
He barely had time to put away his suit and armor
before rushing to the kitchens and bribing the little
kitchen boy once again. Then he ran to the royal
banquet room where the court had already sat down
to eat their supper.*

*"Why, Jack," said the princess when she saw him,
"wherever have you been, and what is that burn upon
your leg?"*

*Jack looked down and saw that the dragon had
wounded him with its fire. He danced about and
performed a silly twirl.*

*"I am a will-o'-the-wisp," he cried, "and
I have floated on the wind to see the king of
salamanders!" . . .*

—from LAUGHING JACK

Jasper wasn't around when Melisande rose in the morning. She pursed her lips when she saw the empty break-

fast room. Was he avoiding her? She'd been blunt the day before—perhaps too blunt. He'd loved Reynaud, she knew, and it took time to recover from such a grievous loss. But it had been seven years. Couldn't he see that his hunt for the Spinner's Falls traitor had enveloped his life? And didn't she as his wife have the right to point this out to him? Surely she was supposed to help him find happiness—or at least contentment—in life. After all the years she'd loved him, after they'd come so far in their marriage, it wasn't fair for him to pull away from her now. Didn't he owe her at least the politeness of listening to her?

After a simple breakfast of buns and hot chocolate, Melisande decided she couldn't bear rattling about the big town house by herself. She patted her hip for Mouse and went with him to the front hall.

"I am taking Mouse for a walk," she informed Oaks.

"Very well, my lady." The butler snapped his fingers for a footman to accompany her.

Melisande pressed her lips together. She'd much rather take her walk alone, but that simply wasn't an option. She nodded to Oaks as he held the big door for her. Outside, the sun had hidden behind a bank of clouds, making the morning so dark it was like evening. But that wasn't what made her halt in her tracks. At the bottom of her front steps stood Mrs. Fitzwilliam and her two children, and Mrs. Fitzwilliam was carrying two soft bags.

"Good morning," Melisande said.

Mouse ran down the steps to greet the children.

"Oh, goodness," Mrs. Fitzwilliam said. She sounded distracted, and her eyes glittered as if from tears hardly held in check. "I . . . I shouldn't bother you. I am so sorry. Please forgive me."

She turned to go, but Melisande ran down the steps. "Please stay. Won't you come in and have a dish of tea?"

"Oh." A tear escaped and ran down the lady's cheek. She swiped at it with the back of her hand like a little girl. "Oh. You must think me a wigeon."

"Not at all." Melisande linked her arm with the other woman's. "I believe my cook is baking scones today. Please come in."

The children looked eager at the mention of scones, and that seemed to decide Mrs. Fitzwilliam. She nodded and let Melisande lead her inside. Melisande chose a small room at the back of the house that had French doors leading into the garden.

"Thank you," Mrs. Fitzwilliam said when they'd sat. "I don't know what you must think of me."

"It's a pleasure to have company," Melisande said.

A maid came in with a tray of scones and tea. Melisande thanked and dismissed her.

Then she looked at Jamie and Abigail. "Would you like to take your scones into the garden with Mouse?"

The children jumped up with alacrity. They contained themselves until they were outside, and then Jamie gave a whoop and ran down the path.

Melisande smiled. "They're lovely children."

She poured a dish of tea and handed it to Mrs. Fitzwilliam.

"Thank you." Mrs. Fitzwilliam took a sip. It seemed to steady her. She looked up and met Melisande's gaze. "I've left His Grace."

Melisande had poured herself some tea as well. Now she lowered the cup from her lips. "Indeed?"

"He cast me off," Mrs. Fitzwilliam said.

"I'm so sorry." How awful to be "cast off" like a worn shirt.

The other lady shrugged. "It's not the first time—or even the second. His Grace gets into tempers. He'll stomp about and yell, and then he'll say that he no longer wants me and I'm to leave his house. He never hurts me; I don't want you to think that. He just . . . carries on."

Melisande sipped her tea, wondering if telling someone they weren't wanted anymore wasn't in some ways worse than hurting them physically. "And this time?"

Mrs. Fitzwilliam squared her shoulders. "This time I decided to take him at his word. I left."

Melisande nodded once. "Good."

"But . . ." Mrs. Fitzwilliam swallowed. "He will want me back. I know he will."

"You said before that you thought it possible he had taken a new mistress," Melisande said in an even voice.

"Yes. I'm almost sure of it. But that doesn't matter. His Grace does not like letting go of what he considers his. He keeps things—people—whether or not he wants them, simply because they are his." Mrs. Fitzwilliam looked out the window as she said this, and Melisande followed her gaze.

Outside the children played with Mouse.

Shew drew in a breath, finally understanding Mrs. Fitz-william's real fear. "I see."

The other lady watched her children, a private deep love in her eyes that made Melisande feel like an intruder.

"He doesn't care for them, not really. And he's not good for the children. I must get them away. I simply must." Her gaze turned to Melisande. "I have money, but he will track me. I may've even been followed here. I need a place far away. Somewhere he won't think to look. I thought perhaps Ireland or even France. Except I don't speak French, and I know no one in Ireland."

Melisande got up and rummaged in a desk in the far corner of the room. "Would you be willing to work?"

Mrs. Fitzwilliam's eyes widened. "Of course. But I don't know what I could do. My penmanship is very fine, but no family will hire me on as a governess when I have the children with me. And besides, as I said, I know no French."

Melisande found some paper, a pen, and ink. She sat down at the desk with a determined smile. "Do you think you could keep house?"

"A housekeeper?" Mrs. Fitzwilliam got up and wandered over. "I don't know much about keeping a house. I'm not sure—"

"Don't worry." Melisande finished writing her note and rang for a footman. "The person I have in mind will be quite lucky to have you, and you needn't take the position long—just until the duke loses your trail."

"But—"

One of the footmen entered the room, and Melisande crossed to him with the folded and sealed note. "Take this to the dowager viscountess. Tell her it's urgent and I would very much appreciate her help."

"Yes, my lady." He bowed and left.

"You want me to become the dowager Viscountess Vale's housekeeper?" Mrs. Fitzwilliam sounded appalled. "I *really* don't think—"

Melisande took the other lady's hands. "I've asked to borrow her carriage. You said you might have been followed. The carriage will go 'round back and wait at the end of the mews. We'll smuggle you and the children in disguised as servants. Your watchers won't be expecting you to take Lady Vale's carriage. Trust me, Mrs. Fitzwilliam."

"Oh, please call me Helen," Mrs. Fitzwilliam said absently. "I wish . . . I wish there was some way I could show my thanks."

Melisande thought a moment before asking, "You said your hand was very fine, didn't you?"

"Yes?"

"Then there is a small thing you can do for me, if you don't mind." Melisande rose and went to the dresser again, pulling out a drawer and taking out a flat box. She brought it back to where Helen sat. "I've just finished translating a children's book for a friend, but my handwriting is deplorable. Could you copy it out fresh for me so that I can have it bound into a book?"

"Oh, yes, certainly." Helen took the box and smoothed her fingers over the top. "But . . . but where are you sending me? Where are my children and I going?"

Melisande smiled slowly, because she really was rather pleased with herself. "Scotland."

MELISANDE WAS GONE when Jasper returned that afternoon. Inexplicably this irritated him. He'd been avoiding his lady wife for nearly a full day, and now that he wanted to see her, she wasn't here. Fickle woman.

He ignored the voice in his head that said he was being an ass and climbed the stairs to his rooms. He paused outside his own door and then looked down the hall to hers. On impulse, he entered her room. Nearly a month ago, he'd come here for answers to who his wife was and had gone away no wiser. Now he'd traveled with her to Scotland, learned she'd had a lover and been with child, made love to her thoroughly and wonderfully, and still—*still*— he felt that she held something back from him. God! He didn't even know, after all this time, why she had married him.

Jasper prowled the room. He'd been ridiculously vain when she'd first presented him with her proposal of marriage. He'd assumed—if he'd thought about it at all—that she hadn't other choices. That she was on the shelf and had no suitors. That he was her last chance at marriage. But now, after living with her, bantering with her, making love to her, Jasper knew that his first vague thoughts were terribly off the mark. She was a quick-witted, intelligent woman. A woman who flamed to life in bed. The kind of woman a man could spend his entire life looking for and never find. But if he did find her . . . then he would make sure he held her and kept her close and happy.

Melisande had had choices. The question was, why had she chosen him?

Jasper found himself in front of her chest of drawers. He stared at them a moment and then bent and pulled out the bottom drawer to find the little tin snuffbox. He straightened with it in his hand. Inside was the same little china dog and the silver button, but the pressed violet was missing. He stirred the items with his finger. Other things had been added to the little cache in place of the violet: a tiny sprig and a few hairs curled together. He picked up the sprig and looked at it. The leaves were narrow, almost needlelike, and small lavender flowers climbed the stem. It was a sprig of heather. From Scotland. And the hair looked like it might very well be his own.

He was frowning down at the snuffbox when behind him the door opened.

He didn't bother trying to hide what he'd found. In a strange way, he welcomed this confrontation.

He turned to face Melisande. "My lady wife."

She closed the door gently behind her and looked from his face to her treasure box. "What are you doing?"

"I'm trying to discover something," he said.

"What?"

"Why you married me."

VALE STOOD BEFORE Melisande with her most intimate secrets in his hand and asked her the stupidest question she'd ever heard.

She blinked and because she couldn't quite credit him with such idiocy, said, "What?"

He prowled toward her, the snuffbox still in his long, bony fingers. His curling mahogany hair was pulled back in a queue that was coming undone; his face was lined and sad, pouches beneath his eyes testament to his sleepless nights. His wide shoulders were covered in a brown and red coat with a stain on the elbow, and his shoes were scuffed. She had never felt so angry at another person and at the same time been aware of how beautiful he was to her.

How perfect in all his imperfections.

"I want to know why you married me, my one and only heart," he said, his complete attention on her.

"Are you stupid?"

He cocked his head at her tone and her words, as if his curiosity was aroused more than his anger. "No."

"Perhaps you were dropped on your head as a child,"

she said sweetly. "Or mayhap madness runs in your family."

He shook his head slowly, still advancing toward her. "Not to my knowledge."

"Then your stupidity is all your own."

"I don't think I'm any more dim-witted than other males." He was right in front of her now, leaning into her face, too close, too personal.

"Oh, yes," she said as she shoved against him violently, "you are."

He didn't budge an inch, damn him. He simply pocketed her—*her!*—snuffbox and tangled the fingers of one hand roughly in her hair. He pulled her head back and placed his mouth, open and wet, against her throat.

"Tell me," he growled, and she felt the vibration of his voice against her skin.

"You are the most *stupid,* lack-witted"—she shoved again and when he still didn't move, balled her fists and hit his chest and arms—"*imbecilic* man in the history of the world."

"No doubt," he sighed against her throat.

He didn't seem to mind or even feel her blows. He tore away the bit of lace at her neckline and lowered his mouth to the upper slopes of her breasts. "Tell me why, my sweet wife."

"I have watched you," she panted, "for *years*. I've seen you look at women—vapid, pretty women. I've seen you choose which ones you wanted. I've seen you stalk them, woo them, and seduce them. And I've seen when you grew tired of them, when your eyes would start to wander again."

He tore at the laces to her bodice, loosening and pulling

aside the fabric of her dress and stays until he reached her bare nipple. He palmed one breast and drew the other into his mouth, sucking strongly.

She cried out.

He lifted his head. "Tell me."

She looked at him and felt her mouth twist in a grimace of rage. Of pain. "I saw you. I saw you take them aside, saw you whisper in their ear. Saw when you left with a particular woman and knew that you were taking her away to bed her."

Her whole face was contorted, tears streaming down, scalding her cheeks, and still he looked at her. His expression was intent, his hands gentle as he thumbed her nipples.

She didn't want his gentleness. The dam had broke, and all the emotion she'd suppressed for years was pouring forth. She held his shoulders, used them as leverage to reach up and bite him on the ear. He jerked his head back and, in a swift movement, swept her off her feet. She screamed, long and loud, as he threw her over his shoulder and bore her to the bed. He let her fall there, the impact cutting off her scream. He was upon her before she could move, his legs over hers, her wrists caught in one strong hand.

A pounding came at the door.

"Go away!" he shouted, his eyes never leaving her face.

"My lord! My lady!"

"No one opens that door, do you hear?"

"My lord—"

"Goddamnit! *Leave us alone!*"

They both listened as the footman's steps left. Then Jasper leaned down and licked her neck. "Tell me."

She arched up, but his legs held her down, and she couldn't get purchase. "All those years . . ."

He pulled off his neck cloth and tied her wrists to the bed rails over her head. "All those years, what? Tell me, Melisande."

"I saw you," she panted. She looked over her head and yanked on the neck cloth. It didn't give. "I watched you."

"Stop struggling," he ordered. "You'll hurt yourself, sweet lady."

"Hurt!" She laughed and it had an hysterical edge.

He took a knife from his pocket and began cutting away her clothes, each rip a sensuous tug against her oversensitive skin. "Tell me."

"You bedded them, woman after woman." She remembered the jealousy, the deep, cutting pain. He pulled the bodice entirely off her. "So many I couldn't even keep track. Could you?"

"No," he said softly.

He wrenched off her skirts and threw them to the floor. Taking off her shoes, he tossed them away as well. "I don't even remember their names."

"Damn you." She was naked now, save for her stockings and garters. Her hands were bound above her, but her legs were free. She kicked at him and hit his thigh.

He fell on her heavily, his hips across hers. His mouth was on her breast again, his hand combing through the curls at the top of her thighs. "Tell me."

"I watched you for years," she whispered. The tears were drying on her cheeks, and heat was building within her. If he would just touch her. Touch her *there*. "I watched you and you never saw me."

"I see you now," he said, licking around a nipple. He trailed his tongue across her breast and to the other breast, circling the nipple there. Delicately. Tenderly.

Damn him.

"You didn't even know my name."

"I know it now." He tested her flesh with his teeth.

Pleasure mixed with pain shot through her, straight from her nipple to where his hand still played. She arched, silently begging, and he relented, sucking the nipple strongly into his mouth.

"You . . ." She swallowed, trying to focus her thoughts. "You didn't know I existed."

"I do now."

And he slid down her body, spreading her knees and draping her calves over his shoulders.

She bucked, trying to dislodge him, but she couldn't budge him any more now than she could before.

He lowered his head and licked her sex.

Her belly contracted in shock, her bound hands fisted, and then she closed her eyes and simply felt. The wet stroke of his tongue, the fingers of one hand flexing on her hip bone, the other petting her mound. He licked and licked again, each stroke slow and intimate. Each stroke hitting her clitoris. She flexed her fingers, feeling the tension build. He moved his hands, spreading her folds, opening her and making her vulnerable.

She bit her lip, waiting, waiting.

And then he set his mouth directly on her bud and sucked. Nibbling, dragging, pulling on that bit of flesh until she couldn't stand it anymore and broke. She arched, thrusting her pelvis into his face, feeling the heat flashing through her, hearing the pound of her heartbeat. He still licked and sucked, his hands heavy, holding her down. Another wave hit and she moaned, the sound loud in the quiet room. Some other time she might care, might feel embarrassed at the erotic sounds she was making, but right now . . .

Oh, God. Right now, she was a creature of pleasure.

He thrust two fingers into her, still gently licking with devastating accuracy, and she trembled. Her whole body tightened, arching, her muscles tensing, waiting. She couldn't. She was too weak, too spent.

And then he moved his fingers within her and sucked again on her flesh. The muscles inside her contracted and released. She came, shaking with the force of her orgasm, shuddering and gasping. White heat spread from her center in a widening pool of pleasure. She went limp with warm relief.

She felt him move. Opening her eyes lazily, she found him lowering her legs. She let them lie on the bed, her thighs spread wide and wanton. He stared at her exposed center as he stood and removed his clothes.

"I can't change the past," he said. "I can't unbed the women I fucked before I knew you. Knew *who* you were."

His eyes raised to hers, and the blue of them was so bright it nearly illuminated the room. "But I tell you now that I will never bed another woman besides you in my lifetime. You are all I want. You are all I see now."

He stepped from his breeches, and she saw that he was erect, his penis standing to his navel in primitive masculine pride. He climbed onto the bed and prowled up her body, straight-armed. His planted fists made the muscles in his shoulders and arms flex and bunch.

She swallowed. "Untie me."

"No," he said calmly, though his voice was a rasp. He bent and scraped his teeth over her throat.

She shivered in erotic anticipation.

He kicked her legs farther apart and lowered his hips, his penis firmly on top of her oversensitive folds.

She gasped.

"You're wet," he growled. "Wet and waiting for me, aren't you?"

She swallowed.

"Aren't you?" He slid his enormous head through her flesh. "Tell me, Melisande."

"Y-yes."

"Yes, what?" He bumped his hips against her, and the shaft of his cock slid through her folds, setting all her nerves alight.

"Yes, I'm wet for you," she whispered.

She tried to move, tried to arch her hips into his, but he was too heavy, his position too firm.

"I'm going to make love to you now," he whispered roughly against her neck. "I'm going to put my prick in your cunny and it will be just you and me, Melisande. All those others, all those memories, they don't matter anymore."

She opened her eyes fully at this statement and watched him. He was above her, his chest sheened with sweat. It had taken a toll on him as well, holding back, and that fact made her smile.

He looked into her eyes. "But I still need something from you."

He moved his hips, and the head of his cock slid back until it just kissed her entrance.

She swallowed, nearly mindless with lust. "W-what?"

"I want the truth."

He shoved and his penis began to enter her.

"I've told you the truth."

He left her and she nearly wept.

He pressed his penis against her clitoris again and bore down. His arms were straight on either side of her, his upper body held apart from her straining one. "Not all of it. Not the whole truth. I want you. I want your secrets."

"I have no more secrets," she whispered. Her arms were shaking, still drawn over her head, and she knew her nipples were hard points between them.

He drew back and shoved his entire length inside her. She hissed. So full, so complete. It was nearly heaven.

But he stopped and held himself still. "Tell me."

She locked her legs about him, holding his thickness within her. "I . . . I don't—"

He frowned down at her and pulled his hips back quite deliberately. Even with her legs around him, he withdrew easily. "Do you want this? Do you want my cock?"

"Yes!" She was past pride, past deception. She needed his flesh within her. She was half mad with wanting.

"Then tell me why you married me."

She glared at him. "Fuck me."

A corner of his mouth twitched, though a bead of sweat ran down the side of his face. He couldn't hold out much longer either, and she knew it.

"No. But I'll make love to you, my sweet, my lady wife."

And he slammed his entire, thick length into her. He

pounded into her wildly, completely out of control. She was past caring. Her head arched back, her eyes closed. She felt his hard body take its pleasure of hers. He leaned down and licked her shaking breasts, and she saw stars, imploding behind her eyelids, sparkling through her limbs. She gasped, and his tongue invaded her mouth. His body shook as his penis plunged into her again and again.

He stopped suddenly, and she opened her eyes. His head was thrown back, his eyes blind, pleasure convulsing his face.

"Melisande!" he cried.

His head thumped to the pillow beside hers, his lungs sucking air. He was heavy and hard, and her arms were still drawn over her head. It didn't matter. She'd gladly suffocate here underneath him. She turned her face toward him and licked the ear she'd earlier bloodied, and she finally said it. She gave him what he wanted.

"I love you. I've always loved you. That's why I married you."

Chapter Nineteen

Princess Surcease was brought her soup, and when she had eaten all of it, what should she find at the bottom of the bowl but the golden ring? Once again, the head cook was summoned before the king, and though the king bellowed and threatened, the poor man knew no more than before.

Finally, the princess, who had been turning the ring over in her fingers, spoke up. "Who is it who chops the vegetables for my soup, good cook?"

The cook puffed out his chest. "Why, I do, Your Highness!"

"And who is it who sets the soup upon the fire to boil?"

"I do, Your Highness!"

"And who is it who stirs the soup while it boils?" The cook's eyes widened. "The little kitchen boy." And what a commotion that caused!

"Fetch the little kitchen boy at once!" cried the king. . . .

—from LAUGHING JACK

Jasper woke the next morning and knew even before he opened his eyes that he was alone. There was a coldness in the pallet where before Melisande's warmth had been against his side. The scent of oranges lingered faintly, but she was no longer in the room. He sighed, feeling the ache of muscles used until exhaustion. She had worn him out, but in the end, he'd heard what he wanted to know. She loved him.

Melisande loved him.

He opened his eyes on the thought. He probably didn't deserve her love. She was an intelligent, sensitive, beautiful woman, and he was a man who had watched his best friend burn to death. In some ways, he bore scars deeper than the men who had been physically tortured. His scars were on his soul, and they still seeped blood now and again. He was hardly a worthy object of any woman's love, let alone Melisande's. And what was worse—what made him truly a cad—was that he had no intention of ever letting her go. He might not be entirely worthy of her love, but he would hold it close until the day he died. He'd not let her change her mind. Melisande's love was a healing salve, a balm upon his scars, and he would treasure it for the rest of his life.

The thoughts made him restless, and he rolled to his feet. He didn't bother ringing for Pynch but washed and got dressed by himself. He ran down the stairs, where he found out from Oaks that Melisande had gone to visit his mother and wouldn't be back for an hour or more.

Jasper felt a vague disappointment, mingled with relief. The discovery of her love for him was very fresh—it was almost too sensitive to bear touch. He wandered into the breakfast room and picked up a bun, biting into it absentmindedly. But he was too restless to sit and eat. His limbs felt as if bees had entered his blood and buzzed through his veins.

He finished the roll in two more bites and strode to the front of the house. Melisande might not be back for several hours, and he couldn't simply sit and wait. Besides, there was a chore he needed to get through, and he might as well do it now. He should finish this thing with Matthew. And if it was another dead end, as he suspected, well then maybe his lady wife was right.

Maybe it was time to let Spinner's Falls go and let Reynaud rest in peace.

"Ask Pynch to come here, please," Jasper said to Oaks. "And have two horses brought 'round."

He paced the hall as he waited.

Pynch appeared from the back of the house. "My lord?"

"I'm going to talk to Matthew Horn," Jasper said. He gestured for Pynch to follow as he strode out the doors. "I want you to accompany me in case of . . ." He waved his hand vaguely.

The valet understood. "Of course, my lord."

The two men mounted the waiting horses, and Jasper nudged his bay into a trot. The day was a grim gray. Low clouds hung overhead, threatening rain.

"I don't like this," he muttered as he rode. "Horn is a gentleman from a good family, and I consider him a friend. If our suspicions are correct . . ." He trailed off, shaking his head. "It will be bad. Very bad."

Pynch didn't answer, and they rode the remainder of the way in silence. Jasper did not relish this task, but it must be done. If Horn was the traitor, he must be brought to some kind of justice.

A half hour later, Jasper pulled his horse to a halt in front of Matthew Horn's town house. He looked at the old bricks and thought of the family that had lived here for generations. Horn's mother was an invalid, confined to this house now. God, this was a nasty business. Jasper sighed and dismounted his horse, then climbed the steps grimly. He knocked at the door and waited, conscious that Pynch stood on a step just below him.

There was a long pause. The house was still, no sound coming from within. Jasper took a step back, glancing up at the windows above. Nothing stirred. He frowned and knocked again, more forcefully this time. Where were the servants? Had Horn told them not to let him in?

He was raising his hand to pound once more when the door creaked open. A harried-looking young footman looked out.

"Is your master at home?" Jasper asked.

"I believe so, sir."

Jasper cocked his head. "Then will you let us in so I may see him?"

The footman flushed. "Of course, sir." He held the door wide. "If you'll wait in the library, sir, I'll fetch Mr. Horn."

"Thank you." Jasper entered the room with Pynch and looked about.

Everything was the same as the last time he'd visited Matthew. A clock ticked on the mantelpiece, and from the street came the muted sounds of carriages. Jasper strolled to the map that was missing Italy to examine it while they waited. The map hung beside two large wing chairs and a table in a corner. As he neared, he heard a sort of whimper. Pynch started toward him even as Jasper leaned over a chair to look in the corner.

Two people were on the floor behind the chairs, a woman cradling a man in her lap. She rocked back and forth steadily, a whispered whimper coming from her lips. The man's coat was fouled with blood, and a dagger still protruded from his chest. He was quite obviously dead.

"What has happened here?" Jasper asked.

The woman raised her eyes. She was pretty, her eyes a lovely blue, but her face was bone-white, her lips color-less.

"He said we would have a fortune," she said. "Enough money to go to the country and open a tavern of our own. He said that he'd marry me and we would be rich."

She dropped her eyes again, quietly rocking.

"It's the butler, my lord," Pynch said from behind him. "Mr. Horn's butler—the one I talked to."

"Pynch, go get help," Jasper ordered. "And see that Horn is all right."

"All right?" The woman laughed as Pynch ran from the room. "He was the one who did this. Stabbed my man and shoved him back here like so much rubbish."

Jasper stared blankly at her. "What?"

"My man found a letter," the woman whispered. "A letter to a French gentleman. My man said Mr. Horn sold secrets to the French during the war in the Colonies. He said we would make a fortune selling the letter back to the master. And then we could open a tavern in the country."

Jasper squatted by her. "He tried to blackmail Horn?"

She nodded. "We'd be rich, he said. I hid behind the

curtain when he asked to talk to Mr. Horn. To tell him about the letter. But Mr. Horn . . ."

Her words trailed into a low keening.

"*Matthew* did this?" Jasper finally grasped the full horror. The butler's head lolled on his bloody chest.

"My lord," Pynch said from behind him.

Jasper looked up. "What?"

"The other servants say Mr. Horn is nowhere to be found."

"He went looking for the letter," the woman said.

Jasper frowned at her. "I thought your man, the butler, had it."

"Nay." The woman shook her head. "He was too smart to have it on him."

"Where is it, then?"

"The master won't find it," the woman said dreamily. "I hid it well. I sent it to my sister in the country."

"Good God," Jasper said. "Where is your sister? She might be in danger."

"He won't look there," the woman whispered. "My man never spoke her name. He only said who had told him to look through the papers in Mr. Horn's desk."

"Who?" Jasper whispered in dawning horror.

The woman looked up and smiled sweetly. "Mr. Pynch."

"My lord, Mr. Horn knows I am your valet." Pynch was white as a sheet. "If he knows that—"

Jasper was already scrambling to his feet, racing desperately for the door, but he still heard the rest of Pynch's sentence.

"—then he will think that you have the letter."

The letter. The letter he didn't have. The letter Matthew

would naturally think was in his house. His house where his darling wife had no doubt returned by this time. Alone and unprotected and thinking Matthew was his friend.

Dear God in heaven. *Melisande.*

"My MOTHER IS an invalid," Matthew Horn said to Melisande, and she nodded because she didn't know what else to do. "She cannot be moved at all, let alone flee to France."

Melisande swallowed and said carefully, "I'm sorry."

But that was the wrong thing to say. Mr. Horn jerked the pistol he held against her side and Melisande flinched. She really couldn't help it. She'd never liked guns—hated the loud explosion when they fired—and her flesh cringed at the thought of a ball tearing through her. It would hurt. A lot. She was a coward, she knew, but she simply couldn't help it.

She was terrified.

Mr. Horn had been a little strange when he'd come to the door. He'd seemed agitated. When he'd been shown into her sitting room, she'd wondered whether he might've been drinking, even though it was still not noon.

Then he'd demanded to see Vale, and when she'd told him that her husband was not at home, he'd insisted on her showing him Vale's study. She hadn't liked that, but by then she'd begun to suspect something was wrong. When he'd rummaged in Jasper's desk, she'd started for the door intending to summon Oaks and have Mr. Horn forcibly removed. Which was when the man had pulled the pistol from his pocket. It was only then, while staring at the big pistol in his hand, that she'd seen the dark stain on his sleeve. As he moved more papers with that hand, she noticed that his sleeve left a dark red smear behind.

It was as if he'd dipped his coat sleeve in blood.

Melisande shuddered and tried to calm her wild thoughts. She didn't know if the stain was blood, so it was no use becoming hysterical over what might be a misunderstanding on her part. Soon Vale would be home, and he would take care of things. Except he didn't know Mr. Horn had a pistol. He might come in the door and be taken completely unawares. Mr. Horn's mania seemed focused on Jasper. What if he intended to hurt him?

Melisande took a breath. "What is it you look for?"

Mr. Horn knocked all the papers from the desk. They fell in a scattered heap, some of the smaller papers fluttering like landing birds. "A letter. *My* letter. Vale stole it from me. Where is it?"

"I . . . I don't—"

He pressed closer to her, the gun between them, and caught her face in his left hand, squeezing painfully. His eyes sparkled with tears. "He's a thief and a blackmailer. I thought he was my friend. I thought . . ." He squeezed his eyes shut and then opened them to glare at her and say fiercely, "I'll not be ruined by him, do you hear? Tell me where the paper is, where he might've hid it, or I'll feel no sorrow in killing you."

Melisande trembled. He was going to kill her. She had no illusions that she would live through this. But if Jasper came home now, he might be killed as well. That realization marshaled her thoughts. The farther Mr. Horn was from the front door, the more time Vale would have to realize the danger when he returned home.

She licked her lips. "His bedroom. I . . . I think in his bedroom."

Without a word, Mr. Horn grasped her by the back of the neck and shoved her into the hall ahead of him. The pistol was still pressed to her side. The hall seemed deserted, and Melisande gave a prayer of thanks. She didn't know how Mr. Horn would react to a servant. He might very well shoot anyone he saw.

They climbed the steps in tandem, his hand pinching the back of her neck painfully. At the top of the stairs, Melisande turned and her heart nearly stopped. Suchlike was just coming out of her room.

"My lady?" Suchlike said in a confused voice. She looked from Melisande to Mr. Horn.

Melisande spoke rapidly before her captor could speak. "What are you doing here, girl? I told you to have my riding habit sponged and pressed by noon."

Suchlike's eyes widened. Melisande had never spoken to her so harshly before. And then things got worse. Behind the maid, Mouse poked his nose out of the room and scrambled into the hall. He raced toward Melisande and Mr. Horn, barking madly.

Melisande felt Mr. Horn move as if to pull the pistol from her side. Mouse was at her feet now, and she acted quickly, kicking poor Mouse away. The dog yelped in pain and confusion and sprawled onto his back.

Melisande looked at Suchlike. "Take this dog with you to the kitchens. Do it now. And make sure you ready my riding habit, or I'll dismiss you this afternoon."

Suchlike had never liked Mouse, but she scrambled forward and hastily scooped the terrier into her arms. She ran past Melisande and Mr. Horn, her eyes filled with tears.

Melisande exhaled when the maid was out of sight.

"Very nice," Mr. Horn said. "Now where is Vale's bedroom?"

Melisande pointed to the room, and Mr. Horn dragged her toward it. She had another leap of fear as he opened the door. What if Mr. Pynch was inside? She had no idea where the manservant was.

But the room was empty.

Mr. Horn hauled her toward the dresser and began throwing Vale's neatly folded neck cloths to the ground.

"He was there when they tortured me. They tied him to a stake and held his head so he had to watch. I almost felt more sorry for him than for me." He stopped suddenly and inhaled. "I can still see those blue eyes of his filling with grief while they burned my chest. He knows what it was like. He knows what they did to me. He knows it took the British army two hellish weeks to deign to ransom us."

"You blame Jasper for your wounds," Melisande whispered.

"Don't be a witless fool," he snapped. "Vale could no more help what was done to him than we could help what was done to us. What I blame him for is his betrayal. He of all people should understand why I did what I did."

Having emptied the chest of drawers, he dragged her to the wardrobe. "He knows what it was like. He was there. How dare he judge me? How dare he?"

Melisande saw that his eyes were ice-cold and determined, and the sight froze her with terror. Mr. Horn was cornered, and it was only a matter of time until he found that she'd lied.

*   *   *

BY THE TIME Jasper made it home, his heart was nearly pounding through his chest with fear. He flung his horse's reins to a boy and leapt the steps without waiting for Pynch. He threw open his front doors and went in, only to skid to a stop.

Melisande's maid was clutching Mouse and weeping in the hall. Surrounding her were Oaks and two footmen.

Oaks turned at Jasper's entrance, his face drawn and lined. "My lord! We think Lady Vale is in trouble."

"Where is she?" Jasper demanded.

"Upstairs," the maid gasped. Mouse wriggled hard in her arms, trying to get down. "There's a man with her, and oh, my lord, I think he has a gun."

Jasper's blood froze in his veins, painful ice crystallizing. *No. Christ, no.*

"Where did you see them, Sally?" Pynch said from beside Jasper.

"At the top of the stairs," Suchlike said. "Outside your rooms, my lord."

Mouse finally gave such a desperate lurch that she gasped and dropped him to the floor. The dog ran to Jasper and barked once before scampering toward the stairs. He jumped to the first step and barked again.

"Stay here," Jasper said to the servants. "If he sees too many . . ." He trailed off, not wanting to say aloud the awful possibility.

He started for the stairs.

"My lord," Pynch called.

Jasper looked over his shoulder.

The valet was proffering two pistols. Pynch met his eyes. He knew damn well how Jasper felt about guns. Still, he held them out. "Don't go up unarmed."

Jasper snatched the weapons without a word and whirled to the stairs. Mouse barked and ran up the stairs ahead of him, panting with excitement. They made the first landing and continued to the second story, where the master bedrooms were. Jasper paused on the top step to listen. Mouse stood by his ankle, patiently watching him. Jasper could hear the maid, still sobbing faintly down below, and the murmur of a deeper voice, probably Pynch comforting her. Other than that, all was silent. He refused to think what the silence might mean.

He crept to his door on the balls of his feet, Mouse silently trailing him. The door was partly open, and he crouched so as to make himself less of a target as he pushed it open.

Nothing happened.

Jasper took a breath and looked at the dog. Mouse was watching him, completely uninterested in what might be in the room. Jasper swore under his breath and entered the room. Matthew had obviously been here. Jasper's clothes were on the floor, his linens ripped from the bed he never used. He crossed and looked in the small dressing room, but although it had been torn apart, no one was there now. When he came back into his bedroom, Mouse was sniffing at one of the pillows on the floor. Jasper looked and nearly fell to his knees.

The pillow had a small streak of blood.

He closed his eyes. *No.* No, she wasn't hurt; she wasn't dead. He couldn't believe otherwise—and remain sane. He opened his eyes and lifted the pistols to the ready. Then he went through the rest of the rooms on that floor. After fifteen minutes, he was panting and desperate. Mouse had followed him to each room, sniffing under the beds and in the corners, but he'd not seemed that interested in any of them.

Jasper mounted the stairs to the next floor, where the servants' bedrooms were, under the eaves. There was no reason for Matthew to have taken Melisande up here. Perhaps he'd gone down the back way and escaped past the footmen in the kitchen. But if so, someone should've heard him. There should've been an outcry. Dammit! Where was Horn? Where had he taken Melisande?

They'd just made the uppermost floor when Mouse suddenly stiffened and barked. He raced to the end of the narrow, uncarpeted hallway and scratched at a door. Jasper followed the dog and carefully opened the door. A flight of wooden stairs led to the roof. There was a narrow parapet up there, but it was mostly ornamental, and Jasper had never been up there himself.

Mouse shouldered past him and raced up the steep stairs, his little muscled body jumping from step to step. He reached the top and stuck his nose to the crack of a small half-door, whining.

Jasper gripped his pistols and mounted the stairs quietly. At the top, he nudged aside the little dog with his boot and stared down at him sternly.

"Stay here."

Mouse laid back his ears in submission but didn't sit.

"Stay here," Jasper commanded. "Or so help me, I'll lock you in one of the rooms."

The dog had no way of understanding the words, but he certainly understood the tone. He tucked his rump down and sat. Jasper turned to the door. He opened it and slipped out.

The skies had fulfilled the promise of rain. It dripped

down, cold, gray, and dispirited on his roof. The door was only meant to provide access to the roof for repairs and cleaning. In front of it was a small square of level tiles, barely wide enough for a man to stand on, while all around was the slope of the roof. Jasper slowly straightened, feeling the wind blow raindrops against his neck. He faced the back garden. To his left was empty roof, to his right more empty roof. Jasper peered over the spine of the rooftop.

Dear God. Matthew held Melisande bent over the low stone parapet in front of the house. The parapet barely came to knee height and would in no way prevent her from falling. Only Matthew's arm kept her from smashing her brains against the cobblestones far below. Jasper remembered her fear of heights and knew his darling wife must be completely terrified.

"No farther!" Matthew cried. He wore neither hat nor wig, and the rain had darkened and flattened his short reddish-blond hair to his skull. His blue eyes glittered with desperation. "No farther or I drop her over the edge!"

Jasper met Melisande's beautiful brown eyes. Her hair had come partially down, and long wet strands clung to her cheeks. Her hands clutched at Matthew's arm, for she had no other purchase. She looked back at him and a horrible thing happened.

She smiled.

Sweet, brave girl. Jasper averted his eyes and stared at Matthew. He raised the pistol in his right hand and held it steady. "Drop her and I'll blow your goddamned head off."

Matthew chuckled softly, and Melisande wobbled in his grasp. "Back away, Vale. Do it now."

"And then what?"

Matthew stared back stonily. "You've destroyed me. I have no life left, no future, no hope. I cannot flee to France without my mother, and if I stay, they'll hang me for selling secrets to the French. My mother will be disgraced; the crown will take all my assets and throw her into the street."

"Is this suicide, then?"

"And if it is?"

"Let Melisande go," Jasper said evenly. "She had nothing to do with what's happened. I'll put down my pistol if you let her go."

"No!" Melisande cried, but neither man paid her any heed.

"I've lost my life," Matthew said. "Why shouldn't I destroy your life as you've destroyed mine?"

He twisted a bit, and Jasper threw himself at the ridge of the roof. "Don't! I'll give you the letter."

Matthew hesitated. "I've looked. You don't have it."

"It's not in my house. I have it hidden elsewhere." All lies, of course, but Jasper put all the sincerity at his command into his voice. If he could just buy some time and get Melisande off the parapet.

"Do you?" Matthew looked warily hopeful.

"Yes." Jasper had slowly straddled the roof, and now he brought his other leg over as well, crouching at the top. Melisande and Matthew were only ten feet or so away. "Back away from the edge and I'll bring it to you."

"No. We stay here until you bring the letter."

Matthew sounded reasonable, but he'd already killed one person today. Jasper couldn't leave him alone with Melisande.

"I'll bring the letter," Jasper bargained. He inched

forward again. "I'll give you the letter and forget the whole thing. Just let me have my wife first. She means more to me than any revenge for Spinner's Falls."

Matthew started shaking, and Jasper rose in fear. Was the man having some kind of fit?

But dry laughter spilled from Matthew's throat. "Spinner's Falls? Oh, God, do you think me the Spinner's Falls traitor? All this and you don't even know, do you? I never betrayed us at Spinner's Falls. It was afterward—after the British army left us to be tortured for two damned weeks—that I sold secrets to the French. Why shouldn't I? I had my loyalty carved out of my chest."

"But you shot Hasselthorpe, you must have."

"Not I, Vale. Someone else shot him."

"Who?"

"Why would I know? Hasselthorpe obviously knows something about Spinner's Falls that someone doesn't want him to tell."

Jasper blinked raindrops from his eyes. "Then you had nothing to do with—"

"God, Vale," Matthew whispered, despair in his face. "You've destroyed my life. I believed that you were the only one who understood me. Why have you betrayed me? Why?"

And Jasper watched with horror as Matthew raised his pistol and aimed it at Melisande's head. He was too far away. He'd never get to her in time. *Christ.* He had no choice. Jasper fired his own pistol and shot Matthew's hand. He saw Melisande flinch as blood splattered her hair. Saw Matthew drop the pistol with a shout of pain.

Saw Matthew shove Melisande over the edge of the parapet.

Jasper fired the second pistol, and Matthew's head jerked violently back. Then Jasper was scrambling on the slippery tiles, a scream filling his head. He shoved Matthew's corpse to the side and looked over the parapet, expecting to see Melisande's body broken below. Instead, he saw her face, three feet down, looking back up at him.

He gasped and the screaming stopped. Only then did he realize that the sound had been real and that he'd been the one making it. He stretched his hand down. She was grasping an ornamental ridge of stone.

"Take my hand," he rasped, his throat raw.

She blinked, looking dazed. He remembered that day, so long ago, in front of Lady Eddings's town house just before they were married. She'd refused his hand to help her down from his carriage.

He leaned farther out. "Melisande. Trust me. Take my hand now."

She gasped, her precious lips parting, and let go of the ledge with one hand. He lunged and grasped her wrist. Then he leaned backward and used his weight to haul her up and to safety.

She came over the parapet and fell limply into his arms. He wrapped his body about hers and held her. Simply held her, inhaling the scent of oranges in her hair, feeling her breath on his cheek. It was a while before he realized that he was shaking.

Finally, she stirred. "I thought you hated guns."

He pulled back and looked at her face. She had a bruise on one cheek, and there was gore splattered in her hair, but she was the most beautiful thing he'd ever seen.

He had to clear his throat before he spoke. "I do hate guns. I loathe them desperately."

Her lovely brows knit. "Then how . . . ?"

"I love you," he said. "Don't you know that? I would crawl through the flames of hell on my knees for you. Firing a goddamn gun is nothing compared to you, my dearest wife."

He brushed her face, watching her eyes widen, and he bent to kiss her, repeating as he did, "I love you, Melisande."

Chapter Twenty

So the little kitchen boy was brought trembling
before the king. It wasn't long before he confessed.
Three times, Jack, the princess's fool, had paid him
to have a turn at stirring the pot of soup—the last
time this very night. Well! The courtiers gasped,
Princess Surcease looked thoughtful, and the king
roared with rage. The guards dragged Jack to kneel
before the king, and one placed a sword against the
fool's throat.

"Speak!" cried the king. "Speak and tell us from
whom you stole the rings!" For naturally no one
believed the short, twisted fool could've won the rings
himself. "Speak! Or I will have your head cut from
your body!" . . .

—from LAUGHING JACK

ONE MONTH LATER . . .

Sally Suchlike hesitated outside her mistress's bedroom. It was late morning, but still one never knew, and she'd hate to go in if her mistress was not alone. She twisted her hands and stared at the little statue of the nasty goat man and the naked lady while she tried to decide, but of course the statue made her mind drift. The goat man did look so like Mr. Pynch and she wondered, as always, if his rather gigantic—

A man cleared his throat directly behind her.

Sally shrieked and whirled around. Mr. Pynch was standing so close she could feel the heat of his chest.

The valet raised one eyebrow slowly, which made him look more like the goat man than ever. "What are you doing, loitering in the hallway, Miss Suchlike?"

She tossed her head. "I was thinking on whether I should go into the mistress's room or not."

"And why wouldn't you?"

She pretended shock. "She might not be alone, that's why not."

Mr. Pynch lifted his upper lip in a faint sneer. "I find that hard to believe. Lord Vale always sleeps alone."

"Is that so?" Sally put her hands on her hips, feeling excitement heat her lower belly. "Well, why don't you just go and see if your master is in his bed alone, because I wager he's not in his room at all."

The valet didn't deign to reply. He just gave her a glance that swept her from head to toe and entered Lord Vale's bedroom.

Sally blew out a breath and fanned her cheeks, trying to cool down as she waited.

She didn't have long. Mr. Pynch reemerged from the master's bedroom and closed the door quietly behind him. He stalked to where she stood and loomed over her until Sally backed against the wall.

Then Mr. Pynch lowered his head to breathe into her ear, "The room is empty. Do you accept the usual forfeit?"

Sally gulped, because her stays seemed a mite too tight. "Y-yes."

Mr. Pynch swooped down and captured her lips with his own.

The silence in the hallway was broken only by Mr. Pynch's deepened breathing and Sally's sigh.

Then Mr. Pynch lifted his head. "Why do you find that statue so fascinating? Every time I catch you in the hall, you're staring at it."

Sally blushed because Mr. Pynch was nibbling along her neck. "I think it looks like you. The little goat man."

Mr. Pynch raised his head and glanced over his shoulder. Then he looked back at Sally, one brow raised regally. "Indeed."

"Mmm," Sally said. "And I've been wondering . . ."

"Yes?"

He nibbled at her shoulder, which made it rather hard to concentrate.

Sally tried valiantly anyway. "I've been wondering if you're like the little goat man all over."

Mr. Pynch stilled against her shoulder, and for a moment, Sally thought that perhaps she'd been too impertinent.

Then he raised his head, and she saw the gleam in his eye. "Why, Miss Suchlike, I'd be happy to help answer your questions, but I think there is one thing we must do first."

"And what's that?" she asked breathlessly.

His face lost all trace of teasing. He suddenly became quite serious, his blue eyes gazing down at her almost hesitantly.

He cleared his throat. "I believe you must marry me, Miss Suchlike, in order for us to continue this discussion."

She pulled back a little and stared up at him, completely at a loss for words.

He scowled. "What?"

"I thought you said you were too old for me," she said.

"I did—"

"And that I was too young to know my own mind."

"I did."

"And that I ought to be looking at other men. Men more my own age, like that footman Sprat."

His scowl became thunderous. "I don't remember telling you to look at young Sprat. Have you?"

"Well, no," she admitted.

It had nearly broken her heart when he'd said those words, for she didn't want to look at any other man but him. The only thing that had saved her, in fact, was that he'd kept creeping up behind her in the mornings and losing his silly wager. Mr. Pynch didn't seem able to stop himself from their flirtation, and she certainly couldn't.

Not that she'd wanted to.

"Good," he growled now.

She beamed up at him.

He stared at her a moment and then shook his head as if to clear it. "Well?"

"Well what?"

He sighed. "Will you marry me, Sally Suchlike?"

"Oh." Sally carefully smoothed her skirt, because of course she wanted to marry Mr. Pynch. But she was a levelheaded girl, and she needed to make absolutely sure. Marriage, after all, was a very big step. "Why do you want to marry me?"

His expression was enough to send most girls into flight, but Sally had been studying Mr. Pynch and his expressions for some time now, and she knew she was quite safe with him. "In case you haven't noticed, I've kissed you every day in this hallway for the past fortnight or more. And even though you are too young and much too pretty for me, and you'll no doubt regret sooner or later being tied to an ugly bastard like me, I still want to marry you."

"Why?"

He stared down at her, and if Mr. Pynch had had hair, he might've pulled it out in frustration. "Because I love you, you silly lass!"

"Oh, good," Sally purred, and wrapped her arms about his thick neck. "Then I'll marry you. But you're wrong, you know."

At that point, Sally was interrupted by the valet kissing her quite firmly and enthusiastically, so it was some time before he raised his head and said, "How am I wrong?"

Sally laughed up into Mr. Pynch's lovely, scowling face. "You're wrong that I'll regret marrying you. I'll never regret marrying you, because I love you as well."

Which only earned her another enthusiastic kiss.

MELISANDE STRETCHED LUXURIOUSLY and rolled against her husband. "Good morning," she whispered.

"Indeed it is," he said. His voice was lazy, with just a hint of exhaustion.

She hid a smile against his shoulder. He'd nearly worn himself out, making slow love to her. He did seem to like waking her in the mornings.

A scratch and a whine came from her dressing room.

Melisande poked Vale in the ribs. "You need to let him out now."

He sighed. "Must I?"

"He'll only scratch more, and then he'll start barking, and Sprat will come to the door and ask if he should take Mouse out."

"Dear God, such a large ruckus for such a small dog," Vale muttered, but he rose from their pallet and padded nude across the floor.

Melisande watched him under lowered eyelids. He really did have the most beautiful bottom. She smiled, wondering what he'd think if she said so.

Jasper opened the door to the dressing room. Mouse trotted busily out with a bone in his mouth. He jumped on the pallet and turned about three times before settling and gnawing his prize. Their pallet had expanded in the last month with the addition of a thin mattress and lots of pillows. Melisande had had the bed removed from her room altogether, and now the pallet took up pride of place against the wall between the windows. At night, with only a candle for light, she imagined that she lay in some Ottoman palace.

"That dog ought to have his own bed," Vale muttered.

"He does have his own bed," Melisande pointed out. "He just doesn't sleep in it."

Vale scowled down at the dog. Of course, *he* had been

the one to give Mouse the bone, so no one in the room took the scowl very seriously.

"Be glad he no longer sleeps under the covers," Melisande said.

"I *am* glad. I hope never to find a cold nose against my arse again." He turned his scowl on her. "And what are you smirking about, my lady wife?"

"I beg your pardon, this is not a smirk."

"Oh, yes?" He began to prowl toward her, all lean muscle and intent, interested male. "Then how would you characterize your expression?"

"I'm admiring the view," she said.

"Are you?" He made a detour to where he'd carelessly flung his coat the night before. "Perhaps you'd like me to perform a gavotte?"

She tilted her head, watching as he dug in the pocket of his coat. "I might like that."

"Would you, you insatiable baggage?"

"I would." She stretched a bit on the pallet, letting her nipples pop from the coverlet. "But I can be satiated, you know."

"Can you?" he muttered. His eyes were on her nipples, and he seemed a bit distracted. "I've tried and tried and still you're eager. You wear a man out."

Her lips curved at his plaintive tone, and she glanced significantly at his cock, standing proud and erect now. "You don't look worn out."

"It's terrible, isn't it," he said conversationally. "You look at me and I become embarrassingly attentive."

She held out her arms. "Come here, you silly man."

He grinned and knelt by her side.

"What have you there?" she asked, because he held one hand behind his back.

His grin faded as he lay down beside her, propping himself on his elbow. "I've something for you."

"Really?" Her brows knit. He hadn't given her anything since the garnet earrings.

He took his hand out from behind his back and turned it over. In his palm lay a small tin snuffbox. It looked a little like the snuffbox she kept her treasures in, except this box was obviously new.

She raised her brows in question and looked from his palm to his face.

"Open it," he said huskily.

She took it from his palm and was surprised at how heavy the little box was. She glanced again at his face. He was watching her with bright turquoise eyes.

She opened the box.

And gasped. The outside of the snuffbox might be plain tin, not ornamented at all, but the inside was glowing gold, set with precious gems. Pearls and rubies, diamonds and emeralds, sapphires and amethysts, jewels she didn't even know the names of. They all sparkled from inside the box, nearly covering the yellow gold with a rainbow of color.

She looked up at Jasper, tears in her eyes. "Why? What does it mean?"

He took the hand holding the box and turned it over, brushing his lips against her knuckles. "It's you."

She looked down at the gorgeous, sparkling box. "What?"

He cleared his throat, his head still bent. "When I first met you, I was a fool. And I was a fool for years before that. I saw only the tin you hid behind. I was too vain, too asinine, too foolish to look beyond and see your beauty, my sweet wife."

He raised his beautiful turquoise eyes, and she saw that they were adoring. "I want you to understand that I see you now. I've basked in the wonder of your beauty, and I'm never letting you go. I love you with all my battered soul."

Melisande looked one last time at the treasure box. It was exquisitely lovely. This was how Jasper saw her, and it rather awed her. She closed the lid carefully and set the box aside, knowing it was the most precious, the most perfect gift he could ever give her.

Then she pulled her husband down into her arms and said the only thing she could. "I love you."

And she kissed him.

Epilogue

The sword pressed very tightly against Jack's throat, but still he spoke up bravely.

"I would tell you who won the rings, my liege," he said, "but, alas, you would not believe me in any case."

The king bellowed, but Jack raised his voice to be heard over the royal rage. "Besides, it does not matter who won the rings. What matters is who holds them now."

And just like that, the king was silent and every eye in the royal banquet hall turned to Princess Surcease. She seemed as surprised as any when she reached into the little jeweled bag that hung from her kirtle and drew out the bronze ring and the silver ring. She placed them with the gold ring already on her palm, and then all three lay together.

"Princess Surcease has the rings," Jack said. "And it seems to me that gives her the right to pick her own husband."

Well, the king hemmed and the king hawed, but in the end he had to admit that Jack did have a point.

"Who will you choose to wed, my daughter?" the king asked. "There are men here from all corners of the world. Rich men, brave men, men so handsome the ladies swoon *when they ride by. Now tell me, which of them will be your husband?"*

"None." Princess Surcease smiled, helped Jack to stand on his stumpy legs, and said, "I will wed Jack the Fool and no other, for he may be a fool, but he makes me laugh and I love him."

And then before the stunned eyes of the entire court and her royal father, she bent and kissed Jack the Fool, right on his long, curved nose.

What a strange thing happened then! For Jack began to grow, his legs and arms lengthened and thickened, and his nose and chin receded into their normal proportions. When it was all over, Jack was himself again, tall and strong, and since he wore the wonderful suit of night and wind and carried the sharpest blade in all the world, well, you can imagine, he was a very fine sight indeed.

But poor Princess Surcease did not like this handsome stranger who stood so tall before her. She wept and cried, "Oh, where is my Jack? Oh, where is my sweet fool?"

Jack knelt before the princess and took her little hands between his big ones. He leaned his head close to hers and whispered so only she could hear, "I am your sweet fool, my beautiful princess. I am the man who danced and sang to make you laugh. I love you, and I would gladly take on that twisted, horrible form again, if only to see you smile."

And at these words, the princess did smile and she kissed him. For although Jack's form had changed so much she no longer recognized him, his voice had not. It was the voice of Jack the Fool, the man she loved.

The man she'd chosen to marry.

"The new master of the historical romance genre."
—HistoricalRomanceWriters.com

Don't miss the next

delightful installment in

THE LEGEND OF THE

FOUR SOLDIERS

series

To Beguile A Beast

AVAILABLE IN MAY 2009

Please turn this page for a preview.

Chapter One

SCOTLAND
JULY 1765

It was as the carriage bumped around a bend and the decrepit castle loomed into view in the dusk that Helen Fitzwilliam finally—and rather belatedly—realized that the whole trip may've been a horrible mistake.

"Is that it?" Jamie, her five-year-old son, was kneeling on the musty carriage seat cushions and peering out the window. "I thought it was 'sposed to be a castle."

"'Tis a castle, silly," his nine-year-old sister, Abigail, replied. "Can't you see the tower?"

"Just 'cause it has a tower don't mean it's a castle," Jamie objected, frowning at the suspect castle. "There's no moat. If it *is* a castle, it's not a proper one."

"Children," Helen said rather too sharply, but then they *had* been in one cramped carriage after another for the better part of a fortnight. "Please don't bicker."

Naturally, her offspring feigned deafness.

"It's pink." Jamie had pressed his nose to the small

window, clouding the glass with his breath. He turned and scowled at his sister. "D'you think a proper castle ought to be pink?"

Helen stifled a sigh and massaged her right temple. She'd felt a headache lurking there for the last several miles, and she knew it was about to pounce just as she needed all her wits about her. She hadn't properly thought this scheme through. But, then, she never did think things through as she ought to, did she? Impulsiveness—hastily acted on and more leisurely regretted—was the hallmark of her life. It was why, at the age of one and thirty, she found herself traveling through a foreign land about to throw herself and her children on the mercy of a stranger.

What a fool she was!

A fool who had better get her story straight, for the carriage was already stopping before the imposing wood doors.

"Children!" she hissed.

Both little faces snapped around at her tone. Jamie's brown eyes were wide while Abigail's expression was pinched and fearful. Her daughter noticed far too much for a little girl, was too sensitive to the atmosphere adults created.

Helen took a breath and made herself smile. "This will be an adventure, my darlings, but you must remember what I've told you." She looked at Jamie. "What are we to be called?"

"Halifax," Jamie replied promptly. "But I'm still Jamie and Abigail's still Abigail."

"Yes, darling."

That had been decided on the trip north from London when it became painfully obvious that Jamie would have difficulties *not* calling his sister by her real name. Helen sighed. She'd just have to hope that the children's Christian names were ordinary enough not to give them away.

"We've lived in London," Abigail said, looking intent.

"That'll be easy to remember," Jamie muttered, "because we *have*."

Abigail shot a quelling glance at her brother and continued. "Mama's been in the dowager Viscountess Vale's household. Our father is dead and he isn't—"

Her eyes widened, stricken.

Helen swallowed and leaned forward to pat her daughter's knee. "It's all right. If we can—"

The carriage door was wrenched open, and the coachman's scowling face peered in. "Are ye getting out or not? It looks like rain, an' I want to be back in th' inn safe and warm when it comes."

"Certainly." Helen nodded regally at the coachman—by far the surliest driver they'd had on this wretched journey. "Please fetch our bags down for us."

The man snorted. "Already done, innit?"

"Come, children." She hoped she wasn't blushing in front of the awful man. The truth was that they had only two soft bags—one for herself and one for the children. The coachman probably thought them destitute. And in a way, he was right, wasn't he?

She pushed the lowering thought away. Now was not the time to have depressing thoughts. She must be at her most alert, her most persuasive, to pull this off.

She stepped from the rented carriage and looked around. The ancient castle loomed before them, solid and silent. The main building was a squat rectangle, with small windows irregularly placed in a flat front. A Gothic arch held wooden doors. High on one corner, a circular tower projected from the wall. Before the castle was a sort of drive, once properly graveled but now uneven with weeds and mud. A few trees clustered about the drive struggled to make a barricade against the rising wind. Beyond, nearly black hills rolled gently to the darkening horizon.

"All right, then?" The coachman was swinging up to his box, not even looking at them. "I'll be off."

"At least leave a lantern!" Helen shouted, but the noise of the carriage rumbling away drowned out her voice. She stared, appalled, after the coach.

"It's dark," Jamie observed, looking at the castle.

"Mama, there aren't any lights," Abigail said.

She sounded frightened, and Helen felt a surge of sympathy. She hadn't noticed the lack of lights until now. Perhaps no one was at home. What would they do then?

I'll cross that bridge when I come to it. Helen tilted her chin and smiled for Abigail. "Perhaps they're lit in the back where we can't see them."

Abigail didn't look particularly convinced by this theory, but she dutifully nodded her head.

Helen took the bags and marched up the wide shallow stone steps to the huge wooden doors. They were almost black with age, and the hinges and bolts were iron—quite medieval. She raised the iron ring and knocked hard.

The sound echoed despairingly within.

Helen stood facing the door, refusing to believe that no one would come. The wind blew her skirts into a swirl. Jamie scuffed his boots against the stone step, and Abigail sighed almost silently.

Helen wet her lips. "Perhaps they can't hear because they're in the tower."

She knocked again.

It was dark now, the sun completely gone and with it the warmth of day. It was the middle of summer and quite hot in London, but she'd found on her journey that the nights in Scotland could become very cool, even in summer. Lightning flashed low on the horizon. What a desolate place this was! Why anyone would willingly choose to live here was beyond her understanding.

"They're not coming," Abigail said as thunder rumbled in the distance. "No one's home, I think."

Helen swallowed as fat raindrops pattered against her face. The last village they'd passed was ten miles away. She had to find shelter for her children. Abigail was right. No one was home. She'd led them on a wild-goose chase.

She'd failed them once again.

Helen's lips trembled at the thought. *Mustn't break down in front of the children.*

"Perhaps there's a barn or other outbuilding in—" she began when one of the great wood doors was thrown open, startling her.

She stepped back, nearly falling down the steps. At first, the opening seemed eerily black, as if a ghostly hand had opened the door. But then something moved, and she discerned a shape within. A man stood there, tall, lean, and very, very intimidating. He held a single candle, its light entirely inadequate. By his side was a great four-legged beast, far too tall to be any sort of dog that she knew of.

"What d'you want?" he rasped, his voice low and husky as if from disuse or strain. His accent was cultured, but the tone was far from welcoming.

Helen opened her mouth, scrambling for words. This

was not at all what she'd expected. Dear God, what was that thing by his side?

At that moment, lightning forked across the sky, close and amazingly bright. It lit the man and his familiar as if he was on a stage. The beast was tall and gray and lean with gleaming black eyes. The man was even worse. Black, lank hair fell tangling to his shoulders. He wore old breeches, gaiters, and a rough coat better suited for the rubbish heap. One side of his face was twisted with red angry scars. A single light brown eye reflected the lightning at them diabolically.

Most horrible of all, there was only a sunken pit where his left eye should have been.

Abigail screamed.

THEY ALWAYS SCREAMED.

Sir Alistair Munroe scowled at the woman and children on his step. Behind them the rain suddenly let down in a wall of water, making the children crowd against their mother's skirts. Children, particularly small ones, nearly always screamed and cried and ran away from him. Sometimes even grown women did. Just last year, a rather melodramatic young lady on Princess Street in Edinburgh had fainted at the sight of him.

Alistair had wanted to slap the silly chit.

Instead, he'd scurried away like a diseased rat, hiding the maimed side of his face as best he could in his lowered tricorne and pulled-up cloak. He expected the reaction in cities and towns. It was the reason he didn't like to frequent areas where people congregated. What he didn't expect was a female child screaming on his very doorstep.

"Stop that," he growled at her, and the lass snapped her mouth shut.

There were two of them, a male and a female. The lad was a brown birdlike thing that could've been anywhere from three to eight. Alistair had no basis to judge since he avoided children when he could. The female was the elder. She was pale and blond and staring up at him with blue eyes that looked much too large for her thin face. Perhaps it was a fault of her bloodline—such abnormalities often denoted mental deficiency.

Her mother had eyes the same color, he noted as he finally, reluctantly, looked at her. She was beautiful. Of course. It would be a blazing beauty who appeared upon his doorstep in a thunderstorm. She had eyes the exact color of newly opened harebells, shining gold hair, and a magnificent bosom that any man, even a scarred, misanthropic recluse such as himself, would find arousing. It was, after all, the natural reaction of a human male to a human female of obvious reproductive capability, however much he resented it.

"What d'you want?" he repeated to the woman.

Perhaps the entire family was mentally deficient, because they simply stared at him, mute. The woman's stare was fixated on his eye socket. Naturally. He'd left off his patch again—the damned thing was a nuisance—and his face was no doubt going to inspire nightmares in her sleep tonight.

He sighed. He'd been about to sit down to a dinner of porridge and boiled sausages when he'd heard the knocking. Wretched as his meal was, it would be even less appetizing cold.

"Carlyle Manor is a good two miles thataway." Alistair

tilted his head in a westerly direction. No doubt they were guests of his neighbors gone astray. He shut the door.

Or rather, he tried to shut the door. The woman inserted her foot in the crack, preventing him. For a moment, he actually considered shutting her foot in the door, but a remnant of civility asserted itself and he stopped. He looked at the woman, his eye narrowed, and waited for an explanation.

The woman's chin tilted. "I'm your housekeeper."

Definitely a case of mental deficiency. Probably the result of aristocrats overbreeding, for despite her lack of mental prowess, she and the children were richly dressed.

Which only made her statement even more absurd.

He sighed. "I don't have a housekeeper. Really, ma'am, Carlyle Manor is just over the hill—"

She actually had the temerity to interrupt him. "No, you misunderstand. I'm your *new* housekeeper."

He remembered that one was supposed to be kind to mental deficients. Why? He wasn't sure.

"I repeat, I don't have a housekeeper." He spoke slowly so perhaps her confused brain could understand the words. "Nor do I wish a housekeeper. I—"

"This is Castle Greaves?"

"Aye."

"And you are Sir Alistair Munroe?"

He scowled. "Aye, but—"

She wasn't even looking at him. Instead, she had stooped to rummage in one of two soft bags at her feet. He stared at her, irritated and perplexed and vaguely aroused because her position gave him a spectacular view down the bodice of her gown. If he was a religious man, he might think this a vision.

She made a satisfied sound and straightened again, smiling quite gloriously. "Here. It's a letter from the Viscountess Vale. She's sent me here to be your housekeeper."

She was proffering a rather crumpled piece of paper.

He stared at it a moment before snatching it from her hand. He raised the candle to provide some light to read the scrawling missive. Beside him, Lady Grey, his deerhound, evidently decided that she wasn't getting sausages for dinner any time soon. She sighed gustily and lay down on the hall flagstones.

Alistair finished reading the missive to the sound of the rain pounding steadily on his drive. Then he looked up. He'd met Lady Vale only once. She and her husband, Jasper Renshaw, Viscount Vale, had visited his home uninvited only a little over a month ago. She hadn't struck him at the time as an interfering female, but the letter did indeed inform him that he had a new housekeeper. Madness. What had Vale's wife been thinking? But then it was near impossible to fathom the workings of the female mind. He'd have to send the too-beautiful, too-richly dressed housekeeper and her offspring away in the morning. Unfortunately, if nothing else, they were protégés of Lady Vale, and he couldn't very well send them off into the dark of night.

Alistair met the woman's blue eyes. "What did you say your name was?"

She blushed as prettily as the sun rising in spring on the heath. "I didn't. My name is Helen Halifax. *Mrs.* Halifax. We are getting quite wet out here, you know."

A corner of his mouth kicked up at the starch in her tone. Not a mental deficient after all. "Well, then, you and your children had better come in, Mrs. Halifax."

*   *   *

THE TINY SMILE curving one side of Sir Alistair's lips
startled Helen. It drew attention to a mouth wide and firm,
supple and masculine. The smile revealed him as human.
Not the gargoyle she'd been thinking him, but a man.

It was gone at once, of course, that smile. He caught
her looking at him, and his expression turned stony and
faintly cynical again. "You'll continue to get wet unless
you come in, madam."

"Thank you." She could feel the blush heating her
cheeks again as she stepped into the dim hall. "You're
most *kind,* I'm sure."

He shrugged and turned away. "If you say so."

Beastly man! He hadn't even offered to carry their
bags. Of course, most gentlemen didn't carry the belong-
ings of their housekeepers. But even so, it would've been
nice to at least offer.

Helen grasped a bag in each hand. "Come, children."

They had to walk quickly, almost jogging to keep up
with Sir Alistair and what appeared to be the only light in
the castle. The gigantic dog loped at his side, lean, dark,
and tall, very like her master. They passed out of a great
hall into a dim passage. The candlelight bobbed ahead,
casting weird shadows on grimy walls and high, cob-
webbed ceilings. Jamie and Abigail trailed on either side
of her. Jamie was so tired that he merely trudged along,
but Abigail was looking avidly from side to side as she
hurried.

"It's terribly dirty, isn't it?" Abigail whispered.

Sir Alistair turned as she spoke, and at first Helen
thought he'd heard. "Have you eaten?"

Helen nearly trod on his toes, he'd halted so suddenly.

As it was, she ended up standing much too close to him. She had to crane her neck to look him in the eye, and he held the candle near his chest, casting the light diabolically up his face.

"We had tea at the inn, but—" she began breathlessly.

"Good," he said, and turned away. He called back over his shoulder as he disappeared around a corner, "You can stay the night in one of the guest rooms. I'll hire a carriage to send you back to London in the morning."

Helen gripped the bags higher and hurried to catch up. "But, I really don't—"

He'd already started up a narrow stone stair. "You needn't worry about the expense."

For a second, Helen paused at the bottom of the stair, glaring at the firm backside steadily receding. Unfortunately, the light was receding as well.

"Hurry, Mama," Abigail urged her. She'd taken her brother's hand like a good older sister and had already mounted the steps with Jamie.

The horrid man turned at a landing up the stairs. "Coming, Mrs. Halifax?"

"Yes, Sir Alistair," Helen said through gritted teeth. "I just think that if you'll only try Lady Vale's idea of having a—"

"I don't want a housekeeper," he rasped, and turned to the stairs again.

"I find that hard to believe," Helen panted behind him, "considering the state of the castle I've seen so far."

"And yet, I enjoy my home the way it is."

Helen narrowed her eyes. She refused to believe anyone, even this beast of a man, actually *enjoyed* dirt. "Lady Vale specifically instructed me—"

"Lady Vale is mistaken in her belief that I desire a housekeeper."

They'd reached the top of the stairs—finally!—and he paused to open a narrow door. He entered the room and lit a candle.

Helen stopped and watched him from the hall. When he came back out, she met his gaze determinedly. "You may not *want* a housekeeper, but it is patently obvious that you *need* a housekeeper."

That corner of his mouth quirked again. "You may argue all you wish, madam, but the fact remains that I neither need nor wish to have you here."

He gestured to the room with one hand. The children ran in ahead. He hadn't bothered moving from the doorway, so Helen was forced to sidle in sideways, her bosom nearly brushing his chest.

She looked up at him as she passed. "I warn you, I shall make it my purpose to change your mind, Sir Alistair."

He inclined his head, his one good eye glittering in the light of the candle. "Good night, Mrs. Halifax."

And then he shut the door gently behind him.

THE DISH

Where authors give you the inside scoop!

From the desk of Elizabeth Hoyt

Gentle Reader,

The hero of my book TO SEDUCE A SINNER (on sale now) Jasper Renshaw, Viscount Vale, had quite a rocky road on his way to the altar. In fact, TO SEDUCE A SINNER opens with Vale being rejected by his fiancée—the *second* fiancée he's had in six months. Thus, it should be no surprise that once married Vale endeavored to pass on some of his marital wisdom to other gentlemen. I'll reprint his advice below.

A GENTLEMAN'S GUIDE TO MARRIAGE AND MANAGING THE LADY WIFE

1. Chose carefully when selecting a bride. A lady with a sweet disposition, engaging smile, and full bosom is a boon to any man.

2. However, should a gentleman find that he has been left at the altar yet again, he may find himself accepting the proposal of a lady of less than a full bosom and rather too much intelligence.

3. Surprisingly, he may also find himself attracted to said lady.

4. The marriage bed should be approached with delicacy and tenderness. Remember, your lady wife is a virgin of good family, and thus may be shocked or even repulsed by the activities of the marriage bed. Best to keep them short.

5. However, try not to be too shocked if your lady wife turns out *not* to be shocked by the marriage bed.

6. Or, even if she is wildly enthusiastic about her marital duties.

7. If such is your case, you are a fortunate man indeed.

8. The lady wife can be a mysterious creature, passionate, yet oddly secretive about her feelings toward you, her lord and husband.

9. The gentleman may find his thoughts returning again and again to the subject of his lady wife's feeling for him. "Does she love me?" you may wonder as you consume your morning toast. Try not to let these thoughts become too obsessive.

10. Whatever you do, do *not* fall in love with your lady wife, no matter how alluring her

lips or seductive her replies to your banter are. That way lies folly.

Yours Very Sincerely,

Elizabeth Hoyt

www.elizabethhoyt.com

♥ ♥ ♥ ♥ ♥ ♥ ♥ ♥ ♥ ♥ ♥ ♥ ♥ ♥

From the desk of Marliss Melton

Dear Reader,

Sean Harlan, the hero of my latest book TOO FAR GONE (on sale now) is a killer. Surprised? I thought you might be. How could such a charming, sexy, fun-loving man with a sunny disposition and a special way with children be a sniper for his SEAL team? How could he be so ruthless and merciless, taking lives without remorse?

Oddly enough, this all began with one of my kids. I wanted to create a hero with the same relaxed and irrepressible charm as my son. So Sean was born. But I did a little research into that "relaxed" personality type and learned something that blew me away: it's the one and only personality type that makes up a natural born killer! Did you know that in battles, only 15 to 25 percent of infantrymen ever fire their weapons? And most fire over the heads of the enemy! Those who actually shoot to kill comprise less than 4 percent of those in battle yet they do half the killing!

When I discovered this, I knew exactly who Sean was, dark side and all. He was a man that was indispensable to the military. After all, without men like Sean, armies would crumble and decisive battles would be lost. But I wanted Sean to be indispensable to a woman who needed him, too; so, I created Ellie Stuart as the perfect foil. As hesitant as she is about Sean's killer instinct, she soon realizes that without Sean, she stands little chance of reclaiming her kidnapped sons. She also comes to see that her mother's instinct makes killing a viable option and that she and Sean are not so different after all.

It is my hope that you'll love Sean as much as I do. Oh, and by the way, my son is a perfectly nice young man . . . so far.

To learn more about Sean and Ellie's personalities, visit the FUN STUFF page at www.marliss melton.com.

Thanks for reading,

Marliss Melton

♥ ♥ ♥ ♥ ♥ ♥ ♥ ♥ ♥ ♥ ♥ ♥ ♥ ♥

From the desk of Lani Diane Rich

Dear Reader,

Most often, when you write a book, people ask you why you chose that particular setting. All I can say about northern Idaho, the setting for my latest book, WISH YOU WERE HERE (on sale now), is that I drove through it once while moving with my family from Anchorage, Alaska to Syracuse, New York, and I was absolutely entranced. Given the hard-nosed business woman Freya was, I figured there would be no greater fish-out-of-water situation for her than being stuck in the middle of all those trees.

One of the challenges of Freya's story was where I'd left her at the end of CRAZY IN LOVE—on a road toward something of a mental breakdown. Like her sister Flynn, I felt it was high time for Freya's life to buck her off like a mechanical dive bar bronco; and so, it was with great relish that I saddled her with a rare "condition" and placed her in an impossible situation. While I was writing CRAZY IN LOVE, Freya was one of those magical secondary characters who just begged for her own book, and it was so much fun to spend this time with her and watch her grow into her own person.

As for Nate, he was a lot of fun to write as well.

Where Freya was hardened and tough, Nate was open, sensitive, and honorable. His relationship with Piper was especially fun for me to write, especially against the backdrop of Freya's relationship with her own father. Nate's a classic cleft-chin hero, but there was a lot of depth under those still waters, which made him a pleasure to write.

I hope you enjoy reading the story as much as I did writing it. Thanks so much!

Lani Diane Rich

www.lanidianerich.com

Want to know more about romances at
Grand Central Publishing and Forever?
Get the scoop online!

GRAND CENTRAL PUBLISHING'S
ROMANCE HOMEPAGE

Visit us at www.hachettebookgroupusa.com/romance
for all the latest news, reviews, and chapter excerpts!

NEW AND UPCOMING TITLES

Each month we feature our new titles
and reader favorites.

CONTESTS AND GIVEAWAYS

We give away galleys, autographed copies,
and all kinds of fun stuff.

AUTHOR INFO

You'll find bios, articles, and links to personal
Web sites for all your favorite authors—and
so much more!

THE BUZZ

Sign up for our monthly romance newsletter,
and be the first to read all about it!